P9-DVV-529

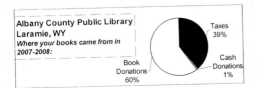

# KILLER
# VIEW

# ALSO BY RIDLEY PEARSON

**Killer Weekend**

**Cut and Run**

**The Art of Deception**

*The Diary of Ellen Rimbauer*
(writing as Joyce Reardon)

**Beyond Recognition**

**The Pied Piper**

**Undercurrents**

# BOOKS FOR YOUNG READERS

*Peter and the Starcatchers*

(with Dave Barry)

**The Kingdom Keepers**

**Steel Trapp**

# KILLER VIEW

## Ridley Pearson

**Doubleday Large Print
Home Library Edition**

G. P. PUTNAM'S SONS    NEW YORK

This Large Print Edition, prepared especially for Doubleday Large Print Home Library, contains the complete, unabridged text of the original Publisher's Edition.

PUTNAM

G. P. PUTNAM'S SONS
*Publishers Since 1838*
Published by the Penguin Group
Penguin Group (USA) Inc., 375 Hudson Street, New York, New York 10014, USA • Penguin Group (Canada), 90 Eglinton Avenue East, Suite 700, Toronto, Ontario M4P 2Y3, Canada (a division of Pearson Canada Inc.) • Penguin Books Ltd, 80 Strand, London WC2R 0RL, England • Penguin Ireland, 25 St Stephen's Green, Dublin 2, Ireland (a division of Penguin Books Ltd) • Penguin Group (Australia), 250 Camberwell Road,Camberwell, Victoria 3124, Australia (a division of Pearson Australia Group Pty Ltd) • Penguin Books India Pvt Ltd, 11 Community Centre, Panchsheel Park,New Delhi–110 017, India • Penguin Group (NZ), 67 Apollo Drive, Rosedale,North Shore 0632, New Zealand (a division of Pearson New Zealand Ltd) • Penguin Books (South Africa) (Pty) Ltd, 24 Sturdee Avenue, Rosebank, Johannesburg 2196, South Africa

Penguin Books Ltd, Registered Offices:
80 Strand, London WC2R 0RL, England

ISBN 978-0-7394-9654-1

Printed in the United States of America

BOOK DESIGN BY MEIGHAN CAVANAUGH

For Marcelle, Paige, and Storey

# ACKNOWLEDGMENTS

Thanks to Gordon Russell for his founding of the Sun Valley Writers' Conference, his continuing support, and, most of all, his friendship and his love of the written word.

Special thanks to Blaine County Sheriff Walt Femling, Hope Stevens, R.N., Dr. Phil Tarr, Dr. Paul Hruz, Brad Pearson, and Roger McGuinn for their expertise on subjects ranging from nursing care to Gamma-Scout radiation detectors. Any mistakes are all mine. Thanks, too, to Nancy Litzinger for office management,

Robbie Freund at Creative Edge for all the IT solutions, Christine Pepe at Putnam for her diligent and patient editing, as well as Amy Berkower at Writers House and Matthew Snyder at Creative Artists for their representation. *Killer View* was written using StoryMill word processing software.

# SUNDAY

# 1

HE SAW HIMSELF AS A CAMERA WOULD, AND often thought of himself in the third person, as if an omniscient eye were looking down on him and his activities. It was no different that Halloween night, as he prepared the syringes. He talked to himself—out loud— narrating every carefully conceived action, as if reading from a script. He could picture himself as one of those guys on the Discovery Channel or A&E.

**"He moves with the utmost care as he makes his preparations, as skilled a technician as he is a hunter . . ."**

The snow was falling to beat hell, which

brought a twisted grin to his scrappy face. Virgin snow—the irony not lost on him, although his education had stopped in the ninth grade and irony, per se, was unknown to him. Fresh-fallen snow erased tracks. No one knew this better than a tracker, and, according to the voice-over, he was among the most accomplished trackers in all of Idaho, all of the West, if you excluded Montana, because there were guys up there who could follow wolves for three hundred miles on foot without a dog. Not him. He used his dogs and their radio collars whenever called for.

**"The final preparations almost complete, he anticipates the events in the hours to come with near-military precision . . ."**

On that night, he was scheduled for a twofer, a tricky bit of timing and complicated logistics, especially given the storm. He intended to get an early start for just this reason, the narrator in his head reminding him of the importance of meticulous preparation and execution.

He arranged the five darts and two syringes, methodically checking dosages, storing them in two metal lunch boxes, the kind he'd once carried to school, the kind his daddy before him had carried into the mine. This one was lined with a gray foam rubber, not a white napkin or sheet of paper towel. He double-checked the charge on the Taser, was half tempted to test the thing on one of the dogs, as he sometimes did. But with Pepper's staying behind, plump with a litter, he couldn't afford to have another one out of commission for the night.

Next came the firearms: the 22-gauge dart rifle; the MAC-10, with its three-speed taped magazines; the double-barreled sawed-off, for under the seat of the pickup. He was careful to separate the Bore Thunder/Flash Bang cartridges from the 12-gauge shot. The flash bangs performed like stun grenades but could be fired from the sawed-off. He kept the right barrel loaded with one of these in case of a run-in with law enforcement; he'd stun the bastard and then shoot him up with some ketamine and leave him by the side of the road, knowing he wouldn't remember what day it was, much less the make or registration of the truck he'd pulled over.

He attached the magnetic license plates over the pickup truck's existing ones—a move as routine to him as brushing his teeth—a necessary precaution when working with his private clients. The plates were registered to a similar truck in Bannock County.

He stuffed some fresh chew behind his molars, hawking a gob of spit onto the garage's dirt floor. Even after being off of crystal meth for six months, at moments like this he found the allure of it tough to resist.

He checked the straps on the wire cages for the dogs. The snow wouldn't hurt them any, and he was in too big a hurry to trade them out for the vinyl carriers that were better in bad weather. He put only one of the weatherproof carriers in the back, the biggest he had. He double- and triple-checked its electric mat, a black sheet of heavy rubber, a wire from which ran to a 12-volt outlet installed in the side paneling of the truck bed; it was warm to the touch—a good sign.

The specially outfitted carrier was large enough to hold a mastiff or Bernese mountain dog, or a mature sheep.

Beneath his stubble, he carried a hard scar on his chin, looking like a strip of stretched pink leather, the result of a meat hook slipping when transferring a she-cat from the pickup to the dressing shed. He scratched at it, a nervous habit, the result of too many hours with nothing to do. He spent far too much of his life waiting for others, a disappointing aspect of being a work-for-hire.

But now he had purpose, a higher calling.

It was time to put things straight. There were enough assholes in Washington to fill a latrine. It was about time they remembered him and others who believed in their country.

# 2

THE MALE CAUCASIAN, TWENTY-FOUR, A SKIER, was said to have been missing for over three hours. A man's panicked voice had made the call to 911: "A friend of mine . . . He never showed up . . . We thought we'd accounted for everyone. I have no fricking idea how we missed him but . . . I think he's still up there."

"Calm down, sir." The county's ERC operator.

"Calm down? WE LEFT HIM UP THERE. We were skiing the Drop on Galena Pass. He never came off that mountain. He's out there somewhere. You got to *do* something."

**Click.**

"Sir?"

Blaine County sheriff Walt Fleming had listened to the Emergency Response Center tape several times, trying to judge if it was a prank or not. It wouldn't be the first time some yahoo had called in a false alarm to Search and Rescue. This one sounded authentic. And hanging up on such calls was, sadly, not that unusual. Guilt could be a powerful motivator. Didn't need to tell a sheriff that.

**A life in the balance.**

A snowstorm. A miserable night.

Walt had set Search and Rescue's phone tree into operation.

Now, standing in blowing snow, in the freezing cold, with only his pale face protruding from the parka, Walt caught his reflection in the glass of a nearby pickup. Where others saw a capable outdoorsman, Walt saw a softness settling in, his desk job taking over. Where others saw a face that could be elected, Walt saw fatigue. No one had ever called him handsome; the closest he'd gotten was "good-looking," and that from a woman who no longer shared his bed. He blamed his sleepless nights on her: the mental images of her riding his own deputy, Tommy Brandon, flickering through his mind. The two of them laughing. At him. After twelve years of marriage, she'd left him alone with their young twins. And as much as he wouldn't have it any other way, it wasn't working. He was failing as a single dad. Barely keeping his head above water as the county sheriff. With the help of only eight full-time deputies, he oversaw law enforcement in a piece of Idaho roughly the size of Rhode Island. Now he faced Galena Summit in a snowstorm when all he wanted was a night playing Uno with his kids, and a decent night's sleep.

He awaited the dogs. Looking through the heavy snowfall, past the bluish glare of halogen headlights thrown from several pickups and SUVs parked in the turnout, he searched for some sign of the Aker brothers. A freak October storm, the forecast calling for eighteen inches above nine thousand feet. They were now above ten thousand, occupying a wide spot in the road along a series of switchbacks that constituted a part of State Highway 75.

Thirteen inches of fresh powder and no signs of a letup.

The conditions were horrible for an organized search, but, statistically, the probability of the missing young man surviving exposure went from bad to worse after the first four hours. They were now well into hour six, so awaiting first light wasn't an option.

Walt saw a flicker of headlights and turned to watch a pickup truck make the hairpin turn in a wheel-spinning ascent and pull into the turnout, parking with the other vehicles. Dogs barked from crates lashed to the bed of the arriving truck, which prompted the other canines to compete. Walt couldn't hear himself think. After another minute, and a lot of peeing, the dogs settled down. Local vet Mark Aker, and his younger brother, Randy, came out of the truck, arguing.

"This coat stinks!" Randy complained, zipping up a winter jacket. "I mean it smells *bad*, bro—amoxicillin mixed with stale beer."

"It takes a moron to forget a coat on a

night like this," Mark said, loudly enough for everyone to hear. By now, the others had climbed out of their vehicles.

"No, it takes a moron to be *out* on a night like this!" Randy replied.

Walt and the Aker brothers went back years. Walt had first met Mark as a teenager, when his family had spent summers and Christmas breaks with his grandparents in Sun Valley. They'd been in a summer camp together, had raised some hell as teenagers on the Sun Valley ski slopes. Now with three dogs at home, Walt basically lived at the vet's. It felt as if he might as well sign his paychecks over to the Aker brothers. Randy's specialty was large animals, horses and cattle; Mark's, primarily cats and dogs. In the glitzy, celebrity-studded Sun Valley community, it was Mark's practice that had soared. With working ranches giving way to showy estates and ranchettes, Randy's large animal practice had nearly vanished in the last ten years, causing some envy and friction between the brothers. Things had gotten more cozy between Walt and Mark when Mark had volunteered his services to Search and Rescue, developing an effective K9 unit. Walt felt more like the third brother than a good friend. Hearing that Randy— the wilder of the two—had forgotten his coat came as no big surprise. He'd probably done it on purpose just to frustrate his more responsible brother. If anything, Randy was a professional thorn in his brother's side. Like most brothers.

Walt and Mark divided up the K9 teams into four pairs. Randy, the odd man out and the most experienced backcountry skier, would work solo, head higher up the road and find his way out to the Drop, from where he would ski the face of the mountain in search of the missing skier. The plan was for him to rendezvous with his brother and Walt midmountain.

The teams headed off without a pep talk or sermon—just a check of avalanche peeps, the radios, and GPSs. Radio checks would be made every fifteen minutes. If the radios failed—and they often did in the mountains—then communicate by flares if the young man was discovered; orange, if you got yourself lost.

**Six hours twenty-five minutes.**

The ache in the pit of Walt's stomach

had nothing to do with the rope tied around his waist, pulling the evac sled.

Now it was all up to the dogs. Mark released Tango, his bitch German shepherd and the best scent dog he'd ever trained. She would go ahead of them searching for anything human, dead or alive.

Fifteen minutes rolled into twenty. A walkie-talkie check produced reports from everyone but Randy Aker, already out of range.

The terrain proved slow and difficult. Walt was in a full sweat, his parka hanging open. It was twenty-eight degrees out. Snow fell in flakes the size of nickels. Steam rose from his neck and swirled around his headlamp like a halo.

"I wanted to talk to you about something," Mark Aker said breathlessly. The falling snow deadened all sound.

"Good a time as any," Walt said. He knew what Mark was up to: he was trying to keep Walt's worry at a manageable level.

"We never talk . . . *politics*," Aker said, testing Walt in a way that made him pay closer attention.

"I run for office every four years. That's enough politics for me."

"Not those kinds of politics."

"I don't pay too much attention to Washington or Boise, if that's what you mean," Walt said. "You ever hear that story—true story, by the way—about some budget committee hearing where the congressman from back east had found a line item listing thirty-five hundred cattle guards and made the recommendation to take them off the federal payroll? Someone had to explain to the idiot that a cattle guard is a couple pipes welded together to prevent cows from crossing a fence line on a road, not a person on a payroll."

"That's the point, I guess."

"What's the point?" Walt asked. "That congressmen are ignorant?"

Mark didn't answer.

At this temperature, over this amount of time, the batteries in the missing man's peep—an electronic device used to help searchers locate someone in the back-country trapped by snow—would fail sometime soon.

It was a human life, and his survival weighed on Walt's every step in the cumbersome snowshoes.

"We're going to lose his peep soon," Walt said, "if we haven't already."

"Hypothermia's the enemy, not the Energizer Bunny."

"Point taken." They continued for a few more difficult yards. "Are you going to explain what you mean by 'politics'?"

But before Aker could answer, both men stopped at the exact same moment.

"Did you hear that?" Mark asked.

"A branch snapping under the weight of the snow." Walt moved his headlamp around. A badly bent and sagging pine bough shed some snow and sprang up. Others seemed to bend lower with each flake of fallen snow.

The two men moved on, Mark Aker with less grace than Walt. He'd spent too much time in the clinic. He rocked forward and back on the snowshoes, wasting energy. But Walt knew better than to try to tell him anything. Mark was a doctor, after all.

"You're thinking it was a gunshot," Walt said. "A rifle. Light gauge: twenty-two-power load or an AR-15."

"It didn't sound like a tree branch to me. Too far away," Aker said breathlessly, winded by the climb. "But you're the expert."

A few nearby branches snapped, surrendering to the snow load.

Hearing this, both men turned their attention uphill. Then Aker trained his headlight directly on Walt, blinding him.

"You're right," Walt said, raising his glove to shield his eyes. "That was a gunshot."

Walt reached for his radio.

**3**

TANGO BOUNDED TOWARD HIM, THROWING UP the snow all around her.

Mark Aker praised the dog and signaled Walt to stop and be still. In the shifting light from their headlamps, Tango circled Aker, tripping over the rear spines of his snowshoes, and sat down excitedly on his left side. Soaking wet and panting, she sank into the snowdrift up to her chest, her whole attention fixed on Aker.

She'd returned only once, forty minutes earlier. On that visit, she had circled Aker twice and then charged back into the dark, following the dull impressions of prior skiers and her own fresh tracks. This was her message to her handler that she'd found nothing.

At that time, Aker had made a point of asking Walt to bump the location into his GPS, knowing it might prove useful later.

But now, with Tango's second return, Mark stood perfectly still, waiting to see what the dog had in mind. Tango stabbed her wet nose into his left glove. She sat back down, then stood up and stabbed his glove again.

"She's found someone," Aker said, rewarding the dog with a treat from his pocket and lavishing praise on her. Tango immediately ran out ahead of them, stirring up her own tracks. She glanced back, her eyes a luminescent green in the lights, and was gone.

The two men trudged off, impeded by the cumbersome snowshoes and limited by their own exhaustion. Walt reported the news and their position to the others but did not call them back. It was critical they find the missing skier, and, until he had more than a dog's excitement, he wanted the search continued.

"No word from Randy," Walt called back to Aker.

"Fucking radios," said Aker, huffing so hard he could barely get a word out.

Walt pulled ahead of Aker as he followed Tango's path through the snow. He snaked his way through a copse of aspen, the barren limbs, gray-white tree trunks, and shifting shadows unusually beautiful in the constantly moving light from his headlamp. His breath formed gray funnels. His thighs ached from dragging the sled, from lifting and planting the snowshoes, the effort clumsy.

Tango's time between her returns warned of a long hike. She would head directly to the target, then return to her handler, before repeating the circuit as often as necessary. She would not stop until her arrival back at the target; then, missing her handler, she would return the full distance, give the hard indicator again, and take off once more. The process, known as yo-yoing, would continue until she led her handler directly to the hard target. Walt calculated that the missing skier was somewhere between twenty and thirty minutes away for her. For a man hiking in snowshoes, it could be double or triple that—an hour or more. He paced himself. Endurance was everything now. Walt was already conserving energy in order to get the missing skier back out of the wilderness.

He came by his wilderness skills honestly, not through textbooks or seminars. He'd grown up in these mountains. With a dad who worked for the FBI and moved the family every two to four years, the Wood River Valley had been his real home. He'd seen it change from a sleepy little destination ski resort into the fashionable, celebrity enclave it had become. And he'd grown with it, finding backcountry skills and survival tactics that had served him well for the past twenty years.

He ate a PowerBar and gulped down some icy water, foregoing the small thermos of coffee—the caffeine was welcome but not its dehydrating effects. He reviewed the work ahead: medical treatment, if they were lucky; sledding him out; recalling the team; getting back down the snow-covered highway to the hospital. It was anything but over.

When he next checked behind him, he'd

lost Mark to the storm, so he waited, as the snowflakes changed from nickels to quarters, suggesting warming. It was the one thing he didn't need right now. If the snow went to slush, the mountain went to concrete and would be more prone to slides. He switched off his headlamp and peered into the dark, finally spotting a pinprick of flickering bluish white light in the distance: Mark. Moving considerably slower. He was weighed down by more than just the backpack and physical exhaustion; Walt knew something was troubling him. It took him back to Mark's mention of politics—a conversation that had been interrupted.

Tango streaked past Walt, bounding down the hill for Aker. Wet, and breathing hard, she passed Walt a few minutes later, charging back up the hill. She was still on the target. Walt checked his watch, bumped the GPS, and estimated the missing boy was now less than ten minutes away.

The moment Aker reached him, Walt headed off, following the dog's zigzag route as it traversed the steep snowfield. He now took a more vertical path, connecting the dog tracks, but climbing more steeply, the steady climb driving his heart painfully.

He pulled a heavy, six-cell flashlight from his pack. Its halogen bulb produced a sterile, high-powered light, which, catching the edges of forest to their right and left, revealed that the snowfield narrowed, ending in a rock outcropping, now a hundred yards straight up.

The Drop.

"Doesn't . . . make . . . sense," Aker said, huffing as he caught up. "We should have seen Randy by now."

In the excitement of the find, Walt had forgotten about Randy. "It's possible he found fresh ski tracks, leading into the trees or something," Walt said. "We wouldn't necessarily see him in the trees."

But he was thinking back to that earlier, unexplained sound, and knew Mark was too.

Now, as they ascended together, Walt's flashlight suddenly caught the eerie glow of animal eyes at the base of the towering rocks. Tango. Her position there suggested a fall.

"Damn," Mark said.

"Yeah."

Despite the drag of the sled, Walt pulled ahead of Aker. People survived falls into snow, he reminded himself, wondering if maybe Randy had fired that shot they'd heard earlier.

Tango bounded from a hole she'd dug deeply in the snow. She raced past Walt to the trailing Mark Aker; then she streaked past Walt on her return.

Walt arrived to her flurry of digging and trained the beam into the hole.

He glanced back at Mark and raised his hand. "Stop there!" he shouted.

Aker ignored him and arrived at Walt's side just as Walt switched off the flashlight.

But Aker's headlamp found the twisted human form in the snow. Randy's head was raked fully around, pointed horribly unnaturally over his back like an owl's, his open, still eyes crusted with ice crystals.

Walt was the first out of his snowshoes. He jumped down into the pit dug by the dog and quickly searched the body for a gunshot wound. But there was no blood, no wound visible. Yet they'd heard a gunshot; he felt certain of it.

Mark was on his knees, sobbing. The snow fell around him like a curtain.

Walt climbed out of the hole and dropped to his knees to block Mark's view of the body. He opened his arms and pulled his friend to him. The sobbing came uncontrollably then.

Tango circled them, whining, with her nose to the hole, her innate empathy steering her nearer and nearer to her master until pressing up against him tentatively and then nuzzling in, as if to keep Mark warm.

# 4

WALT WATCHED THE PICKUP PULL AWAY, SADNESS rattling around in his chest. Mark Aker had barely said a word since the discovery of his brother's broken body. Walt hadn't been as close to Randy but loved Mark like a brother; now that Randy was gone, Mark's loss echoed inside of Walt as well.

Walt's brother, Bobby, had died only a few years before. The tragedy had torn his family apart. Walt and his father, never on great terms, were finally talking again, but it was a relationship often on eggshells. Now, he and Mark shared something unspeakable. Randy, the womanizer, the wiseguy,

the irreverant jokester. The brooding, secretive brother, whose name had crossed
Walt's desk recently—a memo that had
been subsequently buried into a stack. Did
that memo—those accusations— have
something to do with Mark's political refer-
ence made only an hour ago? Grief and
empathy overcame Walt; he looked away
and dragged a glove across his eyes. He
still ached over Bobby's loss. Mark was in
for a hellish few years.

He caught Mark's eye during the loading, his face bathed in the red splash from
the taillights; the vet, so used to death, was
visibly shaken by rigor's unnatural position-
ing of Randy's arms, angled up over his
head. They finally fit the corpse into the
bed of a pickup truck, but only after a great
deal of wrangling. They covered him with a
blue tarp and tied it down with bungee cords.
It was the addition of the cords that got Mark
crying—the finality of fastening them and
the anchoring of the tarp, as if holding down
firewood. Death was in the details, and
those details racked Mark Aker with heart-
break, anger, and frustration.

"Sheriff?" It was his deputy, Tommy
Brandon.

Walt felt as if he'd chugged a soda too fast.

The fact that sheriff's deputy Tommy Brandon was shacked up with Walt's soon-to-be-ex wife kept the men at arm's length.

As far as Walt was concerned, the proper thing for Deputy Sheriff Tommy Brandon to do was transfer to one of the local police or sheriff's departments. Walt certainly wasn't going to resign his office simply because his deputy was doing his wife. But, for Brandon, what was the difference? Walt couldn't fire him without fearing a lawsuit. It was almost as if Brandon was hanging around to torture him. What made things even more complicated and tricky was that Brandon was his best deputy—*goddamn him.* Losing Brandon would hurt the office. But with every small confrontation, every brush of the elbows, every look that passed between them, it seemed increasingly inevitable and necessary. Even the smell of the man's aftershave bothered Walt. Hadn't Gail carried that same smell to bed a few times when they'd still been a family?

Midnight had come and gone: another

two inches of fresh powder lay on the roofs of all the roadside vehicles. None of the dogs had picked up any scents. The searchers were warming themselves in the cabs of their trucks behind fogged windshields, awaiting orders.

"Let's call the search off for tonight, Tommy. We'll start over in the morning. We're going to want the original call confirmed. If possible I want to know who made that call, and I want to talk to him personally."

"Got it."

"We traded a life for a life tonight and that's just plain wrong." For all they knew, the missing skier had found his way home safely.

Brandon moved between the vehicles, speaking with the various drivers. A few minutes later, the pickup trucks began to pull out.

Walt was sitting on the back bumper of the office's Hummer, a vehicle he used for search and rescue. He was strapping snowshoes onto his boots as the last of the trucks departed, leaving only Brandon's big red Dodge SUV. Everything about Tommy Brandon was big, tempting Walt's imagination and begging him to hate the guy.

"Sheriff?"

"I'm going back out there, Tommy."

"Not alone you're not."

"I'm not looking for the missing kid, Tommy. I want some photos before everything's covered."

"Randy skied off the Drop, Sheriff. End of story."

As far back as Walt could remember, Tommy had never called him by anything other than his rank. It made the guy even harder to dislike.

Walt told him about hearing the branch snapping, how his first reaction had been *gunshot*.

The Hummer was idling for warmth, the *slap-slap* of its wipers rising above the grind of the engine.

"But Randy wasn't shot."

"We don't know anything about what drove him off those rocks. Mark and I had to get the body out. There was no time to look around."

He dug into the back of the Hummer and withdrew a broken piece of ski and

tangled metal edging. It was a piece from
the middle of a ski and contained the so-
phisticated mountaineering binding that allowed the heel to be locked down or the
toe to be used as a three-pin binding. The
equipment was different than that found on
recreational downhill skis. A hybrid system,
this gear allowed a cross-country skier to
convert his equipment to downhill on a single pair of skis. He passed it to Brandon,
who shook the water off—the snow having
melted—and studied it.

"So what?" Brandon said.

"The sticker," Walt said, taking the broken piece of ski from him. He pointed out
the ® just below the three pins that secured the toe of the boot.

"It's a patent, or whatever. So what?"

"It's not a registered trademark, Tommy.
It's an *R*, for *right*—as in *right ski* for the
*right boot*. They're paired, same as downhill skis. And this ski was on his *left* foot."

Brandon took it out of Walt's hand and
studied it in the light from the car's interior.
"So he got 'em mixed up. It was dark and
snowing. Big deal."

"You've never cross-country skied, I see.
He'd have known in the first few seconds

he had them reversed. The skis don't track well. They pull to the outside. Drives you crazy and costs you energy. A guy like Randy wouldn't have reversed them in the first place, but, if he had, he'd have stopped and made it right within the first few minutes. Storm or no storm."

"Yeah, but maybe it just didn't bother him, Sheriff." He looked on as Walt fastened the second of his two snowshoes to his boots. "Or maybe he took them off for some reason. Had to take a dump or something. Put them back on reversed. Jumped off the cliff. Who the hell knows?"

"That's what I'm going to find out."

"Then I'm going with you."

"No need, Tommy. I'll be fine. It's late. Get back and get the paperwork started on Randy. I'll call you in an hour, if that'll make you feel better."

Tommy crossed to his truck and returned with his own snowshoes.

Nothing more was said between the two men for over twenty minutes. Walt navigated a more direct route to the Drop, following the GPS. Both men arrived at the top of the rock outcropping winded and sweating. The storm had covered an area of snow greatly disturbed by dozens of prior skiers.

Walt had been right about the snowfall covering any chance to backtrack Randy's movements. It was nearly too late already.

Working on his theory that Randy had taken a bathroom break, Brandon followed a set of ski tracks that deviated from the main route into the woods.

Walt was leaning over the rocks, aiming his six-cell down at the hole, some forty feet below, when Brandon called out over the radio.

"Sheriff? Got something interesting here."

Walt followed Brandon's fresh tracks into the quiet stillness of the forest. They curved to the right, slightly downhill, and aimed southwest—toward State Highway 75. Brandon had traveled a long distance. Walt found him at the base of a tree. With the evergreens acting as giant umbrellas, the snow cover here was only a few inches deep.

The area was heavily disturbed.

"You do this?"

"No, sir. Wolves maybe. I think they may have treed him."

Walt got down on hands and knees. "We didn't see any wolves, didn't hear any, and neither did Tango. Could be dog prints just as easily. They're small for wolves."

"All the dogs were accounted for."

"All of *our* dogs," Walt said.

"Meaning?"

"I don't know, Tommy. I'm thinking out loud. Okay?" He snapped at him, realizing too late that either his fatigue or his resentment of the man was working its influence.

Brandon studied the area. "Well, we're never gonna find a shell casing until spring, if that's what you're thinking. I suppose we'd better mark the tree, though." He took out a knife and carved away a section of bark.

"I'm not connecting the two at all right now," Walt said.

Brandon shined his light on the animal tracks. They came up through the trees in a direct line, now covering Randy's ski tracks, but it was clear the two sets of tracks were connected and had been made at the same time.

"I don't know . . . A pack of wolves makes sense, Sheriff. Randy would have known what he was up against. And it fits with the skis being reversed. They tree him. His skis are down here. Then they take off and hide. He knows what they're about and they know where he is. It's a race. Maybe he tries the radio and it's no dice. So he has to go for it. Gets out of the tree as fast as he can, puts the skis on the wrong feet. Takes off for the Drop, knowing he can outski the wolves if he can get into some downhill terrain. In the confusion, he picks the wrong part of the Drop to jump from. A lot of kids jump off these rocks, but it's the west end, not the middle."

Walt liked the explanation and said so. He ran off some photographs, none of which came out very well. He suggested they backtrack until they discovered where the animal tracks had caught up with Randy's. "I'll want some photographs of that as well."

"I'm going to cross here," Brandon said, pointing to the course of disturbed snow, "and we'll parallel the tracks."

The two separated, staying on each

side of the wide path of disturbed snow. Once out of the woods, the tracks became humped with snow left by the storm. Tracking the pattern was not difficult, but it became less and less clear what they were following.

Walt shuddered at the thought of being pursued by a pack of hungry wolves in a snowstorm. He'd searched Randy for a weapon and hadn't found one, but he could have dropped it during the chase. This would help Walt explain the single report he and Mark had heard.

"If it was wolves," Walt finally said, "then why didn't they scavenge on the body?"

"Yeah," Brandon said. "I was hoping you wouldn't think of that."

Walt popped on the six-cell, flooding the area in a harsh light. The mass of tracks they'd been following separated here. There was no question that the animal tracks joined and followed the ski tracks.

"This sucks," said Brandon, looking down.

Walt crossed the tracks to take a look. A single impression, partly protected by a fallen tree trunk. Its shape and pattern unmistakable.

A snowshoe.

"Motherfucker," Brandon said. "Tell me that's you or Mark Aker."

Walt remained silent as he took a series of photographs, the flashes like small explosions in the overwhelming white. Again, he checked the camera's screen: none of the shots was any good.

"That could have been left earlier today. With all the snowfall, we can't say for sure it's connected to the animal tracks," Brandon said.

He was right: there was no knowing when any of these tracks had been left. Snow blew and drifted; it fell out of trees; it slid down mountains. A print like this, tucked under a log, could be preserved for days.

Walt snapped more photos, informing Brandon he believed the connection between the snowshoe and the animal prints significant.

"Just so you know," Brandon said, "even if it takes all night, I'm following these tracks."

"It won't take all night, Tommy." Walt pointed down a slope to where a stream of white light ran steadily along the tops of trees. A car or truck. The sound of the chains clapping against the pavement, a half mile away.

"That's Highway Seventy-five," he said. "Ten bucks, that's where they're going to lead us."

# 5

HIS SELECTION OF A STOOL NEAR THE END OF the bar was no accident, for it was at the end of the bar where the waitresses refueled their trays. It required patience to wait for the seat right next to the waitress station. Halloween brought out the crazies, and the place was packed. There were two kinds of people who sat at a bar: those waiting for a table or in a hurry; and those with their elbows shellacked to the surface. Thankfully, the two stools to his right were not the thrones of legitimate barflies but only rest stops. Fifteen minutes after he took his place on the third stool, he had migrated to his right and the seat adjacent to the brass bar that segregated the drunken masses from the waitresses.

Reconnaissance had told him that the girl, underage as she most definitely was, was drinking a kir royale—champagne dyed red with crème de cassis. Easy to spot among the beer and vodka of her peers that filled out the tray as the empties returned. Easy to identify, as the bartender placed a fresh one on the bar before turning his skills to the vodka mixes. The decent-looking waitress busied herself with garnishes of lemon and lime; she stabbed a line of three olives onto a yellow plastic stick, dressing the vodka glasses as they surfaced.

The man now sitting on the stool next to her waited for the right moment. The bartender's head came up. The waitress slipped a wedge of lime on the highball's rim. The man pointed to a bottle of single malt, his right arm impolitely extended between the two of them. He asked about the cost and quality of the scotch. As they directed their attention to the bottle, his left hand waved over the top of the kir like a magician's. For anyone looking closely, the champagne briefly fizzed a little more than it had before. A few grains of sediment sank to the bottom of the glass and then vanished.

He was told the scotch was excellent, and cost as much as a tank of gas. He ordered a draft beer, and stayed on the stool long enough to watch the tray make its way through the crowded room, carried high on the end of the waitress's steepled fingers. Waited through half the beer, knowing that a young woman would go to the washroom when her head began spinning. She wouldn't tell her older friends anything was wrong. Might not even ask a friend to join her in the washroom. First, she would try to deal with this herself.

That was when he'd strike.

He finished the beer, placed a modest tip on the bar—neither too small nor too large to be remembered—and freed the stool to one of the many waiting behind him. Working through the busy bar took some time. Given his size and the power of his body, he could have made quick work of it, but invisibility mattered more than efficiency. He took his time, finding openings, and squeezing between the crowded tables, reaching the rough-wood-paneled back hallway. The two restrooms shared a wall across from a gallery of tintypes of mining camps from more than a century ago. An exit at the end led to the back parking lot. It helped that it was snowing heavily, helped that his pickup was parked less than twenty feet from the door.

He saw it clearly unfold in his mind, like watching a film but with him in it. If there was one thing he knew, it was how to hunt, to stalk, to kill. He celebrated his own brilliance, reveled in the warmth that anticipation raised in his bloodstream. Got high on it. *To everything . . . a time for every purpose, under Heaven.*

He admired the tintypes, or at least pretended to: scraggly-looking guys from the 1800s, showing off rows of enormous brook and rainbow trout hanging from laundry lines outside canvas tents. With the alcohol as a catalyst, it wouldn't take long for her to feel it. A swimming head. An unexpected warmth and euphoria. An unfamiliar lack of inhibition, accompanied by a penetrating relaxing of her muscles.

He stole glimpses of her across the bar-room. Each time she laughed, her strapless bridesmaid's dress slipped a little lower on her chest, revealing the remnant of a summer-tan line. She might have paid more attention to this even twenty minutes earlier. But now, light-headed and prone to laughter, she didn't know what she felt except a little too good. Less than five minutes later, just before her left breast completely escaped, her forearm caught the dress, and she pinched the fabric below her smoothly shaved armpits and hiked it back up. This moment of modesty triggered something in what remained of her conscious mind, informing her something was wrong. It couldn't have been more than a glimpse, a flicker, given the dose. But, in that instant, she excused herself, briefly lost her balance, stumbled, burst out laughing, and once again caught the bust of her dress just prior to total exposure. And then, to his pure delight, she headed directly for him.

A syringe occupied each of his coat pockets, making one easily available to either hand. He wasn't going to need the Taser: she was cranked. She reached to the backs of chairs for support as she negotiated her way through the crowded room. The live band pounded through a John Mellencamp song, loud enough to make it impossible to think. She caught the beat, and, smiling sublimely, swayed her hips side to side, now on final approach.

She was an eyeful. Unblemished skin. Thick red hair held high on her head in an elaborate braid. A body ripe and heavy with fruit. Rendered helpless and without a conscious thought, she grinned behind half-mast eyes. Her round hips punched out the beat.

She tripped once more, as she cleared the chairs and tables, and headed for the hallway, where he waited, licking his chops like the proverbial wolf. This was going to be fun. She crashed right into his arms.

"Whoa, there!" he said.

She laughed, looked up, and bent back, as she tried to focus. Eyebrows arched, and then pinched, as she failed to recognize him. And no memory of how she'd gotten there. "Excuse me," she said, some drool running off her lower lip.

He held her by the elbow, knowing she probably didn't feel it. Things would be going spongy now—in crystalline form, this stuff worked quickly.

"No problem," he said, giving his most reassuring smile.

"Just need the little girls' room," she said. She remembered that much but little else.

He took in both ends of the hall. The timing couldn't have been better: they were alone.

His left hand found the syringe in his coat pocket and slipped off the needle guard.

"Maybe a little fresh air," he said, guiding her a few feet closer to the exit.

"You think?"

She stopped. Looked up into his face. Tried to concentrate. "Do I know you?"

"It's cold out. Feels pretty good when you're feeling dizzy."

"I *am* dizzy," she said. "How'd you know?"

"Been there," he said warmly.

She wore five earrings up the curve of her left ear, a rainbow of gems: ruby, sapphire, emerald, two diamonds. An ear worth ten grand. She'd be missing those by morning. She glanced at the word GALS on the rough-hewn door as they passed it, then at her escort, and something registered behind her out-of-focus eyes that the train had missed its stop. But nothing too alarming; it must have felt good to have someone holding her up. "Cold air," she muttered.

"It's snowing. It'll feel good," he encouraged.

She exhaled, suddenly leaning more fully on his arm. Relying on his assistance now, she sagged, her muscles going all creamy, her head bobbing like a marionette's.

"I don't know," she said. "I feel pretty good already."

"No crime in that."

"Real good, actually. Probably too good." That made her laugh. She cracked herself up, her voice still bubbly and light, as the exit door slipped shut behind her.

He checked the alley in both directions. Hard to see more than ten yards in the swirling darkness. He'd knocked out the only spotlight on his way inside earlier. A streetlamp thirty yards to his right showed a cone of snow, large flakes falling heavily.

The pickup's tailgate was already down.

A half inch of fresh snow had collected there. The door to the dog carrier hung open as well.

"What's going on?" she said, a fleeting moment of awareness. But then she stuck out her pink tongue and tried to catch snow-flakes. She giggled childishly.

"We're going to have a good time," he said. "We're going to party."

"I like to party."

One last check in all directions—the snow and the darkness like a privacy curtain. Someone three cars over wouldn't have been able to see them clearly. He hit her in the left buttock with the syringe.

"Hey!" she said, as if he'd pinched her there.

She weighed about a hundred and ten. He picked her up and folded her in half without straining.

"This is a game," he said. "You have to be quiet."

"Shh!" she said, still giggling, as he pushed her inside the carrier and shut its door with a metallic *click* of finality.

# 6

WALT HAD FOLLOWED THE DISTURBANCE IN THE snow back through a mile and a half of woods, to the two-lane Idaho State Highway 75, wondering now if the plan had been for the storm to cover the tracks, removing the evidence. He feared Randy Aker's death was anything but accidental. Proving it would be something else, given that the storm had buried even the circumstantial evidence. So preserving what little hard evidence he believed he had became paramount.

He sent Brandon down the snow-covered road on foot to retrieve the Hummer, while

Walt kneeled, sweating and shivering in the cold, his winter coat spread out and supported by small sticks to make a tent above a section of the turnout where he and Brandon had carefully uncovered a tire print. They'd gotten lucky: the road had been recently plowed before the car or truck had parked in the turnout; its prints had frozen in the quickly freezing slush left behind by the plow.

By carefully brushing away the light powder, he and Brandon had excavated a portion of the icy tire impression. Now that it was exposed, though, the falling snow seemed to be crystallizing on top of it, adhering to it, necessitating the improvised covering. Alongside the impression were two telltale paw prints—a dog's. Not wolf, not coyote. Walt continued to gently brush away the powdery snow, exposing three additional animal tracks—also dog prints. No five-legged dogs, as far as he knew, so there were two or more.

He heard the grind of an engine long before he caught sight of the approaching headlights. The snow was really coming down now, the flakes turning larger and wetter. The kind of warm snow that melted as it fell, covering everything in a pasty slush. A tent twig snapped, and one arm of his coat sagged toward the tire impression and, as the wind caught the coat, dragged it in the snow, perfectly erasing two of the dog prints. Walt did his best to shield the remaining three while struggling to support his sagging coat.

He glanced up somewhat desperately at the headlights and saw two people in the cab, and, as it drew closer and parked, he identified the passenger as Fiona Kenshaw. When he thought of Fiona, in his mind's eye she wore a tight T-shirt and fishing waders; she had her hair trimmed summer short, and she wore no makeup. But as she climbed out of the vehicle, lugging a camera case over her shoulder, he saw she wore a purple downhill ski suit, no hat, driving gloves, and a pair of gray Uggs.

That kind of ski suit was for the Sun Valley set, not Fiona. Maybe it was borrowed, he thought. But even in the headlights, her face was simple and pleasant, with eyes that worked hard to disguise some truth he knew nothing about. Maybe he liked her for this mystery she always carried, maybe for her independence, but he liked her. And, as so often happened in this county, his office relied upon her part-time help.

"Sorry, I was working a wedding," she apologized, cutting off any comments he might make about how she'd dressed. "A freelance thing. Got here as soon as I could."

Brandon explained, "We left her car down with my truck."

Walt directed Brandon to retrieve the blue tarp and tent poles in the back of the Hummer. Ten minutes later, he got his coat back, and, with Brandon holding one of the four corners and Walt the other, with a third corner tied to the bumper of the Hummer, they improvised a tent, under which Fiona went to work.

"You really drive this thing?" she asked him.

"Not often. It was donated by one of our resident billionaires. Comes in handy sometimes."

"All those toys, and you can't take your own pictures."

"I tried. All I got was white on white," Walt explained. "We're going to lose this scene fast. I need as much detail as you can get."

Fiona asked Brandon to hold a bounce screen against his knees, angled to reflect the light off the Hummer's headlights. She set up a large, battery-powered umbrella flash opposite Brandon and ran off a series of shots. She checked the back of her camera, didn't like the results, and rearranged the lighting and tried again. Twenty minutes passed doing four different setups. The snowfall increased, and the wind picked up, lifting ghostly white sheets of powder off the pavement and spreading them around. A thin drift blew across the tire print and briefly covered it. Fiona used a soft lens brush to sweep it off, but it was obvious to all of them they were losing the battle.

"These suck," she said. "No contrast. Bad shadows. You're not going to like them."

"I need this," Walt said.

"Yeah? Well, I need a contrast agent. A dark powder. Hang on." She hurried back to the Hummer, pulled her purse from the car, and dug through it. "Pays that I was at a wedding and wanted to look presentable." She held up a compact case. "Face powder. Who's got a coin?"

She scratched the compressed face powder to dust and blew across it to color the icy tire impression. A few minutes later, she had the shots she wanted and showed them to him on the camera's small screen, before the three of them took down the rigging and piled back into the Hummer.

"Do I get to know what this is about?" she asked Walt from the backseat.

Brandon looked over, curious as to how Walt would answer.

"It's a murder investigation," Walt said.

# 7

HE HUMMED A LITTLE THEME MUSIC IN HIS HEAD as a soundtrack. Real life felt like the movies or television only when you added a soundtrack. The cabin was dark and smelled of wood smoke, and other odors not easily placed: cordite, medicines, old dog.

He'd placed her in his only comfortable chair, next to the woodstove. It had a green Pendleton blanket pulled over the cushions to hide the stuffing that escaped its worn pillows. An unusual footstool—woven cane with deer antler legs—held up her bare feet. He'd bound her wrists to the arms of the chair with plastic ties. He'd left her legs free, for obvious reasons.

"You all right?" he asked her. He didn't care, but he offered his concern as a courtesy.

She giggled—a wet, guttural groan—part of her given to fantasy, part terror. That odd laughing of hers was enough to make him sick. Then again, it aroused him to the point he was needing some satisfaction and that brought him back to the soundtrack, because now he was humming the Rolling Stones. " 'I feel great,' " he answered, speaking for her. One of her eyes lifted partially open as he spoke for her, and only then with great effort. The eyeball spun in her head; her lid fell shut, then blinked open again.

The eye surveyed her surroundings, and she tried to sit up. Her left breast popped out of the dress. She looked down at herself, and some drool spilled from her mouth to her chest and slid into the gulf, the fleshy abyss, and was gone.

" 'Oops!' " he said for her, now laughing along with her as she made that sound again. "'Hey, what's with my arms, any-way?'" he narrated. "'I mean, I can't *feel anything.*'

"Isn't that right?" he asked her. "Numb as Novocain. The good news is, you won't want to remember any of this. Good for both of us. Won't feel hardly anything either, but that's your loss." He rubbed his crotch, and then took hold of it and squeezed it like a rapper. "Old Max is dying to meet you."

His looks must have frightened her on some level, for he was a big son of a bitch, with too much hair and too little grooming.

He waited for her but got only that one wandering eye.

He raised his voice an octave to imitate her. "'I like to par . . . ty.'

"We're going to have fun, all right," he said.

Ostensibly, he was on contract, but he had ulterior motives, information of his own to collect from her. Had she been horsey, he might have gleaned the information and been done with her. But she was a rare thing of youthful beauty—and the ketamine cocktail would erase any memory of these precious hours. As a survivalist, he knew never to waste anything. Put everything to good use.

"'Well, what are we waiting for?'" his ventriloquist puppet asked. Her good eye was locked onto the stove, apparently having lost track of him, but he didn't let that bother him. You didn't lose track of a man with a near-three-foot span to his shoulders and twenty-eight-inch thighs for very long. You just chose to ignore him. But that wouldn't last either. Old Max was coming to attention.

A geometric pattern of light rounded the ceiling and fled down a wall like a ghost, and a car engine was heard shutting off. The cabin door opened a moment later, and, with it, came a gust of cold that turned them both that direction.

"Nice," the visitor said, noticing the gooseflesh on her exposed breast, the tight pucker to her nipple and areola, as he shut the door.

"'Who are you?'" he imagined her asking.

He's who you have to thank for this, he answered himself silently.

The visitor was dressed like a shoe salesman. He removed his Eddie Bauer jacket—black suede peppered with melted snow—and stepped away from the door and into the light. He had uncommon good looks, though his face was difficult to read. He might have once been a high school quarterback or varsity pitcher, the kind of guy that didn't need to drug a girl to get some action. "Stop humming," he said.

The big man went silent and backed away. He could break this guy with one hand tied behind his back, if he had to, but he wasn't about to. Both men knew that.

The visitor stepped toward the woodstove, holding his hands out for warmth. "Kira, you can hear me and understand me?"

"Do I know you?" Her words slurred. It was the first time she'd spoken since leaving the bar. "Help me . . ."

"I will help you. But I need *your* help first. Okay?" He waited. "I'll take that as a yes," he said. The visitor looked over his shoulder and the big man handed him a syringe from the kitchen table.

"You work at the Sun Valley Animal Center," the visitor said.

"Do . . . I . . . know . . . you?" she repeated.

"You're Mark Aker's secretary."

"His assistant. *Ass*-isn't?" she said, amusing herself. "How do you . . . know . . . that?"

The quavering of her voice changed her in the big man's eyes. She looked so incredibly young and childish, all of a sudden. Just a baby in a bridesmaid's dress.

"Tell me about the sheep."

"What sheep? *Which* sheep?"

"The *sheep*. The sick sheep. Why are the sheep so sick?"

"Are we going to party or talk nursery rhymes?" She giggled throatily.

"What's wrong with the sheep?" the visitor asked. "What does your boss think is wrong with the sheep?"

"What sheep?" the narrator inside his head answered. She had said nothing, apparently having lost consciousness, her head now sagging.

*"What happened to the partying, anyway?"* the big man wondered.

The visitor lifted her head by the hair, and the whites of her eyes showed. He held the syringe where she could see it. No one liked a needle. The girl's eyes popped, and she shied away.

"Kira, if you don't tell me about the sheep

I'm going to inject you with this. You will not like what it does. Everything's going to be a lot more real, more clear, for you, once you've had this shot. A lot less fun, I promise. He and I are still going to party with you, Kira, but something tells me you're not going to like it. You see how big a man he is?" The visitor pointed at him. "He gets sloppy seconds. Think about that a minute." He waited for some sign from her. Got nothing. "I need to know what your boss is thinking about the sheep," the visitor said. "I need to know that right now. You can help yourself a lot by telling me."

Did he really think she heard him? Maybe she could see his lips move. Maybe, even, she recognized every other word. But she was too far down, too far back, to fully understand him at normal speed.

"You know . . . you are *really* hung up on these sheep."

The visitor spun around and looked at him. Only then did he realize he'd spoken it aloud into the room.

"What the fuck did you just say?" the visitor asked.

She came to life again, baaing like a sheep. It saved him having to answer. She laughed gutturally as she surfaced. "You aren't, like, one of *those* kind of guys?" She pursed her lips, trying to contain her laughter, but it spilled out of her, along with a good deal of spittle, which the visitor then wiped off his hand and onto his pressed pants. "Can I tell you a little secret?" She egged him closer.

The visitor leaned in to her. The syringe hovered in his right hand, like a preacher's cross at last rites.

She said, "If a guy wants to visit my kitchen door now and then, that's okay with me. I even kind of like it. But if he comes around to my front door, he'd better wipe his feet." She guffawed, rocking up the front legs of the big chair.

"One last try, Kira." He wielded the syringe impossibly close to her face.

She appeared to lock onto it. Perhaps, for just a fraction of a second, she grasped her situation, understood what was to come.

"I want to go home," she said.

"The sheep, Kira. What's wrong with the sheep?" The needle pointed south, aimed directly at her forearm.

"I want to go home."

# MONDAY

# 8

"KEEP TRYING," WALT TOLD NANCY, HIS SECRETARY, the phone clutched under his chin as he kneeled on the kitchen floor, wrestling a small foot into a tight boot.

"It's too tight," his daughter complained.

"Push harder," he said.

"Me?" Nancy asked over the phone.

"No. That's for Emily. You keep trying to reach Mark. I want to hear the minute you find him."

"Got it."

He hung up and set the phone down on the kitchen table and went back to the battle of the boots. He'd been caught by

the fluke fall storm, hadn't had any of the
girls' winter clothes ready. Now he was
racing to get them dressed and into the
car in time to avoid a tardy. He'd managed
four hours' sleep.

"What if I put soap all over it?" he said,
holding her foot. "You think that'll help it
get into that boot?" He tickled the bottom
of her foot and Emily screeched. It was
strange that she should be so ticklish
when Nikki was not. In every other way,
they were identical. Until Nikki had developed a tiny mole by her right eyebrow,
even their parents had had trouble telling
them apart.

"Nooo!" She giggled.

"Olive oil?" he asked.

"Nooo!"

"Snot?"

Emily burst out laughing—a barking
cackle from her gut that was infectious to
anyone within earshot. In seconds, the two
of them were rolling around on the floor,
while Nikki stood away, trying to force the
grin from her face. Nikki had suffered the
most from her mother's abrupt departure.
It was she whom Walt worried about on
his sleepless nights.

The morning report from Nancy was pretty typical for the day after a storm: five highway collisions throughout the early-morning hours, none fatal; three DUIs issued; a ski shop had found a back window broken and was conducting an inventory; a nineteen-year-old girl had been reported missing by her parents.

A few months earlier, he'd not needed phoned-in reports from Nancy; he would have already been at his desk by now. He resented Gail for every intrusion in his routine. There was no seam in their family life her indiscretion had not penetrated and infected. It was as if the waning gifts of a young face and tight body had compelled her to prove herself still attractive, with no regard to the three she had left behind.

With Nancy's help, he'd dispatched a team of twelve Search and Rescue to continue looking for the missing skier. He felt he owed his energy to Mark Aker and the investigation into Randy's death. He was the only trained investigator for a hundred miles in any direction. As such, he also asked for more on the missing girl. Nancy told him that Kira Tulivich attended a wedding, had gone out drinking with friends, and had not come home. Walt assumed she would stagger home sometime later in the day, with apologies, but he knew to consider it a crime first and to be happy if it turned out differently.

"My coat won't zip," Nikki complained, all trace of humor gone from her face.

"Okay, okay," he said, Emily's foot finally sliding down into the boot. A small victory. He tried Nikki's zipper, but she was right: the coat wouldn't close around her.

"Damn."

"Daddy said a bad word!" Nikki announced loudly. This time both girls giggled.

"Daddy's tired. I shouldn't have said that."

Lisa, the sitter, would pick them up from school, get them home, and start dinner. She worked for a flat daily fee, not hourly, and she gave him all sorts of breaks, doing everything from picking up dry cleaning to running to the supermarket—and never charged him. She'd made his transition to single parenting doable, though he had miles to go. He felt like a failure most of the time, as if, no matter how hard he tried, no matter how much he cared, he moved backward. He held himself to higher standards than what he was capable of. He was digging in sand, and, worst of all, he thought the girls knew it.

There was nothing much to do about the jacket. New winter outfits were needed. He tried the snaps; got the middle two to hold. "That's going to have to do."

"But it won't zip."

"It's the best we can do for now." Talk of the zipper reminded him of Randy Aker's body bag. He thought he should probably hurt more for Randy's loss. In truth, he felt bad for Mark, but it was difficult to take the victim's death personally. That emotion had been trained out of him, clipped from his DNA. Even Bobby's untimely death had hit him much the same way. He grieved not for the dead but for the living.

"I don't want to wear it if it doesn't zip," Nikki said.

"Don't. Please, don't. Not this morning. Okay? We've got to get to school. We'll fix it later. Maybe you can go shopping with Lisa." He was thinking how expensive kids' winter clothing was. Maybe he'd get lucky and find a secondhand jacket at the Barkin' Basement.

Despite the best intentions, he went from fuming mad to blind anger as he made the short drive to Hailey Elementary. Gail had cited a dozen reasons for leaving him—his time on the job, the nature of his work and the fear it forced her to live with, her unfounded jealousy of other women— but they both knew the real reason: the two girls in the backseat. Motherhood had not only not come naturally; it had barely ever come at all. He had watched her descend from the initial glow of motherhood to the reality of being overwhelmed. Year by year, she had grown more resentful of losing her own freedom. She might have survived a single child, but the needs of two proved too much. When early frustrations had evolved into resentment, manifested as screaming rants and threats that shaded dangerously close to child abuse, she'd done the only thing available: removed herself from the home. She'd used the affair with Tommy Brandon to keep friends and neighbors in the dark, as well as to renew her own sense of self-worth; but he suspected her failure as a mother was rotting away what little chance at happiness she dreamed of. For him, whatever feelings he'd had for her had dissolved with her inability to cope. In the end, he'd realized he'd never really known her. Never mind that the added burden of single parenting drained him. Never mind that her departure and absence influenced every moment, his every decision, even something as simple as a drive to school. They had reached a disconnect. With divorce now inevitable, he reminded himself to keep it from getting bloody: the girls had to be protected at all costs.

BY THE TIME he reached the sheriff's office, an unremarkable one-story brick building with the jail's coiled-razor-wire exercise area slung off the back side, he pushed Gail aside, expecting that Nancy would have found Mark Aker while hoping she might have word on the missing teenage girl as well.

Instead, he saw Tommy Brandon and two other deputies across the street from the office, the lights of one of their cars flashing.

Walt parked and joined them, his heart sinking. Crazy Dean Falco was chained to a tree.

"The sheep are all dying!" Falco shouted for Walt's sake. "The environment is a killer. All corporate profiteers should be hanged!"

Falco himself had been arrested and tried no fewer than six times for similar stunts. He usually found a small group to join him, but, typically, in the summer months, not in twenty-degree winter weather. The chain was big and thick, and was padlocked with a hardened steel lock that would be hell to cut. Using an oxyacetylene torch might scar the tree, giving Falco added ammunition to his cause.

He began shouting his message again, though louder—animals in peril, the poisoning of the environment—causing Walt to check behind him, wondering at his audience.

He saw Fiona, with her camera gear, and a reporter, Sue Bailey. They crossed the street, suppressing grins. Everyone knew Dean.

Falco strained the chains, working himself up to a lather.

Brandon was on his cell phone, working with Elbie's Tire and Auto to bring a cutting torch up there; no bolt cutter was going to handle that heavy-gauge steel.

Walt's father, Jerry, enjoyed ridiculing his son about the small-time nature of his sheriff's job. Though Sun Valley had grown into an internationally recognized playground for the rich and famous, big-city crime had, for the most part, not found its way here yet. The *Wood River Journal* still carried stories on its front page about bands of sheep stopping traffic and the Senior Center's vending machine being robbed. Jerry Fleming made fodder from all of it. For this reason, Walt hoped to avoid being in any of the photographs. Jerry subscribed to both local newspapers, the *Mountain Express* and the *Wood River Journal*.

He shuffled over to Fiona. "I know you're wearing another hat at the moment," he said, "but I'd sure appreciate it if I didn't end up in any of the pictures."

"Keeps your name in front of voters," she suggested.

"Makes me look like all I've got time for is babysitting tree huggers," said Walt. "If I arrest him, I'm antienvironment; if I don't, I'm a flaming liberal."

"What if you just set him on fire?" she asked.

He barked a laugh and then hid his smile behind his hand. "A reasonable reaction, I think."

"Or, better yet, just leave him. Do nothing."

"You think like a cop," he said.

"He'll freeze his butt off out here with no one to preach to."

"I think I'll take your advice," he said, squeezing her arm—a nice, firm arm. He headed for his office.

Nancy offered him a grim look. "Nothing on Mark," she said.

"Cell phone?"

"Not answering."

"Work?"

"They don't open until ten. I tried the emergency number, but the woman who answered hadn't heard from him. She reminded me—unnecessarily—how close he was to Randy. She said he may have just shuttered himself in for the morning."

"I doubt that."

Despite the mountain of paperwork, Walt had to admit that he loved his office.

It gave him an excuse to shut the door and lock the world out. Yet these days, thanks to Gail, he would catch himself behind his desk, staring into space, ten minutes lost to the black hole.

"What about the Runaway Bride?"

*"Bridesmaid,"* Nancy corrected. Her sense of humor stopped when she occupied that chair. "Her name is Kira Tulivich. No, still no word."

He'd made up his mind. "I'm going over to Mark's," he said.

"I've called," she reminded. "We could send a cruiser by, if you'd rather."

"No, I'm doing it myself." Before he left, he gave Nancy his wish list: he wanted more on Kira Tulivich, all her friends, boyfriends, and fellow bridesmaids; he wanted to know why the ERC had not yet provided the caller ID for the Search and Rescue call that had sent them up Galena in the first place; and he wanted photos from Fiona of the tire tracks.

"Got those," Nancy said. "She just dropped them by." She handed Walt a manila envelope, and he double-checked the contents.

"If you get a minute, call the Barkin' Basement and see if they have a kid's winter coat, Nikki's size. Zipper, not snaps."

HE DROVE the four miles north to the Starweather subdivision, marveling at the beauty of a fresh snowfall sparkling in the sunlight. A sky of perfect blue. Sugarcoated evergreens bowing to gravity.

Highway 75 ran north-south, bisecting the twenty-mile-long valley. It was the only road that connected the three main towns: Bellevue, Hailey, and Ketchum/Sun Valley. For most of the drive, the south faces of the mountains were without trees. Covered in a fresh snowfall, they looked like giant marshmallows, forming a V with Sun Valley near the tip that pointed north. Dozens of smaller roads, all hosting million-dollar homes, led east or west off the spine of Highway 75.

He drove his department-issue Cherokee down a small hill into a forest of aspen trees. Starweather formed a large oval through the woods.

Aker's driveway hadn't been plowed. Snow slipped down into Walt's boots and melted around his ankles, as he headed from the Cherokee. The multiple tire tracks he followed suggested vehicles coming and going at a very early hour. When Walt had arrived home just after two A.M., the snowfall had still been steady. The tracks he was following had been left somewhere before three A.M., when the storm had stopped completely.

The driveway curved to reveal a modest one-and-a-half-story log home with a river-rock chimney. About an acre of trees had been cleared around the house, and Walt knew from many summer evenings spent on the back deck that it overlooked a small lawn, leading to the edge of the Big Wood River.

A magpie floated overhead on fixed wings, landed between Walt and the house, and then took off again. No motion in any of the windows. A pair of spotlights, on the corner of the roof nearest the garage, left on. Another light glowed by the front door. Combined with the lack of any interior lights, Walt didn't like the look of the place. It was possible, of course, that a grieving Mark Aker had turned off all the phones and was sleeping in. Possible, but unlikely.

As a small-animal vet, Mark lived with death. No matter his emotions, he was not a person to hide himself away. And even if he had needed some time, Francine would be fielding calls.

He rang the front bell to no success. Maybe they'd headed south to Mark's parents and the family farm.

He walked around back and tried to see into the kitchen. He knocked loudly on the living room's French doors. But there was no sign of life.

He tried the back door. Locked. Tried it again. Stared at it.

Mark never locked his doors. The fact that he'd done so now and had apparently left town—in the middle of an awful night—told him something was terribly wrong. Mark not answering his cell phone also needed explanation—he was on call 24/7.

The more Walt looked at this, the more it stank. Mark had brought up politics the night before, had done so with difficulty. They never talked politics. Coincidental or related? Had it had something to do with Randy?

Returning to his Cherokee, Walt took a minute, sitting on the back bumper with the tailgate up, to clean the snow out of his boots and brush off his socks.

The rumors about Randy had to do with big-game poaching. Hunting violations belonged to Fish and Game, so Walt had steered clear.

No doubt, Mark had heard the same rumors, might even know of Randy's associates. Was he trying to protect the family name by running?

Or, knowing Mark, was he determined to handle this himself?

**Politics?**

Back behind the wheel, Walt drove fast now, intent to keep his friend from exacting vengeance yet having no idea where to begin.

# 9

ELBIE, OF ELBIE'S TIRE AND AUTO, WAS A STOUT man with a potbelly whom Walt had known since back when the man had hair. Elbie greeted Walt with a calloused right hand that had the feel and texture of a gardening glove left outside for the winter.

"Come on in," he said. "Show me what you got."

An air gun rattled periodically from the garage, interrupting music playing on an oldies station. Since when had Talking Heads become oldies? Walt pondered this, as they reviewed Fiona's photograph.

"I need the make of the tire," he explained, "and what kind of vehicle I might be looking at."

"I repair flats and do alignments. We've got a special right now on wiper blades."

"Please?"

"It's a Toyo tire." Elbie had the nasty habit of making a whistling, wet, sucking sound between his teeth when he paused to think. He led Walt across the garage, past three kids in soiled jumpsuits who were busy with machinery, and he tugged a tire down from the rack. "They call it the Observe. See this center pattern? Easy to spot. It's a good, solid tire. Expensive, though."

"Vehicle?"

"It's a truck tire. Pickup. SUV."

"That doesn't narrow it down much, does it?"

"We sell a lot of them. And they come standard on some Toyota all-wheel drives."

"This same size?"

"You scaled the photo with a glove, Walt. Kinda hard to pinpoint a particular size."

"Anything at all to help me narrow it down?"

"It's underinflated. See how wide it's spread?" Elbie said, pointing to the photo. "And it's worn to the outside. Overloaded *and* underinflated. Or maybe someone just wanted better traction in all this snow. It'll hold better this way, but it'll cut the life of the tire in half if it's not corrected."

"An overloaded pickup truck driving on snow," Walt said disappointedly. "Only a couple thousand of those to pick from."

"I can put you into a new set of wiper blades."

Elbie noticed Walt eyeballing one of the workers.

"Listen, Walt, I know Taylor's history with you. With your office. But he's a hardworking kid, and I'm giving him a fresh start."

"Did I say anything?" Walt asked defensively. "I'm glad to see him gainfully employed. But what the hell happened to his face?"

"Said he hit a tree, skiing this morning."

"On the mountain?" Walt said sarcastically. "At sixty bucks a day? Taylor Crabtree? He's doing four hundred hours of community service for mounting a webcam in the girls' bathroom of the Alternative School. You really think he's spending a lot of time on the mountain, Elbie?"

"He hit a tree. That's good enough for me. He does afternoons for me. Kids this age . . . a boy like this, basically on his own. You know how it is in this valley, Walt. Hell, a guy with a real job can't afford to live here anymore. A kid like Taylor? It's not easy."

Crabtree sneaked a look in Walt's direction. Walt read all sorts of things into that look, among them avoidance and fear. But there was something else as well. A searching expression, as if Crabtree wanted to talk to him.

"Listen," Walt said. "Do you have any ink or oil or something that would give me a print of this tire's tread pattern?"

"I probably have a picture of it in one of the books."

"Could you give a look for me?"

Elbie glanced from Walt to Taylor and back again. "Go easy on him. That's all I ask."

As Walt crossed the garage, Crabtree lowered his head and tried to look busy. Up close, Walt could see that the bruised eyes and split lips were clearly not the work of a tree. There were no scrapes; he'd been hit, once, real hard.

"Take a break with me out back," Walt said.

Crabtree set down his tire iron and followed like his boots were two sizes too big. Once outside, Walt checked for anyone within hearing range. The effort won Crabtree's attention.

"How many hours are left on your community service?" Walt asked.

"Two hundred eighty-two."

"But who's counting, right?" Walt said. He'd hoped to win something other than a scowl but failed. "I could use your help with something, maybe cut back some of those hours."

"Do I have a choice?"

"Have you heard about any recruiting going on after school?"

The kid shrugged, avoiding eye contact.

"They call themselves the Samakinn," Walt said. "It's a Blackfoot word for 'spear.' Word is, they want to recruit high school kids to do their dirty work. Get someone else to commit the felonies. Guys like that, they talk about the Mexicans having ruined everything. Taken all the jobs. Crowded the schools. Get someone mad enough, they'll do about anything. You know anything about it?"

Crabtree's eyes met Walt's. His were swollen and bruised, and Walt knew what kind of a blow it took to leave that kind of damage.

"Maybe they've roughed up kids that disagree with them."

Crabtree shrugged.

The Idaho Bureau of Investigation had put out an alert on the Samakinn for central Idaho. It was said to be a small but determined cell.

"You and I might disagree on a lot of stuff, Taylor, but no one wants this kind of thing around here."

"Don't know nothing about it."

"This is nothing but a small group of bozos, hiding behind the Blackfoot's good name. There's no proof they're even Native Americans. They want their manifesto heard, make a name for themselves. They think violence—sabotage—is going to get them heard. They're said to be interested in recruiting kids your age. Get them hooked on meth. Get them to do stuff for them, like dropping power lines, blowing up bridges. Stuff like that. Front-page stuff. That if they do enough of that, people will listen." He gave this a moment to sink in. "Maybe they beat up the ones who won't play along?"

Crabtree lit a cigarette. He played the scene deadpan.

Kids saw too many movies, Walt thought.

"Thing of it is, Taylor, I could probably convince a judge to cut that two hundred eighty-two hours in half, if you were to give me something that led me to these guys. If we got a conviction, he might make that time go away completely."

Crabtree stared at the scuffed toes of his winter boots. He flicked the long ash off the cigarette and finally inhaled.

"Maybe you didn't hit a tree. Maybe you can identify one or two of these guys from photos."

"I hit a tree." Eyes still fixed on the ground.

"They threaten you? I can help with that."

He huffed out a laugh and some smoke with it.

"Why don't you ask someone else?"

"Because most kids are afraid of them." Walt gave that a few seconds to sink in. "You don't strike me as a kid who's afraid of much, Crab."

Crabtree glanced up briefly from the toes of his boots.

"I'd like to know how many there are. What they drive. Where they're staying. Who they know. Anything along those lines. You think you could do that?"

He shrugged.

"Community service can't be too wonderful this time of year. What do they have you doing, shoveling sidewalks at Rowan House? Cleaning the dog shit off the ski trails? I can make that go away."

"You're the one put it there in the first place."

"Was I the one who broke into that laundry to steal chemicals? Don't put that on me."

Elbie banged on the inside glass of the door to the garage and held up a three-ring binder.

Crabtree snuffed out his cigarette and shuffled back inside, Walt trailing behind. Walt took the manufacturer's product description—the sheet included a print of the tread pattern—and thanked Elbie. There was no mistaking its similarity to the tire tread in Fiona's photo.

As he climbed back into the Cherokee, Walt caught a glimpse of Crabtree's bruised face through the filthy gray glass of the garage doors.

# 10

MYRA, WALT'S SISTER-IN-LAW, SAT ON THE ONLY free chair in Walt's crowded office. Pushed back into a corner against a bookshelf, she faced his desk, her skinny legs crossed, a solemn expression dominating her shrunken face. Her awkwardly cropped brown hair was held out of her eyes with a pink plastic clip. Brown eyeliner was smudged over her right eye.

"To what do I owe the pleasure?" he asked, giving her a peck on the cheek as he crossed to his desk. She returned the kiss, and then grabbed his arm and worked the thumb of her left hand against his cheek to remove the lipstick left behind.

"You look tired."

"I am," Walt answered. "And I'm busy, Myra. A lot on my plate." He'd received an update from Search and Rescue: forty percent of the mountain below the Drop had been searched, with no sign of the missing skier.

He didn't want to say how she looked. And he didn't want to get her talking. Once started, she was like an avalanche.

There had been a time, three years ago, back before the death of Walt's brother, when she'd had some weight to her breasts and hips. Had even turned a few heads. But grief had freeze-dried her, and there was no reconstituting that original Myra. Robert's death had cost Walt too—his marriage, among other things.

Myra kicked the office door closed. Walt rarely shut his office door; he could almost hear the gossip begin on the other side of it.

"You asked Kevin about something going on at school."

"I'm talking to a bunch of the kids," he

said. "Just spoke to Taylor Crabtree a few minutes ago."

"You could have told me."

"It's kind of quiet right now. I asked Kevin to keep it between us."

"If you're turning your nephew—my son—into an informer, I'd like to know about it."

"And if it gets that far you will." Walt shuffled some papers. "You and Kevin have dinner plans?"

"Now we do. Eight o'clock?"

Walt smiled. "Good."

"Girls okay?"

"Nikki needs a new coat. Emily's growing out of her boots." He looked up exasperated. "I suck as a father."

"Not true."

"Work is taking over again."

"It goes in cycles. You know that. You're tired. Give me the girls for a couple days. Catch a movie or something."

"Yeah, right."

"You can't be everything for everyone. There's no one complaining but you. The girls are happier. You're better off than you were with Gail around. At least things are

consistent. That's a major improvement."
She picked some lint off her sweater. "Have
you cleaned out her stuff?"

Walt hit her with an icy stare.

"I can't, Myra. Not yet."

"That's where it starts, Walt. I offered
before: I can do this for you. You come
home from work, it's done."

He shook his head, pursed his lips. "No
thanks."

"Open-ended offer."

"Let's change the subject."

She stirred; he hoped she might get up
and leave, but it wasn't to be.

"And what about the primary? What if
you lose?" Myra asked.

Walt closed his eyes and pinched the
bridge of his nose. He dreaded the election cycle. Every four years, like a plague.

"Have you thought about what happens
if you lose this election?"

"Myra, I'm a little busy for this."

"It's not as if there are other sheriff jobs
in this valley. If you and Gail sell the house,
and you end up unemployed, you're going
to be forced out of the valley like every
other worker. Who can afford these prices
anymore? Then what? Will the court let

you take the girls out of state? Courts love the mother."

"The mother doesn't want them."

"Not now, she doesn't. But just wait until she sees you with another woman. Sees you happy. She'll do anything to stop that."

"That's not going to happen anytime soon," he said.

"Then it'll be when you challenge her for custody. But the day is coming when she's going to regret all this. Mark my word."

He swallowed that one away, hoisted a pile of pink messages. "I'll figure it out. I've got a ton of work here, Myra."

"You need this election."

"I'll give it more thought. We'll talk about it at dinner."

She stood. No one could take that chair for too long. "You give me the word, I'll have every trace of her out of that house in twenty minutes." And she meant it.

# 11

WALT WAS EN ROUTE TO RANDY AKER'S CABIN when the call came in. Kira Tulivich, the missing bridesmaid, was in Emergency at St. Jude's. He reached Fiona and asked her to meet him there.

"She wandered in through the front door about four-thirty this morning," the attending desk nurse told Walt. "She didn't know who she was or where she was," the nurse continued, "and there was some confusion on our end in contacting you, as I understand it, because we thought we might be dealing with a minor. We've cleaned her up and examined her. Brought in a SANE nurse."

Sexual Assault Nurse Examiner. This told Walt all that he wanted to know. "She gave us her name about an hour ago. She's nineteen. Doesn't want her family notified, and we have to honor that."

"You do, but I don't," he said. "We'll let them know."

The nurse seemed relieved. He placed a call to Nancy and asked her to inform the family. As Fiona came through the doors, he guessed they had fifteen to twenty minutes before the onslaught.

They waited quietly in seats alongside a set of automatic doors that errantly reacted to the slightest motion. Walt felt paralyzed, reeling over Mark's disappearance.

A tall artificial tree stood in the corner of the waiting room, its dust-colored silk leaves looking pathetic. One of the seat cushions bore the artistic efforts of a child with a purple marker. The walls were covered in a sand brown corduroy fabric.

"You're awfully quiet," she said.

"I called the Hailey mortuary on the way up here. Mark's never called."

They sat in silence. Walt checked his watch, then the wall clock, then his watch again.

"I don't love the idea of photographing this woman. Can't the doctors do that?"

"The nurses. Yes. You'll only be shooting her face and hands and belongings. Believe me, the quality of their pictures leaves a lot to be desired, and you're the best we've got."

"I'm the only one you've got."

"I have a hidden agenda: I'm required to have a woman deputy in the room with me, and you were the closest."

"Last time I checked, Walt, I was also a civilian."

"Consider yourself deputized. Seriously. It's done."

"I want a badge," she said. "And a car with a siren."

"So noted."

They were shown into a brightly lit examination room that held an array of colorful machines hung from stainless steel stands, yards of clear plastic tubing, and three boxes of different-colored examination gloves.

Fiona saw the young woman's face and gasped.

Her reaction turned Walt toward her. "Listen, if you can't handle this—"

"It's not that!" she countered in a whisper. "I *know* her, Walt. From the wedding. Last night's wedding. On the dance floor. She was there, for heaven's sake."

"Can you do this?" he asked.

"Of course."

The girl's knees were raised beneath a white cotton sheet adorned with pale blue bees, her head elevated by several pillows. Beneath the blotchy complexion and runny nose, she was a pretty girl of nineteen, but with a tormented sadness in her dull eyes that cut to the quick. Her red hair was a tangled mess. Her makeup was smeared down her face. There were bundles of oversized paper bags on a rolling table to the left of the bed. Her clothes and belongings. One of those bags would contain a bedsheet she would have stood on while undressing—Walt wanted a look at any debris that had fallen off her.

The nurse was an attractive woman in her late forties wearing the name tag HOPE on the chest of her scrubs. She spoke in a dry, husky voice.

"Her behavior when we admitted her was consistent with date rape. Catatonic. Possibly a result of shock, but more likely the drugs. I wouldn't be surprised to find either Rohypnol or ketamine. Bloods are cooking in the lab. Injuries are consistent with oral, anal, and vaginal penetration. We'll run a rape kit on her next, but that can take hours. I was told to wait for you guys first."

"I'd like to talk to her, if possible," Walt explained. "And I've asked Deputy Kenshaw to take a few pictures—face and hands."

"I've got no problem with that." She leaned over the victim. "Kira? The police are here."

The girl squinted open bloodshot blue eyes. She didn't focus well. Her pupils were completely dilated, making him think of Roman death masks with coins placed over the eyes.

Walt kept his voice low. He made introductions. "Can I ask you a few questions, Kira?"

"I don't remember anything," she said, sounding doped. She took a sip of water from a straw offered by the nurse. Tears followed tracks down her cheeks.

"Sometimes we know more than we think. What's the last thing you recall?"

"We were at Whiskey's . . . dancing. Then I woke up in this car." She pinched her eyes shut tightly. "He dropped me out front, I think."

*"He?"* Walt asked the girl. "Do you know whoever drove you?"

She opened her eyes and looked at Walt as if she'd never seen him. "Who are you?"

Walt reintroduced himself and Fiona. "Did you get a good look at the man that dropped you off? Do you know him, Kira?"

She stared right through him.

"A friend? Family? Someone from the wedding?" he asked.

He thought he'd lost her. Her eyes rolled up and her lids closed. Her chest rose and fell heavily. "KB's," she whispered almost inaudibly.

KB's was a burrito shop in town. Two restaurants: one in Hailey, one in Ketchum.

"Someone you know from KB's?" Walt asked, a jolt of energy pulsing through him.

Her head rocked faintly side to side. Or maybe she had just nodded off.

"A person who works there?"

"KB's." Her lips moved silently.

"KB's," Walt repeated back to her.

Her head moved infinitesimally.

"She just nodded, yes?" he asked Fiona, who shrugged. "Kira?"

A minute or two passed. It seemed much longer.

"My two cents?" the nurse said.

Walt nodded.

"The bruising indicates violent assault. This wasn't a frat house rape, or, if it was, it was multiple partners. It was a violent assault. If that helps you any."

"I need her last twelve hours," Walt said, his voice cracking. "It's important."

"I doubt you'll get it. Not if the bloods come back positive for Rohypnol."

"May I?" Walt said, indicating the girl's hands.

He donned a pair of gloves and a pair of glasses, then picked up her limp right hand, leaning close.

He asked Fiona for some photographs and she went to work.

"She was bound," he said, addressing the nurse. "Wire or plastic tie. You'll scrape the fingernails, as part of the kit?"

"Absolutely."

"I'd like her fingernails clipped and bagged, please, if that's possible."

"Of course."

He indicated the paper bags on the stand.

"Her dress, a piece of panty hose. Shoes. I've held off on the rape kit, as I said." She sounded a little defensive. "She's wearing a strapless bra. It was not in place, and I've left it where it was. There's bruising visible on both breasts. No underwear. Probably torn off during the attack."

The possibility of evidence left behind at the scene sparked a moment of optimism in him.

"Alcohol was also involved," the nurse said, interrupting. "She tested point-one-four upon arrival." She answered Walt's inquisitive expression. "We ran a Breathalyzer as part of admittance."

"Point-one-four?" Walt said. "That's juiced. Well over the limit."

"A good wedding, I suspect," agreed the nurse.

Walt and Fiona exchanged a glance.

Concerned over the chain of evidence,

Fiona donned a pair of surgical gloves and photographed the clothing and personal effects in the bags without removing them.

"You never can have too much documentation," Walt said.

Fiona went about this methodically, bag to bag.

"I still need her last twelve hours," Walt repeated, as if no one had heard him the first time. "What about security cameras?"

"I know there are some here, outside ER," the nurse said. "I'm not aware of any out front, but maybe."

"No one beats a woman and then drives her to the hospital," Fiona said with the sound of authority. "That just doesn't happen."

"That's why we need the driver," Walt said. "If he wasn't involved, why abandon her?"

The nurse crossed her arms tightly and looked at the girl sympathetically. "Unfortunately, Sheriff, I don't think she's going to tell you much."

"Then maybe this will," Fiona said, pointing into the white paper evidence bag.

Walt saw two dirty high-heeled satin shoes. "Mud," he said.

The shoes were caked in it.

"She didn't just step in some road sludge," Fiona said. "She sank up to her ankles."

"Her legs are the same." The nurse gently and carefully pulled up the sheet to reveal the girl's lower legs. They were splattered with dried mud.

"But the ground is frozen solid," Fiona said. "Has been for a couple days at least. A week or more." She ran off several photographs of the shoes in the bag, then glanced up at Walt. "So where was she?"

# 12

THE ICY SURFACE OF THE ROADS CARRIED A THIN skim of melt. Walt drove cautiously—there was little more embarrassing than the sheriff needing to be towed out of a snowbank. Ketchum, the town that serviced the Sun Valley hotels and condominiums, was nestled at the base of the ski mountain. In the 1960s, the north-facing slopes had been developed along Warm Springs Creek and a like-named road, surrounded by desirable real estate. Warm Springs continued as a dirt track for some twenty miles, past the small village of ski shops and restaurants that had grown to service the condominiums and second homes. A hundred years earlier, the road had provided access to small mines that had never proved lucrative. Despite the avalanches that closed the road regularly in winter, a few daring souls had built past Board Ranch, which for generations had been the last stop on the road. They'd left Fiona's Subaru at the hospital, ostensibly because of the remote location and the treacherous road conditions. But there was an undercurrent of something more to her request for the ride, a sense she had something on her mind.

Walt, even more socially incompetent than usual, couldn't find a way to prime the pump. Fiona tried to pick up the slack.

"Couldn't it just be that they wanted to grieve as a family? Together? That they've gone off on a retreat—a friend's ranch—to pull themselves together?"

"Possible," he said. "But I don't know . . ."

The road wound through stands of lodgepole pine, spruce, and aspen, all covered in a dusting. Strong sunlight, slanting through the limbs, forced harsh shadows onto the undisturbed rolling white carpet of fresh snow. A pair of magpies flew across the road and landed on an old rail fence. High overhead, a jet's vapor trail cut a pure white line across the rich blue sky.

"Times like this," she said, "I could just keep driving." She caught herself, embarrassed by the sentiment. Opened her mouth to say something but then coughed out a self-conscious laugh and turned toward the side window.

"It's real pretty," Walt said. He wondered if his boot would fit in his mouth along with his foot.

He four-wheeled, following car tracks out to some natural hot springs. Fiona remained in the car as Walt surveyed the area. The year-round hot springs were well known to locals; it made sense that a drunken wedding or Halloween party might have driven out and skinny-dipped during a snowstorm. Made sense that this might have been where some guy had assaulted Kira Tulivich, out where no one would hear her screams.

To Walt's disappointment, he found no signs of recent activity around the pools. No mud. With no tracks leading to the pools, and no sign of the telltale mud, Walt had to rethink his theory.

Another mile out Warm Springs Road, they reached Randy's cabin. It had been part of the Board Ranch, a cattle-and-horse operation that had gone bust in the 1960s. The owners had wisely retained the property, selling off fifty-year leases, most of which had been sublet a dozen times by now. Its eight hundred acres lay directly in the shadow of Bald Mountain. A satellite dish hung beneath the south-facing eave, and somehow broke the romanticism of the setting. Walt and Fiona followed tracks—fresh tracks—to the cabin's door. They found it unlocked, which was not at all surprising. Until recently, locals had commonly left their keys in the ignition while at the grocery store. On frigid days, cars were left running out in the parking lot. Much of that had changed with the white flight from Los Angeles in the early 1990s. Celebrities had followed their affluent friends and agents who'd come to Idaho in response to the riots and wildfires. With Sun Valley in the tabloids, ten years of constant development had transformed a modestly popular ski resort into an enclave of the very rich and very famous. All of which had pushed locals like Randy Aker to less expensive housing on the outskirts of the town.

"Start shooting when you're ready," Walt said, banging the snow off his boots and stepping inside. "I'm going to look around. I want everything in here documented. Anything and everything."

They stood in a single open room, with a woodstove in the right-hand corner, a small love seat facing it. A TV, on a low table, viewable from the couch. Bookshelves along the near wall, crowded with videos, DVDs, and books. A small kitchen was just beyond, its U-shaped countertops framing a butcher-block island. A small table for two that backed up to the love seat. The bedroom and bath were to the left. Electric baseboard heat fought to keep the temperature in the low sixties, the woodstove no doubt contributing when lit. Walt kept his coat zipped but removed his winter gloves in favor of a pair of latex.

"Looking for anything in particular?" Fiona asked.

He shrugged. "We'll know when we find it."

She started making pictures, her camera flashes annoying him. To the left of the front door was a narrow harvest table and a laptop computer.

More flashes.

"Don't you think it's a little weird for a veterinarian to have animal heads on his walls?" There was a bull elk, a buck deer, and, more of a surprise, the head of a mountain goat, a protected animal.

"Anyone local—and the Akers are local—hunt. They do it for food. For tradition. Because their granddads taught them to."

"I still think it's strange," she said. "They heal them Monday through Friday and kill them on the weekends?"

"I doubt they'd see it that way," Walt said, having trouble taking his eyes off the goat head. Mountain goat hunts were by lottery, with only a few tags sold each year. And they were the most expensive tags offered, along with bighorn sheep and moose. He thought he would have heard from Mark if Randy had bagged a goat. Considering the dust on the elk and deer, the goat was a recent trophy.

He searched all the kitchen cabinets,

the refrigerator and oven, knowing people hid things in strange places. He tapped the plank flooring, listening carefully for a hollow sound. If the rumors about Randy's illegal poaching were true, Walt expected to find some evidence. The goat head wasn't proof of anything. He wanted a bank account, checkbook, or a cashbox. He planned to take the laptop with him.

"You know anything about radio collar hunting?" he asked Fiona, as she clicked off more shots.

"Isn't that where these rich golfer types hire someone to tree a cougar, then fly out to shoot it?"

"Exactly. The guide uses dogs to hunt down the game. It can take days. When the dogs get a cougar treed, they look up at it, barking, and keeping it there. The poachers follow the signal to the tree. They phone their client—it can take most of a day for him to get there—then he climbs out of the helicopter and is handed a rifle. He shoots the cougar, then flies off. Single shot. Ten minutes, max. The cat is taxidermied and shipped to him a few months later."

"And that's called hunting?"

"It's called *poaching*. The collars are illegal to use, and the cats require a tag from Fish and Game. So the whole thing is one violation after another. A hundred-thousand-dollar fine, and up to five years in prison. So it's an expensive way to hunt. The client pays about ten grand an animal."

"Why are you telling me this?"

"Randy's name surfaced in a bust in eastern Washington. It reached me through a friend. Word was, he'd begun taking clients on his own. And that kind of thing can get a man killed out here."

"And Mark?"

"Probably knew. He has his ear to the ground."

"That couldn't have been easy. And you're looking for a possible connection," she said.

"*We* are. Yes."

"That's right: I'm deputized."

"Don't let it go to your head."

"You want the contents of the kitchen cabinets?" she asked.

"Why not?" he answered.

Walt searched the tiny bedroom and small bath while Fiona sparked flashes in the kitchen. Frustrated by a lack of evidence, or even anything interesting, he climbed on a chair and lifted up all three game heads in succession, hoping an envelope or paperwork might have been hidden behind the trophies. All he got was dusty.

"Here's a curiosity," Fiona called out.

Walt joined her in the kitchen.

She pointed to the kitchen cabinets. "Box of nongluten pancake mix. Several boxes of pasta, also gluten-free. And a breakfast cereal—all corn. Lots of rice and rice noodles. No pretzels or chips."

"So he's gluten-intolerant," Walt said. "Where's the crime in that?"

"Check it out, Sherlock." The toe of her boot pointed at an open drawer. There were some potatoes, a bag of onions, and a loaf of bread. "What's he doing with the loaf of bread if he can't eat gluten?"

"Just because he doesn't eat it doesn't mean he doesn't serve it." But she'd raised his curiosity. He bent down and retrieved the loaf from the drawer. "And it's moldy, to boot. Probably forgot he even had it."

He balanced and bounced the loaf in his hand a couple of times, weighing it.

Unusually heavy. "I want a record of this," he said as he placed the loaf on the cutting board. He didn't like that he had missed this; liked it even less that she had pointed it out to him. But there was no changing that now; and he wasn't going to ignore it simply because she had brought it to his attention, though the thought crossed his mind.

"Pictures of you opening a loaf of bread? Seriously?"

"Just shoot it, please."

She ran off a series of shots, as Walt unfastened the plastic clip and opened the wrapper. His gloved hand reached in and pulled out the first few slices.

The center of the loaf had been hollowed out. A brick of money wrapped in stretch plastic wrap filled the cavity.

*Click, click.* Fiona gasped while running off more shots.

Walt peeled back the stretch wrap, revealing one-hundred-dollar bills. Three inches high.

Walt whistled. "There's got to be thirty or forty thousand dollars here."

"Good Lord," she said. "I've never seen that much cash."

"His own little in-joke. *Bread? Dough?* And that's where he hid it."

"Poaching?"

"It's got to be dirty," Walt said. "But he's a doctor, don't forget. It could be poaching. It could be drugs. Abortions. Blackmail, I suppose."

"And we'll never know," she said.

"What are you talking about?" Walt said irritably. "Of course we'll know! It's my job to know. To find out. Don't say things like that, you'll jinx it."

"You? Superstitious?"

"Careful, is how I think of it. The weirdest things can squirrel an investigation. Never speak ill of the dead, and never, ever claim you've got a suspect until the court case is over and he's behind bars."

"Sage advice for a freshman deputy?"

"Just take the pictures, *Watson*, would you please?"

Walt began counting the money.

# 13

WALT LOVED TECHNOLOGY. HE DIDN'T UNDERSTAND it half the time, but the beauty of good technology was that he didn't have to understand it. Just use it.

His patrolmen were currently taking advantage of a quiet evening by updating the score of *Monday Night Football* over the police band radio, mistakenly thinking their boss off air, otherwise, they wouldn't have dared do it. In fact, Walt was a Seahawks fan, so, on the ride home, he listened in guilty pleasure.

Lisa had been kind enough to stay with the girls while Walt had dropped Fiona back at her car. He'd then spent thirty minutes talking to employees at Mark and Randy Aker's veterinarian practice.

Jillian Davis was Mark's head nurse and sometime bookkeeper. She led Walt into the "family room," where, for an additional fee, boarding pets were treated to a "home environment" that included two couches, some throw rugs, and a television running all the time. The room's popularity with customers spoke to the excesses of Sun Valley. Mark had turned wealthy guilt into a profit center for his boarding clinic.

Jillian worked to keep her composure. A sturdy woman in her early forties, with kind eyes and a severe brow, she wore blue scrubs with a pilled cardigan sweater. He'd caught her at the end of what had to have been a long, difficult day. He cautioned her that, for both their sakes, he was going to speak directly, warning her that anything discussed must not leave the room. She agreed, then turned up the television to cover their voices.

"I have circumstantial evidence that Randy was involved in poaching," he said. "High-stakes stuff. Probably mountain goat, cougar, and bear. Any talk around here to that effect?"

She nodded reluctantly. "Only that: talk. It came up when our inventory was off. Incapacitating meds that we rarely use were found to be in short supply."

"So Mark knew." He made it a statement.

"I'm sure he suspected, as did I. To my knowledge, no one else. And before you ask: if Mark confronted Randy, I never heard about it."

"Would Mark have considered the whole subject matter of hunting tags and fees *political*? Did he look at it that way?"

"I've heard both of them talk about their childhoods, when there were no restrictions on hunting. Some limits, to be sure, but the state wasn't running lotteries and such."

"Does Mark talk politics with you?"

"No. Just business. We're very busy here—all the time, these days."

"Was he doing anything political? Volunteering? Fund-raising?"

"Not that I'm aware of."

"Did you see anyone, anything, bothering Randy? Giving him trouble? Visitors that you wouldn't have expected? Phone calls?"

"Nothing like that. We all loved Randy. He was a terrific guy. Really good with the large animals."

"Any conflicts in either of their practices lately? Threats? Lawsuits?"

"Nothing out of the ordinary. Business was down on Randy's side."

He could read it in her face: she was holding back. "But?" he said. She hesitated. "By talking to me, you're helping him, Jillian. You have to believe that."

"Mark's been up to something." It came out of her like a confession; she hung her head, as if ashamed of herself. "Secretive. Brooding, at times. You know how up he usually is. That kind of went out of him lately."

"Trouble at home?"

"No. At least, I don't think so. He spent a lot of time here, at the clinic, after closing. And he wasn't training. Wasn't doing paperwork. The one time I checked on him, he was in the lab, and he blew up at me for surprising him like that."

"Any idea—"

"No. That's just the thing," she said, interrupting. "None. He's been spending a lot of time at their cabin in Challis. Been going there a lot lately. Sometimes overnight. Was he following Randy or something? I don't know. Some of our deliveries . . . he'd put them straight into his truck, and that was always when he'd go north for a day or so."

"Do you know what was in those boxes?"

"No clue."

"Receipts?"

"I could check with Sally, our book-keeper. There might be records."

Walt had forgotten about Mark's cabin, and chastised himself. "It's on Francine's side. The cabin? I didn't think they used it, some family battle they got embroiled in. A relative lived up there, didn't he?"

"You're right. Her brother. But he moved to Maine, I think it was. This is like a year ago, and Mark and Francine took over caring for the place."

"So he'd been going up there to fix it up."

"Initially, yes. But then he and Randy started using it . . ."

"To hunt," Walt said, when she failed to finish.

"Yeah. You knew about that? They didn't exactly want that to be public knowledge. Bad for business."

"I've known Mark a long time," Walt said, still angry at himself for having forgotten about the cabin. "Do you know where it is, exactly?"

She shook her head. "Randy's death was an accident, right?"

"Sure looks like it," Walt said, not wanting to start anything, "but we have to investigate it, anyway."

"They were superclose. It doesn't surprise me Mark's gone off like this." Tears formed in her eyes. They weren't the first.

"Who else might know?" Walt said. "About the cabin? Anyone who works here?"

"I doubt it. Francine, of course." As she met eyes with Walt, a spark of realization ignited in hers. "She's missing too, isn't she? Oh my God. You can't find either of them."

"As you said," Walt reminded, keeping his voice level, "they probably just need a day or two in private to grieve. My guess is, we'll find them at the cabin. I might give them another day before trying."

Her eyes softened, thanking him, and she nodded. "Good people," she choked out.

"Yeah."

The tears finally spilled, and she laughed at herself out of embarrassment, saying, "I thought I was done with this." She dabbed her eyes with tissue.

"If Sally could get back to me about those deliveries . . ." he said.

"Will do."

As Walt stood, the dozen dogs in the room hurried to him, nosing him and whining.

She laughed. "We kind of spoil them in here."

"I'll say." He pet several.

"You might try Kira," she said.

"Excuse me?" he said. Mention of the name turned Walt around sharply to face Jillian.

"Mark's assistant, Kira. I suppose there's a chance she might know how to find the cabin."

Walt felt it like a blow to his sternum. He took a moment to recover, to clear his head, so that his voice didn't give away his surprise. "Kira Tulivich?" he asked. He'd left her in the hospital only hours earlier.

"You've already spoken to her?"

"Kira's Mark's assistant?" He tried to keep the shock from his face. He had a good deal of practice with such things, but this one hit him hard and he was afraid he'd shown his cards. "I didn't know that," he said.

"You know, she didn't show up today either." She paused. "You don't think Mark and Kira . . ."

"Absolutely not," Walt said. The idea swam around in his head. "Do you?"

"No, of course not."

Walt needed some time to think this through.

"I doubt she knows anything more than I do," Jillian said. "Whatever he was up to, he wasn't sharing. And, yes, I thought it might have something to do with Randy— you know, because of the inventory. But that was never anything more than a wild hunch."

His cell phone rang, and he chased a decent signal across the room and out the door. He took the call in a back lot used for animal exercise and training.

His office informed him that AmeriCell had traced the emergency call that had sent Search and Rescue into the mountains the night before. The owner of the cell phone that had made the call had a billing address in West Ketchum.

He returned to the door, thanked Jillian, and asked that she keep their discussion private. "You know about this valley and rumors," he said. "Mark doesn't need that on top of everything else."

"I wouldn't think of it," she said.

AS WALT PULLED DOWN Bird Drive in West Ketchum, a KPD patrol car pulled away from the corner and followed him. Out of courtesy, he'd called ahead to his friend, Cory Limon, the Ketchum police chief, detailing his intention of making an arrest, and Cory had assigned the backup.

Walt and one of the KPD officers approached the front door of a gray-and-white, board-and-batten single-family residence while the other officer sludged through the snow to cover the back. The clutter of snowboards, mountain bikes, and other gear on the covered porch suggested a rental property. Walt rapped sharply on the door and called out: "Sheriff's Office. Open the door, please."

It took another try before the door finally was opened, by a girl in a tight-fitting T-shirt, black Lycra stretch pants, and gray wool socks. Walt and the officer stepped inside. For the time being, Walt ignored the faint smell of pot, looked past the clutter of pizza boxes and the clumps of clothes on the floor. A dormitory room.

"May I help you?" she asked, a little taken aback by their entering.

"I'm looking for Charles Jones," Walt said, glancing around.

"CASEY!" she shouted over her shoulder. Then, more softly, "Can I help you?"

"Do you live here?" Walt asked.

"No. Just a friend. We all went boarding today. Amazing powder."

"You might want to take off," Walt said. "I'm only interested in Charles—Casey. But Officer"—Walt read the man's name tag—"Shanklin might have an interest in the *incense*."

"Got it," she said, and immediately went searching for boots and a jacket. She was out of the house before the boy arrived downstairs.

"Charles Jones?"

"Yeah?" he said.

He was a gangly boy with curly, unkempt hair, a skier's tan, and a failed attempt at facial hair. Like most of the kids his age that Walt encountered, he did not cower at the sight of law enforcement. He carried his shoulders straight and high, and his mouth remained small as he talked, like he'd been sucking on a lemon.

"Your cell phone placed an emergency call to the county's ERC—the Emergency Response Center—at six thirty-two P.M. yesterday."

The boy appeared to be chiseled out of marble. For a moment, he didn't breathe and didn't blink.

"Think carefully . . . Casey," Walt warned. "Can I call you 'Casey'?"

"Yes, sir." The shoulders hunched forward. Eye contact was broken.

"Think carefully about how you answer. These next few minutes are critical. Do you understand me?"

"Yes, sir."

"Your cell phone bills are being sent to this address," Walt said. "That's how we found you. You've cost this county time and money. The money will have to be repaid. But whether or not we treat this as a crime . . . well, that depends on you and how forthcoming you are."

"Yes, sir."

"Was it a prank? A dare?"

Jones looked up, his face a pool of shame.

"It wasn't, was it?" Walt said. "A thing like this . . . you get one chance and one chance only. That chance is to tell the truth. You lie to me, son, and you'll pay for it for the rest of your life. So you want to think about that, okay? You want to think about your parents, your friends, your family, and how this is going to reflect on all of them. Because there are no second chances. You lie to me and you'll start a progression of events that you'll look back and regret forever. I need to know you understand that."

"Yes, sir."

"All right, then. There are two ways to do this. I can arrest you, right here and now. If I do, Officer Shanklin here is likely going to search your residence and that may complicate your situation, judging by the odor in the air. The situations of others living with you as well. So that's one way. The other is to talk this out for a few minutes, for you to tell me the truth. For me to decide where to go from here. You agree to do that and Officer Shanklin goes back to his cruiser and waits for me. Do you understand? It's just you and me. But I'm only interested in door number two if you're interested in sharing the truth with me. In my line of work, you get so you can spot the truth, son. So don't even think about trying to lie to me. The choice is yours: door one or door two? Time's up, so which is it?"

Shanklin shut the door on his way out.

Walt took a seat on the spongy couch, moving an Xbox controller out of the way. Jones took the dilapidated, overstuffed chair across the coffee table from him.

"You all set?" Walt asked.

The boy nodded.

"Did you make that call to 911?"

"Yes, sir."

"Was it the truth?"

"No, sir."

"There was no skier left behind on Galena?"

"No."

Walt fought back the emotions that set his teeth grinding.

"Why'd you do it?"

The boy wouldn't answer. Walt asked a second time.

"I was paid. By the government."

"The government?" Walt said, unable to disguise his astonishment.

"A guy from, you know . . . I don't know . . . some agency. He told me, but I forget exactly which one. He said it's, like, routine to check the response time of Search and Rescue teams. That with caller ID, and everything, the government can't make the calls, because then people know it's a test, so they ask common citizens—like me—to make the calls for them."

"You were paid to make the call."

"Exactly. Then they time the search and rescue . . ." His voice trailed off. "What are you saying, exactly? This guy was for real, right?"

Walt removed his notebook from his uniform's breast pocket. "Can you describe him, please?"

"I don't know. About my height, I guess. Khakis. Coat and tie. Mustache. Kinda short hair. Your color—you know, kinda sandy and gray. Normal-looking dude."

"He told you what to say," Walt stated. *Gray?* he wondered.

"Yeah. Said it had to be done a certain way to make all the tests comparable. He had it typed out."

"He had the message you were to read typed out?"

"Yeah."

"And you read it exactly as he'd written it."

"Yes."

"And do you have that . . . I don't know . . . card, sheet of paper, currently in your possession?"

"He took it back."

"Of course he did," Walt muttered.

"What's that?"

"Nothing."

"Did I fuck up or something?"

"How much did he pay you for this service?"

"A C-note."

"A man offered you a hundred dollars to make a phone call and you didn't question it?"

"I questioned it, all right. I demanded to see the money up front."

Walt hurried out to the car and radioed in to call off the search. He took a minute to settle himself, reeling over the wasted manpower and the risk to the searchers.

When he returned inside, his voice was irrationally calm.

"How 'bout credentials? Did you demand or did he show you any credentials confirming he was with the government?"

"He flipped open some ID when he first came up to me. Not that I took that good a look or anything. I wasn't going to blow off some government dude. And then when he got explaining it, it sounded good to me."

"But not too good to be true?"

"What's that?"

"Would you recognize him if you saw him again? A photo maybe?"

"I don't know. I guess so."

"Lay off the pot for a while, okay? I need your memory clear."

If the boy could have dissolved into the chair, he would have. Eyes to the dirty carpet, chin down, he said nothing for a moment. Then he looked up. "I take it he wasn't with the government."

"Mr. Jones, you're not to leave the county

without my permission. You do so and you will be considered at flight. Is that clear?"

"Is that legal?"

"You want to involve the courts? I'm happy to do so."

"It's clear," the boy said.

"I want a written statement from you. Exactly what happened. Where, when, who, what. Every detail you can recall: accent, clothes, mannerisms, expressions, shoes, car, glasses, gloves—I don't care how insignificant you think it might have been. I want that on my desk, in Hailey, by six P.M. this evening. Is that clear?"

"Yes, sir."

"No excuses. No delays. No makeups. Six P.M."

"Does it have to be typed?" Jones asked.

Walt shook his head in frustration. "It has to be truthful. I don't care if it's a podcast; I just want to know what happened. In your words, to the best of your ability." He dug himself out of the couch and made for the door. "And I'd lose the weed, if I were you. Ketchum police will be watching you now."

He headed out the door and, as he did so, he tugged on his jacket against the cold.

The process of pulling the jacket up onto his shoulders instantly took him back to Randy's coming out of the pickup truck the night before. Randy and Mark had been throwing jabs about Randy borrowing the coat.

Walt recalled Randy's complaining about the smell of the winter jacket and Mark's chastising him for forgetting a coat of his own in the middle of a blizzard. It had been Mark's coat that Randy had been wearing up on the mountain. A loaner. A coat carrying Mark's scent, not Randy's. Walt had all but proven that dogs had been involved—the prints found alongside the tire track.

What if Randy had been pursued by dogs meant to target Mark?

**We never talk politics.**

Mark had tried to discuss something. Walt had joked about it, had failed to listen.

The same complaint he'd gotten from Gail on her way out the door.

# TUESDAY

# 14

ROY COATS LEFT THE DOGS BEHIND THIS TIME. he didn't need to track some guy through a snowstorm. He didn't need a cage to hide a girl.

Pulling a sled, he rode the snowmobile, a Yamaha Phazer, several miles up Sunbeam Road, pulled it into the trees, and locked and chained it. To some, this was the middle of nowhere—fifty miles past Galena Summit in a national forest of four million acres, so vast that it included the one-million-acre River of No Return Wilderness Area, the largest wilderness in the continental United States.

He could have called upon the others to help him, but he was the best shot. He pursued this alone.

During the "work" on the girl, with the client in the other room cleaning himself up, Coats had made promises to her that he'd be gentler than the visitor had been. He'd won a moment of compromise on her part. She'd mentioned the doc's frequent trips to a cabin in Challis. She didn't know anything about any sheep but knew he'd been hauling mail-order gear up there. Coats had still done her, but he hadn't yanked her hair or slapped her around the way the client had.

Now, he snowshoed the final mile, following nothing more than his internal compass, working from memory, having viewed a topographical map only once. He ascended a steep mountain ridge, holding just below the tree line, and then dropped down into thick forest, as the cabin came into view.

He picked up the fresh tracks of an elk herd and stayed among them for the sake of covering his own prints in the snow. He carried a CheyTac Intervention M-200 slung over his right shoulder. The weapon carried a Nightforce scope, which could be upgraded all the way to a digital device that plugged into a PDA and gave the weapon an effective range of twenty-five hundred yards—well over a mile—that accounted for wind speed and atmospheric pressure. The newspapers called it a *sniper* rifle. To enthusiasts like himself, it was an *antipersonnel* rifle, providing long-range, soft-target interdiction. He'd replaced the muzzle brake with an OPSINC suppressor. It wouldn't scare a chickadee in the next tree over, if he had to use it.

His choice was not to use it, because it would be one hell of a tricky double shot. He had it sighted for two hundred yards. If needed, his target would never have a clue to his position. The target would not hear a thing until the wet *thwack* of his own shredded flesh. Thankfully, the contracted inventory included only the adults, and excluded any children. He didn't have any desire to chalk a kid.

Tied onto the left side of his day pack was a D93S cartridge-fired rifle that he often employed in his private client work. With his special loads and the four-power scope, he could accurately project a dart from one hundred twenty-five yards. A single-shot rifle, it weighed eight pounds but was worth every ounce. The D93S was his weapon of choice for the work that lay ahead, but it was the CheyTac that made him feel secure.

He rubbed his sore knuckles through the glove, mulling over his recent mistakes. How he'd killed the wrong brother was beyond him—the dogs didn't make such errors. He pushed that from his mind and stayed with the elk tracks, huge half-moons the size of horse hooves. As hard as it was to get past his mistakes, they had given him time to rethink his own priorities. He had his own uses for the doctor.

He climbed a tree to verify his position, keeping the pack and both rifles with him. From his position thirty feet up, he had an unobstructed view of a cirque of rock to the south, bejeweled and glistening in the spectacular afternoon sunlight; to the east, a semiforested expanse that trailed down toward the small town of Challis, just the roofs of a few small buildings visible. Dead center, looking southeast, stood a small log cabin in a sea of white, alone at the top of an escarpment, looking to him like a mole on a man's bald head.

Carefully scanning the area with a pair of binoculars, he spotted the elk herd slightly north, watering at a spring above the bald man's left ear. A mighty herd at that—thirty to fifty head. He located the herd's only buck, carrying a monstrous twelve-point rack that he'd have loved to have on the wall of his own cabin. But that was for another day.

He returned to the snow and moved deeper into the forest, working his way silently to the very edge of the trees, less than fifty yards from the front of the cabin and the apron of snow that surrounded it. The snow was deep, so he climbed fifteen feet into a lesser tree and found a perch. He sighted the CheyTac and strapped it to a branch so that it was firmly locked onto the lower-left corner of a window to the left of the cabin's front door. At this distance, he could have shot a screw out of the door hardware, if he'd chosen to.

Next he readied the dart rifle directly alongside the CheyTac, slinging a pouch at his waist carrying four extra darts. It was a double shot: the CheyTac would shatter the window so the dart could travel through smoothly and on target, a difficult, technical shot that only made it all the more attractive to him.

He had no plans to kick in the door. Playing Bruce Willis was definitely Plan B. Patience was a hunter's true gift. His best tool: the ruse. He doubted he could coax the good doc to come outside onto the porch, but that was why he'd brought the two rifles. The double shot would do the trick.

He rechecked the sights of both rifles—the CheyTac was strapped in place, the dart rifle free. He spent fifteen minutes getting the setup just right: the CheyTac would be triggered with his left hand; the D93S aimed and fired from his right. He'd have just the one chance because of the single dart. After that, like it or not, he'd have to pull a Bruce Willis on the cabin. The narrator inside his head favored this second option. The hunter opted for the first.

With a piece of Velcro holding the barrel of the dart rifle in place, Coats produced a double-reed elk bugle from his pack and held it to his lips. The bull elks bugled when in rut, and, though the season had just passed, the snow had come early, and it was not impossible that a male might still be out here, sounding his call. A vet would know this. Only the most effective bugling would ensure success.

But he was a professional hunter. Few understood the art of duplicating the wailing oboelike sound of an adult bull elk as he did. He believed any vet, any hunter, would be drawn by the chance to see a bull elk up close. There were few animals as beautiful and regal.

The procedure took some practice: sound the bugle; secure the device in his belt, reach for the D93S, and pull his eye to scope. Bugle, belt, rifle, scope. He waited. He tried another dry run. It took five seconds for him to get the bugle stashed and his eye to scope. It would take a person in that cabin at least a few seconds to get to a window upon hearing it.

Bugle, belt, rifle, scope.

He was ready.

He let out an enormously loud bugle, quavering with tremolo—more of a shriek than a cry. His eye focused on the cabin window . . . waiting . . . waiting.

No one came.

Another try: a second loud bugle—a trill up and down an out-of-tune scale, a screech, like fingernails on a blackboard.

Eye to the scope.

Light shifted on the far side of the window. It was an incredibly subtle change, but something was moving inside the cabin. Coats exhaled and then drew in a deep breath, his index finger moving from the trigger guard to in front of the trigger.

**Demonstrating the patience of a martial arts master, our hunter slows his bodily functions in apprehension of the shot.**

**Steady.**

**His trigger finger never falters as he holds himself as still as a statue.**

Another change of light. A slight movement of the curtain.

There! The curtain was pushed aside. Seen through the scope, the hand looked gigantic. A head moved into the frame: a man. Middle-aged. He could see the day-old whisker stubs on the man's cheeks.

Aker.

The scope's crosshairs stopped a few centimeters from dead center. He trained this magnified empty space on Aker's chest, his own heart thumping wildly. His left hand came up and found the CheyTac's trigger. He had yet to breathe, still working on the same breath. He squeezed: left, then right.

The CheyTac's recoil ripped it off the limb, but that scraping sound was the only noise it made. The D93S popped, sounding like one strong handclap.

Through the scope, he saw flashes of blinding light as the window shattered. Pieces of glass rained down both inside and out. The curtain fluttered.

Then nothing.

No indication of success.

No indication of failure.

Nothing.

He jacked the CheyTac into place, ready to unload the magazine, if need be. If he'd missed with the dart, if the doc made a run for it . . .

He waited. One minute . . . Two . . .

He had no choice.

**Time for Uncle Bruce**.

# 15

THE BARREN, SNOW-COVERED HILL ROSE STEEPLY from the locked gate like a bubble of shaving cream. A primitive road had been cut into the winding hillside, jutting out like a frown. Walt saw what might have been tracks—it could have been game or people—but there was too much drifting snow to know for certain.

The top of Mark Aker's four hundred acres abutted the western edge of the Challis National Forest. A quarter mile to the west ran Yankee Fork Road, a dirt track, snowed in for the winter, that connected the town of

Challis to the abandoned mining town of Sunbeam. To the east were a few sprawling ranches. This was God's country, the last vestiges of community before the National Forest spread north and east for hundreds of square miles.

"No sign this gate's been opened recently," Brandon complained. "You still want to go through with this?"

A sharp but distant rifle report sounded. Small-gauge, Walt thought, as he connected the sound to the one he'd heard the night of the search: *like a limb snapping.* If anything was the Wild West, it was Challis, Idaho; the sound of a rifle, even out of hunting season, would normally have been of no interest. The reverberating dull echo prevented Walt from determining the direction of origin, but its proximity to Aker's cabin put a spur in his backside.

"Hurry!" It had taken him all morning to round up Brandon and to make the three-hour drive. The sound of a gunshot fueled his impatience. It made sense that Mark might hide his family here—with the property listed under Francine's maiden name there was little chance it would be connected by others to Mark—but maybe they hadn't been the only ones to figure it out.

They vaulted the gate. Walt pulled his snowshoes through and was strapping them on as Brandon beat him to it and started up the unplowed road.

Walt charged off and quickly caught up, the technique more familiar to him. Larger and heavier, Brandon sunk down more deeply and couldn't find a rhythm to his mechanics. Within a minute or two, Walt found his pace and passed Brandon. Brandon then leaned into the hill and regained lost ground, pulling even with Walt. It didn't escape Walt that they were acting like schoolboys, but it didn't slow him any either.

After a quarter mile of climbing, steam pouring off them, and just as they rounded the last of three ascending turns, the buckle on Walt's snowshoe popped loose and he went down into a face-plant.

Brandon glanced back but didn't slow down.

Walt sat up and tried to make sense of the equipment failure. He couldn't find the buckle. He knotted the straps together, as tightly as possible, and took a few steps. It held.

Ahead of him, Brandon was closing in on the tiny cabin. It had a covered porch that wrapped around two of its sides. A stovepipe jutted out of the roof, no smoke coming from it. The one window on this side was blocked with a curtain.

"Hold up!" he hollered to Brandon. Procedure dictated they approach the structure with one man covering.

But his deputy took this as Walt's attempt to fix the race and continued ahead.

"Stand down, Deputy!" Walt tried again.

Brandon glanced back, grinned, and then bent over to loosen the snowshoes. He came out of them fast and climbed up onto the porch, banging a shoulder into a wind chime. Light flashed from the spinning metal, and the tinkle of bells carried on the wind.

A spurt of blood burst from Brandon's shoulder, and the exterior wall of the cabin splintered with a *thwack*. He spun, reached out, and pulled down the wind chimes with him as he fell to the deck.

"Tommy!" Walt dove into the snow, rolled onto his back, and dumped his gloves in order to lose the snowshoes. He fumbled with the straps, finally kicking the snowshoes loose. Beretta in hand, he belly-crawled toward the cabin. "Stay down!" he shouted. "And don't move!"

He stole a glimpse up the hill toward the woods, believing the shot had come from somewhere out there. Fresh tracks led through the snow in that direction. Then he lowered his head and continued his belly crawl, staying below the snow's surface. He crawled . . . paused . . . listened. It felt as if the cabin was moving away from him; as hard as he crawled, he didn't seem to get any closer.

"Fuck!" It was Brandon, from the porch.

"Stay down!" Walt shouted.

"I'm hit."

"Stay down and don't move."

"Shut the fuck up! I'm hit."

"I'm coming."

"The fuck you are. He'll pick you off."

There'd been only the one shot. It offered two possibilities: a shoot and run or a shoot and hunt to the death.

Walt needed cover: he saw the move,

as he finally drew closer. He jumped up onto the deck, spun, back first, to the house, tucked himself into a ball, hands over his face, and vaulted backward through the window. The glass exploded and rained down around him. He hit a table, caught a lamp with his toe, and brought both down on top of him. He scooted away from the glass, came to a standing position, and rushed the front door.

The other window was shattered too, glass on the inside. Had that happened when Brandon had been shot? He didn't recall the sound of breaking glass, only the bells of the wind chime. He reached the open window and peered out past the jagged frame.

Brandon lay below him, faceup. The man's glove was gripped high on his left arm, which was blood-covered and still oozing.

"You okay?"

"Dandy," Brandon answered with a grimace.

"I'm going to pull the door open. We're going to do this fast, on three. You with me?"

"Three," Brandon said, and he started to slide on his back toward the door.

"Shit!" Walt said, as he yanked open the door, reached out, and found the man's right shoulder. He dragged him—the man was heavy—through the door and slammed it shut.

"Motherfucker hurts!" said Brandon. "Goddamn it!" He ran through every expletive he knew, as Walt opened the jacket and worked it off the man's left arm. As wounds went, it was pretty awful. The bullet appeared to have missed the bone, but the exit wound was twice the size of the entrance, leaving a hole the size of a golf ball. The bleeding was severe, possibly arterial. The wound wouldn't kill him but the blood loss might. With Brandon compressing the wound, Walt stripped a shoelace out of the man's boot.

"No," Brandon said.

"I'm going to tie it off."

"The hell you are," Brandon said. "Once we do that, we can't go back. The toxins'll kill me if we loosen it, and, if we don't, they take the arm. Fuck that. Compression for now. We only go to tourniquet if I pass out and you see no other choice."

"There *is* no other choice."

"I'm not losing my arm, Sheriff. Nice try."

"Tommy!"

"No . . . fucking . . . way. I've done the course, Sheriff. I'm not losing this arm unless I have to."

Walt looked around the room, as if someone might arrive to help him.

"You've got to go after him," Brandon said.

"The hell I do."

"Yes, you do." Brandon couldn't point, so he shook his head in the direction of the door.

It took Walt a moment to see the plastic dart canister wedged into the intersection of the wall and floor.

"They got him, Sheriff. That's what we heard with that first shot. We're maybe, what, fifteen, twenty minutes behind him?"

Walt processed everything Brandon was saying and his eyes were telling him. "Darted him *inside* the cabin? I don't buy that."

"Who the fuck knows? That's a dart, and, unless I'm mistaken, no one's home."

"You're bleeding out."

"I can get down the hill. It's easier than going up."

"Bullshit."

"Give me the keys."

"This isn't going to happen, Tommy. I'm going with you."

"We'll use the radios," Brandon said. "I'll keep talking. As long as I'm conscious, you keep heading up there. I go silent, then, sure, come back and be the hero."

"Give it a rest. There's procedure, Tommy. I'm evacuating the wounded."

"You're pursuing the hostage. The first twelve hours, Sheriff. You know the drill."

"*If* someone took Mark, they'll be on snowmobile. I'm on foot, Tommy."

"And when I get down to town, I'll send a deputy up Yankee Fork on a snowmobile looking for you."

"Got it all planned out, do you?"

"Yes, sir, I do."

"Mark's a vet. The dart could be his," Walt said.

"Could be." Gripping his arm tightly, Brandon said, "I'll need help with the snowshoes, and you'll need a pair of gloves."

"We're going to clean and wrap the

wound," Walt said. "We can get a lot of compression with the wrap."

"Well, fucking hop to it!" Brandon said. "He's got a head start on you."

Walt passed him the keys.

# 16

WALT FOLLOWED THE TRAIL OF PACKED SNOW for only the first fifty yards, then gave one final look back at Brandon before cutting to his right and entering into a stand of towering lodgepole pine that formed the southwestern boundary of the National Forest. He had first learned to track in Boy Scouts; but where other kids picked up footballs or soccer balls, Walt had spent his school-day afternoons in the wilderness with his head down. A man named Jeff Longfeather, a Blackfoot Indian who worked as a farmhand for his maternal grandfather, had seen the boy's passion and had taught him the natural state of indigenous flora and fauna, the different ways and speeds that mud dried, the forces behind impact prints. Taught him the feeding, watering, and mating habits of big game. How to bugle an elk to within fifty yards. How to construct a blind. To survive in the woods for days at a time, eating pine nuts and edible roots, and burying his own scat. In the process, Walt had come to respect the environment in ways that wouldn't be popular for twenty more years, but his reverence had paid off. Jeff Longfeather turned a wet-behind-the-ears Boy Scout into a fine tracker who could stalk a bull elk or deer for days without revealing himself. Walt had not stayed with scouting, but he'd visited the family farm weekends and school holidays and had come to view Jeff as something of an older brother, spiritual adviser, and mentor.

He disappeared now into the woods, his mission twofold: to track the man who had kidnapped Mark Aker, for there was only one set of snowshoe tracks coming and going, and to make certain no one tracked him.

Brandon's ramblings crackled on in his earpiece, as his deputy descended from Aker's cabin toward the Cherokee. The reception wasn't great, but he continued to hear Brandon's voice, which was all that mattered.

The snowpack was thinner inside the woods, most of it caught by branches. He doubled back on his own tracks, removed the snowshoes, and climbed rocks to break his own trail from being followed. He climbed trees for surveillance and never left the confines of the forest, even when the tracks he was following reached across acres of snowfield. He located and climbed two trees that had clearly been used to scout the cabin; they'd been climbed by a strong man with a good-sized leg spread—a man with coarse black hair, judging by the strands he found stuck to the pine sap. At the top of one of the trees, he found a rubbed spot on a stout branch that suggested an object had been braced there—a rifle or monocular—the location offering an unobstructed view of the cabin's porch.

Brandon had not been shot from such an elevation, but the dart on the floor of the cabin lingered in Walt's mind.

What was Mark involved in? Why would anyone want, first, to try to kill and then, later, kidnap a local veterinarian? If he'd been willing to shoot Brandon, why not Mark Aker? Why the dart?

Being up a tree helped with radio reception. Brandon had reached the vehicle and felt able to drive himself into Challis. They signed off, with Brandon promising Walt a snowmobile on Yankee Fork Road in short time.

Walt returned to the snowfield and stayed parallel to the tracks. Jeff Longfeather had taught him about time and patience; where possible, he stole into the center of the well-traveled elk trail and reestablished the snowshoe tracks—the man was pulling a heavy sled. Mark? He'd clearly made good time, establishing himself in Walt's mind as big and strong. He was also an expert with a sniper rifle, keeping Walt mindful of his cover.

An hour and a half passed before his radio barked again. The Challis sheriff and a deputy were waiting nearby on Yankee Fork Road.

Walt discovered some cigarette ash, dancing on the snow. The butt had been

GI'd, or packed out, leaving only the rolling worms of ash as evidence. The man towing Mark had paused here, had come back to the sled and done something—had administered more drugs, maybe, or delivered a warning. Walt followed the tracks and soon met up with two men on snowmobiles. They wore sheriff patches.

A track of a snowmobile towing a sled was evident. It headed not toward Challis, as he'd expected, but deep into the National Forest.

Introductions were made. Steam poured from Walt's clothing. The two eyed him apprehensively; he sensed reluctance in them that he didn't understand.

Riding a snowmobile would chill him down quickly, so he took a moment to strip down to his bare chest and change into a fresh Capilene undershirt. He redressed in his uniform shirt and zipped up his jacket, shifting on his feet to get his body heat back. The conversation never stopped as he caught up the Challis sheriff, a man with whom he'd had a major falling-out over the killing of a wolf a year earlier. There was no love lost between them, and he thought that that explained their mutual reluctance.

The Challis sheriff established that they'd crossed no fresh snowmobile tracks. "This guy's headed back the way he came."

"But what's out there?" Walt inquired.

"Not much. Not for a long ways, anyway," said the sheriff.

"Sunbeam or Clayton, I suppose," the deputy said with a bit of a twang. His face barely showed out of the tightened hood and ski goggles. "Nothing else between here and there but a shitload of snow."

"And your odd summer ranch on grandfathered parcels," the sheriff added. "Would be a hell of a lot faster to head back to town and drive down to Clayton than punching through on Yankee Fork Road."

"But the only sure way to know where he's going is to follow the snowmobile track," Walt said.

"Can't argue with that," the sheriff said. "I'm just saying there ain't many places a fella can meet up with Highway Seventy-five, and Clayton's the most likely of 'em."

"But not the only one," Walt said.

"I think we established that," the sheriff said indignantly.

"You mind if I borrow one of your

machines?" Walt asked. "I'll follow on the trail while you get your guys down to Clayton. It wouldn't hurt to roadblock Seventy-five at the turn to May."

"Radios won't do shit in there. You've got maybe a mile of coverage. Nothing more."

Walt tapped his pack. "Satellite phone," he said, raising a snarl in his counterpart. The Challis sheriff's office wasn't at the forefront of technology. "My deputy has the number."

"You sure you want to do Yankee Fork Road?" the deputy asked one final time. "There ain't nothing out there for thirty miles, Sheriff."

Walt saw red. He didn't like his decisions being questioned. He'd had that a lot over the past six months. People had expected him to fire Tommy Brandon. Myra had expected him to dump Gail's clothes out the front door.

Minutes later, he found himself riding the snowmobile at forty miles an hour, following in the tread impressions that played out before him. It wasn't until he caught a glimpse of himself in the snowmobile's vibrating rearview mirror that he understood the reluctance he'd seen on their faces: mucus from his nose had frozen in twin lines on his upper lip; his eyebrows were white with frost, as were his eyelashes and some hairs on his neck and lower ears; his cheeks were an unnatural red, and some drool was frozen to his chin. He looked like a wild mountain man.

He rubbed his face clean with his glove. You couldn't tow a sled at the speed he was going, which meant he was making up time. But he was riding fast, and often blind, into the path of a sniper who wasn't shy about shooting cops.

He began slowing down at every curve and wishing the snowmobile didn't whine like a chain saw, announcing his approach.

# 17

INSPIRED BY THE PANORAMIC VIEW OF PRISTINE wilderness, the soundtrack from *The Sound of Music* played in his head—no narration, just the gentle strains of Julie Andrews's bell-like voice.

He took something of a risk in leaving the vet down there in the sled, as he climbed a mountain ridge overlooking a long bend in Yankee Fork Road. Strong winds had blown away the snow, leaving scrabble rock and patches of ice, which he negotiated with care.

**The ascent is carried out with precision, the timing critical, as he leaves**

**his captive bound and unconscious far below. To make even the slightest mistake now can cost him everything, and so he goes about his mission with great care.**

He loved grenades. It was well worth the climb to achieve the godlike sense of power associated with kicking an avalanche. He carried the CheyTac, as a measure of precaution: he could shoot the eye out of an eagle at half a mile with the thing. But it was the two grenades that really warmed his nut sack.

He stopped several times to catch his breath in the thin air. Looked down at the snowmobile and sled, a quarter mile beyond the turn. No one was going to come down this road, unless they were after him, but, if anyone did, he'd covered the unconscious vet with a blanket to hide the sled's contents.

**People had seriously misjudged the man. They took him for a hick and an incompetent. But in doing so they had allowed him to overhear the girl's interrogation. They had given him a way out of this mess. The doctor was the witness he'd longed for. A simple double**

**cross and his mission—his message—was saved.**

He sat down on a rock to quiet himself. It wouldn't do to handle grenades in this state. He smoked a cigarette and took in the scenery. His plan was a simple one: as a precaution, he would kick an avalanche and cover the Y in Yankee Fork Road, making it impassable. Snowmobiles would be blocked by a giant wall of ice and rock and, to the right, a precipitous drop-off. No one would get through here except on foot.

He heard a buzzing in his ears as he removed the concussion grenade from his satchel, pulled the pin, and heaved it well out into the snowfield. Moments later, he heard its soft cough. Watched as the center of the slope calved and caved simultaneously, an enormous shelf of snow sinking and breaking free from the uniformity above. Snow rippled as the newly created shelf pushed against the snow below, looking like age lines on an elderly face.

The sounds came next: a deep groaning, like the awakening of some great beast. This was interrupted once again by

the buzzing whine of an insect, the contained anger pulsing past his ears.

The crack in the slowly shifting shelf of
snow widened.

Then he saw what appeared to be a little black bug shooting along the road, and
the insect sound took on an entirely new
meaning: a snowmobile.

It was barreling down Yankee Fork
Road, coming from the direction of Challis. Alone. It all but ruled out the cops; they
always traveled in pairs or groups. No, this
was some poor shit out on a nature ride
who'd chosen the wrong day and the wrong
route.

All at once, the snow slid in a massive,
beautiful display of the raw power of nature. It was like a dam bursting.

He gloried in the moment, feeling the
earth shuddering at his feet, hearing that
sound, now more like a jet taking off.

It buried the buzz of the snowmobile,
wiped out the soundtrack, silenced the
narrator.

It moved first as a unit, as if the whole
side of the mountain were falling. But then
inertia and momentum collided, and a

central chute rose, in a massive upheaval, a wide river of flowing snow, rock, and ice, gorging out the center of the slide and sucking more and more snow and debris down with it. Two huge trees at the edge of the far hill snapped like matchsticks and were carried down, swallowed whole.

And there, still unaware, came the black bug of the snowmobile, curving slowly around the long bend, headed directly into its unforgiving path.

# 18

IT BEGAN AS A SHUDDER, AS IF HE'D PUSHED THE snowmobile too hard, had thrown a belt or burned up some bearings. Walt felt it first in his legs, then his waist, and finally some spinal signal reached his brain that told him to look to his left.

His greatest fear was death by fire, with asphyxiation a close second. This included drowning. But more than drowning, being buried in an avalanche. He'd led enough Search and Rescue teams, both success-ful and not, to know the horror stories, and to see the results firsthand. If you were lucky enough to survive the churn—and few were—then you found yourself in a sea of blackness, disoriented and buried alive. Death came slowly: as your body chilled into hypothermia, your own breath contaminated what little air existed in your icy tomb and you suffocated, thrown first into hallucination, and, finally, a lung-bursting death.

His first thoughts, as he saw the mountain collapsing toward him, were not thoughts at all but images. He'd pulled out bodies, the faces frozen in looks of madness—terror-ridden masks of inescapable panic.

Then, for just a fraction of a second, above the fluid hillside cascading toward him, he made out the silhouetted shape of a man standing on the distant ridgeline. It might have been his imagination or wishful thinking: wanting to attribute this devil's work to a man instead of synchronicity, his being in the wrong place at the wrong time.

It was too big a slide, traveling too fast down the hill, to try to cross its path. The one bit of luck working for Walt was that he'd slowed considerably as he'd headed into the curve, cautious of the range of the sniper's rifle. He was not quite midslide, an area that looked to cover about two hundred yards. The first boulders of snow tumbled onto and across the cut of the roadbed, itself already buried in four feet of fresh snow. He jacked the handlebars, threw his left leg out, and gassed the accelerator, fishhooking the snowmobile into an about-face and cutting a deep rut that threatened to swallow the machine. Ironically, a snowmobile only worked well in deep snow if moving; if stopped or slowed significantly, it bogged down and was stranded.

The time consumed in turning it around cost him. More chunks of snow—two and three feet across—bounded on the road; the tremendous grinding sound of the slide overwhelmed him and literally shook the mechanized sled beneath him.

The avalanche came down the hill not as an arrow but as a snake's tongue, its forks faster and more charged than its center. Beyond the road's man-made, twenty-foot-wide patch of level track, the hill dropped away again precipitously, covered with trees and rock out-croppings.

He wasn't going to make it: the snowmobile had slowed as a result of the turn and the rush of snow now coming down pushed across the road as a unit, shoving Walt and the snowmobile sideways out in front of its headlong force. He had to make it at least another sixty yards to clear the turn and it wasn't going to happen.

Walt tugged on the handlebars and jumped the sled off the road. The snowmobile plowed into a drift, and Walt came fully off the seat, attached only by his bloodless grip. Behind him, the roar was unlike anything he'd ever heard: the open throat of a monster. The vehicle pulled up and out of the drift; Walt slammed back down onto the seat and twisted the accelerator, the full force of the avalanche now only yards behind him—a rising wall of debris shoved ahead of its unchecked force. Above the din, he heard the explosions of trees succumbing. The speed with which it now traveled dwarfed his own; one glance back told him as much.

There was no outrunning it.

At an incredible speed increased by the pull of gravity, he slalomed the sled down the hillside, narrowly missing tree trunks and dodging rocks. He tried to back off the accelerator, but it was no use: the whole hillside was moving out in front of that force, like he was riding a carpet being tugged out from under him. With the snow that carried him now itself in motion, the steering became unresponsive; he was no longer in control of the vehicle—the movement of the snow dictated his direction.

He faced a huge snow-covered rock to his right and a stand of massive trees straight ahead. He goosed the accelerator, yanked on the steering yoke—and nothing happened. The snowmobile carried him, as if on tracks, right for the tree trunks.

He leaped free and rolled, scrambling for the lee behind the rock outcropping. It was like swimming in sand. The crush of the avalanche lifted the snow beneath him and he rose like riding a wave. It firmed as it rose, the packed mass out in front, shelving up from under the fresh powder. He came to his knees like a surfer, measured his speed against the fixed position of the intractable rock outcropping, and dove.

Never the most athletic person, Walt nonetheless managed the perfect jump.

Now behind the enormous rock that towered some twenty feet overhead, he scrambled on hands and knees to hide in its lee.

The snowmobile crashed into the trees. Walt reached the shelter of the rock face, hugging himself to the stone and gripping it with both gloves. It divided the avalanche, the ice and snow flying past in a deafening roar that terrified him more than the snow itself. Some rocks and chunks of ice flew overhead but landed beyond him, the outcropping fully screening him from the downthrust of the slide. It seemed to last an hour; in all, it was just over four minutes.

Walls of snow now rose fifteen feet on either side of him as the avalanche advanced down the hill. He thought he would be buried. And then, without warning, it stopped. As still as concrete.

All sound seemed to stop along with it, replaced by the quiet calm of a winter forest. Some wood creaked. He heard the chittering of a squirrel followed by the irritated call of a western magpie.

He slid down to a sitting position on a slight cushion of snow in the protection of the rock and gave a prayer of thanks.

Then, suddenly, he heard the distinctive buzz of a snowmobile.

It was running hard, traveling away from him, fading slowly behind the frantic pulse of blood in his ears.

# 19

WALT CALLED OUT ON THE SATELLITE PHONE AND a challis deputy picked him up on Yankee Fork Road an hour later. Once in town, the Challis sheriff vented his frustration over Walt's destruction of their property and the dispatching of his men on what turned out to be a wild-goose chase: no one towing snowmobiles or matching Aker's description had been turned up at the now-defunct roadblocks. Walt's promise to replace the destroyed snowmobile failed to gain him much ground. The wolf incident a year earlier lay between them.

Brandon had been driven to a hospital in

Salmon, Idaho, which, as far as Walt was concerned, was the kiss of death, given the community's isolation. The polio vaccine was considered advanced medicine in Salmon. Brandon's only hope was that Salmon probably saw plenty of gunshot wounds.

Walt and the sheriff organized a team of four to revisit the Aker's cabin and collect evidence. There was much to be done, from photographing tracks, the broken window, and the cabin's interior to searching beneath the trees for shell casings. Walt called in Fiona's services and waited the two hours for her arrival.

It was agreed that Walt and Fiona could initially work the cabin.

Instead of snowshoeing up, everyone teamed up on snowmobiles. Fiona climbed on behind Walt. Her gloves were too thick for the strap on the seat behind him, so she ended up wrapping her arms around his waist, and she and Walt bounced their way up the road.

He leaned over his shoulder and shouted above the machine's roar. "Everything we have points to a kidnapping."

She shouted back. "This thing just gets crazier and crazier."

Walt hadn't told her about the avalanche, only the possible abduction and Brandon's shooting, which seemed enough information to process.

A few minutes later, they entered the cabin, and Walt propped the broken door shut to try to contain some of the warmth from the propane heater.

They circled the cabin's main room, Walt pointing out areas he wanted photographed.

They hadn't been inside but a few minutes when she asked, "Do you know a guy named Roger Hillabrand?"

"I know *of* him, sure. Extremely wealthy. Well-connected."

"I met him at a wedding I was shooting."

"And I need to know this because . . . ?" Having worked the floor for one full turn, Walt directed his attention to the furniture and the walls.

"No reason. Just wondered."

"I don't believe that," he said from the opposite side of the room.

"No reason," she repeated.

"Women don't mention other men for no reason."

"You're the sheriff. That gives you an insider's position when it comes to people like Roger Hillabrand."

"He's not a serial killer," Walt said. "That I'm aware of."

"Thank you."

"Now you're mad at me."

"No, I'm not."

"If you want me to be jealous, I'm considering it."

"Furthest thing from my mind, I promise you." She hesitated. "Why would I want *you* to be jealous, anyway?"

"My mistake," he said.

"It most certainly was."

"Government contracts. Like Halliburton. That kind of thing. Iraq. Afghanistan. Domestic work as well. Site clean-ups. Nuclear facilities. He attends the Cutter Conference—that's how I know all this. Has a very . . . professional . . . security detail around him."

"Was that sarcasm or cynicism?"

"Ex-military. *All* of them."

"Is that so unusual?"

"Yes, as a matter of fact it is. Ex-cops is more typical. Big-city cops: New York, Chicago, Miami. Those are the guys these guys hire. They've got the résumé, and they maintain good contacts. An effective security detail needs access to other law enforcement. Hiring military discharges gives you brawn but no brains, in terms of connections."

"Discounting the Pentagon."

"Knowing someone in the Pentagon doesn't tell you who you can trust in the NYPD to get your guy across town safely."

"But nothing bad? Roger, I mean. Does he have a reputation?"

"As a ladies' man? A drinker? A gambler? Not that I've heard, no. But he's in that upper echelon of power brokers, and, from what I've learned, they all dip their toes in that water, whether they're known for it or not."

"That's a little harsh, don't you think?"

"Over here," he said. She crossed the room and studied where he was pointing. Four pushpins framed an empty space on the wall. Three more pushpins were on the floor. They'd missed those pins the first time around, something neither mentioned but both were thinking.

Fiona readied her camera, changing some settings.

"Something was pinned up here. A photo maybe. Or a calendar. Or . . ." He reached out and gently moved a red push-pin, tilting it. A small triangle of torn paper swung down from where it was stabbed by the pin. There was a light green border on the white paper, along with a series of numbers.

"Money?" she said.

"If I had to guess, I'd say maybe a map. A topo map."

"Don't you have to guess?" she asked.

"As little as possible," he answered. "Those numbers on it will help us iden-tify it."

The cabin was constructed of three-sided logs, with the milled face on the interior. Walt pointed out three distinct pinholes at the center of the four others, which, to him, represented corners. He told her he wanted a lot of coverage on these, including a way to reconstruct it to scale.

He pocketed the torn corner of paper, protecting it in an evidence bag, and left her to work.

They were thirty minutes into it when Walt stomped his foot down onto the area rug in the small bathroom. His ear had

picked up a difference in sound and it did
so again. His thumping brought a curious
Fiona. He peeled back the area rug, which
was tacked on one end but loose on the
other.

It covered a hatch that had a recessed
handle carved out of the top. He pulled out
the Beretta for good measure, signaled
Fiona to step back, and yanked it open.
His penlight led the way as he climbed
down into the dark. He found a light switch,
and a compact fluorescent glowed.

It was a small, square space, eight feet
by eight feet—two sheets of plywood on
each wall. It had been dug into the earth
but was built only with wood, not concrete.

Mark had installed the equipment for
solar power down here: an inverter, a battery bank. There was a French-made
instant-hot-water device, an air pressure
tank, and a composting toilet that smelled
of peat moss. And two lawn chairs. A por-
table radio. Five-gallon jugs of spring water. A variety of freeze-dried foods. A camp
stove. Two sleeping bags—though not
enough room to unroll them.

Steep ladder steps led down, ending
near the battery bank.

Fiona clicked off several shots by lying down on the floor above. "A safe room?" she asked.

"Looks that way. Not originally, of course. But he'd made it into one. Check out the bolt," he said, indicating the open hatch.

She photographed the three large steel bolts on the underside of the hatch, making note of the steel plating that had been installed on not just the hatch but across most of the ceiling of the room.

"Jesus," she said. "Built for an invasion."

"Francine could have been down here," Walt said, noticing a partially eaten protein bar.

"When?" Fiona asked.

"When Tommy and I arrived. I never had time to look around. Tommy was shot and . . . the shooter . . . And we both took off. Shit! Francine could have been down here the whole time."

"We don't know that."

"I fucked up," he said.

"Your deputy was shot."

She was making excuses for him and he didn't like that.

"It's pretty crowded down here. Let me

get out, and then why don't you take pictures of everything you can?"

"Everything?"

"Cover it. I'm going to alert the Challis
deputies to be looking for a set of tracks
leaving the area. If Francine was here,
she's gone now. She's had several hours'
head start."

"But why would she take off?" Fiona
asked.

"It's bulletproof; it's not soundproof. It's
conceivable she heard her husband go
down. Heard someone take him away. Can
you imagine that? Then we arrive. More
shooting. I'd have taken off too."

"God . . ." she said.

"Work it like the crime scene it is," he instructed, as he climbed out of the space.

She was lying on her stomach on the
floor above as Walt climbed the ladder.
When they were face-to-face, Walt paused,
and, for a moment, they both just stared.
"Hillabrand *does* have a reputation," he
said, in more of a whisper. "He's suppos-
edly a good guy, someone who doesn't
throw his weight around and who gives
back to the community, which is more than
you can say for most of the people up

there in his income bracket. The Semper Group does billions a year."

"Okay," she said. "Thanks." Her breath smelled sweet, like chocolate.

LEAVING HIS CHEROKEE for Brandon to use, Walt rode with Fiona. The long drive through Stanley and back over Galena Pass forced the memory of Randy Aker's broken corpse back on him, as they passed the turnout where the tire tracks had been found. Twice he caught himself falling asleep but woke up, despite Fiona's encouraging him to rest.

She dropped him at his house.

Lisa had been with the girls since the close of school. Nikki had a runny nose, Emily a stomachache. Walt promised Lisa a bonus for her overtime—a false promise, they both knew, but his intention seemed to mean a great deal to her.

The clock on Mark Aker's abduction was running. The blood on the dart's needle could be used to confirm blood type, but Walt wasn't waiting. The sled had carried weight. That was enough for him. Lisa agreed to drop the twins off with Myra on her way home. They'd spend the night there. He battled his guilt. He'd fought like hell for joint custody, but, with no legal opinion yet returned, he proved his own worst enemy. It would appear he had little to offer the girls beyond an unreliable schedule and multiple handoffs to a variety of caregivers. Not the most stable environment. If he'd caught Gail treating them this way, he'd have brought it as evidence against her. She might do the same to him. He had to work out a balance.

He had just come out of a hot shower when he heard the crunch of breaking glass at the back of the house. It didn't sound like a window; more like a lightbulb, on the back porch. Still dripping wet, he slipped into some workout pants, grabbed the Beretta, and headed stealthily through the house, working his way quickly to the kitchen. He sneaked a look out onto the back porch, surprised to see the light working, then cut quickly to the door and yanked it open, keeping himself shielded behind the doorjamb. With the gun now in both hands, he broke outside for a better look, immediately hopping to his left when his right foot took a shard of broken glass.

Footsteps in the snow. Walt hadn't shoveled the back path since the storm and he'd had no reason to be back there. He pulled the shard from the ball of his foot and headed down into the snow in his bare feet. He couldn't take the cold for more than a couple of seconds, but it gave him a chance to follow the tracks with his eyes out into a stand of aspen that separated him from his neighbor's house. A silhouette flickered there, tucked into the trees.

"Hey!" Walt called out.

Whoever it was took off at a run. Walt made it about ten yards in that direction before his frozen feet stopped him. A short adult, or someone young.

He returned to the porch and studied the broken glass there. It was thin glass, smashed around a cylindrical plug of milky ice. He avoided it, returned inside, and came back out dressed for the cold.

Had his visitor dropped it? Stepped on it?

He had returned wearing a pair of evidence gloves, collected the pieces of glass into a paper bag; the plug of ice went into a Ziploc. Handling the tight curve of the pieces, he tried to fit them together in his mind's eyes. A test tube?

Mark Aker, he thought.

How long had it been out there? Had it arrived frozen or had it frozen on its own? Had the freezing of the contents broken the glass and *then* someone had stepped on it or had his visitor just now crushed it accidentally? Most important: what was its significance?

**Mark** . . .

The lack of any note or instruction confused him. Had his visitor been interrupted and a ransom note gone undelivered?

His cell phone rang from inside the house, and he ran to answer it.

The hospital lab: the blood recovered from the dart, a dart carrying a barbiturate cocktail typically reserved for bull elephants, had come back a match for Mark Akers: O positive. Adding to the lab's confusion was the fact that the chemical composition of the dart's drug matched another they'd processed earlier in the day: that of the patient Kira Tulivich.

# WEDNESDAY

# 20

BY ONE P.M. WEDNESDAY, WALT WAS BEGINNING to work the evidence. The first was the result of Randy Aker's blood workup out of Boise. It confirmed both medetomidine and ketamine, the same doping agents used on Kira Tulivich and Mark Aker.

The second was the broken glass and plug of ice—now melted—that he'd had one of his men hand deliver to the Boise lab. Its contents might suggest who'd left it. He suspected it was a gift from Mark Aker; but, with little to back that up, he hoped for the lab's clarification.

The third piece of evidence was the torn

triangle of paper found stabbed into the wall in Mark's cabin.

Nancy entered his office and unrolled a topographical map across the mounds of paperwork piled on his desk. This was, in part, a comment on the neatness of his desk.

"Took no time at all," she said. "The librarian recognized it immediately by the shade of green. She's a hiker. Uses topos all the time. Sent me over to the Elephant's Perch and it was the same thing there, only, this time, because of the number printed on it, they pulled the exact map. We matched the torn corner to it."

"Mark had a topographical map of the Pahsimeroi Valley hanging on his cabin wall?"

"Correct."

The map did not include his cabin's location, which intrigued Walt. It covered the valley forty miles to the southeast. He turned the map right side up, putting what would have been the torn piece into the lower-right corner.

"Get Fiona," he instructed Nancy. "Tell her I need the reconstruction of the cabin wall. She'll know what that means."

By two P.M., Fiona and Walt had overlaid the topo map, already pinned to corkboard, with the photographic enlargements, all done to scale. Seven eight-by-ten printouts had been taped together to form a whole. These were fitted over the map, using the torn corner piece and the three other corner pushpin marks as references. With the map now fully covered by high-resolution shots of Mark Aker's cabin wall—the coarse texture and yellow color of rough-sawn timber—it looked as if they'd removed a piece of the wall and had brought it with them. It was the three black dots, like fly-specks, that interested Walt.

He double-checked the alignment of the photos over the map. Allowing for the fact that three other corner pins might be off by a quarter inch or so, it looked like a good job.

Fiona eyed it proudly. "You realize the map went on the wall, not the other way around? Shouldn't we put the wall behind the map?"

"Yeah, but I want to use the holes that were in the wall to mark our map. We saw three pushpins on the floor. What if they were marking certain spots?" Walt withdrew a pushpin from the side of the corkboard and answered her by carefully poking the pin's needle through each of the three black specks. He then removed the photographs, leaving the map with three new pinholes in it.

Fiona went quiet as she watched him work. He crossed to a computer and called up a mapping website that included hybrid images of maps overlaid onto satellite imagery. A few clicks later he had zoomed in on the Pahsimeroi Valley, with small, circular green dots, each the product of a pivot irrigation system—a huge, wheeled sprinkler arm that irrigated a quarter square mile of ground. These identified working ranches. He then cross-referenced the two maps and used the cursor on the computer to give him latitude and longitude for each of the pin markings.

He wrote down the three locations, knowing they held significance for Mark Aker. It was possible that Aker had visited them, either professionally or otherwise.

"How'd you do that?" she asked.

"You just saw me."

"No. I mean, how'd it occur to you to do that?"

"It's what I do," he answered.

"Three pinpricks in a log wall. Are you kidding me?"

"Three ranches," he said, standing and studying the topo map. "A vet," he reminded.

The discovery that Aker had pinpointed the ranches intrigued Walt. As a vet, the man did plenty of house calls without marking them on maps. He'd been told of Mark's secretive ways over the past month, of Mark's spending extra time up at the cabin. But no one knew he'd actually been at the cabin; he could have easily been over in the Pahsimeroi.

He opened the door to the incident room and called out loudly for Tommy Brandon, startling Fiona with the sharpness of his voice.

Brandon appeared, his left arm in a sling. It was the first the two had seen each other since the shooting. Other deputies would have taken a week's leave, but Walt had received no such request on his desk and knew Brandon would give him no excuse to be put on leave.

"You okay?" Walt asked.

"Fine."

"Want to take a ride?"

"Where to?"

"Randy Aker was shot with a ketamine cocktail before he dove off those rocks. He was wearing his brother's jacket—his brother's scent. Now, come to find out, Mark was drugged by the same cocktail. And he was interested in three ranches over in the Pahsimeroi. He marked them on a topo map he had pinned to his cabin wall. Whoever took Mark probably took the map as well."

"Count me in," Brandon said.

# 21

BEFORE HE GOT OUT OF THE BUILDING, WALT WAS grabbed by the officer on duty and introduced to a gorgeous woman from the Denver office of the CDC. Lynda Bezel was in her early thirties and wore a dark blue suit. It wasn't a look typically seen in Hailey, Idaho. The Sun Valley look was Patagonia and Eddie Bauer; faded jeans, hiking boots, and clinging tops. She had a creamy complexion, and pale eyes that opened wide as she spoke.

"This might be better discussed in confidence," she said. She had a raspy bedroom voice and the coy smile that went along with it. She sat in Walt's intentionally uncomfortable visitor's chair. She crossed her legs with a whisper of panty hose.

"I've come here as a courtesy," Bezel began, comfortable with taking the lead. "Daniel Cutter is on probation, as we understand it. Because he's in the system, I thought it only right to pay you a visit and let you know I intend to question him later today."

Walt had a history with Danny Cutter that went back several years. Patrick Cutter, Danny's older brother, now ran a billion-dollar cellular company. Danny, whom Walt liked better than his far-more-successful brother, had a prior arrest and conviction on drug charges. He'd spent time in a federal minimum security facility before returning to Ketchum, just in time to be caught up in a murder investigation—the valley's only murder in six years. He was a womanizer, a hard-partying boy who had cleaned up his act and, as part of his attempt to reestablish himself, had founded a bottled-water company, called Trilogy Springs, based in Ketchum.

"Concerning?" he asked.

"We were contacted by a Salt Lake City

hospital. Two of Mr. Cutter's employees have taken ill. Their condition is listed as serious. Doctors have not been able to stabilize them. I'm here to interview Mr. Cutter about his company's role, if any, in these illnesses and to question him about his actions. We have a full inspection team on the way to the Trilogy Springs bottling facility, near Mackay, Idaho."

"What actions?"

"It has come to our attention that Mr. Cutter may have flown the two employees in a private jet to Salt Lake City while possibly denying them medical care locally."

"You think he tasked those two down to Salt Lake to avoid being found out? That doesn't sound like Danny. Listen, Salt Lake's the better health care. All our Life Flights go to Boise or Salt Lake."

Bezel jotted down something into a small notebook. She looked comfortable in the chair. Maybe she was into yoga; she looked it.

"You said you came to me as a courtesy," Walt said, somewhat suspiciously.

"Exactly."

"Is there a probation violation?"

"He traveled with the employees out of

state. I assume that was with your knowledge and permission?"

He was getting the idea now. Beneath
the superfeminine façade was a bulldog.
"I'm not his probation officer."

"But, as a felon, he's required to notify
your office if he intends to travel out of
state, is he not?"

"He is."

"Did he do that in person or by phone?"

Walt felt cornered. He wasn't going to
lie for Danny Cutter, but he didn't like the
idea of the CDC playing babysitter.

"I could check with his PO."

"Would you, please. The point is, if he
entered this facility—your offices—there's
the possibility of contagion."

"The illness is contagious?"

"There are two patients with similar
symptoms. Tests are being conducted.
Doctors have not yet identified the illness.
We've asked both Mr. Cutter and his assistant to keep themselves isolated prior
to my arrival. My job is to track their movements since their contact with the indi-
viduals in question. We've also notified
the pilots as well as employees at the

Fixed Base Operation that serviced the plane."

He read between the lines. "Are you saying this is somehow terrorist related?" He'd had the recent warning from Homeland concerning activity by the Samakinn. "Was Trilogy contaminated intentionally?"

"We don't know what we've got, much less how Cutter's employees might have contracted it. But, with your permission, we'd like to pass out tags to everyone employed here." She produced what looked like a car air freshener, a round disc in a cheap plastic frame divided into six wedges of different-colored paper. It dangled from her fingers like a Christmas ornament. "And we'd like both physical swabs of the environment and a few blood samples."

"Jesus."

"Your deputies and staff come in contact with the public. Should any one of these indicators change colors, no matter how subtle, we need to hear about it."

Walt knew from recent training that such indicators had been proven to help field investigators narrow down searches and limit exposure. He had a box of similar tags in a cupboard in the incident room. He'd never had use for them.

"Sure," he said. "I don't have a problem with that."

"We'd appreciate it if every member of your staff—"

"I get it," said Walt, interrupting. "Leave them with me. I'll see to it."

"Companies in your county are aware of their obligation under federal guidelines to notify both you and our center in the event of suspected contamination or un-explained illness, are they not?"

"I would assume so. We've spread the word, and there's been a lot of literature."

"Can you think of any reason Daniel Cutter would elect *not* to notify either of us?"

"They're guidelines, recommendations, not requirements, if I'm not mistaken."

"But you'd think with his history—"

"This is the first I've heard of it. I'm sure if you ask him, he'll tell you. Danny isn't what you'd call shy."

Bezel said, "Please instruct your officers to remain alert for flulike symptoms and nosebleeds."

"You make it sound like Ebola."

"We don't know what we're dealing with," Bezel said, her face suddenly severe, her husky voice an octave lower. "I wouldn't be making any jokes."

"Nerves," Walt said. "I'm not real comfortable with biological agents."

"Neither are we, Sheriff," Bezel said.

# 22

"IT'S REALLY QUITE SIMPLE," THE MAN SAID, OVER the sound of wood popping and crackling inside a woodstove. Aker sat, tied to a ladder-back chair, wearing a black hood. A syringe and some vials sat in an enamel tray on a game table to his left. A dog was curled up by the woodstove. The ceiling was vaulted to the cabin's roof, the scissor trusses exposed. The air smelled strongly of coffee and, less so, of the distinct but foreign odors of pharmaceuticals.

"We need you to write up a report on what you found," he continued.

"Found where?" Mark Aker asked through the fabric of the hood.

"The sheep. Don't play dumb with me."

"Writing a paper requires lab work, research, *patience*, and a lot of time," he said.

"You've done all that."

"I did some. It's true. But I need more time. If you release me . . ."

"All I'm talking about is a discovery of findings."

"I'm a long way from that. It's true, I have theories. If you want me to stop my research, I will. No questions asked."

"To the contrary: I need you to scientifically confirm what I already know. You can help me here. I want you to publish what you've found, not hide it." He paused. "You think I'm trying to fuck you, don't you? I'm not! I want you to publish."

"If you want me to do that, I will. But first you need to drop me off near a hospital and you need to do it real soon, if you're going to avoid manslaughter charges."

"I'm not going to kill you. Relax. This isn't about stopping you from doing your research; it's about publishing it. You're misunderstanding. Publish what you know and we'll release you."

"It's you who's not understanding, asswipe. See, I'm an insulin-dependent diabetic. In a couple of hours, if not sooner, my heart rate's going to increase, I'll start breathing rapidly, and I'll pass out. I'll go into shock. And if I don't receive medical care, I'll die. As for your report: I won't live long enough to write the first paragraph. Get me to a hospital; I'll do whatever you want."

A dark musical score ran through his head; it had begun with the mention of diabetes. He untied Aker's feet and wrestled to bring his unwilling body out of the chair. Aker fell sideways and the chair crashed to the floor. Aker thrashed, and landed a kick to the man's left ear, before he was restrained. The man unfastened Aker's belt and pulled his pants down.

Aker's left buttock was riddled with circular bruises, the result of insulin shots.

"Motherfucker!" the man shouted. He snorted and paced the small area angrily.

"I need insulin, Coats," Aker said.

During the ruckus, the hood had come off.

Roy Coats heard his name spoken. He stared at his hostage. *How in the world?*

"R. Coats, right?" Aker said. "And she would be Dimples," he said, referring to the dog, now by the fire. The dog had gotten close enough earlier for Aker to see down through the opening at his neck. And he'd recognized her. "Front right paw bitten by a rattlesnake . . . what, two years ago? You owe me a hundred and eighty bucks for that, Coats. I tend not to forget the customers who don't pay."

"Shut the fuck up."

"What are you going to do, kill me?" he said, amused. "I'm going to die here, Coats. And let me tell you something: it won't be pretty."

"You're not going to die. You're going to write your report."

"Would if I could, but I don't think so. I don't remember how you got me here. I don't even remember how you found me. Ketamine?" he asked. "Headache tells me it's ketamine. But there's not a sound anywhere near us. Not even planes going over. So I've got to think we're a long way from anywhere. And that doesn't bode well for me. Challis? Salmon? The Pahsimeroi?

Stanley? You're never going to get the insulin in time."

Coats paced between the stove and back again, his head hanging, the fingers of his right hand tugging at whiskers in his beard. Then he stopped and addressed Aker, who remained on the floor. "The islets of Langerhans," Roy Coats said.

Aker couldn't conceal his astonishment.

"My mom was type 1," Coats explained. "I know all about acidosis."

Aker's focus changed as he took in the cabin walls, all floor to ceiling with books. Hundreds, perhaps thousands, of them.

"The second coming of Ted Kaczynski?"

"I'd watch my mouth, if I were you." Coats began searching the stacks for a particular title. "There's a cow, two pigs, and some chickens out back."

"I'm a little old for a petting zoo. I'll pass."

"Last warning about that mouth."

"What exactly do you think you're holding over me, Coats? Without insulin, I'm on my way out."

"Bovine and pig insulin kept diabetics

alive for decades. It wasn't until the nineteen fifties that they synthesized it."

"You cannot be serious," Aker said. "Oh,
I get it: you're Frederick Banting, not Ted
Kaczynski."

"Both the pig and the cow have a pancreas, and that's all we need." Coats pulled
a book from a shelf, returned it, and se-
lected another. "All I've got to do is keep
you alive until the next radio check. We
stay off the airwaves. Only check in once
a day. You're the vet. You want to live, doc,
you're going to have to earn your supper."

# 23

TWO MOUNTAIN PASSES THAT WOULD HAVE BEEN available to Walt in the summer months were closed by snow for the winter, forcing him to travel southeast around the ends of three mountain ranges that pointed like fingers into central Idaho's vast, arid plain. He and Brandon said little on the two-hour drive that took them through Carey, Arco, and, finally, the tiny town of Howe, which consisted of a Church of Latter-day Saints, a post office, and a general store. He drove northeast into the Pahsimeroi Valley. With long, subzero winters, and only enough surface water to support a dozen ranches, the Pahsimeroi existed in a time warp, virtually unchanged for a thousand years. Majestic mountains surrounded a valley floor of rabbitweed and sagebrush. Aspen and cottonwood trees lined its few streams and creeks. Herds of antelope flashed their white tails like garden rabbits while red-tailed hawks sailed effortlessly on the steady winds that made this place so inhospitable to man.

A two-lane road, dead straight, plowed through a tablecloth of white, splitting the valley in two. It was as breathtaking a piece of Idaho scenery as could be found, and Walt never grew tired of looking at it.

"You get over here, it's like another world," Brandon said.

"My father used to hunt here."

"You don't hunt," Brandon said, as if it had just occurred to him.

"No."

Brandon tracked a handheld GPS, the topo map unrolled on his lap, his actions awkward due to the sling. He cross-checked the map with the device, occasionally glancing over to the right, where he imagined the first of Mark Aker's three pinholed locations.

"You think I'm nuts coming here," Walt said.

"Did I say anything?"

"It's all we've got to go on: three pin-holes in a map."

"Maybe it's enough," Brandon said.

Walt gripped the wheel more firmly. The tension he was feeling had nothing to do with the snow floor he was driving on.

"There was a time I wanted her back," Walt said.

Brandon took the opportunity to check the GPS and then to look out the window for the umpteenth time.

"If I fire you, I look resentful. Maybe you sue me."

Brandon reached for the door handle. "I could walk home from here; it's only a couple hundred miles."

"It's the girls I'm thinking about," Walt said. "First and foremost, it's the girls."

"Shit," Brandon whispered. "Can we stop this?"

"You want to fuck my wife, that's your business. Your risk. But you're fucking me along with her, and you should have thought about that." He glanced over at Brandon.

"You think I didn't?"

"Ketchum has an opening for a deputy. Bellevue, maybe."

The suggestion hung inside the car as it raced up the empty two-lane road. Walt felt insignificant and small.

"My guess is," Brandon said too loudly, acting as if the recent exchange had not happened, "we're not going to get in there because the road won't be plowed."

"It'll be plowed," Walt said. He answered Brandon's puzzled expression. "Mark visited here. He called on a client. And, in this valley, it's either cattle or sheep. They'll keep the road open in winter in order to feed. The satellite map had four or five pivots clustered out there. That's a ranch, for sure." Walt having said that, an interruption in the plowed bank appeared a quarter mile ahead. He slowed the Cherokee.

"She complains, I'll bet," Walt said. "About your trailer being so small, about your work hours."

"Is that why you asked me along, Sheriff? Make sure I log in a lot of OT?"

"Yup."

Brandon winced. He hadn't expected the truth.

He was squirming inside, right where Walt wanted him.

"Did you notify the Lemhi sheriff?" Brandon asked.

"I might have forgotten," Walt said.

"Because?"

"Lemhi's a different kind of county. You can't throw a stick without hitting someone's nephew or cousin. It's too cozy. I don't want to give him a chance to rehearse anything."

"What would he rehearse?"

"How would I know?"

"Then why say that?"

"Something got Randy killed. Maybe it was the poaching, but I'm not so sure. I think it was the coat he was wearing: Mark's coat. And now that Mark's been abducted, and we've found the same date-rape cocktail in Randy's blood, I'm guessing Randy's death was some kind of misfire. So it's all on Mark and whatever he was hiding up in his cabin, which means one or all of these ranches are involved."

"No shit."

"What gets a vet in trouble? One thing keeps coming to me: mad cow. That's something any rancher, and especially these good old boys out here, would make damn sure to keep quiet."

Brandon was no longer paying attention to his GPS. He was leaning in his seat toward Walt, hanging on his every word.

"So what they'd be rehearsing," Walt said, "is some piece of fiction to provide cover for Mark coming out here, and tracking their ranches, and sticking goddamn pushpins in a map to mark their homesteads, something that has nothing to do with whatever was the original reason they called him out here in the first place."

"Mad cow."

"It's got to be something along those lines. Something big. Something that makes the truth too expensive."

"So why go to the trouble of abducting him? These old boys are plenty used to the rifle. I don't see them getting all sentimental."

"Who knows? Could be they wanted to establish if he'd told anyone. How far along he was in his findings. Could still be their plan to kill him. He could be dead right now."

He wished he could take back what he'd just said. Saying such things gave them weight. He drove through an open gate in a wire fence and bounced the Cherokee across a cattle guard. Thing rattled to beat hell. A pair of steel grain sheds rose from the snow like gray hats to his left. He drove past a hundred-acre field that was probably knee-high with alfalfa in the summer. Black veins of meandering cow trails cut through the deep snow. A herd of seventy or eighty Angus was wedged tightly into the field's southwest corner, their backs to the wind.

Walt directed the Cherokee toward the granaries, two wood barns, and a two-story gray clapboard house with white trim. He studied the cows for signs of illness but didn't know what he was looking for: they all looked mad to him.

In the field directly ahead, sheep fretted, dancing nervously back and forth, as Walt's Cherokee drew closer. White on white, broken by black legs and black heads. Puppets on unseen strings.

"The thing I'd never get used to about living on a farm like this," Brandon said, sniffing the air, "is the stink."

"It's usually not so bad in winter," Walt said. "I've got to admit: that's funky." It was a horrid, bitter smell. Sour and permeating. It only hit them now, as they drove close to the buildings.

"A smell like that," Brandon said, "no wonder they called a vet."

# 24

LON BERNIE MET THE CHEROKEE WITH FOUR dogs at his side. In his late fifties, with a florid complexion and soft gray eyes, he wore dirty canvas coveralls, a smudged cowboy hat, and large rubber-coated gloves. His nose carried a curved scar the size of a thumbnail, as pink as Pepto-Bismol. A front tooth had been chipped in a bull-riding championship when Bernie was nineteen. He still wore the belt with the oversized silver buckle to dances at the Grange Hall on Saturday nights, after a steak at the Loading Chute.

"I see a sheriff's car coming, I expect it

to be Ned," the rancher said, tugging off his glove and offering his calloused hand to both men. His voice sounded like a gearbox with broken parts. "You're a long way from home."

"Couple questions, is all, if you've got the time," Walt said.

Brandon banged his boots together, already cold. Windchill was pushing the mercury into the single digits. "Ain't got nothing but time, this time of year."

Lon Bernie looked out over Walt's head—the man was a giant—surveying his animals. He reminded Walt of Hoss Cartwright. Walt sensed in him a cautiousness, a reluctance. It felt for a moment as if the rancher might be considering inviting them inside or to follow him on his chores. Something flickered in his gray eyes as Lon Bernie sucked some air through his top teeth.

"Be my guest," he said.

Walt shot a quick glance over at Brandon. His deputy stopped banging his boots together.

"Mark Aker, Sun Valley Animal Center, did some work for you recently."

Lon Bernie's gray eyes iced over. There

was no change in his otherwise-pleasant expression. A fog fled his mouth on each exhale. Lon Bernie: a steam engine climbing the hill.

"Had a cow down with the bloat," the rancher said. He didn't seem to feel the cold. Walt was freezing. "Mel Hickenbottom was busy up to Challis. He's usually the one I'd call. This Aker fellow stepped in. You can't wait too long with the bloat."

"Well, that's a good start for us. You remember how you paid him?"

Lon Bernie briefly lost his composure. "I paid him good, I'll tell you what. It's a long drive over here, and he charged by the hour. How is it my livestock is any of your business, anyway, Sheriff? You going to answer me that?"

"The vet's brother was killed two nights ago. Now the vet's gone missing. Mark's last business brought him over this direction." Lon Bernie's face remained expressionless. "Mark doesn't often tend to the bigger animals. That's his brother's job. Seems he made an exception. That interests me. The appointment book shows it was Mel Hickenbottom who called the center. Said your sheep were suffering.

Your sheep, not your cattle. No mention of bloat."

"Could be right," Lon Bernie said, without missing a beat. "Coulda been the way you say. Maybe it was Mel handled the bloat and the Glitter Gulch vet the sheep."

The nickname for the Sun Valley area was not new to Walt. The valley's wealth and glamour offended people like Lon Bernie, and there was nothing to be done about it. Most of the resentment stemmed from jealousy and ignorance and was therefore undeserved. Most but not all. Not by a long shot. Lon Bernie was letting him and Brandon know they were outsiders here and therefore unwelcome, business or not.

"Was it the cattle or the sheep?" Walt asked pointedly.

"I said one of my cattle had the bloat, didn't I? Something's always sick around here."

"What specifically was wrong with your sheep?"

"If I'd known that," Lon Bernie said, "I wouldn'ta needed no vet, now, would I?"

"Did you get an answer? A diagnosis?"

"You ever been around sheep, Sheriff?"

The rancher looked to his right and the hundreds of thick wool coats milling about. "Dumb as paint. You look at 'em wrong and they take sick. Or they throw themselves in the irrigation ditch and their coats get too heavy and they drown themselves in two feet of water. I leave 'em to the vets. A couple of shots and they're right as rain. I pay my bills on time, and that's about all there is to it. I'm not asking for no diagnosis, just results."

"The sheep are better now, then? Did Mark Aker have success with the sheep? Or was he working on your cattle?"

Lon Bernie's eyes went stone cold. A grin twitched at the edges of his cracked lips.

"Maybe what happened," Walt suggested, "was that Mel called Mark about the sheep, but then, when Mark got here, it turned out Mel had misspoken and it was actually the cattle having problems."

"You think I don't know which of my animals is having problems, Sheriff? You got a dog? A cat? You can't tell the difference? Not me. A head of cattle had the bloat. That's all."

"My brother," Brandon said, "once had a

cow with bloat. Stuck his Swiss Army knife
in the cow and about the worst smell I've
ever smelled came out. But that cow stood
up five minutes later and went on her way.
He never even called the vet."

"Cattle's got three stomachs, son. Depends which one catches the bloat. I put
a knife to our cow three times. Doggone
pincushion. Got nothing. Then I called
Mel. I thought I was the one called your
Glitter Gulch fellow, but, maybe you're
right, it could have been Mel. Don't see
how it matters."

"Mel took care of the bloat. Mark worked
with the sheep," Walt stated. He did not
ask.

"Hell, it has been a month or more,
Sheriff. What do I know?"

"Have you heard of any illness at your
neighbors' ranches? Sheep or cattle?"

"No, sir, I have not." The man's answer
came out much too quickly and sharply.
He'd been expecting that question.

"Would you happen to have a bill
handy?" Brandon asked. "Could we maybe
get a look at it?"

"I pay 'em and I throw 'em out, son."

"It's 'Deputy,' or 'Deputy Sheriff,' not

'son,'" Brandon said, making no effort to conceal his contempt. "The vet, Hicken-bottom, would have records?"

"Might have. You'd have to ask him."

"We will." Brandon withdrew his note-book and scribbled in it.

"I don't see what all the fuss is about," Lon Bernie said.

"A man's dead," Walt reminded. "That's fuss enough for us."

The wind picked up. At a certain tem-perature, it seemed it couldn't get any colder, but it always did. Lon Bernie still didn't seem to feel it.

"Ever had any sign of mad cow over this way?" Walt asked, hoping for a reaction.

"That's never come down from Canada, as far as I know."

"And the last time you called upon either vet would have been . . . ?"

Lon Bernie cocked his head toward Walt, as if he had only one good eye. "A while," he said.

"Can you be more specific?"

"Out here, time kinda runs into itself. Drive a man half mad, this time of year. Maybe more than half."

"Cattle bloat from eating too much green grass," Walt said.

"A month ago, we had green grass. Early winter this year. Moldy hay'll do it too. You trying to make a point, Sheriff? 'Cause you're going the long way around the barn to find the door." He looked first at Walt, then at Brandon.

"I'll tell you what I need: I need the truth, Mr. Bernie. And I don't believe I'm getting it."

"You calling me a liar, Sheriff? 'Cause, over here, that's not terribly neighborly. Listen, I've got chores to do." He never flinched, as he maintained eye contact with Walt.

He turned and walked toward the barns.

The foul smell had not been apparent while Walt and Brandon had been out of the vehicle, but as they drove away from the ranch it filled the car again. Complaining, Brandon rolled down the window.

That seemed to only make matters worse.

Like burning hair.

# 25

ROY COATS TRUDGED AROUND BEHIND THE CABIN along a path shoveled through four feet of snow that created a trench with six-foot-high walls. He avoided the piles of frozen dog excrement, as if they were land mines.

The narrator in his head wouldn't shut up.

**The rebel soldier must learn to improvise if he is to survive. The needs of the few give way to the needs of the man. Faced with the possible death of his hostage, he's willing to make a sacrifice.**

Coats called the two cows and the pig

by their names: Bess, Tilda, and Pinky. He
didn't think enough of the chickens to
name them. He had, on many occasions,
launched into rambling diatribes with only
these three as his audience. He'd gone on
about the injustices to society brought on
by the immigration influenza, the disease
of poverty eating into society like a cancer.
He had stood on the milking stool and lec-
tured for ninety minutes at a time, his voice
carrying over their heads and fading into
the thousands of acres of empty wilderness that surrounded his homestead. The
government had lost its way, focused entirely overseas, when there was cleaning
up to do at home. He'd chosen the name
Samakinn carefully, never mind that his
recruitment had not gone well. A spear
was needed. The Romans, the Croats, the
Uzbeks, the Hutus all had the right idea:
ethnic cleansing. But it started with being
heard, being taken seriously. The government thought they could silence their
voices by denying their acts. But once the
people heard of what they'd done, how
powerful they were, the Samakinn's message would be heard. Supporters would
swell their ranks. Change would be at

hand. He sought legitimacy, nothing less: credit where credit was due. The doc would make his report—who didn't believe a doctor?

He had a long night ahead of him, dressing out whichever beast he decided to kill. It was a great deal to ask of him. The sacrifice had begun.

As prearranged, the daily radio call didn't happen until midnight; that meant it would be a while before Gearbox could arrive with the insulin. He had no choice but to act, compounding his resentment.

The cows gathered on the other side of the fence, expecting a feeding. Pinky was smart enough to wait inside the pen. He hadn't realized how difficult this would be. Like killing a house pet. He was willing to see Aker or others die for his cause but not one of his stock.

He considered Pinky first. He had no great rapport with the sow and considered her a dirty, though lovable, companion. But the size of the pancreas mattered, and that quickly took her out of consideration. It was either Bess or Tilda, and Bess's condition demanded it be her.

He used a can of grain to lure her through

the side door of the ramshackle shed at the corner of the paddock, the chickens making noise in the coop as if a fox were on the prowl. He wanted her as close to the block and tackle as possible, knowing he'd have to rig some kind of motor or winch to hoist all eight hundred pounds of her.

He got a harness on her head while she was still standing. Attached a length of chain to the front ring and secured it to a two-ton pickup truck that hadn't run in years. She was chewing on the grain, the first she'd had in a long, long time, and he knew that for a cow this was as close to heaven as it got.

So he scratched her on the head between the eyes, feeling the hard bone beneath the tough skin. Dust rose from the black-and-white hair. It had formed a permanent layer on both animals.

"You've been a good girl all these years, Bess," he said, his throat tightening. "Your being pregnant is your downfall. What can I say? No greater honor than to fall a martyr for a cause. I ought to know that. I expect I'll be seeing you soon."

He stabbed the knife in sharply at the

jugular. Dragged and twisted its blade until she sprayed, her eyes pure white, as she reeled and cried out. Leaned his weight into it, pulling for her windpipe, wanting this over with.

Resentment filled that part of his heart emptied by grief. He would see the vet dead for this, after he'd written the report.

# 26

WALT STOPPED THE CHEROKEE BESIDE THE closed fence gate. He could see the end of a double-wide trailer, some outbuildings, and curved mounds in the snow about a hundred yards past the gate.

"Looks like snowmobiles been running in and out," Brandon said. The track started on the other side of the closed gate and had been beaten down by a good many trips.

"Roads are all snow floor," Walt observed. "A snowmobile's as good as a car."

Walt leaned on the horn, and they waited

for some sign of life from the ranch. When none was forthcoming, they left the Cherokee parked where it was and went in on foot. As they neared the cabin, they saw that the snowmobile track connected with others, forming a network of beaten-down paths leading to and from various outbuildings.

Walt shouted, "Sheriff's Office!" It wouldn't have surprised either man to be greeted by the wrong end of a shotgun, and Brandon walked with his good hand resting on the stock of his pistol. The cold dry snow squeaked beneath their boots.

When their knocks on the door went unanswered, they checked the neighboring outbuildings. One was a working garage, the other a storage shed overrun with junk.

A snowmobile track continued past a granary, leading toward the fence line.

"I know you think she's using me to get at you, but that's not the way it is," Brandon said, as they trudged through the snow.

Walt stopped and turned to make sure Brandon heard him. "You're my best deputy. You think that's coincidence?" He turned and walked on.

"You two were separated."

"She convinced herself she was a lousy mother. She envied how easily the parenting came to me. It isn't about you. It's about the kids. She's having second thoughts now. She's going to fight for them. Are you ready for that?"

Brandon stopped short, and the distance between them grew. He had to hurry to catch back up.

"I want to work for you. This is where I belong."

"Grow up."

The rancher was a pack rat. The mushrooms of snow seen from a distance turned out to be junk: dishwashers, farm implements, tires, car parts, tractor parts, furniture. It surrounded every building, looming mysteriously out of the snow.

"Damn," Brandon said.

"You notice what's missing?" Walt asked.

"Human beings?"

"Listen."

The two men stopped. Absolute silence.

"It's quiet enough," Brandon admitted.

"And then some." Walt led Brandon

along one of the snowmobile paths to a fence line. The snow out in the pasture was rippled and dented by interconnecting seams, not flat and pristine. It reminded Walt of a brain. But there was no recent activity. All of the wandering seams connected into a single point down the fence line near yet another outbuilding.

"Those lines mark where the snow was trod down by livestock," Walt said, pointing toward the shed. "Then a fresh snow covered them up."

"So where's the livestock?"

"That's the point, Deputy. Moved 'em off the place." Walt pointed to where all the paths connected. His eyes couldn't make out a gate there, but he expected to find one. "I'd say it was probably to another field, but we're not hearing them."

"Who moves their livestock in winter?"

"It's a pain," Walt agreed. "Unless a water line froze or the snow got too dry. They might move them to make feeding easier."

Walt started down the fence line through the knee-deep snow.

"What the hell?" Brandon called out, hesitating to join him.

"Check the trailer again. Another reason

the livestock would be moved is if someone died."

Brandon mulled that over. Walt kept on
walking, trudging with difficulty through the
snow.

"Are you mad at me, Sheriff? For what I
said?" Brandon called out.

"Shut up and check the trailer."

"Yes, sir."

The farther down the fence line he went,
the tougher it got for Walt, his legs growing weary from the deep snow. Sweat ran
down his rib cage, despite the harsh cold
that whipped his face, but there was something else he felt: an unease brought on
by the utter stillness of the place, and the
growing sensation he and Brandon were
being watched.

As he drew closer to the shed, he picked
out the outline of a feed trough, a double-
hung gate, and a pair of automatic waterers. He arrived to the feed trough and saw
it was filled with snow, suggesting the animals had been moved sometime between
the two most recent snowstorms—in the
last five to six days. He studied the sweep
of the gate, the way it had pushed the prior
snowfall ahead of it as it had been opened.

This too confirmed his time line. Mark Aker had made a twoday trip to his cabin a few days earlier, just before the search and rescue that took his brother's life. Had this ranch been a stop for him during those two days? What had he found? Why had the livestock been moved?

Fighting the deep snow, he wrestled open the shed's large door far enough to squeeze through. It was dark inside, shafts of sunlight appearing as Walt kicked up dust from the dirt floor. A milking station and some stalls. A squeeze chute, used to isolate an animal for doctoring or branding.

He slipped back through the door to the outside. He might have missed it had he not visited the shed, for only now did he get a good look at the automatic waterers.

The waterers were clear of snow but dry. Warmed by a thermostat in winter months, with a float valve to control the water level, the devices were used to save the rancher from fighting ice and trying to keep his cows drinking. Walt studied the jerry rigging: on each device, baling wire had been twisted to hold the float valve up so the bowl wouldn't refill.

He pulled off his glove and tested the metal bowl; it was warm to the touch. That explained the snow having not collected on it but not the floats being wired up.

Some kind of problem with the waterers would explain the livestock having been moved. A frozen line, or intermittent power.

Chicken or the egg: had the livestock been moved and then the water turned off or had the water been turned off and then the livestock moved?

The unexpected visit at his office from the CDC woman—*what was her name?*—replayed vividly. Danny Cutter's employees, sick as dogs. Flown out in a private jet—literally, under the radar. Danny's most recent enterprise was Trilogy Springs: spring water from a source "two miles deep."

Maybe it wasn't mad cow after all. Something to do with the water?

To his left, Walt noticed an area that had been blocked from view by the shed.

Walt plodded along, ten yards, twenty, thirty. A hundred. He climbed a fence, where a snow-covered trail led through a gate. He was soaked through with sweat now, his breathing heavy. But there was more to it: his nerves all ajangle.

Maybe it resulted from the frank talk with Brandon. Maybe those wounds weren't meant to be reopened.

His thought was interrupted by the sound of animals—a sound so unique and, prior to that moment, missing.

As he crested the hill and looked down, he saw five hundred sheep—a half a band—spread out along the edge of a fog-shrouded creek. The fence crossed the creek in two places and rose to include another twenty acres on the far side. The sheep had been fed hay from the far side of the enclosed pasture. Some of the hay remained scattered. Mist rose from five holes in the creek ice, each hole roughly chopped open with an ax. The rancher had traded more difficult feeding conditions for easier access to water, explaining the empty pasture behind him.

But it drew his attention back to the condition of the water. The sheep were now being offered surface water in conditions that likely required grunt labor to keep the iced-over water holes open and accessible. If a line had frozen in the waterers behind him, then it made some sense to move the sheep.

He retraced his own tracks through the deep snow to the waterers. Slipped off his gloves. Began untwisting the wire used to keep the floats up.

If the waterers were broken, then moving the sheep made practical sense.

But if the waterers worked, then why had the rancher chosen labor-intensive surface water over automatic waterers? That might require an explanation.

The last twist freed the wire.

Walt released it and watched.

# 27

ROY COATS'S APRON AND BOOTS WERE COVERED in blood, as he returned to the cabin, sweat running down his face. Aker was asleep, his head slumped forward, the rest of him still tied to the ladder-back chair. His breathing sounded sharp and fast and shallow. As Coats shut the door, Aker lifted his head. His skin was sallow, his eyes bloodshot.

Coats hoisted the freezer-sized Ziploc bag. Inside it, Bess's unborn calf's pancreas slid around like a dead fish. "Now what?" he said.

Aker's eyes rolled in his head.

Coats crossed the room, stiff-legged and fast, and took Mark Aker by the chin. "Do *not* pass out on me! I've done my part. Now, you tell me what's next. You hear me?" He raised his voice. "Doc! You hear me!?"

Aker vomited into his own lap.

Coats stepped back, grumbling. "Jesus!"

"Not doing real well," Aker managed to croak out.

"Shit!"

"Fluids," he mumbled.

Coats cut him loose and poured him a glass of water. Aker gagged it down. But he shook his head, as he handed the empty glass back to Coats. "From here, I dehydrate. The vomiting won't allow me to keep the water down. I'm going to lapse into a coma at some point. Be ready for that. You'll have to do this on your own, Coats. Have some sugar water or juice ready, because you probably won't get the dosage right." His eyes bobbed. "You got all that?"

"You gotta stay with me, Doc."

"I'm trying."

"Grind it?" Coats asked, indicating the baggie on the table.

"Mortar and pestle. Coffee mug'll work. Handle end of a screwdriver, but you'll need to boil it first. Ten minutes. Do you have any saline?"

"Contact lens solution."

"That'll work. You may need that. Not much. Enough to liquefy. Then get the extract into the syringe."

"I mush it up. Add the saline. How much do I give you?"

Coats was already over at the stove. He dropped a screwdriver in the kettle of boiling water kept there to throw moisture into the air. He located an oversized coffee mug, rinsed it with some of the boiling water, and put the contents of the baggie in the cup. It looked like a piece of liver but was, in fact, pancreas.

Aker muttered. Coats returned to him and put his ear by Aker's trembling lips. "If I start sweating and shaking . . . this is *after* the injection . . . then you gave me too much. I need the—" Aker vomited, pitched forward, and passed out. Coats shook him, but it was no use: he was unconscious.

"You need *what*?" Coats screamed at him.

Coats didn't have ten minutes to steril-
ize the screwdriver. He used a pair of bar-
becue tongs to fish the screwdriver from
the boiling water; he dried it on a clean
dish towel and used the butt end to smash
the tissue in the mug. In a matter of minutes, he had the tissue reduced to a mushy
gruel. He added a small amount of the
contact lens solution, and then he tipped
the mug and drew the extract into the same
syringe originally intended to get Aker to
cooperate.

The fluid was a horrible color and con-
sistency. He couldn't see how this could
do anything but kill someone, but Aker was
on his way out as it was. He pulled down
Aker's loose pants and stabbed the syringe into the man's flank and gave him 20
ccs.

Aker's reaction was surprisingly quick.
Less than two minutes after the injection,
he snapped awake, lifting his head. Color
had returned to his face. He glanced around
the cabin. "Interesting," he said.

Coats noticed beads of sweat forming
on the man's brow.

"You're sweating."

"Juice," Aker said. He grabbed the arms

of the chair as his limbs began to shake. "Get the juice, you moron!" he shouted. The entire chair was shaking now, dancing on the floor.

Coats had neglected to have this ready. The only juice he had was frozen orange juice. He placed the can into the sink and ran water on it. But Aker's chair was going like a paint shaker. It tipped over and crashed to the floor. Coats fumbled with a water glass, spooned sugar in it, and filled it with water. He stirred it up, and slopped it out of the glass as he hurried to Aker. Sat Aker up and got him drinking, the water spilling down his front.

Aker returned to the living, and, unable to measure his blood sugar, took inventory of how he felt. Five minutes after he'd been going like an earthquake, he sat calmly in the chair.

"We can expect some secondary problems, Coats," Aker said.

"Such as?"

"The extract will be weak. I'll need injections every few hours. But we'll have enough for that. Dosage is obviously going to be the problem. There will be warning signs: I'll know when I need more. But the bigger issue will be the allergic reaction to the extract. Possible infection at the site of the injection. That's basically a given. The reactions can be anything from some discomfort, in the form of a skin rash, to something much more severe. We won't know until we see them. And we *will* see them. You'll want to watch me fairly closely, and I'll do my best to monitor how I'm feeling. Tell your guy I need Lantus. One dose lasts for twenty-four hours. Until we get the Lantus, we're not out of the woods. Not yet."

Coats barked out a laugh. Some spittle escaped onto his beard and he wiped it away.

"Something funny about that?" Aker asked.

"Doc, we are so deep in the woods it would take an army to find us." He amused himself. "A very *big* army."

"Get me a clean shirt," Aker said, testing how much leverage he'd gained over his captor. "Mine's filthy."

Coats hesitated a moment, unsure how to respond; but then he crossed to a footlocker by the only bed in the room and dug around in it for a shirt.

Mark Aker did not allow his captor to see the smile that slowly formed. Coats had done as he'd asked.

There was hope yet.

# 28

SENATOR JAMES PEAVY'S WHITE HAIR ESCAPED from beneath his cream-colored, beaver-felt Stetson, his blue, steely eyes never leaving Walt as he paced the living room of his homesteaded farmhouse. He was the fourth-generation Peavy to run the twenty-thousand-acre sheep ranch and he looked the part, with his large belt buckle, the pressed blue jeans, and the pair of Tony Lamas.

"That's a hell of a question, Sheriff," he said.

"It's simple enough, Senator." The man

hadn't been a senator for twenty years, but respect where respect was due.

"What's your man doing out there?" Peavy asked, his back to Walt as he faced the window.

"You said he could look around."

"He's walking across my pasture."

"He's an overachiever," Walt said. "Let's not worry about him."

"We use Mark—Sun Valley Animal Center—exclusively. It's not as if it's unusual for him to pay us a visit."

"It's not as if you're answering the question," Walt pointed out.

"We run nine band of sheep, Walt. That's nine thousand head. I have a ranch foreman, an overseer for each band. It's not as if I know every time we call a vet or what the ailment was."

"So you don't know why Mark was called? That's simple enough." Walt stood from the couch. "Maybe you could introduce me to your staff?"

"Sit down," Peavy said, his voice suddenly too loud for the room. He moved to another window, still fixated on Brandon's activities. "Enough of what Mark Aker did or did not do for us. What difference can it make? What's important here is your next election. That's what I thought you came here for. Let's get down to brass tacks: what can I do to help?"

"You've always been more than generous, Senator." Peavy supported sheriffs in at least three counties, including Blaine.

"I hear you have some real competition this time around in Richie Dunik."

"Well-organized."

"And I hear you're . . . distracted by this divorce. Damn sorry to hear about that. Talk about bad timing."

Walt clamped his open palms between his knees and leaned forward, trying to keep from saying something offensive about Peavy's insensitivity.

"I could arrange for each of my bosses to make contributions, Walt. Up to the accepted limit. There are ten to twelve who would do this, if I asked."

"I don't think I'm supposed to talk about ways to get around the election laws, Senator."

"Christ! Do I look like I'm wearing a wire? I'm making you an offer. I'm trying to help."

"Help is always appreciated."

"If you need financial help, I can arrange it. That's all I'm saying."

"I need to know what brought Mark Aker out here. I need to identify whatever it was that made your sheep sick."

"Who said my sheep were sick? Don't go jumping to any conclusions, Walt. I'll tell you what. Mark comes out here as much to vaccinate and geld and deliver calves as he does to doctor."

"Did you know he'd recently made house calls to two of your neighbors?"

"Should that surprise me?"

"There's no paper trail for any of these visits over here. His office knows next to nothing about them. This, from a type A, meticulous professional who, I'm told, would never have made a trip this distance without billing for it. Much less three such trips."

"And this interests you because . . . ?"

"If I could just say something here, Senator? That is, that every time I ask you a question, or say something about Mark Aker's visits, instead of an answer I get a question. We both know what a skilled orator you are, but, frankly, you've never treated me the way you're treating me today. I find it offensive. I'm sitting over here wondering what the hell is going on."

Peavy abandoned the windows for the time being, moving into the center of the room. It was a luxurious living room, with leather couches, a Remington sculpture, some western landscapes on the wall. The hearth was stacked stones covered in a patina of black carbon surrounded by a wire-mesh spark screen. The hearth had the original wrought-iron hook for warming pots. Peavy stopped on an enormous sheepskin rug that was covered by a tan pelt of some four-legged creature that, without its head, was impossible for Walt to identify.

"I heard about Randy. He's come over here for us as well. I assume your questions about Mark, being that it's you asking and you're a long way from home, must have something to do with that tragedy. I don't know what it is exactly that you're asking me, Walt. Mark's visits to my neighbors is news to me. Maybe we all got a bad batch of vaccine or something. Maybe it's something contagious I have yet to hear about. I just don't know. I'll ask my boys and I'll get back to you. That's the best I can offer."

"Can't argue with that."

"I'm serious about helping out your campaign."

"Much appreciated."

Lingering on Walt's tongue was a question about the quality of the senator's water supply. He kept that to himself for now.

Peavy stepped closer to shake Walt's hand. He had a firm grip, for an older guy, and he looked Walt in the eye. Walt sensed he was about to say something as well. They shook hands for a little longer than was comfortable. If that was supposed to communicate something to Walt, he missed it. Gail would be the first to tell anyone who would listen that Walt's communications skills were lacking.

Peavy opened his mouth. Once again, Walt expected him to say something. The senator shook his head, more of a twitch than anything else, and exhaled deeply.

*What?* Walt wanted to ask.

But his host left him guessing, as he ushered Walt to the door and saw him off.

Brandon was tromping through the snow, making his way back toward the farmhouse. He picked up his pace when he saw Walt waiting by the Cherokee. The house was a mile behind them before Brandon broke the silence of the car's interior.

"There are five automatic waterers in that field, all over by the hay shed, in the southwest corner." He paused to adjust his arm in the sling, which Walt thought was more for dramatic effect than anything else. "Not one of 'em's working."

"Not working or not turned on?"

"Dry. And the same's true of three more over by one of the barns. I tried to get into that barn to check the stalls, but a Mexican basically kept me out, saying, 'Mr. Jim. Mr. Jim.' Meaning Peavy, I assumed. I passed a stop and waste on the way back. Get this: *locked*."

"The stop-and-waste valve was locked," Walt repeated. A stop and waste was a freestanding water spigot that ran year-round.

"You've been in Idaho ten times longer than I have, Sheriff, but I've never, ever—not once—seen one of those locked. For one thing, that's about the only absolutely guaranteed water in winter, in case of fire, since those things never freeze."

"The senator skillfully avoided lying," Walt said, his hands gripping the wheel more tightly.

Far in the distance, but presumably still on Peavy's ranch, rose a charcoal gray plume of smoke. Probably ranch hands burning off slash, thought Walt. Winter snow made for the safest time to set such fires. It looked beautiful in the slanting afternoon light, lifting and coiling into the blue sky.

"Damn!" Brandon said, rolling down his window. "That's that same funky smell."

Walt sniffed the air and knew Brandon was right: a sour, bitter stench. Memorable. He turned the wheel. The car skidded on the snow floor. He backed around in a three-point turn and headed for the fire, stopped ten minutes later by an unplowed road. Brandon consulted the topo map: the road they traveled showed on the map as dirt. It went unplowed in winter.

Brandon's thick finger traced a second road—also marked as dirt—that accessed that same area from Peavy's ranch.

The stench was noticeably stronger there, at the end of the road, the connection to the fire inevitable though unconfirmed.

The two men got out of the car and climbed the snowbank. Walt slipped his hands into his pockets to fight the cold. Brandon tried to warm the fingers that protruded from the sling.

A sign on a fence warned PRIVATE PROPERTY, NO HUNTING, NO TRESPASSING.

"The senator couldn't keep his eyes off you the whole time you were out in his field."

"What was that about?"

"He kept what he told me very controlled, but I was much more interested in watching him."

"What's this about, Sheriff? You think it's something to do with the water? That makes the most sense, right?"

"Makes the most sense," Walt agreed.

"You think we're going to find Aker? Alive, I mean?"

"We sure as hell better."

"You think he's over here somewhere?"

"I haven't the slightest."

"You think the senator knows?"

"No. For whatever reason, I doubt that. I didn't get any sense of that."

"But he's involved." It was a statement.

"He basically offered to single-handedly pay for my reelection," Walt said, taking his hands out and rubbing them together vigorously. "He's definitely involved." Walt turned around and looked back over the vast expanse of the valley, stunning in its emptiness. A neighbor might see such a fire, but he'd never smell it, not given the distances between ranches. "There's something connecting the three ranches. Mark knew what it was and it got him kidnapped. Got his brother killed." He headed back to the car. "You hungry?"

"I could eat a horse," Brandon said.

# FRIDAY

# 29

"ARE YOU GOING TO COME INSIDE OR JUST SIT out there all night?" Walt held the phone pressed to his ear while staring out his front window at Fiona's Subaru.

During the long silence that followed, Walt could imagine her backing out and driving away, trying to pretend she hadn't been parked out there for nearly twenty minutes. Nearly two days had passed since the drive to the Pahsimeroi. With Mark Aker still missing, it might as well have been a month for Walt. He battled the fatigue of twenty-one-hour days while trying to maintain a father's patience for the sake of the girls. He'd put them to bed after twenty minutes of reading, during which he'd fallen asleep, not them. They'd tickled him awake. He told them a bear story and then turned off the light.

He slogged through his daily paperwork and meetings while exhausting every resource in his bid to find Mark Aker alive. Predictably, the Challis-led investigation into Brandon's shooting had produced nothing; if Brandon had died up there, with their history, Walt might have been accused of it. Francine Aker had failed to surface. The lab was taking its sweet time, as always.

The car arriving at his house, and just sitting there, had immediately won his attention, the midnight visit to his back porch still kept firmly in mind. But with the Subaru out front identified as Fiona's, he'd given her a liberal amount of time before calling her.

He heard footsteps approach the front door, and he put away the phone. He greeted her and invited her inside. She stood by the open fire, warming her backside. He studied her body, in silhouette against the fire, his first unhurried appraisal of her. Despite all the time they'd worked together, only now did he really see her narrow hips, athletically lean figure, and the muscular curve of her backside.

"Sorry," she said.

"For?"

"Sitting out there."

"No charge for parking." A pause. He added, "I'm terrible at jokes."

"The night of the search and rescue—Randy—I was skiing with Roger Hillabrand."

"I don't think that's any of my business."

"I was flattered. Enchanted, even. No, charmed. I was charmed."

"I don't doubt it."

"He sent a guy of his out to deliver a message. This is after the search and rescue. Late, late, I'm talking about."

"Fiona—"

"No. You've got to listen. You've got to help me make sense of this." She turned away to face the fire. "He invited me to some gala event in San Francisco. He was flying private. I was supposed to drop everything and join him."

"You and I were at the hospital the next day."

"Exactly. I turned him down." She moved to her left, standing in profile now, the reflections of the flames bouncing off her chest and below her chin. Her face flashed orange. "So now he tells me he didn't go. He canceled the trip because I turned him down. At least, that's what he told me. This, while he's inviting me to dinner—"

"I still don't see—"

"Can you just listen?"

The question hurt. Gail accused him of constantly interrupting.

"Please," she added. A word Gail had seldom used.

"I'm listening," he said, wishing she would get back in the Subaru and leave him the hell alone.

"He invited me over for tea this afternoon. Tea, just so he could ask me out for dinner. This guy is a very smooth operator." She turned again. "But not too smooth. He gets a phone call after I'm there less than five minutes. There's a phone right there in the living room, but, of course, he takes it somewhere else. Leaves me to watch the light on the phone glow for the duration. After fifteen minutes, I ask to be driven home."

"Driven?"

"He lives halfway up Baldy. His people drive you up from the bottom of the hill. I've got all-wheel drive, but they won't even let me try it. The gate is locked at the bottom. So I tell his guy Sean—Sean Lunn—it's either he drives me or I walk. And he drives me. What's interesting is, Sean doesn't interrupt the boss and tell him I'm leaving. He just drives me down the mountain."

"And that's interesting because . . . ?"

She snarled. "Because Roger was going to rip his head off when Roger found out he let me leave."

"Let you."

"You know . . ."

"Maybe not."

"Are you listening?"

That was another line borrowed from the Gail playbook. He was beginning to wonder if Gail hadn't sent her here to torture him.

"My role in this is?" he asked.

"Oh, God. I'm sorry." Her expression moved through embarrassment to a feverish glance at the door. "I'm *so* sorry. I didn't mean to . . . But . . . The reason I had to see you . . . I don't think he's as interested in me as he is in you."

"What?"

"My working for you."

"That's ridiculous."

"I wish it were. But I'm not so sure. He and I have so little in common. I admit that. He flirts with me at a wedding I'm shooting. I wanted to think that was for real, but I'm not so sure. He takes me that same night skiing down Baldy—*very* romantic—but doesn't make anything like a pass. I have to leave him because you call me up to the search and rescue. He barely objects, and he isn't surprised when I tell him I work part-time for you. Not surprised at all. And another thing: I got that wedding at the last minute. Who waits to hire a wedding photographer until the day before? Not in this town. Not in any town. Just isn't done. Sean, his guy, is waiting for me when I get home that night—this is in a snowstorm, don't forget. Parked outside the fence. Scares the hell out of me, coming up behind on foot. Says he's there to invite me on the private jet the next morning. Hello? Ever heard of cell phones? You think a guy like Roger Hillabrand can't get my cell number?"

"Checking up on you, maybe? Hillabrand could have been trying to find out if you ditched him for another guy. Sends his boy to see how many are in your car, how many cars in the drive. It doesn't spell conspiracy; it spells hormones. You're pretty. You sparkle. Men go crazy for that."

Hearing this from him clearly caught her off guard. *"Sparkle?"* she asked. "Did you say I sparkle?" She stepped closer, laid her hands on his shoulders. "Listen to you!"

Her palms felt warm through his uniform. She smelled of lilac and cinnamon, and, for a moment, she was everything—all he could smell, all he could sense.

A noise from out on the porch surprised them both. He jerked his head in that direction, still skittish from the encounter out back a few nights earlier.

*Gail.* Her face pressed to the glass and framed by open curtains; her expression that of a voyeur caught in the act. Walt immediately saw the scene from Gail's point of view: the fire burning. Fiona's hands on his shoulders, their bodies close. Gail, the most jealous woman he'd ever known. Jealous, no matter what. Almost a matter of pride.

She hurried off the porch. Walt ran to the front door and burst outside, calling her name. The car door thumped shut. Tire rubber whistled on the ice and then gripped. Walt charged up the shoveled path, shouting her name. The car shot back out into the street, fishtailing. He saw only taillights then, as he stood in the middle of the empty street. Still shouting for her to stop.

Since the split, Gail hadn't come by the house unannounced. Not once. For her to have done so meant . . . something. His awkward talks with Brandon came to mind. Had Brandon carried the conversation home? Had she wanted to weigh in? Negotiate a truce?

A neighbor, Mrs. Shunt, had ventured out onto her porch to see what all the shouting was about. The sheriff, in full uniform, stood in the street without a jacket, shouting at a departing car. A familiar car. The curtains at the Fridlers' house moved: the old bird had been spying on him as well. The sheriff's marital problems were well known, but this was the first time he'd been seen chasing his soon-to-be-ex wife's car down the street and shouting at her.

Worse, when he turned, there was Fiona at the open front door, partially backlit and actually glowing. Looking radiant. He imagined what Gail must have imagined.

He arrived at the top of the steps, wearing the porch light like a crown, a harsh shadow cast down on him, turning his eye sockets black and hollow. He stood there for a second, wondering if his actions had looked as childish as they now felt. Afraid to go inside with her. Too cold to do anything otherwise.

"That was her?" Fiona asked.

"Yeah."

"You think she . . . I mean . . . we weren't *doing* anything."

The last thing he wanted, the last thing he could handle right then, was a discussion.

Then his mouth betrayed him. "She gave me a lecture about not setting the girls against her. This, despite her bailing on them. When they visit her for a night—a rarity—it's at a friend's, never at Brandon's. She has this all worked out, as long as it's her way. And seeing us just now . . . Oh, boy."

Fiona approached him. He held up his hands to stop her advance. With the porch light overhead, it felt as if they were both on stage, acting out some melodrama.

Fiona had no intention of embracing him. Instead, with a panicked look on her face, she reached through his defensive pose and grasped the CDC biosensor tag clipped to his uniform's right chest pocket. She angled it up and into the porch light so that they both could see it.

One wedge of the white hexagon— separated by plastic dividers—was a distinct lavender, on its way to purple.

"You've been exposed to something."

For a moment, Walt couldn't get past the Gail fiasco. Exposed to the wrath of an ex-wife. But taking notice of the purple triangle, the cold intensified.

Fiona instinctively stepped back.

**Contaminated.**

Each of the six sections represented a different contaminant. He understood what it meant. "There's this CDC woman; might still be in town. She'll know what's next."

"Jesus, Walt."

"You'd better keep back. In fact, you'll need to stay here until it's sorted out." He paused, still processing what it all meant. "This is not good."

# 30

WALT FRANTICALLY SEARCHED HIS CLUTTERED desktop, distinctly remembering being handed a business card. He'd left Fiona at his house, awaiting his call. The discovery of the triggered biosensor had panicked him. An unfamiliar reaction. He had no love of hospitals; abhorred the early hours of a flu or head cold.

Never mind he felt perfectly normal. Unable to distinguish fever from panic, he began to work himself up. The call to Brandon had gone unanswered. He'd left a message for his deputy to check his own biosensor and to quarantine himself—and Gail—if necessary. Procedure dictated stringent guidelines. Walt was stretching those procedures by visiting his office.

He found the business card at last. Called the cell number and got voice mail. Called the business number and was told by recording that Dr. Lynda Bezel was out of the office until Monday. She was likely still in the valley—Danny Cutter's water source and bottling plant were located in the Lost River Range, east of Mackay, a three-hour drive each way this time of year. He guessed her investigation would require trips to the plant. Cutter was Walt's best shot at finding her. More voice mail. He felt feverish and sick to his stomach, his skin itched, his bones ached, his head hurt. He donned a blue hazmat suit over his clothes in the privacy of his office, grateful that, given the hour, he had to walk by only the duty officer. He hurried outside to his Cherokee and drove, determined to find her.

Driving north took him into money country. Ketchum/Sun Valley wasn't just rich, it was superrich, with more per capital wealth concentrated in such a small area than possibly any place in the country. He was accustomed to driving past the second-home estates, each the size and look of a country club. He arrived at Patrick Cutter's fifteen-thousand-square-foot vacation home, in which his younger brother occupied a suite in the eastern wing, wearing his impatience and disgust openly on his tormented face.

Patrick Cutter's estate consisted of five New England barns, all authentic timber-frame structures disassembled and moved from New Hampshire and Vermont and re-assembled into an interconnected master-piece. It was landscaped, even in winter, as if it had been standing for thirty years, and was surrounded by a privacy fence. Walt drove up to the closed gate, his headlights shining across the heated terrace-stone driveway. The only car he saw parked out front was a blue sedan with Boise plates and a rental-car sticker on the bumper. He knew the identity of the renter without running the registration, and, judging by the lack of interior lights, the house looked closed up for the night. Patrick used the place as a second home, spending less than six weeks a year here. His younger brother currently called it home.

Walt tried the phone number again, elected not to leave a second voice mail, and then called in on the gate box. Danny Cutter answered on the fourth ring. Walt announced himself and asked for Dr. Bezel.

"She's right here," Danny said. "We were just reviewing inspection reports."

*I'll bet you were.* Danny had a reputation. It was a few minutes past ten. "I need to speak to her."

He was buzzed through the gate and parked in front of the rental. Danny Cutter answered the door barefoot, his polo shirt untucked, his hair tousled; but it didn't necessarily mean anything. Danny was a young Jack Nicholson in training.

"Sheriff, you look like a housepainter," Danny quipped. "Come in."

"I'll be in my car," Walt said, turning.

"I didn't mean to offend you!" Cutter called after him. Walt didn't bother answering.

Bezel had put herself together quickly. She'd thrown on a pantsuit that was either similar to or the same one he'd seen her in previously. She'd pulled her hair back and had even managed to apply lipstick. But she'd forgotten the perfume, and her strong scent revealed far too plainly what Danny Cutter had been inspecting. An awkward, embarrassing moment lingered as long as the interior light, which finally dimmed and went dark. Walt reached up and switched it back on. She'd been too self-absorbed to notice his paper suit. But now she did, and some of the red left her face.

"Sheriff?"

He unzipped the hazmat suit, reached in and picked the biosensor off his chest pocket. He handed it to her. "I'm supposed to report this."

"Jesus . . ." She threw open the car door and stood outside in the cold. She knocked for Walt to put down the passenger window. "Shit, Sheriff, there's protocol involved here! Procedure. What the hell were you thinking?"

"That you were the closest expert."

"You're supposed to isolate yourself and call the 800 number. You know the drill."

"This is a small community, in case you hadn't noticed. If a van full of space aliens shows up at my front door—and we both know how the government reacts to these situations—it's going to throw this valley into a panic. My first and most important job is maintaining the peace, not causing riots. What's that thing trying to tell me? I'm perfectly willing to do whatever's necessary."

She left the car and walked over to the light at the front door. Walt caught sight of Cutter inside, keeping his eye on developments. She turned the biosensor in the light, called inside to Cutter, and he handed her purse to her. She made a call on her cell phone. Walt was thinking he'd made the right choice—it was better if the space aliens showed up at Patrick Cutter's isolated mansion than on Third Avenue South in Hailey. She returned to the car and climbed into the passenger seat. For the first time in about an hour, Walt felt some relief.

"Mild exposure to low-level radioisotopes," she stated.

"I'm radioactive? Seriously?"

"If it had been a darker shade, there'd be reason for concern. The tags were modified post nine-eleven to be supersensitive.

That way, if a container inspector, for instance, had had contact with even ultralow levels of radiation, it would be detected. Yours isn't exactly ultralow, but it's not high. You can lose the suit. We'll ask that they run a few tests at the local hospital, but you've got nothing to worry about."

Walt leaned back against the headrest and let out an audible exhale.

She said nothing for a moment. "Must have scared you."

"You think?"

"About my being here . . ." It became clear she'd had no intention of finishing the sentence when Walt made no attempt to interrupt her.

"About your being here," Walt said, taking unexpected pleasure in her awkwardness.

"I'm a big girl. I can separate the two."

"I'm not saying you can't."

"But you're thinking it."

"I know Danny's history."

"Preliminaries aren't in. If there's biological contamination at the bottling plant, we're having a hell of a time finding it. Much less ID'ing it."

"Do you carry one of those?" he asked, referring to his tag in her hand.

"Of course."

"Did you wear one at the plant?"

"Yes."

"And?"

"Nothing."

Walt considered this. He had a scenario in his head that he wasn't willing to voice without a lot more proof. Her tag coming up blank didn't sit well with his theory. "Have you asked Danny what he did out at the plant before your arrival?"

"Meaning?"

"What if his brother's private jet happened to have flown in a wet team?"

"You're saying he deep-cleaned the facility prior to my inspection?"

"You sound so shocked."

"That's illegal."

"I doubt that. More like it violates some regulation."

"Same thing to us."

"Maybe so. But not really."

"There's protocol. I questioned Mr. Cutter. He answered me faithfully and to my liking."

"You're not on trial, Dr. Bezel. And drop the 'Mr. Cutter' crap, will you? Ask again," Walt said. "That's all I'm saying."

"Are you telling me my job?"

"I'm telling you your sugar daddy can sweet-coat anything, can sweet-talk anyone, can fast-talk the best of them, and I put nothing past him. I'm betting he professionally hosed down his facility before you arrived, and that if you had a tape of your Q and A—which you don't, I'm guessing—that you'd find he never lied to you but failed to tell the truth." He paused. "Meet Danny Cutter, Dr. Bezel."

She blinked repeatedly, pursed her lips, turned her face toward the house, and then trained her rage on Walt. "What is it with you people out here?"

"Ah, come on. He dodges a few questions. No one's ever done that? And, at least for an evening, he's managed to take your mind off work. Score two points for Danny."

"Stop it!" Her lower lip was quivering. She looked ready to bite his head off.

"Test the plant for low-level radioisotopes," Walt said.

Her neck made a cracking sound, she spun it so quickly. "You're saying you were there? At the bottling plant?"

Walt considered how to answer this. "No, I wasn't," he said. "And that's the hell of it."

# SATURDAY

# 31

ROY COATS'S WIDE SHOULDERS FILLED UP ONE side of A booth table in the dim recesses of the back corner of the Mel-O-Dee steak house in Arco, Idaho.

The woman who entered, fanning at the smoke-filled air, had aged fifteen years in the past twelve months since he first recruited her. The meth had dragged bags under her once-pretty eyes, melted her gums, and had turned her skin a pasty gray. But she still had the tight body of a thirtysomething.

She couldn't help the way she walked—and not many men missed it. All without an ounce of self-awareness. If she'd had a face to go with it, she wouldn't have been walking into this bar. But the small head and pointed chin, the turned-in teeth, and pixie nose had all suffered under the effects of the meth. She wore a mask of melted, sallow skin, and carried a haze of disrespect, like an out-of-work whore. At a glance, you'd never have imagined her an atomic physicist.

"Evening," he said. "Buy you a drink?"

She shrugged.

Roy signaled the waitress, a sixty-year-old former rodeo queen with a beer belly. Without asking, he ordered his guest a double vodka on the rocks with a twist of lime, himself a draft beer.

"Do you have it?" he asked.

"Not yet. But it won't be a problem." She paused, then asked, "Do *you* have it?"

"You're two weeks late."

"So sue me. It's tricky. They're watching everyone like a hawk. You have only yourself to blame for that."

"I need it. Soon," he added.

"Yeah. And I need it now." She leveled her eyes on him. Jaundice was setting in.

"You gotta take better care of yourself,"

he said, caring nothing about her long-term health. "They're going to figure you out. You don't look so good."

"When anyone asks—and it isn't often—I tell them I can't shake the flu. I can handle myself." Her right hand trembled, and she tucked it in her lap.

They both went quiet, as the old cow approached and delivered the drinks. She asked if the younger woman wanted a menu and the younger woman laughed. She didn't understand the concept of eating. Not anymore. The cow trundled off.

"Listen, I gotta have a backup plan. We lose this chance, no one's going to listen."

"I told you: I don't know."

"I'd hate to miss my next delivery," he said.

Her hand clasped the glass more tightly, turning the skin beneath her unpainted fingernails a bloodless white. Her face remained impassive. "As if," she said.

"Don't push me."

"I'm on it. It's not easy." She leaned across to him, her breath giving lie to the myth that the smell of vodka went undetected. "It's an atomic research facility, Roy boy. What do you expect?"

"Delivery," he said equally softly. He despised the nickname, despised her weakness, despised most everything about her but her body. Her talking in that husky voice aroused him. "All those degrees of yours . . ."

Her eyes went off someplace over his head. He wondered what was going on in there, if she could grasp even a glimpse of her decline at the hands of the meth. He'd taken her from a lonely, bored, successful physicist and reduced her to a skeleton-eyed addict who showed no remorse over her breaches of security. Maybe it hadn't been him or his cause but instead the tedium of a professional life that required total secrecy, performed in the middle of an enormous desert. The government contractor daily bused three thousand specialists just like her in from Pocatello—nerds with their laptops—a Mormon town where the idea of an exciting night out was a decaf latte at Starbucks. She'd walked into a four-year contract and had burned out within six months. She'd been waiting for someone like him to come along.

He passed the paper bag beneath the table. Collected no money for it. If she'd thought about that, it might have given her pause. He'd never charged her for the meth. He understood the ways of an addict. If she wasn't totally behind his cause, she was at the very least accustomed to his keeping her high.

His knuckles brushed her knee under the table. Her hand met his and she took possession of the bag, and, with it, an eagerness flashed across her otherwise-dull, yellowing eyes.

"I could take a room at the Lazy Horse," he said. "You wouldn't have to wait. To risk smoking in the car. We wouldn't want you to get busted."

She no longer rode the bus from Pocatello. She'd moved to a double-wide near Moore, a few miles down the road. This to be away from her coworkers, thrust into the roaring nightlife of Arco, Idaho, population one hundred and fifty. The movie theater ran two shows every Friday night.

"I think I can make it seven miles down the road, Roy."

He wasn't so sure. "But you wouldn't have to," he said. "Not if I took a room."

"What else do you want from me?"

He smiled.

"Oh, Roy, what are we going to do with you?"

"Just about anything you want," he said.

She upended the vodka, leaned close to him, and whispered again, "You terrify me. Whenever we meet, I leave shaking. A pit in my stomach. You scare the piss out of me, Roy. You scare everyone who meets you."

He heard all that, but he barely reacted, because she rose and pumped her way back to the EXIT sign. Next time, he would withhold the meth. Next time, she would pay for that mouth of hers.

# 32

DESPITE THE PROMINENT SIGN—PLEASE TURN off your cell phone, this is a no cell phone environment—Walt was on the phone for a good deal of the time his physical was being conducted. Dr. Royal McClure, a good friend who sometimes wore the hat of pathologist for Blaine County, drew his blood and ran him through a variety of tests while Walt raised his own blood pressure trying to locate a Geiger counter. Nancy was on the receiving end of his irritation, as it became increasingly clear to him that Idaho State University owned two such devices but didn't loan them out; the state's environmental agency used a lab in California; and buying a Gamma-Scout would cost five hundred dollars. After a number of calls back and forth, he relented and approved the purchase. He asked her to call the Idaho state crime lab and confirm that they'd tested the mess of broken glass and ice discovered on his back porch for radioactivity.

While Walt was sitting on the edge of the examination table, the paper liner crackling beneath him when he buttoned up his uniform, his cell phone rang as he was putting it away. McClure glowered at him. Bothered, Walt barked his name when he answered: "Fleming!"

"Sheriff Fleming?"

"Speaking."

"Hold for Congressman McMillian, please."

The line clicked.

"Sheriff?"

"Congressman?"

"I don't believe we've met."

"No, sir."

"I was speaking with George Carliner and your name came up."

"If this is about my suggestion we drop party affiliation as a requirement for—"

"It's not," the congressman interrupted.

"I told the attorney general it was an idea still in its infancy," Walt said.

"Nothing to do with that. Let's put a pin in that and come back to it another time."

"Yes, sir."

"I'm calling about the National Law Enforcement Conference here in Washington next week. I don't know if you've heard but Mel Tooley has had to withdraw at the last minute."

"I hadn't heard."

"His wife, I think. Something medical."

"I'm very sorry to hear that." Walt liked Tooley, who was sheriff of Ada County, one of the fastest-growing counties in the nation.

"George and I were discussing a replacement. You've headed the Western Regional Sheriff's Association, as I understand it. You held two terms as president, and you gained high-profile status in that fine work you did involving Vice President Shaler."

"She hadn't been elected at the time,

Congressman. She was a candidate. And
I really didn't—"

McMillian cut him off again. "The point
is that George has recommended you to
replace Mel Tooley at the conference. To
represent the state for us. I wish I were
asking here, Walt—may I call you Walt?—
but I'm not. The state needs you. I need
you. The federal government is at the start
of a major reorganization of everything,
from communication to hardware assets
for state law enforcement. A lot of us want
them to keep their hands off. We need you
there. You're respected. You're recogniz-
able, and George and I think others will
listen to you. I'd like you out here by Friday. My people will work through the talking points with you, and you'll come out to
our home in Bethesda for some meetings
over the weekend. You'll hit the ground
running Monday morning on the Hill."

His head was spinning. To be seen on
the national stage was certain to open job
opportunities. It was just the kind of appointment he could see his father arranging for him. Elizabeth Shaler, now the vice
president, had told him she could use him

in Washington; he wondered if this appointment had anything to do with her. He wondered if Mel Tooley's wife was actually ill or if Mel had been asked to step aside so that Walt could be offered the appointment. Wheels within wheels.

"Can I think about it, sir?"

"Hell, no. You can pack your bag, and you can thank me later. One of my guys will be in touch shortly to iron out your itinerary. The state picks up the bill for everything, Sheriff. Make the necessary arrangements on your end. You'll hear back from us by the end of the day." The line went dead.

"Good news?" McClure asked.

Walt stared back at him, dumbfounded.

"Unexpected," Walt answered honestly. Unexpected and slightly unbelievable, he thought. In spite of his accomplishments on a state and regional level, there were at least a half-dozen more-senior sheriffs in line for such perks. Whether Mel had dropped out or not, the chiefs of Boise, Pocatello, Coeur d'Alene, and Moscow would typically have been considered first. Should have been considered first.

Someone had gotten to the congressman and had convinced him to put Walt's name in ahead of others.

One thing seemed certain: it had been carefully orchestrated. The more he thought about it, the more he knew he couldn't attend the conference. Worse, he saw no easy way out of it.

McClure prescribed iodine tablets and wanted a follow-up exam in two weeks.

Walt thanked him and headed out to the parking lot. He called Nancy from the Cherokee and asked for a list of all financial supporters of both his opponent and Congressman McMillian.

"I was just calling you," Nancy said. "The lab called back almost immediately. The sample in the broken test tube—"

"It came back positive for radiation," Walt declared, as if he'd received the call himself.

"What's going on?"

"Mark Aker left me crumbs to follow and I almost missed it. A test tube of water, instead of just writing me a message. Why, I'm not sure. Left it on my back porch. Someone stepped on it the other night and

I heard them and found it. I don't know who. But now I get the message: its contaminated water—radioactive water. And I know someone who can clear this up for me."

# 33

AS THE SHUTTLE ESCALADE ARRIVED AT ROGER hillabrand's electronically controlled gate, Fiona Kenshaw checked her face once more in the Subaru's rearview mirror. She saw the face of a traitor. She'd felt compelled to accept Hillabrand's invitation to lunch, despite her better judgment. She'd changed clothes three times before settling on blue jeans, a tailored cranberry shirt that offset her dark hair and eyes, and a black boatneck sweater. Over it all, she wore a sheepskin coat that was her most prized, and most expensive, garment. The attention to her clothing informed her of her desire to impress him, which only served to further undermine her disposition. As she climbed out of the Subaru and headed across the squeaky snow to the black Escalade, she didn't like herself very much.

The driver's-side door opened and Sean Lunn climbed out, though begrudgingly. She moved quickly to avoid him opening the door for her. There were times such gallantry was a compliment and other times it felt demeaning. Lunn was not doing this out of respect but because his job required it of him. Fiona took exception, hurrying now.

"I've got it," she said.

Lunn didn't put up any fuss, immediately returning to his place behind the wheel.

The SUV stood high off the ground; she looked down to find the step rail. What she saw there knocked the wind out of her: mud. A grayish brown mud.

She wondered if she hesitated too long, how much of her reaction Sean Lunn caught. Had there been a recent thaw, had the road they now traveled up to the mountaintop estate been rutted, she might have quickly written this off. But neither of those was the case. More important was the mud's distinctive color.

He was speaking. Talking to her. Saying something. She wasn't listening, her thoughts locked on that mud. It was the same color mud they'd found on the dress shoes of the rape victim, Kira Tulivich—a sickly, unnatural gray. There was no mistaking it. She had a photographer's eye. She knew color the way a painter did. It might not be the same mud. But what if it was?

". . . do you think?" he said, finishing a sentence.

"I'm sorry?"

"Never mind."

"No, please."

"It was nothing. Weather talk. I was wondering if it'll warm again or if we're in for a very early winter."

"Looks like winter to me," she said.

"Am I driving too fast?" he said, noticing her expression—a mixture of shock and contemplation—and easing back on the accelerator. The private drive twisted and wound its way steeply up the mountain. Lunn knew it well enough to drive fast. Some of the turns were indeed terrifying, though her mind was elsewhere.

"No . . . no. I'm fine."

He kept the speed steady. "I probably shouldn't say this, but this—your being asked up to lunch—is not normal. In case you're wondering. I can't name the last time Mr. Hillabrand had a woman up to the house for lunch."

"Do I look that nervous?" she asked.

"Preoccupied, is how I'd put it."

"It's a little unusual," she said. "His home instead of a restaurant." But Lunn had read her correctly; her mind was on the mud and where and how the Escalade had picked it up.

"When he dines in town, he's constantly interrupted. He knows everybody and everybody knows him. Besides, he loves showing off his place. You want to score points with him, compliment him on the house."

She wondered if part of Lunn's job description was to soften up Roger Hillabrand's potential conquests. That was suddenly how she felt. She'd struggled with accepting the invitation. What signals was she sending by attending?

"Do you suppose the dirt roads will thaw or are they frozen now through winter?"

She tried to sound nothing but curious. When he didn't answer right away, she lied: "I ride horses occasionally, and the dirt roads—like Lower Broadford in Bellevue—are the best."

"Stays this cold, I don't see anything thawing."

"Good point."

She wondered how many of Roger Hillabrand's employees drove the Escalade. One of them might have driven the same road or area where the girl had been raped. The silence between her and Lunn felt increasingly uncomfortable. Had her question about the thawing roads silenced him or had they simply run out of things to say?

When the vehicle finally pulled to a stop, Fiona made a point of dropping her purse as she opened the door. As she bent to retrieve it, she chipped a chunk of the mud off the rail. She slipped it into one of the purse's outside pockets. As she stood, she noticed Lunn suddenly looked her way, and she wondered if he'd seen any of that.

She tried to cover her excitement by expressing insecurities over having come here. Lunn said nothing.

In fact, the invitation to lunch had taken a distant backseat to the discovery of the mud. All she really wanted now was to get back down the hill and to connect with Walt as soon as possible.

# 34

"WALT, YOU MAY WANT A PART OF THIS."

Walt was in the middle of a bite of pizza at Smokey's on Sun Valley Road, his children and their sitter, Lisa, at the table with him. He put down the pizza.

"Part of what, Chuck?" He'd recognized the smoker's voice on the phone immediately: Chuck Webb, director of the Sun Valley Lodge's security.

"Front desk got an anonymous call that one of our guests might be in need of medical assistance. Gave us a room number. I responded. It was Danny Cutter, stoned out of his mind. I've called SVPD just now. A requirement. But I know the history of you and Mr. Cutter, his probation and all, and so I'm also calling you."

"You're holding Cutter?"

"I'm in the room with him."

"Can I speak to him?"

"He's way out of it, Walt. In and out of consciousness."

"Any drugs?"

"Found what looks like an ounce of a white powder taped under the sink."

"An ounce?" If it tested positive, it would carry twenty years for Cutter, given his current probation. Walt felt a pit in his stomach. "The call to the front desk? Was it recorded?"

"No."

"Anonymous."

"Yeah."

"Afraid for Cutter, was that it?"

"That was the claim. But it's not right. He's more than just stoned. He's out of it." He paused. "What's Danny Cutter doing in my hotel when he lives here in town?"

"Who's it booked to?"

"A John Greydon. Paid cash. We cleared the card for five hundred in incidentals. I can start a trace on the card."

"What's the condition of the room?"

"Bed's made. That's the stink of it. I know he has a history of drugs, Walt, but this doesn't feel right."

"Yeah . . . Okay." Walt looked into the curiously sad eyes of his children, who understood his tone of voice well enough to know what this call meant to them. "I'll be right there," he said into the phone, trying to think of some new way to say what he'd said to his kids too many times before.

INVESTIGATIONS COULD spiral out of control. Walt did his best to keep things simple. But the more threads that were added, the more tangled they became. Randy Aker had been darted and had died, possibly because he was mistaken for Mark. Mark had run away, been found, and then abducted. A test tube had been left on his own back porch—a water sample that tested positive for low-level radiation. A CDC investigation had looked into Danny Cutter's bottled-water company. Now, after two years of being clean, Danny Cutter was embroiled in a drug bust.

And, in the middle of it all, he'd been invited to a conference twenty-five hundred miles away.

Walt found himself giving Danny the benefit of the doubt as he approached room 223, on the second floor of the lodge. The plush carpet absorbed his footfalls. Framed black-and-white photographs of Gary Cooper, Clark Gable, Jamie Lee Curtis, and Clint Eastwood lined both walls.

Sight of the celebrity photographs reminded him of the two worlds he served: the obscenely affluent residents of Ketchum/Sun Valley and the locals that provided services for them. It was a medieval caste system with him in the middle, keeping the peace. The Sun Valley Lodge was the castle.

He knocked and a moment later was admitted. Danny Cutter lay on his back on a love seat, a pillow under his head, his eyes shut. There was a white smudge on his upper lip; his hair was a mess. He wore blue jeans, penny loafers, and a maroon cashmere sweater. Webb showed Walt the tape job under the sink. The baggie was thick with a white substance.

"Heroin?" Walt suggested.

"But taped under the sink? What is this, the *Rockford Files*?"

"Christ," Walt said, taking in the room once again. "Happy hour downstairs?"

"Yeah. Macaroni's playing." He meant Joe Macarillo's jazz trio.

"You called Sun Valley?" Walt asked.

"Be here any minute."

"How much did you tell them?" Walt found himself considering tampering with the evidence, and, having never done anything close to that in his years in law enforcement, he wondered what motivated him. He owed Danny Cutter nothing; he'd given the man a number of breaks.

"I told them I had a guest needed medical attention, that maybe drugs were involved. They'll be careful about it. Won't make a big scene."

"I can't remove those drugs," Walt stated, "even if I wanted to."

"No one said you should."

Walt met eyes with Webb and stared. And stared. Having not touched his phone, Walt said, "My cell's got shitty reception in here. I'm going to try the hallway." He did not break the eye contact. "You've helped out guests before, yeah? Covered up an infidelity or two, I would imagine."

"That's obstruction," Webb said, glancing into the bathroom.

Walt said nothing, still staring.

"I had a call girl describe a scene to me one time," Webb said. "This was in Portland, back when I was on the job. She and her pimp would Mickey a prospective john, get him up to the room, and lift his wallet. While the pimp hit the ATM, the girl pinched the john's nose and covered his mouth until he was damn-near suffocated. Then she put a deep spoon of coke to his nose and released her fingers. John gasps for air and takes down a huge hit of coke. He's now going to test positive if he involves the police. Not one of those guys ever fingered her or the pimp. They had a nice little thing going and it just kept on going."

"So, in case we miss the smudge on his nose, they give us the ounce beneath the sink."

"I don't know. That's an expensive way to do things. Why not a dime bag?"

"Because it's got to stick. It's got to be something we can't ignore. And it's got to

look big—the way Danny Cutter does everything."

"What if they covered themselves? What
if there's video and we've got it wrong?"

"That could do us some serious damage," Walt agreed.

"Cameras these days—the size of a
shirt button."

"Yeah."

"His prints are going to be on the bag,"
Webb said.

"Yup."

"He'll go down for it."

"Yeah, I think so too," Walt said.

"And we're supposed to just stand here
and let it happen?"

Walt shrugged. "We could be completely
wrong."

"But we aren't." Webb leaned his head in
the bathroom. "Thing of it is, when this
door's shut and the light's off in there, no
camera's going to pick up anything." He
paused. "I thought you had a call to make."

"I can't back you up on this," Walt
warned.

"I'm a big boy. Go make your call."

"Remember, Chuck: if this comes out
that Danny's culpable, he goes away for it,

so don't get your prints on that bag. You hear? And keep it somewhere handy. I may need it."

"Hurry," Webb said. "Before I lose my nerve."

# 35

ROY COATS CAME THROUGH THE DOOR OF THE cabin, looking like Bigfoot. He was wrapped in layers of frost-coated clothing, his beard and mustache were white with globs of snotty ice, his face windburned from what had to have been a long snowmobile ride.

"Nice trip?" Mark Aker asked.

"Have you finished your paper?" Coats hung various pieces of clothing on wall hooks and the backs of chairs, in a semi-circle around the woodstove. The Samak-inn member who had delivered the insulin and stayed to watch Aker—Coats had called him Gearbox—he began dressing for outside. With the return of Coats, Gearbox was assigned perimeter patrol.

"Haven't started it," Mark Aker replied. "If it's to be credible it has to be scientific. That takes time."

Gearbox took off. Coats installed himself on a footstool in front of Aker, his left elbow up on the room's only table.

"You're stalling," Coats said. "You've got all the insulin you need. We brought everything in from your cabin with us, so you've got your papers. Don't push your luck, Doc."

"They're searching for me by now."

"I wouldn't be so sure about that."

There was something about his confidence. Aker studied him carefully. "You have contacts in the sheriff's office?" He waited for even the faintest of signs. "Challis?" He sighed. "So it's Challis, is it?"

"I didn't say anything," Coats reminded.

"Didn't have to. Your heartbeat gave you away. Your interior jugular vein. It runs continuous with the sigmoid sinus. A barometer to the soul, and your soul was disturbed when I mentioned the Challis sheriff's office. So that much we both know: you've got an insider with Challis. And perhaps they might have ways of knowing what Custer or Lemhi County is up to. But do you think they could possibly know what Blaine is up to? Walt Fleming has trained with the FBI. Did you know that? His father *invented* the first SWAT team ever. You think he's going to let Custer or Lemhi know what he's doing? You think? Seriously? You know the toys he's got available to him, all that money down in Blaine? Have you been listening for flyovers, Roy? Your boy out there on patrol—what kind of a heat signature does he throw off when he's out there? How about this cabin? Your snowmobiles? You think Walt Fleming's working with satellite images? I do. How long do you think you can keep this up?"

Coats turned, ostensibly to adjust his jacket on the back of a ladder-back chair, to help speed up drying. More than anything, he didn't want Aker reading him like that. Not only did it creep him out, that someone could read his neck, but giving anything away cost him.

He settled back onto the footstool, facing his hostage with a calm, almost serene face.

"You ever heard of Shays' Rebellion?" Coats asked.

Mark Aker stared back, his eyes flat.

"You know your American history?"

"Don't do this," Aker said.

"This was near the end of the war, the Revolutionary War. The Boston merchants pressed the state legislature to levy a tax on all the farmers. And they couldn't pay the taxes—same as we can't pay 'em today. Shays organized an open rebellion, put together an army of some eight hundred–odd and went after them, pitchforks and rifles. What they did was against the law, and they paid mightily for it, but that rebellion is considered the last battle of the Revolutionary War because it changed opinion forever. The federal and state governments realized they had failed at representing the people. The People, Doc. Capital *P*.

"Now, I'm not saying we aren't breaking the law, because we are. And I'm not claiming to be a tree hugger. Not hardly. I'm more what you might call a militant libertarian." That won a bemused smile. Mark eyed all the books again, his opinion of his captor changing. He'd read about

Stockholm syndrome, had no desire to go there. "But we did what we did for a reason. A purpose. Our government should not be dictating to other countries about things it doesn't have under control itself. Plain and simple: someone's got to show the people what's going on."

"And that's you? You're Shays? That's supposed to justify this?" he said, indicating his own situation.

"Shays' Rebellion was put down. Eighteen were given death sentences. Two were actually executed. I understand what's in store for me. But, goddamn it . . ." he said, raising his voice. His intensity lit up the air between them. Then his face softened. "I'm giving you a real chance here. All I'm asking from you, Doc, is to tell the truth. I'm not some raghead holding an AK, trying to put words in your mouth. That's the beauty of it: I don't have to. The truth will hang them. Whether they hang me or not."

"Okay," Aker said.

Coats did a double take. He looked Aker over like it was someone else sitting in that chair. "You'll write it," he said to himself. He tried to contain a childlike enthusiasm.

"I said I would. And I mean it this time. But I've got to ask: is any of what you just told me for real?"

"All of it," Coats said proudly. "That's our heritage, Doc."

"Because I've got a story for you."

Coats leaned in toward Aker a little too close, a changed man, gloating over his victory.

"Have you ever heard of Aker's Rebellion?" Mark asked.

Coats's brow knitted. At the last second, he seemed to anticipate what was coming, to understand that Mark Aker had drawn him into a trap. But it was too late.

"Now you have." The doc moved with the quickness of a snake.

A sudden heat flashed in Coats's thigh, followed by a searing pain that bent him over. The doc had been concealing a pair of scissors behind his back. As Coats fell forward with the pain, the doc drove both elbows into his back and forced his face against the cast iron of the hot stove. The smell of burning hair and blistering skin filled the air as Coats sat upright, at which point the scissors plunged deeply up and into his left armpit, remaining there as the doc let go and grabbed a chair. He swung the chair and a light-headed Coats ducked to avoid the blow, only to realize too late that he was not the intended target. Instead, the sheet metal stovepipe dislodged with the chair's clanging contact and the small cabin immediately filled with acrid gray smoke. The doc snagged Coats's winter jacket and threw it on the stove. It smoldered only seconds before melting and smoking. The doc seized his own jacket from the wall, grabbed a flashlight from the windowsill, and was out the door.

Coats vomited. The skin on his burned face felt as if it were shrinking and tightening on his skull. His beard was singed off on that side, and, in its place, branded on his cheek at an awkward angle, were the reversed letters: SGNITSAC—VERMONT CASTINGS, the embossed name on the stove.

He dragged himself toward the door, his leg wound bleeding badly, his arm in pain. The doc had known exactly what he was doing: both wounds immobilized him.

He reached the door, a blood trail painted behind him. Hacking. Unable to breathe for the pain. He tried to get to his knees, to reach the doorknob, but his leg wound wouldn't let him. He grabbed hold of the knob, only to realize his bulk was blocking the door. He collapsed back down to the floor. Reached for his ankle. A .38 revolver, in a calf holster.

Fired off three rounds. Waited.

Debated using the last three. Decided against it: if Aker returned, Coats wanted some rounds left for self-defense.

"FUCK!" he screamed. Smoke swirled just above his head. He coughed and gagged, and forced himself up through insurmountable pain toward the door.

The doorknob.

It was Gearbox, horrified. He wretched at the sight of Coats's face.

"Air!" Coats groaned, as he tasted blood at the back of his throat.

The cold came through the door like a hammer.

"The doc," Coats mumbled. Right before he passed out.

# 36

MARTY, WALT'S FOUR-YEAR-OLD GOLDEN, BANGED against the fire screen and sent one of Emily's mittens flying. The mitten landed on a fresh ember and soon the wet wool began to smolder, producing a god-awful stink.

The foul smell brought Walt from the kitchen. To the twins, who knew they weren't supposed to play fetch indoors, their father's expression came as a complete surprise. Not one of anger but curiosity. Laughing, they ran for cover behind the couch. But the admonishment never came.

Instead, a moment later, they overheard him speaking on the phone with Lisa and they mistakenly believed his leaving was the punishment for their crime.

"Could you possibly come over and get them to bed?" he asked. "Something's come up at work."

"THE SMELL?" Brandon asked, nursing his arm in the sling from the passenger seat of the Cherokee.

"A wool mitten. Yes. At first, I was pissed at the girls. Same old same old. But then I recognized that smell; I remembered that smell. Lon Bernie's ranch. Remember that stink?"

"Impossible to forget."

"Burning wool," Walt said. "That's what the smell was: burning wool."

WALT KILLED the headlights way out on the plowed two-lane state road and continued on by the dim glow of a fingernail moon. They parked the vehicle a half mile from the driveway leading onto Lon Bernie's ranch and went on foot, both sporting day packs, six-cell flashlights that doubled as nightsticks, and their 9mm Berettas.

They made quite the pair, throwing night shadows in the soft moonlight. Walt, cursed with DNA that got him to five foot ten only with boots on, had compensated by working the weight room until he was as wide in the chest as he was tall. Brandon, meanwhile, shopped the Big and Tall Guys stores. Now the deputy was one-winged and walking awkwardly because of it.

They held to the left of the road, putting the fence as a screen between them and Lon Bernie's farmhouse.

"Does it bother you that we have no authority in this county?" Brandon said, his words puffing out from his mouth as gray fog.

"I wouldn't say *no* authority, but it does make things a little tricky."

"Tricky? If he's up to something he'll shoot us like dogs and ask questions later. Welcome to Lemhi County."

"I'm aware of that," Walt said.

"Oh, and this just in: he wasn't real thrilled to see us *last time*, in *daylight*."

"Point taken."

"Are you trying to get me killed in the line of duty?"

Walt didn't dignify that.

"It's midnight, Sheriff. Couldn't we have—"

Walt cut him off. "If we'd come by day, all we'd have accomplished was to tip him off to our interest in his burn pit. He'd have snuffed it, buried it, and it would have froze solid, leaving us waiting 'til April or May to dig for evidence." Walt tugged on Brandon's sheriff's coat, pulling him lower as they drew closer to the gate. "It has to be now, when we can get a good look at whatever's in there. We owe that to Mark."

When the wind shifted, the putrid smell hit them both at the same moment.

"Damn," Brandon said.

They turned onto the property, staying low. The burn pit was on the far side of the ranch, requiring them to pass the farmhouse and the outbuildings to reach it. Walt assumed there would be dogs—there were always dogs on ranches—but that wild game was more likely to wake dogs than humans, and so the trick was to move quickly and keep to shadows.

It was bitterly cold, somewhere in the teens. Each light breeze penetrated and burned their faces. Ducking, they hurried through the dry, crunching snow. As barking erupted from inside the farmhouse, to their right, they ran across the plowed driveway and ducked into the deep snow behind a hay swather. If Lon Bernie was awakened by the barking, he might think he had a shot at poaching an elk or deer from his bedroom window.

They waited. Brandon began to shiver, though didn't say a thing.

Finally, the dogs stopped their noise. Walt held Brandon there another few minutes—long minutes—knowing that Bernie could be moving window to window in hopes of spotting some trespassing game. Then they stood, returned to the plowed driveway, and moved together toward the far side of a toolshed. From there, around a granary, and, from the granary, around the far side of the main barn. Here, Walt picked up tractor tracks—dualies—two tracks of double tires, each pair four feet wide, running parallel to the barn and disappearing like train tracks into the dark. He and Brandon followed these away from the glow of the mercury lamp, out into an artificial dusk, and finally into the coal black night, clouds having moved in to mask the moon, the hideous smell growing stronger with every step. They never dared use their flashlights for fear of being spotted. At times, they stopped, awaiting a cloud to pass by the moon, the surrounding dark so intense, the silence so complete, that, had it not been for his heartbeat in his ears and the stinging cold in his toes, Walt might have thought he'd died.

It took forever to reach the burn pit. Nearly an hour had passed since they'd left the Cherokee by the side of the road. Finally, the tractor tire tracks gave way to a wide disturbance in the velvet field of snow just as the stink from the pit achieved epic proportions. The pit appeared before them as a square black shadow amid the white glaze of snowfall. Slash had been pushed into a pile on the left side, a tangle of dead limbs and detritus stacked well over ten feet high. The pit itself had been dug crudely into the brown earth some years before, a catchall of burnable waste, which to a rancher meant anything from plastic pesticide containers and fertilizer bags to household paper trash and spent gearbox oil. Walt kneeled and, cupping his flash-light to mute its light, aimed a diffused beam down into the pit.

Brandon projectile-vomited down into the pit, staggered, and stepped away. Normally he was a man of a strong constitution, but his reaction reflected the horror there: an assortment of limbs, bodies, and heads of dozens of sheep, all blackened, the burned skin peeling back in leaflike flakes, the scabbed, unmoving eyes bulging or missing, having exploded from the heat. Fuel had been poured over everything and lit, further discoloring the skin and patches of wool, and leaving a mass of twisting limbs and burgeoning flesh, ripped open by the gases of decomposition to expose frozen pink tears in the carbon wasteland of dead animal.

The smell was of everything bad in the world: excrement, burned hair, lost life.

Walt dug around in his day pack, withdrew the Gamma-Scout and a Dell laptop that was part of his office's mobile command center.

"Jesus," Brandon said, pulling himself together. "Sorry about the hurl, Sheriff."

"It ain't pretty," Walt said.

"And then some."

"Get rope ready."

Brandon slipped his day pack off. "You're not thinking what I think you're thinking."

"Stop thinking so much."

"You can't be serious."

Walt had the Gamma-Scout plugged into the laptop; the laptop powering up. "The cord isn't near long enough."

"Sheriff . . ."

"I've got to go down there. Look for a decent hold. Try that fence post."

"Sheriff . . ."

"You don't burn your hoof stock. You sell its meat. The *only* reason you wouldn't sell the meat is if the meat is contaminated. Wholesale slaughter like this? Come on! It's the only explanation. But we've got to prove something's going on. And you've got one good arm, Tommy. You can't go down in there and you can't pull me out. So get that rope tied off. And do it quickly," he said calmly. He lifted his chin, indicating the distant ranch. "We may have company."

Brandon spun around. A flickering light

appeared in flashes between the outbuildings. A powerful flashlight.

"Probably the dogs barking," Walt said. "When a guy like Lon Bernie's got something to hide, he sleeps a lot lighter."

"Turn that laptop around so the screen faces away," Brandon said.

Walt did so. His gloves were off, his fingers stinging. He doubted the screen would show at such a great distance given that they were surrounded by higher walls of moved snow, but it was a worthy precaution. A rancher out at midnight was not yet cause for alarm. It could be anything from a sick animal that needed checking to a freeze patrol—making sure all the heaters were working prior to turning in. Even if Lon Bernie's guilt had gotten the better of him, there would be no reason to look beyond the barns and outbuildings. A vision flashed in Walt's imagination: the twin chevrons of the massive tire treads that the tractor had imprinted in the snow. He and Brandon had followed the tracks out here, no doubt leaving a trail of boot prints.

"We should keep going," he encouraged.

"Rope's tied off."

There was no way for Walt to climb down the rope with the laptop in hand, so he put it back into the day pack but without fully closing the screen so it would remain running. Then he lowered himself down the dirt wall and into a piece of semifrozen hell. Brandon trained the light down on him. Walt arrived at a muddy layer in the corner of the pit where the pile of carcasses left a gap. Despite the freezing temperature, the smell wafting up from the decomposing carcasses was as bad as anything he'd ever experienced. He zipped his coat up over his face so that only his eyes showed, one-armed the day pack around to where he could dig the laptop out, and, balancing the laptop on his left forearm like a waiter would a tray, handled the Gamma-Scout with his right hand. He trained the Geiger counter on the nearest bloated carcass. Its digital readout fell well within the range of the acceptable amounts of radiation. He'd expected to see a much higher reading.

Gagging from the odor, he aimed the Gamma-Scout up the carcass toward the rotting, burned head. The bloat had cracked

open the animal's blackened skin with expansion, and this is where the meter's numbers edged up slightly—the frozen, exposed
flesh.

*Water,* Walt thought.

"Sheriff! We got company!" Brandon
called down into the pit, his hand cupped
so tightly over his mouth and nose that
Walt barely understood him. "An ATV,
maybe. Two small headlights."

Walt set the Gamma-Scout onto the
keyboard and dug around the day pack
with his free hand. He came out with a
hunting knife with a six-inch serrated blade
of carbon steel. He hesitated only briefly
before plunging the tip through the hardened shell of burned skin. The bloated
carcass spit through the rent and hissed
out a gas that made Walt retch.

"Christ Almighty!" Brandon complained,
the stink quickly reaching him.

The meter's readout jumped significantly, this time to dangerous levels.

"Light!" Walt called out.

Brandon, in monitoring the approaching
vehicle, had neglected his responsibility.
Now the light caught Walt, and the sheriff

glanced down at the fresh biosensor tag he had clipped to his uniform a day earlier. The same wedge was shaded a ghostly purple, indicating additional exposure to radioactivity.

"Check your tag!" Walt hollered up from the pit.

"Shit!" Brandon said a moment later. "I'm hot."

His voice was now overcome by the whine of the ATV's motor.

"How close?" Walt shouted.

"A minute. Maybe less."

"Bury the rope in the snow. Hide yourself in that slash pile."

"Hide?"

"Now, Tommy. That's an order!"

Walt felt the same way as his deputy: it was not in his nature to hide. But for a rancher to burn this many sheep—to throw away that kind of money—the stakes had to be extremely high. High enough to kidnap or kill? A rancher like Lon Bernie was likely to shoot first and ask questions later, and Walt had no great desire to test that theory. If Lon Bernie figured out his burned sheep had been discovered, he and Brandon might wind up buried along with them.

Walt slapped the laptop shut and zipped it and the Gamma-Scout in the day pack. He kept the pack in front of him, as he curled down into the corner of the pit, his head lower than the nearest sheep, and huddled there. The sound of the ATV grew progressively closer and louder, like the buzzing of a bee. The cold penetrated, as he held his head between his legs, offering only the back of his jacket to the night sky. Bernie would have to shine a light and look right down at him in order to see him.

The ATV arrived and quieted, its motor idling.

Out of the corner of his eye, Walt caught the light from the headlights shifting, as the driver moved the vehicle to spread the light around the edges of the pit.

Walt believed he'd discovered the boot prints behind the barn, had followed them out to the pit. So now, finding no one, Bernie had to wonder if they were fresh tracks or if a couple of his hands had come out here on foot. It was the wrong time of year to go marching around the ranch on foot.

Bernie—or whoever was driving the ATV—would be trying to reconcile things.

At last, Walt heard the dry crunch of footfalls. The driver was off the ATV and heading toward the pit. Silence followed. Walt could picture the man up there, studying the pile of bloated carcasses, troubled by the sensation that all was not well. Walt had been there enough times himself: trusting his senses more than his reasoning.

He heard something unexpected: a stream of water. Lon Bernie, or whoever was up there, was urinating into the pit—not a pleasant practice in these temperatures. But then Walt's nose took over: not urine but petroleum. Diesel fuel.

A shudder rushed through him.

The driver of the ATV had not come looking for them; he'd come to douse the pit and burn the sheep in the dead of night. With the pit dug as deeply as it was, the flames would show as no more than a glow at night, the rising black smoke not revealing itself to the distant neighbors. Only a plume would linger by daylight. Burning trash and debris was a year-round practice on any ranch. A little smoke wasn't going to raise eyebrows. The ATV held a drum of fuel oil. It was hand pumped, and it showered onto the carcasses. None of the fuel fell directly on Walt; it was concentrated toward the pit's center and the heaped carcasses. But it came, gallon after gallon, the stench alone enough to choke him.

And then, minutes later, the match.

The pit lit on fire all of a sudden. Diesel is a slow-burning fuel. There was no great explosion, or even a *whoosh*. Flame simply ran across the pile, chasing the spent fuel. The heat increased. The flesh began to pop.

Walt knew Brandon would be anxious, might ruin things by leaping to Walt's rescue, but then the ATV's motor whirred. And grew faint.

The rope struck Walt on his back.

"Jesus, Sheriff!"

The concentration of flames was well away from Walt, but the heat was intense and the fire was spreading. He grabbed on to the rope, placed his feet on the wall of the pit, and drew himself up and out, where Brandon offered his one good hand and pulled hard.

The ATV's taillights receded down the access road.

"You're out of your mind," Brandon said, his face aglow in the light of the fire. His skin shined from the sweat of anxiety. His eyes flashed white, wide with anger that he disguised as outrage.

"I would have called for help if I'd needed it," Walt said offhandedly.

"Jesus! How was that possibly worth it, Sheriff?" Indignant. "How is that possibly—"

Walt patted the day pack. "It was well worth it, Tommy." He looked back at the burning heap of flesh, popping and bubbling. He was thinking about Mark Aker and how much time had passed since his abduction. He was thinking that in these temperatures fire connected one person to another, one ranch to another, one life to another, and that somewhere out there Mark Aker hopefully was near a fire just like he was. Walt's chance of finding and rescuing Mark Aker came down to efficiency, of turning a number on a Geiger counter into hard evidence, of uncovering an evidence trail that could connect the

discolored biosensor to the missing veterinarian.

He understood where that trail would
start and, rising to his toes, could almost
see it in the blanket of darkness that
stretched for miles up this nearly uninhabited
valley.

Senator James Peavy's ranch lay just
out of view.

# 37

MARK AKER WAS SURPRISED BY HIS OWN strength. HIS legs felt good. Adrenaline, perhaps. He walked in the snowmobile track because it was easier going. It followed what appeared to be a road, given the lack of trees and shrubs. Not only could he move faster on the track, but he was less likely to leave tracks to follow. The moon turned the snow lavender. He heard shouting behind him, coming from the cabin. Coats and Gearbox. These first few minutes were critical. They wouldn't know where he'd gone: around back to the shed, toward the woodpile, or up the snowmobile track. They'd search for tracks leading into the woods.

It wouldn't take them long—five minutes, maybe less—to realize he hadn't headed into virgin snow, that he must have taken the snowmobile track. And then they'd come after him.

He'd hurt Coats badly with that burn. Would Coats stay and lick his wounds or join the hunt? The answer came immediately, as more shouting erupted behind him, and the coughing of the snowmobile trying to start rumbled through the woods.

Aker had yet to turn on the flashlight, still negotiating by the light of the moon. If he left the snowmobile track, his prints would give him away. But if he stayed, he was only minutes from being caught. He could try jumping off the track, making his first prints in the virgin snow as far off the beaten track as possible, but he knew Coats to be a professional tracker. He had to outsmart him.

**Think!**

At the first curve, the snowmobile track left the road and weaved through the thick forest of lodgepole pine and aspen, no doubt following a shortcut only available in winter months. He passed a dozen or more trees before he heard the chain-saw-like buzz of the snowmobile's motor catching life. They'd be on him in less than a minute.

He stopped. Turned. His mind counting down the time he was wasting. Then he saw it: a branch.

The track cut incredibly close to a twisted pine that had once been struck by lightning. It was a craggy old tree with a few sparse branches low enough to the ground to reach by jumping. Aker squatted and leaped, but his gloves slid off the only branch close enough to reach. He tried again, and again, but could not grab hold.

Now the snowmobile was crying out, well under way.

He jumped a fourth time and managed to hook his hands and lace his fingers over the branch. He walked his feet up the trunk, hooked a knee over the branch, and struggled up to a sitting position. With the adrenaline spent, he was far weaker than he'd first thought. He continued to climb, following the tree's natural ladder. Two, three, four branches up; and now, looking down, he saw only branches. He moved himself higher, and on the opposite

side of the tree from the track. He strad-
dled the branch and kept himself against
the trunk.

The snowmobile's headlight winked
through the woods, as the grind of the motor drew nearer. It was traveling slowly, and
now a second light was revealed: a flashlight, searching both sides of the track.

Aker caught himself holding his breath
as it came into view, staying in the track.
*Two* men. Gearbox was driving, Coats,
straddling the motorcycle-style seat behind Gearbox, holding the flashlight.

The snowmobile purred up the track approaching Aker's tree, the flashlight alter-
nately illuminating the forest on both sides,
throwing harsh shadows that moved around
in a jarring dance. It continued past.

A red taillight now. Nothing more. The
sound grew more and more distant.

A person on foot was no match for a
snowmobile. It would only take them minutes to realize they'd missed him.

Aker climbed down out of the tree as
quickly as humanly possible. He landed
back on the track and took off for the cabin.
He tried to run but wasn't up to it. It seemed

to take forever to reach the camp, but it was only minutes. But how long until the snowmobile returned?

Inside the cabin now—the smell of burned hair and flesh, a nauseating stink—he stole a backpack, ripped a regional map off the wall, and stuffed it and other items into the zippered compartment: canned foods, matches, a church key, can opener, saltshaker, a fork, and a kitchen knife. He snatched up the syringes from the table and took the vials of insulin and the medication Coats had used to subdue him: opiates and narcotics. A pair of wool socks hanging by the woodstove. A wool cap. He grabbed a pair of snowshoes from a peg.

The sound of the snowmobile was suddenly louder. Closer . . .

He'd heard the two talk about spotting a cow elk by the salt lick. That meant game, which meant a game trail to follow. Out back, he briefly risked the flashlight, the moon having hidden behind the fast-moving clouds overhead. He couldn't find the salt lick. The unbroken snow that formed an apron beyond the shed trapped him as neatly as a fence.

Leaving any tracks would give him away.

And there, in the flashlight's beam, came his answer: two woodpiles, one for the split logs, neatly stacked very high, and, beyond it, a pile of ten or twelve massive tree trunks, ready for cutting and splitting. Small animals had greatly disturbed the snow in and around the logs; his tracks wouldn't be easily noticed. By daylight, they might spot his route, but, if he hurried, he could be far gone by then.

He struggled up the pile of stacked wood, winded and weak. He fumbled his way over it and fell to the other side. Next, he took two great leaps in succession and reached the pile of felled trees. He clambered over this pile as well, the whine of the snowmobile fast approaching.

In all, he'd left but two prints in the deep snow, between the stacked wood and felled trees, both hidden by the woodpile itself. He crept under a tree's snow-laden branches and out to the other side. Crawled under the branches of the next tree, to hide his tracks. He was at least twenty yards from the shed now.

The snowmobile's engine coughed to

silence. Coats shouted: "Fuck this! He can't be far!"

Aker strapped on the snowshoes. His pursuers searched the far side of the cabin first, buying him precious time.

He found a rhythm in a half-speed run, leaning forward slightly to compensate for the added weight of the backpack. The adrenaline was back, and, with it, some needed energy.

He had no compass and no idea where he was. But he was no stranger to the outdoors and he knew where he was headed: as far away as he could get.

# SUNDAY A.M.

# 38

WALT STRUCK THE BRASS KNOCKER SHARPLY against the plate on the front door. Despite a career of getting used to it, he was put off by the grandeur of the farmhouse and generational wealth it represented.

Brandon stomped his boots on the porch, trying to feel his feet.

"You sure about this, Sheriff? It's almost three in the morning."

"We're not driving back over here to-morrow."

"No offense, but you don't smell so good."

Walt smacked the door knocker—a

brass cowboy boot—against the door again.

Standing beneath the porch roof, they didn't see a light go on in a second-story window, but the snow behind them lit up from the glow, and Walt stepped back.

The door rattled and opened.

Senator James Peavy wore a pair of blue jeans with a sweater turned inside out. He squinted into the brightness of the porch light. His head of wispy white hair was thin on top, a fact usually hidden by the ubiquitous Stetson.

"Sheriff?" Astonishment. "Deputy?"

"We need a minute of your time," Walt said.

"You come in here smelling like that, obviously you must," said Peavy, waving them inside. "Come in."

The parlor could have been from a homesteading museum. Peavy motioned for them to sit. Walt wanted to stand, but he took a seat on a blue velvet love seat with ruby piping. Brandon took the end of the piano bench, facing into the spacious room. Sheer curtains hung on the windows of air-bubbled, imperfect glass.

Peavy remained standing, an act that infuriated Walt. Perhaps sensing this, the rancher then sat down on the edge of a blue-and-white-crocheted slide rocker. He moved gently forward and back.

"So?"

"Why would Lon Bernie burn fifty head of sheep? And why in the dead of night?"

Peavy's life in politics mixed with time spent in the great outdoors afforded him a wonderfully expressive face, gracious and kind and handsome. Even half awake, he possessed the countenance of a minister and the composure of a therapist.

"You want to talk about Lon Bernie's sheep?" he said.

"I'd rather not dance around the issue. Mark Aker's life is in play. Something's going on here, and before I tear the lid off this thing I wanted to give you a chance to break it to me gently."

"So you're here out of thoughtful consideration, are you? At three in the morning?"

"This was a convenient time."

"Not for all of us."

"Radiation contamination," Walt said.

Peavy scowled, an expression impossible to read as anything but surprise. "Jesus, what is that smell?"

"Help me out here, James," Walt said. "What's going on?"

"This is your party."

"The invitation for me to go to Washington. That was your doing. Why?"

"Because I think you're underrated, Walt. Sometimes we control the timing of the events in our lives, sometimes not. The vice president is eager for you to serve on a national level. Don't think this was just me. You have more friends than you're aware of."

"One of them's dead. Another's missing."

An uneasy silence. The piano bench squeaked under Brandon's weight.

"You called Mark to take care of your sheep."

"We've been over this."

"I thought it was the hay or grain. Mad cow, or something like that. Come to find out, it's the water."

Peavy asked to speak with Walt privately, and Walt told Brandon to stay where he was. He wanted a witness to anything discussed and he said so. Peavy winced, part disgust, part concession.

"Sheriff, if you have a crime to charge me with, please do so. Otherwise . . ."

"Senator . . ."

"I understand your concern over Mark Aker. I share it. I know nothing about his disappearance. Do you hear me, Walt? Nothing. As for your suggestion, this other subject, I can tell you this: there is a good deal of money involved when a rancher loses a head or two of livestock. What you're reporting with Lon, twenty-five, fifty head, that's not just a backbreaker, it's a *bank* breaker. That's forty-five thousand, plus the loss of the ewe producing for you. Probably a hundred grand, all told. On our margins, that's your operation, or damn near. Think about that, Walt. Consider that very carefully. It isn't entered into lightly. You're assuming the invitation to Washington somehow benefited me. But what if it's me, or people in high places, trying to protect you? What if that's how wrong you've got this?"

"If there's a crime, then you're a victim—Lon Bernie's a victim. Why won't you come forward? How can you not come forward?"

The senator arched his brows. "Your explanation, not mine."

"Then what's yours?"

"I don't have one. Don't need one."

"Mark came out to these ranches because of sick sheep. He discovered radiation poisoning in the water. He kept his work away from his office because he understood the politics. He tried to warn me about the politics."

"And you're not listening."

"This can't be you talking, Senator. We've known each other forever. I consider us friends," Walt said.

"If I knew anything about Mark Aker, I'd help you. But I don't."

The two men's eyes met.

"No one is going to help you. I'm trying to protect you, Sheriff. Take the trip to Washington."

"Protect me?" Walt's face was scarlet, his voice too loud for the room.

"The Lon Bernies of this world make their own laws. You and I both know a badge doesn't mean much in this valley. Ironic since we've both served the law ourselves.

But it's different over here. You know that. If it wasn't for the vehicles, it could be a hundred years ago."

"Maybe they buy off the local sheriff, but I'm not the local sheriff."

"Worth taking note of."

Walt stood, took a menacing step toward an unreasonably calm James Peavy, and caught himself, as Brandon rose off the piano bench.

Peavy said, "Maybe by finding Mark Aker you find your answers, I don't know. But by looking for him, you put yourself at risk, Walt. Hear me on this. Hear me good. This valley isn't a safe place for you. Go home. Keep to your side of the mountains. You'll find nothing but trouble over here."

"But if you're a victim, why not report it?" Walt repeated, now exasperated. "Since when can someone intimidate James Peavy?"

Peavy didn't speak again. His expression suggested not resignation but determination, which confused Walt.

He walked to the door and opened it for them. As cold a night as Walt could remember.

# 39

THE OUTSIDE OF THE ENVELOPE BORE HIS NAME, handwritten in a lovely script, although Walt couldn't actually touch the envelope, as it was sealed in thick, red-tinted plastic. BIO-HAZARD was printed on the front in large letters.

The desk sergeant explained that the envelope—hand delivered to the office by Fiona Kenshaw—had tripped the elec-tronic sniffer used on all incoming mail.

Contaminated.

He was working on forty-five minutes of sleep. He'd showered, shaved, changed his uniform, and had eaten the scrambled eggs Lisa prepared for him. She'd slept on the couch, and had let the girls brush her hair and put it into a ponytail, so that she looked somewhat disheveled, as she washed dishes while Walt ate. It felt weird having her in the house. He hadn't thanked her. Hadn't said much at all. They'd met eyes at one point during the morning confusion, just before she'd left. Her eyes had said something about feeling sorry for him while all he felt was impossibly guilty. He'd driven the girls to school, because this was their routine. They'd played a word game on the way—the animal game—and Walt found himself not wanting to stop. Maybe just keep driving, his eyes on the two faces in his rearview mirror. When he'd let them out, he'd run around the car to hug them. Both girls appeared embarrassed by the gesture, though neither complained.

"Radiation?" he asked his desk sergeant.

"No! It was indicated as only biohazard," she said. "The machine doesn't get specific. If an item alerts for radioactivity, it goes in that box they gave us. Biohazard gets the red bags."

After 9/11, the Blaine County Sheriff's

Office had received a threatening letter containing a white substance that eventually came back as arsenic but had been believed to be anthrax. The feds had required the installation of the sniffer—a fifteen-thousand-dollar machine subsidized by the federal government—and it had been SOP ever since to test each piece of mail arriving at the office. The letter, bearing Fiona's unmistakable handwriting, had been the first ever to trip the sensors, and the desk sergeant seemed more excited than frightened by the event.

"You want me to issue a BOLO?" asked the desk sergeant. *Be on lookout.*

"I'm not arresting her," Walt said. "She works for us."

The desk sergeant held her tongue, but her eyes reminded him it was procedure to arrest anyone suspected of attempting to contaminate the offices. It was also procedure to involve the postal inspectors.

He answered that look of hers. "This wasn't sent through the mail. It wasn't an intentional contamination, and my guess is, it's one big misunderstanding. Before we call anyone, I'm going to clear this up."

"And what do I do with this?" she said, lifting the red bag by one corner.

"Give it to me," he answered, accepting the bag.

WALT HELD a morning meeting with his two lieutenants, during which he passed along the day-to-day so he could continue working on Aker's abduction. Nancy called Fiona, and, when Fiona arrived, Walt led her outside, and they walked around the block, circumnavigating the former courthouse and city hall, a grand, three-story brick building built in the late 1800s. It now housed the DMV and county records. He didn't bother with a jacket; it was already in the upper forties. The early bite of winter seemed to be mitigating, at least at the lower altitudes.

He produced the red baggie from his coat pocket.

"I didn't want to discuss this in the office. But can you please tell me why you left me an envelope that tripped our biosensors? You might have warned me."

She stopped abruptly.

"My letter's a *biohazard*?"

"I thought you'd given it to me because

you knew it was contaminated, that it was related to Mark's work somehow."

She told him then about being picked up by Sean Lunn at Hillabrand's. About spotting the dried mud on the Escalade's step rail. About how the unusually pale color had reminded her of the dried mud on the rape victim's clothing.

Walt unsealed and opened the plastic bag, as she explained its contents. He tore open the envelope and saw that it contained both a note and a small amount of a pale brown dirt.

"Roger Hillabrand?"

"The mud was on his car. I was going to suggest that you have the lab compare this to what we found on the girl's shoes."

"That's certainly available to us."

"Roger—or, more likely, Lunn—drove that car somewhere near where that girl—"

"Tulivich. Kira Tulivich," he provided.

"—had been."

"Ohio Gulch or Triumph," Walt said. "The two most likely spots in this valley where you'd find contaminants: the dump and the old Triumph Mine. But the fact is that Kira Tulivich was at the wedding at Hillabrand's.

You're the witness on that. Mud on his rails and her shoes—odds are, it's from his house, or at least somewhere on his property."

"Everything's frozen solid and covered in two feet of snow," she reminded him.

"Maybe not everything," he said. "You want to help?"

"Of course!"

"Can you get yourself invited back up there?"

"You want me to *spy* for you?"

"Once we've confirmed we've got a match, my guys and I can work Ohio Gulch and Triumph, and we will. But ruling out Hillabrand would be the first step in any kind of an investigation. You start with the most obvious: that she was in those shoes, on his property, the night she was raped. The mud may have absolutely nothing to do with anything, other than she attended the reception. You're not 'spying,'" he said, putting it in finger quotes, "you're eliminating him from consideration."

"I attended the reception and I didn't come home with any mud on my shoes."

"I'm just saying that's where it starts. If I come at Roger Hillabrand with a request to collect evidence, there will be a line of attorneys at my door ten deep."

"Okay. I accept. I'll spy for you," she said.

"It's not spying. It's just looking for some mud. He has a pond up there. But this would more likely be around a hot tub or along the edge of a heated driveway."

"But contaminated?"

"I'm not saying I have the answers. I'm just telling you where we start."

"I'm not going to find any mud up there, Walt. It's frozen solid. The Escalade's the connection. If you ask me, Roger's guy, Sean Lunn, was at the same afterparty, the same bar—the same something—as Kira was. He probably doesn't know it, but he's the one who can help you. Not that he ever would."

"Women's intuition?"

"Don't patronize me, Walt. Roger will never allow it. He'll stick his boy on the private jet and send him to Brazil for all eternity rather than get involved with something here that can't possibly do anything but sully his company's name."

"You've gotten to know him, I see."

"Jealousy doesn't suit you."

Walt felt his face flush. Was he jealous? It struck him that maybe he was.

She spared him further embarrassment. "How long for the lab to compare the two dirt samples?"

"Several weeks, I would think. It's never fast."

Her face sagged.

"But we may not need it," he said. "We already have a sample of the mud from her shoes. We took it at the hospital. I'm thinking all we need to do is run that sample through our mail sniffer. If it kicks as hazardous, that's good enough for me: that gives us probable cause. We can send it off to the lab, but we don't need to wait for specific results."

Fiona nodded. "I'll bring my camera. That gives me the added excuse to look all around. But it can't be a hot tub. It's on the Escalade's step rail. It was thrown up onto the car when the car was going at a good clip. It's got to be a road or a driveway, and the only thing that makes sense to me is that the contaminants are salts that keep the ground from freezing."

"Like I said, that's Ohio Gulch or Triumph. We're on it." Maybe it was the repetition, or her stating so confidently that it was salts keeping the ground from freezing, but, standing there, he suddenly knew exactly where and with whom to begin this discussion.

He'd nearly had his chance a few nights earlier.

# 40

"DO NOT RAIN," WALT CHANTED TO HIMSELF, staring up through the Cherokee's windshield. For an area that saw three hundred sun-filled days a year, the skies had picked this particular Monday to threaten, and it was in the low forties—the one time he was out searching for preexisting mud.

He could remember a time, not long ago, when the road out to the landfill had been a poorly maintained dirt track, leading to a giant, unsupervised pit in the ground. But now he drove on asphalt all the way out to a series of excavations, all surrounded by chain-link fence, monitored by an attendant in an entrance booth.

"Hey, Ginny," Walt said, his elbow out the window, the Cherokee perched on a concrete slab, a vehicle scale large enough to weigh tractor trailers.

"Walt."

"Just need a look around."

"Not dumping nothing?"

"No, ma'am."

"How're the girls?"

"Wild. More like teenagers every day."

"Sorry to hear it."

"How's your mother doing?" he asked.

"Same old same old. Nothing going to kill her."

"Nor should it."

"Second cancer in two years, but she's still doing her own shopping."

"The way it should be."

"I hope I'm that strong when I'm eighty."

"Right there with you."

"Anything new on Mark Aker?"

"Working on it. Everyone in my department."

"Is that what brings you here?"

"No. I'm just sightseeing."

"Yeah. True beauty. And the smell is certainly worth a visit."

"An aroma coma. May I pass?"

"Be my guest." She tripped a button that lifted the red-and-white-striped barricade, and Walt drove off the scale and onto dirt. The surface was crushed granite, like nearly every road in the county, rock chips and sand mixed with a good deal of clay, the color of coffee with cream. He was no great judge, considered himself mostly color-blind, but the dried mud on Kira Tulivich's shoes had been a pale pasty brown, almost gray. The dirt he saw here wasn't close to that color.

The landfill pits were constantly being dug up, covered over, and redug, bringing every kind of unwanted thing to the surface. He drove into a big, open field of dirt, patches of litter trapped on the surface, leading to a sharp edge, beyond which a well-graded ramp carried the big Caterpillar tractors and loaders fifty feet down into an organized mass of trash and household debris at the bottom.

A light drizzle struck his windshield, and

he cursed aloud in the confines of the car.

SEVERAL MILES NORTH of Ohio Gulch, Walt arrived at the turn for East Fork, a valley canyon running east of the highway and parallel to a like-named creek. East Fork represented the dichotomy of the valley, a crossroads where the blue-collar community of Triumph, situated on an abandoned mine site, met the multimillion-dollar homes that bordered the creek. The mine had been dug and exhausted a hundred years earlier, leaving behind vast fields of chemically poisoned gravel and clay tailings so toxic that nothing, not a single weed, would grow. The steppes of tailings, each the size of several football fields, rose in three successive levels, thirty to forty feet high, just as East Fork Road left the affluent neighborhoods behind.

A hippie community had sprung up in Triumph in the late 1960s, squatters willing to risk living on the top tier of the toxic mine tailings. For thirty years, Triumph had been listed as among the nation's top five most toxic sites on the EPA's Superfund list. No cleanup money had ever been allocated. Despite health warnings, the residents stayed. As land values escalated, the squatter shacks grew to trailers, mobile homes, and even a log cabin or two. The result was a ramshackle assortment of dwellings whose occupants had reputations as eccentrics, renegades, and, in some cases, outlaws.

Senator James Peavy's warning echoed in Walt's ears, though he was much closer to home: people made their own laws. There were places in this county that a uniform felt more like a bull's-eye than a designation of authority, and Triumph was one of them.

The road rose more steeply on the final approach to Triumph. Remains of ancient mining equipment jutted out of the hill. The road ascended to a cluster of dwellings, a desolate, desperate landscape juxtaposed against stunning views to the west.

As Walt made the drive, he noticed that each terraced steppe changed color. The lowest was a black-gray clay, the middle gray-green, the top grayish yellow. Even half color-blind, Walt saw the similarity to the dried mud on Kira Tulivich's shoes.

He drove through the neighborhood

carefully. He hadn't been up here in a while and was surprised to see some decent-looking homes interspersed with the trailers. Wood smoke spewed from stovepipes. A few dogs patrolled.

Parked next to a broken-down RV he spotted an old beater Subaru that he recognized as Taylor Crabtree's. Walt's office had impounded the car twice. Even from a distance, he could see discoloring along the side of the car.

Now it added up: Crabtree, a repeat juvie offender; his face, a battered mess; now, mud on his car. Walt parked alongside the Subaru. The mud was the same grayish yellow as Kira Tulivich's shoes.

Walt saw his own face in the reflection off the glass of the driver door, as he stole a look inside: the dark "snow tan" hid any evidence of fatigue or lines of concern, the sunglasses masked his eyes. Only his cracked lips and stubble beard offered a glimpse into the strain of the past several days.

Walt squinted, pushing closer to the glass: on the Subaru's dashboard was a sticker: KB'S BURRITOS. Kira Tulivich had offered only one, seemingly irrelevant piece of information from the examination table: "KB's"

Walt broke off a chunk of the mud and bagged it, then slipped the Beretta out of its holster. Walt ducked down alongside the Subaru and triple-clicked the radio com clipped to his uniform's epaulet. This signaled to his dispatcher a low-voice communication: he or she was to answer in clicks, not voice. Walt reported his location in a whisper and requested backup, using the radio code to signal no lights or sirens. He released the mic's button and waited.

Two clicks. Backup was on its way.

After two minutes passed, Walt lost patience waiting for backup to arrive. He reminded himself that Crabtree was just a kid.

He edged around the car, crossed to the RV, and put his ear to the door. If the kid dived out a window or climbed out a skylight, Walt would regret not waiting. But he hammered on the door just the same. "Crabtree! It's Sheriff Fleming. Open the door, please!"

The RV moved and squeaked on its springs.

"Crabtree!" Walt called loudly. "Don't be stupid."

The door swung open.

"Keep your hands where I can see them."

Crabtree wore blue jeans and the denim shirt from Elbie's. His hands were stained black from work, his hair a rat's nest. His beat-up eyes were filled with contempt and soured with distrust.

"Yeah?"

"Step outside," Walt said, backing up. "Okay, now . . . hands against the RV and your butt back." Walt frisked him. "Good. Fine." He holstered the Beretta and asked Crabtree to turn around.

"I don't know nothing about any guys trying to get people to join anything."

"It's not about that," Walt said.

Crabtree shrugged.

"Do you know a girl—a young woman—named Kira Tulivich?"

"Sure I do."

The admission surprised Walt. Crabtree was the kind of kid who'd deny everything. "You know her from where?"

"School. From around. You know."

It started to rain again. Walt ignored it. Taylor Crabtree checked the sky a couple times, shedding more light onto his cut-up face.

"Know her *well*?"

"Nah. Just know who she is. Her type and me, we don't exactly mix."

"Her type? You mean she's older, or pretty, or what?"

"Rich," he said. "That's the way it is at school: us and them. You know?"

"When was the last time you saw her?"

Crabtree's hesitation belied his answer. "I don't know."

"You know what we're going to do, Taylor? We're going to put a forensics team from Boise on your car. You ever seen *CSI*? Like that. They vacuum the car. Develop prints. Lift some. Photograph others. They'll be looking for hair and fibers that connect back to Kira Tulivich. That mud on the car. All that evidence—some of it you can't even see—is going to bring you down like a ton of bricks. You want to get ahead of this, now is your chance."

Crabtree wasn't paying attention. Walt followed his line of sight: spotting a couple of pickup trucks coming up East Fork Road and then, in the far distance, a cruiser. His backup, still a mile away.

Walt thought he could use this. "Running out of time here. When was the last time you saw Kira Tulivich?"

Crabtree refocused on Walt's stern face.

"When I seen her, I thought it was her, but I ain't never seen her all dolled up like that." The boy's eyes drifted back to the advancing patrol car.

"Forget about that," Walt said. He radioed the unit to hold off. The cruiser pulled to the side of the road just as the two pickups drove out of sight. "You saw her?"

"I said I did, didn't I?" Crabtree sounded irritated, and more nervous than a few minutes earlier. "Walking . . . on the side of the road . . ."

"Walking? What road?"

"And I stopped to . . . you know."

"Let's assume I don't know," Walt said.

"She got in. But she was fucked-up."

"You knew this how?"

"Because she was fucked-up. Shit, Sheriff. Fucked-up. You don't know fucked-up?"

"In what way?"

"High. Real high. Barely recognized me. Barely standing up. That kind of fucked-up. *Real* fucked-up."

"Intoxicated."

"No. More than that. High. Boozed-up, yeah, but fried, you know? Spaced. And I say, 'Get in,' and she gets in, like it's cool. You know? With me. I mean, that's like totally not happening. And I say, 'Where to?' And this is, like, I don't know, the middle of the fucking night."

"And she was on which road?" Walt asked.

Crabtree looked as if he'd been slapped. "This road," he said, pointing. "East Fork. Headed down toward the highway."

"And you were headed where at that time of night? The middle of the night?"

"I don't know. Don't remember. Smokes, I suppose? Mountain View," he said, referring to a gas station quick stop.

"Okay."

"And once she's in the car, you know, I see she's all messed-up. The dress is toast. Her face looks like shit, like she's been beaten real bad. Her left tit comes out of the dress and she barely notices. Stuffs it back in and looks over at me with these creeped-out, dead eyes. And now I'm thinking she's loopy because someone hit her too hard or something. Like my moms used to get . . . And I'm no longer asking her, 'Where to?' I'm booking it for the hospital."

"You took her to the hospital?"

"I dropped her there, yeah. I thought about taking her in, you know, but what was going to happen to me? I'd be talking to you. The way I am right now. And no one would believe me, just like you don't believe me. That's how it is with me. That's how it always is, so fuck that. I just dropped her. Let her figure it out."

"You came to my house the other night," Walt said. "The back door."

"That wasn't me." Spoken too quickly, and with his eyes to the ground.

"Were you thinking about telling me about Kira?"

The boy had tipped. He was bursting to tell all. Wished for a quiet room, other circumstances. But Crabtree looked at the cruiser again and the light went out of his eyes. He fumbled for a cigarette. The moment had passed.

"There are a couple things that need to happen now," Walt said.

"I promise you, it wasn't me. I didn't do shit to her, Sheriff."

"You don't have to go down for this. But I need more. Did she say anything to you? A name, maybe?"

Crabtree tightened. He took a long drag off the cigarette, and the smoke disappeared inside him. "You look scared, Taylor. Real scared. Of me? Of the possibility of prison? Or something else?"

It took Crabtree a long time to speak. "Something else."

"A rape conviction puts you in the sex offender database. It'll follow you the rest of your life. People will put posters up on telephone poles near your house. They'll cross the street to avoid you."

Crabtree twitched at the mention of rape, his eyes narrowing: he hadn't known. A weight lifted from Walt. A smile slipped across his face, but he wiped it off with the back of his hand.

"Blah, blah, blah." Crabtree glanced around again, either afraid to make eye contact with Walt or plotting an escape.

"Don't try it," Walt said.

"What?"

"Whatever it is you're planning."

"Are we going to do this or not?" He held out his hands to be cuffed.

"Work with me, Taylor."

Crabtree looked Walt squarely in the eye. "Fuck you and your posters."

"Please," Walt pleaded.

"Do what you gotta do," said Crabtree.

# 41

THE TERRAIN ROSE UP THROUGH THE TANGLED forest, the dark bark of the trees like burnt offerings against the sparkling, sun-dappled snow. A snowmobile whined as it followed a game trail, its motor straining, its tread spewing ice and elk scat in its wake. The irritating sound grew fainter as it was swallowed by the landscape.

Along that same route stood a majestic fir tree, battle-scarred from a lightning strike forty years earlier. It was split from the first long-dead limb to its four-foot-diameter base. While half the tree had died as a result of the strike, new growth extended up the other half, with gnarly, tightly grouped branches, scarred with veins of charcoal, running like arrows toward the sky. The split gave the trunk a charred, inverted V shape that, at its base, looked like a door to a teepee. It was just wide enough for a man to squeeze through, which was exactly what Mark Aker had done hours earlier. He'd done so without leaving the game path, without causing any prints or impressions that might reveal his hiding place.

Forcing his way through the split in the tree, he'd fallen into the cavity, two feet below the snow's surface, and onto a bed of leaves. Aker had burrowed down into the leaves, using them as both insulation and camouflage. He passed the coldest hours of the night drifting in and out of sleep, knees to the chest. The buzz of the snowmobile woke him, steadily approaching like a nagging insect. As it tore past his hiding place, he realized that at least for now he was safe. And, though he was regaining strength, if he hoped to save his feet from frostbite, he would have to get moving soon. At some point, he'd have to leave the game trail for deeper snow, even though it would create a path for his captors to follow.

He waited over forty-five minutes for the return of the snowmobile, sunlight blazing on the very tips of the trees he could partially see through. Coats had stripped him of his watch, but he was guessing it was late morning or early afternoon. The horrid machine came back more slowly than it had gone out, Gearbox no doubt at the controls and paying closer attention, attempting to track him. Aker hoped he'd done his job well enough; and when the snowmobile's whine grew faint, he allowed himself to relax and plan his next move.

# 42

WALT WAS REELING WITH REGRET WHEN HE
turned crabtree over to booking. The kid
was eighteen now; Walt could no longer
protect his record.

He ate a muffin to settle his stomach,
but the lukewarm coffee chaser only added
to his discomfort. Among his many phone
messages were several he found impossible to ignore: a pair from Congressman
McMillian, inquiring about Walt's participation in the national law enforcement conference, and another from James Peavy.
He couldn't ignore them. He was an elected
official; he needed both the support of his

party and his party leadership, especially given that it was an election year.

"McMillian first?" Nancy asked him.

"Let's hold off on that. Any word from the people out at the INL?"

The possibility of radioactive water had led Walt to the obvious call: the Idaho Nuclear Laboratory, a facility covering nine hundred square miles in the center of the state and containing over thirty active or retired reactors.

"I've called a couple different people out there. They've all refused appointments. They were polite enough about it. But I get the feeling it's not going to happen."

"Okay, one more time: get me the director out there."

"Now?"

"Now." Walt stood there while Nancy made the call. She was put on hold several times before she eventually thanked someone and hung up. "Unavailable. He'll return the call when he's free."

Walt considered the situation. The smart move would have been for them to take the meetings and calls and issue a string of denials. By refusing him, it implied they needed time to coordinate their denials, and that seemed to him the most advantageous time to strike. "Get hold of Fiona. Find out if she's available for me later today. It may involve night photography, so tell her to bring the appropriate gear, and tell her to dress warmly."

"Should I contact the Butte County sheriff and let him know you're coming?"

"No. Call over to Sun Valley Aviation and see if you can get me a time for a tow."

Nancy looked up at him quizzically. "The glider?"

Walt smiled for the first time all day.

WALT AND THE PILOT of the towplane coordinated the release of the glider. As the Cessna banked slowly to the right, diving below and away, Walt piloted the glider higher and slightly left.

"It's noisier than I'd imagined," Fiona said from behind him.

"Are you okay?"

"Fine," she said. "I told you: I have no problem with small planes."

Walt had flown gliders since his early twenties, his interest born out of an envy of eagles and hawks and a budget that couldn't afford renting single-engine airtime.

The glider suddenly caught an updraft off the base of the hills and gained a hundred feet in a matter of seconds, leaving both their stomachs somewhere up on the Plexiglas cockpit cover.

"Still okay?" Walt asked.

"I'm getting used to it."

He saw the towplane now. It had come fully around, on a line with the Arco airstrip about twenty miles ahead. As arranged, rather than returning to Hailey, it would wait in Arco for them.

"Are we high enough?" Fiona shouted, to be heard over the roar created by wind over the wings. There was no motor, just the rush of the glider slicing through the sky.

"I'm working on it."

Walt worked the glider into a wide spiral, climbing into an azure sky, carried aloft by thermals generated by the mountain landmass below. Killer view, Walt thought. To their right, the vast central plain of Idaho stretched out like a lake of desert sand, interrupted occasionally by volcanic cones dormant some ten thousand years. So random were these buttes, they appeared artificially placed. They saw bunkerlike buildings surrounded by tangles of pipes and aprons of parking lot. So secret was the work done here, so important to national security, that the entire area was grayed out on Internet-accessed satellite maps. Not even the topography was properly mapped—and it was the terrain and topography that most interested Walt.

Rivers and streams flowed out of the mountains roughly west to east. For Walt's theory of contamination to hold up, there had to be underground water flowing northwest from the INL. He'd made a quick study of the massive northern Rocky Mountain aquifer that stretched from Canada all the way to Mexico, but it too flowed predominantly south and slightly east. He wanted a bird's-eye view, to validate or invalidate his theory, but the INL airspace was restricted and those restrictions strenuously enforced.

His decision was to stray over the airspace, what he would call "a regrettable but unavoidable piloting error." He counted on the evening thermals to hold the glider aloft long enough for him to maneuver into position. Pursuing more altitude, he continued the elegant, half-mile-wide spiral ascent. At eleven thousand feet above sea level—six thousand aboveground—Walt kept the glider shy of an altitude requiring supplemental oxygen.

"Everything ready?

"Yes. Good to go."

"I have no idea what they'll do when we enter their airspace, but I don't see them shooting us down or anything."

"Well, that's reassuring."

"Get everything you can, everything we discussed."

"Will do."

"And if we are forced down, whatever you do don't surrender your equipment. Under no circumstances will you take that camera off your neck. They will claim all sorts of rights, but I think they'll stop short of actually physically removing the camera."

"And if they think otherwise?"

"We'll move it up a level to the attorneys."

"And if the attorneys fail?"

Walt said nothing.

"Walt?" she said, trying for an answer. Then it hit her. "Oh! Goddamn you! You wouldn't stoop to something . . . You wouldn't *use* me like that."

"Like what?"

"You were the one who told me Roger's company, Semper Group, is under contract with the government to manage nukes, among other things. The INL is a Semper contract, isn't it?"

"It is, but—"

"Did you honestly think I'd call Roger for you if you get busted in here? Is *that* why you asked me along? I'm your safety valve? How self-serving is that?"

"It never occurred to me. I just need photographs."

"But you didn't need me to take them."

"Of course I did."

"You're banking on my relationship with Roger to get you out of trouble. It's despicable."

"You're overreacting." He directed the glider toward the alluvial plain, the sun bloodred as it edged ever closer to the western horizon. "I thought you'd like it up here."

A difficult silence followed. It was too loud for him to hear her preparing her equipment. She said, "It just so happens that I do."

Walt smiled to himself, eased the joystick forward, and the glider quickly picked up speed as it dove, racing now into the restricted airspace.

# 43

ROY COATS BROUGHT THE MAUL DOWN ONE-
handed, splitting the log in a single stroke
and sending a shudder of pain through his
wounds. Standing a few feet off to the side,
Gearbox eyed the sharpened edge of the
maul, as it caught the mottled sunlight.

"I have to meet with her." Coats spoke
cautiously through a clenched jaw. Any
movement of his facial muscles sent white
pain down his neck and into the scissor
wound in his armpit. His unmoving lips resulted in a menacing tone. "She makes
the drop, and we don't give a shit about
this guy. Let him freeze out there. But I

can't count on her making the drop. So I'm not leaving here until I know we have a backup in place. That means you've got to *find him*." Coats wound up the maul and split another log, again in a single stroke.

"As if we haven't been trying."

"Find him," Coats repeated. He took off his glove and gingerly touched where the stove had branded his cheek. There was yellow pus on the tip of his finger. He wiped it off on his jeans. The burn needed medical attention, a primary reason he wanted the vet recaptured. "He's on foot in a fresh snowfall. We're on snowmobiles. Are you fucking kidding me?"

"But, with the dogs . . ." Gearbox said.

"We don't slow down, waiting for them."

"But Bill said—"

"Fuck Billy! If the dogs get here, they get here. But every minute he's out there, he's farther away. And you know what's worse? It's worse if he dies out there. Until I say otherwise, we need him."

"I'm open to suggestions," Gearbox said.

He cowered as Coats turned slowly. The maul swung like a pendulum at his side.

"We've been up and down that track a dozen times," Gearbox complained. "The game trails too. Without the dogs, we got nothing."

"Fuck the dogs!" An idea hit him. "Okay," Coats said, his anger briefly subsiding. "You remember that time we lost the cat over in eastern Oregon?"

"Sure," Gearbox said, nodding.

"We're going to do it like that: a pattern search. All we've gotta do is cross his tracks at some point. He can't be far."

"Okay," Gearbox said. He didn't sound convinced.

"I've got to keep that meeting with her. Are you listening? If she delivers that drum like I asked, within a week there's not one person on this planet won't have heard of the Samakinn. They've got, what, ten thousand of those drums stored out there? Twenty? All containing 'low-level waste,'" Coats said, making finger quotes in the air. "You think they're going to miss one? It'll be the first time it's ever been done. Shit, that kind of thing doesn't make news; it makes history."

He couldn't stop the grin from finding its way onto his face, but, this time, the accompanying agony was well worth it.

# 44

MARK AKER'S BEST CHANCE TO OUTRUN HIS pursuers was to find a river, someplace he wouldn't leave behind tracks or a scent to follow. He used the trees effectively, dodging under the umbrella of green branches that reduced the accumulated snowfall to a dusting. He would cut across the base of a tree, dragging a sprig behind him and erasing his tracks as he went. When the trees were positioned closely enough together, he could make it fifty yards or more without tracks to follow. But eventually he was faced with deep snow again, forcing him to reveal his route. In summertime, he would have been nearly impossible to follow, he wouldn't have been battling the elements, and he would have had an abundant source of water and food. As it was, he was sweating, cold, hungry and thirsty, and still trying to hold off using any of what he'd stolen from the cabin for as long as humanly possible.

Then came the sound he'd been outrunning all day: the distant whine of the snowmobile. It wasn't that they were close; it was their determination that ate away at his confidence.

What he saw next intrigued him: a low, inverted semicircle amid a rock escarpment, fifty yards to his right. The formation began low and grew into a collar that wrapped around a small hill. Seeing the rocks rise out of the snow, and that small semicircle of dark in particular, gave him another idea. If he could reach the windblown rocks, he'd leave no trail to follow.

He spent fifteen minutes creating a fake route south to the edge of a copse of trees, before carefully backtracking and returning to where he'd started. Then he worked his way below a cornice where the snow was only an inch or two deep, again dragging an evergreen limb behind him and brushing his tracks away. The effect was outstanding: there was no way to tell he'd headed toward the rocks. He climbed through the escarpment. The farther he made it, the more confident he was that he'd created an effective diversion.

He approached the dark inverted curve, just above the surface of the snow, cautiously, the vet in him having identified the cave from a distance. He crept quietly to the opening, stuck his nose to the hole, and sniffed the air. Excited by the dank, sour smell, he searched the backpack for the concoction Coats had used to subdue him and liberally charged the syringe. With the syringe in his left hand, he shined the flashlight through the hole, daring to stick his head inside.

He trained the light from side to side, working progressively deeper into the narrow hole, picking up the sharp lines in the frozen mud, immediately knowing he'd guessed correctly. What he was about to attempt was suicidal—and few knew that better than a vet—but his choice had been made and he wasn't going to turn away from it. He carefully dug into the snow blocking the hole, removing as little as possible, not wanting to draw attention to the hole or the small cave it now revealed.

He pushed the pack through and followed, twisting and moving his body to delicately slip between the gap he'd widened. The stench increased exponentially. He was on his knees now, his head tucked down. The space was small, the air thick enough to gag him, a combination of rancid bacon grease and scat. Still holding the syringe, he put his left hand over the flashlight's lens to soften its beam. He ran the diffused light across the cave's wall, holding to where the mud floor rose to meet it. Even after two decades of working with animals of every kind, his heart fluttered as he discerned the bear's coarse brown hair. It was a big black, perhaps six hundred pounds, curled into an enormous mound of slowly rising and falling fur. Its head was tucked beneath its front paws, like earmuffs. The paws themselves were the size of a kid's baseball mitt, ending in mud-caked, curled black three-inch claws.

Hibernation was not unconsciousness; a bear's heart rate drops from fifty to ten beats a minute during hibernation, yet the animal retains its senses and can awaken—though slowly—if threatened. By now, the bear had smelled him, was aware of the intruder. Aker had from two to eight minutes, no more than ten, before the bear would rise to defend his den.

He'd misjudged the dose significantly, not figuring on such a large animal. He scrambled with the pack to fill the syringe with an additional 30 ccs, emptying the vial; all or nothing. The bear's paws slipped off his head and his sad eyes popped open. Awake but barely conscious. Still, the ferocity in those eyes terrified even someone as comfortable around animals as Aker. The scratch marks in the frozen mud and on the rock were warning enough.

He had to squat and finally lie down in the cave's tight confines in order to reach the animal. One of the bear's legs twitched. Its eyes blinked open wider. It was late fall; the animal wasn't yet fully settled into the metabolism that would carry him through the long winter. He was coming awake far more quickly than Aker had anticipated. A giant paw lunged out, though awkwardly and with dull reflexes. Aker tucked into a ball, rolled, and plunged the needle deep into the thick fur coat. He depressed the plunger, emptying the syringe. He left it stuck in the animal, rolling away toward the mouth of the small cave.

The bear blinked behind heavy eyelids. Its front leg twitched, the massive paw clawing the air where Aker had just lain. Several long minutes passed, Aker not knowing if his plan had worked. The bear blinked once again before his eyes eased closed. A hibernating bear maintains a body temperature of over eighty degrees Fahrenheit. Aker rolled, and he pushed his back up against the mass of the sleeping animal. Within a matter of seconds, his back began to warm. Then his legs. Soon his whole body responded, shaking at first, then steadying, as the cold was gradually overcome. The drugs would keep the bear out for several hours. In a state of hibernation, despite its enormous body mass, it might remain unconscious for a day or more.

For the first time since his escape, Aker felt almost safe. He doubted the cave would be discovered by Coats or Gearbox. The chance to rest would strengthen him.

Though the cave was foul-smelling, he'd found both shelter and a heat source. He could remain here for at least four hours, possibly longer. At first, he fought off sleep, focusing his attention instead on the mouth of the cave and listening for the sound of the snowmobile. Encouraged as he was, he knew his survival ultimately relied upon Walt Fleming's efforts to find him. If some form of help didn't arrive soon, Aker would be forced back into the elements, back into the hunt, where the odds were against him.

# 45

A FLIGHT OF MIGRATING SANDHILL CRANES approached off the glider's right side, a ballet of slowly beating wings and out-stretched necks easily mistaken for geese or swans from a distance. But, seen closer, they were too elegant for the former and too large for the latter. They moved as a black arrow, an undulating wave, like a single organism against a backdrop of a once-royal-blue sky now flaming out in resignation to a setting sun.

Walt pointed out the formation to his passenger, appreciating her hand then tapping him on the shoulder in acknowledgment, secretly enjoying the brief contact. She seemed to understand this was not a moment to raise one's voice above the roar of the wings. He liked her all the more for it.

The V drew nearer, as if drawn by curiosity or mistaking the glider for one of their own. The cranes flew close enough that Walt could briefly make out not only the delicacy of their individual feathers rustled by the steady wind of their efforts but the beady stares of their unflinching eyes. They passed, and, like a curtain opening, revealed not the expanse of the desert below, simmering in the blush of dusk, but the menacing, insectlike form of a military helicopter, obscured until that moment.

Startled by the sight, Fiona jumped in her seat, bumping her head against the Plexiglas canopy.

It was a jet-assisted chopper—what Walt thought of as a gunner ship—capable of both tremendous speed and aerial agility. Both men in the cockpit looked like insects as well, as the copilot pointed to the bulbous black headphones mounted over his Air Force helmet.

Walt had purposely changed radio fre-
quencies to avoid being contacted by Air
Traffic Control and ordered out of the restricted airspace prior to Fiona taking the
pictures. He had forced their hand, necessitating the scrambling of an intercept. But
he acknowledged the request with a gesture and quickly reset his radio. He checked
in with ATC, announced himself, and was
told to immediately switch to yet another
frequency, where he could communicate
directly with the helicopter pilot.

The anticipated warning was issued with
authority: Walt had violated federal airspace; he would land the glider at the Arco/
Butte County airport, a tiny strip where the
towplane now waited. He could expect to
be boarded and detained. The standard
"boarded" line brought a grin to his face:
the glider's cockpit barely fit its two passen-
gers; no one would be boarding his aircraft.
But the mention of detention was more significant. He planned to withhold his trump
card—his status as law enforcement—until
reaching the ground. But the carefully
worded caution implied the government
would exercise its right to search.

"They're going to look at your equipment," Walt shouted back to Fiona. "If they find we've been spying instead of joyriding, we'll be in some serious trouble. I don't want that for either of us. You'd better erase anything of the INL site. Keep the landscapes; we need to justify the gear."

"How long do we have?"

"They're escorting us. I need to land right away."

"But how long?"

"Five, ten minutes. I'll need to come around for the wind. They're not going to shoot us out of the sky or anything. Why?"

"Can you make it more like ten?"

"How long does it take to erase some photographs? I would have thought—"

She interrupted. "Walt, I got some terrific shots of that construction site. I'd hate to lose them."

Ten minutes earlier, they'd flown over an area of excavation, busy with large earthmoving machinery, the hole being dug alongside one of the bunkerlike buildings. The area was a beehive of activity, especially given the late hour: past seven

P.M. The overtime work suggested an intriguing urgency. He'd circled the excavation, possibly putting him onto radar. Fiona had run off dozens of shots, including some of the Pahsimeroi Valley to the northwest. Walt wanted time to study the shots, but not at the expense of arrest.

"Not worth it."

"They're stored on an SD chip. The thing's the size of a fingernail. You really think they're going to search us that thoroughly? I could put it in my bra or something. They are *not* going to strip-search us." When Walt failed to respond, she added, "Are they?"

"This is the U.S. military. Who knows what they'll do? But if they find that chip, especially hidden on you, we would be in the deep stuff. These people don't mess around."

She was quiet for a moment, as she considered their options. "What if I encrypted them? I can password-protect the camera."

"Child's play for them. Besides, the more we look like we're trying to hide something, the more heat we're going to draw. We don't need that. Erase them. I'll buy you the ten minutes."

"And if I can save them?"

"I'm telling you, it's just not worth the risk. They'll find them."

"Not if I e-mail them *before* I erase them. My phone's a PDA, Walt. It takes the same SD chip as the camera. You buy me enough time and I can switch out chips and e-mail at least a couple of the shots. They'll be in cyberspace by the time we land. Keep your eye out for a cell tower. If you see one, try to stay close. I can do this."

For the next ten minutes, Walt juggled stalling the air patrol's increasingly heated demands he land the glider with Fiona's run-on narration of her progress. She switched out the chips and had started e-mailing out the photographs, but the transmission speed of the photographs—all large-graphic files—was incredibly slow over her mobile phone.

Walt landed the glider a little hard—a little out of practice—causing Fiona to yelp from behind him. He rode the momentum off the strip's lone runway and onto the first of three ramps. The helicopter set down just ahead of them, so close that the wind from the blades pushed the glider around like a toy, driving it back several feet and nearly damaging the tail. The chopper pilot killed the engine, and, as the blades slowed, two white SUVs with federal decals on their doors sped out to meet them.

"Where are we?" Walt called back to Fiona.

"I need more time," she called out anxiously.

"Forget it. Just erase them."

"The chip's out of the camera; there's nothing to erase. But I can't erase them off the phone until they're done sending and it's taking forever."

A uniformed officer pounded on the Plexiglas.

"Pocket the phone," Walt instructed her, as he bent down low to make it appear he was busy shutting down the glider.

"OPEN UP!" the officer hollered.

"They'll focus on the camera, not the phone," Walt said, softly enough that the officer wouldn't hear him through the cockpit dome.

"They will when they see there's no chip in it," she countered. "Wait! I've got a spare . . . Okay . . . okay . . . Buy me thirty seconds."

She then bent over to where, in the tight space, her back screened her hands and the camera from view.

The officer pounded again.

"Ten seconds," she pleaded.

Walt slid open the small triangular air vent on the side of the dome and moved his lips closer. "She's feeling a little airsick. My passenger needs a moment."

"Open this aircraft or I'm instructed to break it open for you."

"Just let her get her sea legs, would you?" Walt pleaded.

"I'm okay," she announced, sitting up and waving at the officer. She leaned forward, her chin on Walt's shoulder, and whispered hotly, "The phone is still sending."

"Purse," he said, covering his lips as if itching his nose.

Walt unlocked the cockpit releases, and the officer instructed them to climb out of the plane. If caught, Walt thought his badge would bail them out. But seeing how serious these guys were, he wondered if he'd dragged Fiona into something he would soon wish he hadn't.

She busied herself, collecting her gear.

"Please don't touch anything, ma'am. We'll get your belongings for you."

"You most certainly will not," Fiona protested. "He was the one flying the thing. It was his idea for a sunset sightseeing date. Why I agreed, I have no idea. Some date! I felt nauseated enough, and then you people came along? Who *are* you people?"

"You were flying in restricted airspace," the officer said matter-of-factly. He pointed to her headphones. "Did you hear our communication with the pilot?"

"All he told me," she said distraughtly, still clinging to her purse and camera bag, "was that we were being forced down. And the funny thing is, I probably should be thanking you. I think you just saved me the trip back to Sun Valley."

"Put the bags down, please, ma'am. Leave them there."

"It's my camera," she protested.

"We'll want a look at that," he said.

"Walt! Do something. You're the sheriff."

The officer whipped around his head to take in Walt, who then introduced himself. "Blaine County sheriff," Walt added, proffering his ID wallet. The officer examined the wallet, his eyes flashing between his two subjects.

"Are you over here on business, Sheriff?" the officer asked.

"No. Just an evening flight, trying to impress a woman."

"You really go all out," Fiona said. "What do you do for the second date?"

Even the officer cracked a smile. He wiped it off quickly. "We're going to want to talk to you," he informed Walt. "Both of you," he said, then looked at Fiona. "If it all checks out, I'm sure you've got nothing to worry about."

Fiona cracked open her purse. "May I make a call?" she said, reaching the phone before the officer could move to stop her.

"It's all to remain in place," he said, holding out an open palm.

Fiona shot a sideways glance at Walt. She turned the face of the mobile device so that Walt could see it. His view of the colorful menu led him to believe the photographs had completed sending. "Can't

I call someone to come get me?" she asked
the officer.

Walt understood then: the photographs
had sent, but she hadn't had time to erase
them off the chip. The evidence remained
in her hand.

"Apparently not," Walt answered. "And I
think they want your phone."

As she handed it to the officer, she managed one more look in Walt's direction—a
serious look, one of deep concern. He
took this as confirmation of his suspicions:
the photographs were still on the phone's
memory chip.

"Maybe they'll let you call once we get
to wherever they're taking us," Walt suggested.

The officer didn't contradict him.

"Who said they're taking us anywhere?"
Fiona complained. "All he said is, they
want to talk to us."

"People like this," Walt said, "people like
*me*, we always take you somewhere when
we want to talk to you."

Looking at Walt fiercely, she said, "Tell
me this was all cooked up to impress me.
Tell me this is your screwed-up attempt at

a joke." She then looked at the officer, as if he might confess to the conspiracy.

The officer said, "Afraid not."

"As far as dates go," Fiona said to Walt, settling into her role a little too easily he thought, "this one really sucks."

# 46

"THE GLIDER'S RADIOS ARE FULLY FUNCTIONING. did you know that?" Walt's interviewer, a man who introduced himself as Russell Amish, was an unshapely man in his mid-forties who spoke his vowels in a nasal tone and carried a liverish blemish on the side of his neck like an abscessed high school hickey. A man who had once been physically strong, he'd gone soft, like fruit left in the bowl too long. His black eyes revealed a contempt for Walt's badge.

Walt had met other wannabes: private

security employees who feigned authority, wishing their threats meant something. This guy wanted to play the fed when in fact he was merely contracted to Semper, which, in turn, was contracted to the government. He wasn't powerless—far from it—but Walt's position trumped his, and both men knew it.

He and Fiona had been separated immediately, put into separate cars and driven out to a nondescript, one-story cinder-block building that carried an American flag out front. It was part of a small cluster of buildings surrounded by a vast expanse of desert. Other buildings looked like parking garages. They might have been entrances to underground tunnels, or storage facilities, or served any number of other purposes. Nuclear testing was a world Walt knew nothing about.

"I believe we call that pilot error," Walt said, taking a look around the briefing room. Acoustical ceiling. Video surveillance in two corners. A vinyl-topped table that held a cassette recorder.

"I don't know much about gliders, Sheriff, except that while they're dependent on wind and air currents to maintain altitude, the wind does not determine direction of flight."

"We were blown off course," Walt said. "At right about ten thousand feet, we were caught up in winds out of the north that drove us into your airspace. You must have had me on radar. Check my flight pattern. I was beating upwind ever since, trying to work my way back to the highway." He paused, searching the man's eyes to see if he'd checked the radar. "When you fly a sailplane, Mr. Amish, you like having a strip of pavement in sight. Despite the beautiful view your restricted airspace offers, I'll take the safety net of a flat stretch of pavement under me any day."

"You were or were not on official business?"

"Was not. I'm out of uniform, Mr. Amish. I'm coming out of a marriage, which I'm sure you're able to confirm, and," he said, lowering his voice, "I was trying to get into something new, if you catch my meaning. I was going for the wow factor: *Top Gun* meets *National Geographic*. If I hadn't made her sick, if you guys hadn't interfered, I might have had a chance."

"I doubt it," said Amish. "Not your chances but the story." He shifted some papers. Guys like him did that just as a matter of habit. "You're a long way from home, Mr. Fleming."

"Not so far as the crow flies."

"Your towplane pilot reports you requested a release over Craters of the Moon. You strayed quite far from that release point."

"Have you ever seen the park from the air? The huge flows of lava, like somebody spilled black ink and it froze in place. You want to impress a woman, Mr. Amish, show her Craters at sunset. Land in Arco. Buy her a steak at the Mel-O-Dee and have the towplane waiting to fly you home. Knocks their socks off, and, if you're lucky, other pieces of clothing as well."

Amish fought back a grin. For a moment, Walt allowed himself to believe he was regaining some credibility. But it was a grin of satisfaction, as it turned out, not one of agreement.

"Ms. Kenshaw is your department's contracted photographer, Sheriff. She boarded your romantic escapade with two camera bodies, five lenses, a light meter, and a

variety of filters. And, oh . . . infrared ca-
pability. You flew into our airspace and
stayed off com for twenty-seven minutes
before being forced down by the Air National Guard. The only photographs on her
camera are of what appears to be an
assault—a young woman, badly beaten,
and some colorful clothing. A prom? A
wedding? They're dated less than a week
ago. So what you're telling me is you
brought her up on this 'date' to photograph
the sunset and she got, what, so caught
up in your smooth talking that she forgot
to shoot any photographs?"

"You'd have to ask her."

"We are."

Walt wondered if she could possibly
hold up under the scrutiny and realized he
should have created a story for them both
to stick to. Amish likely knew of his attempts to reach the director by phone.
Even so, proof was proof. No matter what
Amish believed, he could not prove intent.
"The glider's not much different than a
parasail. You've never had parasailers
over your airspace?"

"We'd rather work with you than against

you," Amish said. "We're all on the same side here."

"I'll take that to mean you don't want me calling the vice president about it," Walt said.

"I'm aware of your relationship with Vice President Shaler. I'm aware of your service record. You're something of a hero, Sheriff. I get that. Doesn't make my job any easier."

"You're retired military," Walt said. "That's a burn wound on your neck—chemical, maybe. Desert Storm, I'm guessing. There were compounds used in that war that few of us ever heard about, weren't there? You don't strike me as military intelligence, Mr. Amish. You have field experience, I'm pretty sure. Marines, maybe." There was a flicker in the man's eyes that was his tell: an ever-so-slight lifting of the eyelids that Walt guessed he'd worked hard to control. "Your boss worked under George the First when he headed up Langley. Your boss's boss I'm talking about: Roger Hillabrand. He was a Marine, wasn't he? A big player in Desert Storm. Hired his men to work for him, once he entered the private sector, and formed the Semper Group. So you're long on loyalty, short on questions. We can spend three or four hours in here and all I'm going to do is lose my chance at Ms. Kenshaw. These are tricky waters because your boss's boss has a personal relationship with Ms. Kenshaw—and if he had anything to do with our grounding, if any phone calls were exchanged, this is going to look personal. Mixing business with pleasure. Using his power . . . to derail any attempt at a date. I thought I could take off the uniform, fly her up over Craters, and make a good impression. Maybe score a few points. But maybe Hillabrand thought different. This could be embarrassing. You called in the Air National Guard, Mr. Amish. Over a woman. Why don't you release us and let me try to salvage what I can of an evening gone horribly wrong and we'll both forget all about this?"

"Your glider will be impounded until further notice. Our people will take it apart—piece by piece, if we have to—in order to determine there were no cameras hidden in it. I can only assume you think you're doing good, Sheriff. But we both know that do-gooders typically do more harm than good."

"I was out on a date. I was trying for some romance. You want to arrest me for that? Guilty as charged."

Amish's eyelids flared again. His jaw clenched, as he fought to keep his mouth shut. But Walt egged him on with a shit-eating grin intended to make the man feel as small as possible. Interrogations could go both directions.

"This facility is under constant surveillance," Amish said proudly. "We are watched"—he pointed to the two cameras in the room—"recorded, scrutinized, and investigated. We are held accountable to six different federal departments. We report to the NRC, the Nuclear Regulatory Commission. I know it's easy to see a place like the INL as a conspiracy in progress, given the materials we work with and the secretive nature of the research conducted here. On-site protests and demonstrations remind us of this on a regular basis. We offer up a fine target for the Greens. But this lab lit the first city in the world with atomic-powered light. The nuclear submarine engine was developed and tested at this facility. Critical situations like Three Mile Island were successfully resolved because we had a working facility in which to simulate repairs. This place matters. And if you work here, you can't pick your nose without a Senate subcommittee hearing about it. We are not a rogue facility. No matter what people like Sheriff Walt Fleming think. There is nothing here that's going to help you with this murder investigation of yours." He answered Walt's expression: "Read the pages, Sheriff."

Walt wanted to take a swing at the guy, more out of frustration than anger, but it wasn't going to happen. Amish's confidence was disconcerting. There was a knock on the door followed by the arrival of a man who leaned into Amish's ear.

Amish said, "You'll go home tonight, but we're not done here. We'll report this violation to some of those six departments, and I'm sure you'll be hearing from more than one of them. This was a stupid stunt to pull, Sheriff. You've fooled no one."

If he was being sent home tonight, then they hadn't found the photographs.

He waited another hour to be released and around nine P.M. was led outside to a

vehicle that drove him and Fiona back to
the Arco airport, where the towplane
waited.

They didn't speak while in the car and
under escort. After having been dropped
off, the shuttle vehicle then leaving the airstrip, Walt turned to her.

"So?"

Her lips pursed. She tugged the strap of
her camera bag higher onto her shoulder.
"I made the call. You know?"

"E-mailing the photos, you mean? Yeah.
That was incredibly fast think—"

"The *other* call," she said. "How do you
think we got off so easily?"

"Hillabrand?"

She nodded spitefully.

"But . . . they didn't have us on anything," Walt protested. "Why drag Hillabrand into this if they were going to
release us, anyway?"

"Let me get this right: you're *mad* at me
for getting us out of there?"

"I'm not *mad* at you. But they had no
evidence."

"They had us locked up in interrogation
rooms. They had my phone. *My* phone,
not yours. All the photographs were on my

phone. Besides, don't give me that: it's why you brought me along, right? We established that earlier."

"It's *not* why," Walt countered. "I hadn't even thought about Hillabrand until you brought him up."

"That's not true," she said.

"It *is*! I asked you along because I needed photographs shot. If we hadn't been forced down, I'd have gone in there on foot tonight. To that construction work. But, listen, I never once considered using your . . . relationship . . . with Hillabrand to my advantage—our advantage. Your mention of it actually amused me, Fiona. You don't know me very well if you'd think I'd do such a thing."

"There is no *relationship* with Roger. Just FYI. I'd say that pretty much just came to an end tonight. I felt like a teenager calling Daddy. Who knows what he thought. Ten minutes later, we were released. You can thank me later."

She hurried off toward the towplane, where the pilot was standing by. Walt packed in with her behind the pilot, and they sat pressed shoulder to shoulder for the short thirty-minute flight. She never said a word to him. He tried twice to break the silence but failed. At the FBO in Sun Valley, she marched to her parked Subaru, climbed in, and drove off without looking back.

Walt arrived home, depressed, and wondering if the INL would take legal action. Hillabrand being dragged into it complicated matters.

He parked the Cherokee out front as he almost always did, despite a garage around back. He liked the police cruiser being seen sitting in front of the house. He hurried up to the front porch, concerned—but not overly so—by the front porch light being off and the rest of the house being so dark. He always encouraged Lisa to keep several lights on.

He managed to key open the door in the dark and flip on the lights.

"Lisa?" he hissed softly.

The couch was empty. He usually found her dozing there at this hour. She'd probably fallen asleep next to one of the twins while reading a bedtime story.

"Lisa?" he repeated more loudly.

His chest tightened.

He hurried through the house, carefully

opening Emily's bedroom door first. *Empty.* Then Nikki's. *Empty.* He checked the face of his cell phone: eleven messages. He had assumed them all to be work related; consumed with the events of the evening, he'd planned to answer them once he got home.

He tried the master bedroom.

Dark and empty.

He had the phone to his ear now, the first of the messages replaying. With no way to skip messages, he was forced to endure the mundane while anticipating the worst.

Finally, he heard Lisa's voice, bordering on hysterical: "Walt? It was Gail. She was . . . I don't know . . . I've never seen her like that. She said you two had an agreement about no women. I thought she meant me. I tried to reason, but she just stormed right past me, saying how she was the mother. The girls are fine. She has them. Please call me. I didn't know what to do, Walt. I didn't know what to do."

He threw the phone. It skipped off the dining-room table and hit the window and broke the glass.

Walt hurried to the door; he knew exactly

what to do: get his children back. He caught himself on the threshold, reconsidering. The girls had had enough for one night. Gail wouldn't have taken them to Brandon's—that was indeed the agreement.

He stepped back inside, slammed the front door shut, and locked it. Switched off the light so he didn't have to see how empty it was without them. He heard the sounds of his own labored breathing. He extracted a single truth from the depths of his depression: they'd crossed a barrier, arriving at a finality to the truce that had been maintained for far too long.

# 47

THE HAILEY LIBRARY HAD BEEN A SUPERMARKET in its former life. Walt came here often enough with the twins, but he still couldn't shake the memory; he expected to smell fresh coffee and doughnuts. Instead, he passed the front desk and a table displaying NEW ARRIVALS. There was an end cap on the nearest stack devoted entirely to Hemingway. Walt wished the fame and lore of Hemingway could have been attributed to the work of the great writer when he'd lived in the valley, but, instead, most of the fame of the place came from the fact he'd died here. Being known as a

place where a famous writer ate the wrong
end of a shotgun was nothing but trouble
for the county sheriff. Others had come
here for like purpose. Not so great to be
*the* trendy suicide locale.

He'd never paid any attention to the library's conference room. It held an oval
table that sat ten, with just enough room
behind each chair to slip past. There was
a pull-down whiteboard at the end of the
room, carrying notes written in pink marker
that appeared to have something to do
with a book sale fund-raiser.

He didn't appreciate being made to wait,
but Danny Cutter had sounded frantic on
the phone, and Walt made it a point to
tread lightly with the billionaires and their
families. And so he waited. Five minutes
melted into ten.

Finally, the door opened.

Danny Cutter had that tanned, outdoorsy
thing working for him. He wore blue jeans,
a pressed white shirt, and an Orvis out-
door coat, black fabric with a brown leather
collar and trim.

"Sorry I made you wait," he said, shaking hands with Walt only after he'd locked
the conference-room door and twisted the

blinds closed. "I thought if someone followed me, they wouldn't see you entering
*after* me, and that just felt better."

"Someone's following you?"

Cutter shook his head with a look of disgust. "Who knows?"

"Sit," Walt said.

Cutter took the chair next to Walt and
spoke quietly. "You know about the charges
at the hotel? The violation of my parole?
Chuck Webb said you knew about it, said
it could have been worse—much worse—
and that I had you to thank for that."

"Wouldn't know what he's talking about,"
Walt said, stone-faced.

"Someone called it in to the Sun Valley
police. Said I was drunk or stoned or both.
So I ended up under suspicion, and they
required a blood test because of the parole and I had coke in my system—coke I
have no memory of doing, I might add.
And that puts me in violation."

"Chuck told me most of this," Walt allowed. "I didn't know the blood workup was
back."

"None of this matters to you, I know, but
the blowback that followed is what counts."

"What kind of blowback?" Walt asked.

He was feeling edgy all of a sudden, like the room was too small.

Cutter glanced nervously toward the locked door. He lowered his voice, forcing Walt to concentrate on his every word.

"I shouldn't tell you this. I know that. You, of all people. Damned if I do, damned if I don't. But the thing is, they warned me if I violate the NDA I signed I'm shit up the creek. The way my probation reads, you're supposed to be informed of any possible violations, so I'm taking a big chance, Sheriff. That's my point: a very big chance."

"Slow down, please. You signed a non-disclosure agreement?"

"I've been bought off. Fifty thousand dollars *plus* all legitimate expenses arising from the contamination. I was told that if I accepted the money, the parole violation would eventually be dropped, that Trinity could return to production in as little as two weeks, and that I'd be reimbursed for lost inventory and gross revenue for the period in question. All I do is show them our books for the past three months and they'll average my revenue stream."

Walt couldn't help but remember the

stench of the burning sheep and Peavy's reminder of the loss of money that any mass grave would mean for the rancher.

"Who offered you this?"

"No idea. A call to my cell phone. A private number. I tried to trace it. I even called my brother—he owns the cell company, after all. Dead end."

"A hoax," Walt proposed.

"The next day, five grand was in my checking account—my personal checking account, not my company account. I checked with the bank: the deposit was cash, made through an ATM. Totally untraceable." He glanced back at the door again. "Second phone call said the five grand was just to prove the offer was for real."

"The terms? What did they want from you?"

"They'll provide a script for me. I'm to stick to the script."

"And the CDC?"

"Dr. Bezel's report will apparently support whatever it is I'm supposed to say."

Walt attempted to process all that he'd been told. Who could control the CDC like that? "Why me, Danny?"

"Why you?" he blurted out, laughing and grimacing at the same time. "I'm already in violation of my parole—this coke thing—which, incidentally, was a *total* frame job. I'm not saying I expect you to believe that, but the way it happened—"

"I believe it," Walt said, interrupting. "Tell me about the payoff."

"I've told you everything. Two calls. Sign the NDA. The five grand up front. It all goes away."

"Who can promise such a thing?" Walt blurted out.

"My thoughts exactly."

"What did you tell them?"

"I signed. Are you kidding me? You know the hit I'm going to take? My inventory destroyed. My line shut down. I'm not insured for this kind of thing. Who is? I was sunk. I mean totally screwed. And then this phone call. Fifty K, on top of costs. And they made it clear that if business is off for a while because of this, they'll take care of me."

"But . . . why tell me?" Walt repeated.

"I've got to be breaking a dozen laws, right? I had a chance to think about it and I came to you. As sweet as this deal is, if it means another twenty months in prison, I'll pass, thank you very much."

"It's nothing my office would have anything to do with, beyond the parole violation."

"But that's the point: it's a clear violation of my parole, right? Doing anything like this?"

"Enlisting in a cover-up? Yeah. That would be federal time. But it's apparent that whoever is making the offer has a long reach. It could be genuine. And, how do I say this?" He paused. "You aren't the only one to receive such an offer."

"They came after *you*?"

"Me? No!" Now it was Walt glancing toward the door. He stood and peeked out the blinds. No one. With his back to Cutter, he said, "What's important to focus on here, Danny, is that whoever is making the offer is the same person, or persons, who set you up for the coke."

"I know that."

"And this just escalates things, doesn't it? I mean, after this, they'll have you on accepting a bribe, avoiding a CDC investigation—any number of charges. If they want."

"That's why I'm here, Sheriff. Did they frame me on the coke thing just to make sure I'd take this offer or am I being set up now to take a bigger fall? Someone's coming after me, and I'm screwed either way."

"I don't have the answers."

"I'd rather go bankrupt than return to that damn facility."

"But you agreed to take the money."

"Yeah, but it's only the five grand so far. And I've come to you to cut a deal. Buyer's remorse. I don't care about the money. I've told you everything. Honestly, I have. I will keep the money in escrow, not spend a cent of it. I'll wear a wire, allow you to tap my phones—whatever you want. I do not want to get on the wrong side of this. Now, I understand I've already done that," he added quickly, "but this is my attempt to fix it."

"If these people can deliver, then I'm no use to you," Walt admitted.

"They've got to be government, don't they? I mean, who can make such promises?"

"Or big business," Walt said, speaking what he was thinking, never a good call.

Cutter leaned back in his chair. "You

know who it is," he said, unable to conceal his surprise.

"I don't."

"You have an idea."

"I imagine you do, too," Walt said.

"But I don't! Government, as I've said. A private firm, no matter how big, can't guarantee legal charges dropped. Who in the government cares about my company staying in business? This guy promised my probation violation would be expunged. The NDA gave no hint of who was behind it. I don't have any idea. Honestly."

"I think we're done here, Danny. For both our sakes."

"Done? I'm not done."

"I appreciate the information. As to the offer, there's nothing I can do without warrants, and, if I seek a warrant and it gets back to whoever is making you this offer, that's not good for anyone." He thought a moment, working the corners. "I'd like to hear from you if they make contact. If you go the informer route, it's done through the U.S. Attorney's Office. I could help with that. But if we go to the wrong guy, my guess is the offer will be pulled and you'll be back in a federal facility. The coke charge was about discrediting you, Danny. They've laid the necessary groundwork so that whatever you say in public can be quickly written off as a desperate man making cheap allegations. It's been very carefully thought out."

"Yeah," Cutter said sarcastically, "let's admire their work."

"I didn't mean it like that."

"Since when is the government that smart?"

Walt cracked a smile. He stood up from the chair and said, "Good luck, Danny."

"I came to you in good faith, Sheriff. You can't just walk."

"I've got problems of my own, Danny. I have no choice but to walk. You waited too long. I needed to be brought in before you signed the NDA and agreed to take the money."

Cutter looked devastated.

Walt scribbled out a name. "Andy Hamilton's in the U.S. Attorney's Office in Seattle. Andy can't be bought." He passed the name to Cutter. "Use my name."

"Thanks, Sheriff."

"Tread lightly, Danny. And don't speak a word of this to Dr. Bezel. I don't see how, but she may be part of this."

Cutter looked as if Walt had hit him.

"Do we even know if she's actually with the CDC?" Walt asked. "I never checked her credentials."

"Sweet Jesus!"

"Trust no one, Danny," Walt said. His voice continued inside his head: *Not even me.*

# 48

"MAYBE I'M NOT EXPLAINING IT RIGHT." JOHN borton was a big, bearish man, with red hair, wide eyes, and an unexpectedly kind and soft minister's voice. He'd started out as water master for the water district, inspecting headgates on irrigation canals, reporting violations, and locking flows at levels where they belonged. Then he'd served as an inspector for the state's adjudication process—the redistribution of stream and river water to private landowners—that had taken five years and nearly cost a few lives. Now he was the water master for the central district, and, as such, ruled like a feudal lord over million-dollar ranches and their century-old legal rights to tap into and drain both the surface waters as well as the underground aquifer that flowed for thousands of miles, from British Columbia to Mexico.

His office was small, even by government standards. The water district was housed in a building that also leased space to the Nature Conservancy.

Walt and Borton were leaning on a work-table that held Fiona's aerial photographs, a satellite image of central Idaho, and a topographical map of a fifty-square-mile region surrounding Craters of the Moon and reaching to the Pahsimeroi Valley.

"Think of it as an eddy," Borton said. "Just like in open water, but, in this case, it happens to be underground. You've got this tremendous flow of water, sometimes thousands of feet below the surface, moving like a river north to south. Huge volume. It pushes up quite close to the surface for much of the route. But we know it always seeks the path of least resistance, as well as the lowest spot it can find. This range," he said, indicating a spur of mountains that pushed toward the alluvial plain and the desert that housed the Idaho Nuclear Laboratory, "acts as a barrier, just like a levee or breakwater."

"But you said the flow of the water is north to south," Walt reminded. "And the elevation of the Pahsimeroi is higher than the desert. My interest is whether water could get from here," he said, indicating the desert, "to here." He pointed to the center of the Pahsimeroi Valley.

"And, logically, that's impossible. How can water run uphill?" Borton dragged the satellite image closer. "But some rivers flow to the north in the Northern Hemisphere, don't they? And so do some aquifers. In this case, it's the result of a subterranean fault and a promontory." He pointed out a mountain spine on the satellite image. "This looks like a weather map, but these gray swirls are actually the underground water—part of the Northern Rocky Mountain Intermontane Basins system—that exists thousands of feet below the surface and is one small part of a freshwater source that stretches from Canada all the way to Mexico. The Big Lost River disappears completely under the desert here and doesn't resurface for hundreds of miles. But the force of that downward pressure has the same effect as a narrowing river: increased speed. That pushes a great quantity of water west and around this underground promontory. The flow is further restricted by faults on both sides, and, with nowhere to go, it flows north for nearly seventy miles, until most of it is absorbed into the more porous strata of the upper Pahsimeroi."

For security reasons, the satellite image had grayed out the surface topography of an area that included the INL, but Walt pulled Fiona's photograph alongside the image and visually compared the two. The long, feathered flow that was the rogue branch of the aquifer curled and turned directly beneath the area where he and Fiona had spotted the after-hours earth-moving equipment. For a moment, he just stared.

"This help any?" Borton asked, made uncomfortable by the long silence.

Walt looked up at the man, then back to the various pictures. "Does the water in the aquifer ever reach the surface of the Pahsimeroi Valley's floor? Is it part of the groundwater?"

"That's a much bigger question," Borton said, running his stubby finger across the satellite image, "because there's a constant surface flow north to south—all the winter melt slowly finding its way down through sediment and into the valleys. But that water can prove itself seasonal and intermittent, as we know, and the reason this gets more complicated is that some of the ranchers have drilled very deep wells. Those deeper wells, eight hundred to as much as ten thousand feet, are directly tapping into the aquifer, not the surface water. It presents a particularly difficult issue for us."

"Do we know the locations of those deeper wells?" Walt asked.

"We would have a list of at least some of them in the state, because they've been the subject of adjudication."

Not once had Borton asked what any of this was about, though Walt sensed his curiosity.

"How hard would it be for me to get hold of that list?" Walt asked.

"It's a public record," Borton returned quickly, having anticipated the request. "I don't have those documents here, but the state water board should have copies."

"That helps."

"I do happen to have computer access," Borton said with a twinkle in his eye. "And a printer. But any data that proved useful to you would have to eventually be sourced elsewhere. It didn't come from me, Walt."

"Understood."

Borton glanced around the quiet office. "Wait right here," he said.

# 49

WHEN WALT'S ATTEMPTS TO REACH GAIL FAILED, he resisted using the power of his office to find her, knowing any such personal use would be held against him. Instead, he sought out his divorce attorney, Jan Wygle, in an attempt to get his daughters returned.

As he sat in the officer's reception, an NPR report out of Boise caught his attention.

"Today, the state senate's environmental impact committee will hear public comments on the Semper Group's management of the Idaho Nuclear Laboratory. Conditions of Semper's contract with the federal and state governments require semiannual review of health and safety issues in the workplace. Semper took over management of the nuclear facility from the troubled General Industries two years ago and was instrumental in the fifty-square-mile facility's third name change in just six years. More now from our Capitol correspondent, Lisa Laird."

The reporter continued the story, reminding listeners of the controversial shipments of overseas nuclear waste to the INL. Said to be for temporary storage, much of the Japanese and Korean low-level waste had been held in drums above ground in central Idaho for nearly a decade. Semper was said to be in negotiations to extend the program by accepting Russian low-level waste. Walt's ears pricked up when Hillabrand's name was mentioned. He was to be the committee's chief witness, testifying at three P.M. A public forum.

He faced a two-hour drive or a thirty-minute flight. His first phone call was not to Nancy, nor to Barge Levy, who he hoped might fly him over to Boise now that his own pilot's license had been suspended. It was instead to Danny Cutter. His request caused Cutter to invoke a moment's silence on the other end.

"You want *what*?" Cutter had asked.

"You heard me right," Walt answered.

"I don't know if that's possible."

"Find a way," Walt told the man. "Both our futures may depend upon it."

WALT ARRIVED AT the statehouse in Boise wearing a crisp, heavily starched uniform, his shoes and belt polished to gleaming, his hardware sparkling. It was three-twenty by the time he slipped through the door of the hearing room, where a dais held five state senators, four men and a woman. The room's interior was a magnificent throwback to the grand statehouses of the nineteenth century: aged mahogany and walnut panels, a marble floor, and brass chandeliers. Roger Hillabrand sat at a long table, front and center, with his back to the main doors, the fabric of his suit shining. He took no notice of Walt's entrance.

The same could not be said for James Peavy. The dignified-looking rancher sat on the aisle in the fifth row of bench seating.

He wore his trademark Stetson, a blue blazer, and a white oxford. He glowered at Walt. There was no mistaking that look. He shook his head faintly, like a reminder of his prior warning, and his eyes tracked Walt, as he found a seat.

Most of the hearing centered on the proposed expansion of the so-called temporary storage of offshore low-level nuclear waste, and, when the hearing was thrown open to public comment, the room became hostile toward Hillabrand. At last, the chairman relieved Hillabrand by stating that the floor was closed to questions regarding that particular issue, and the room emptied quickly. There were fewer than ten people in attendance when the chairman opened the floor to any other questions for Mr. Hillabrand and Semper's management of the INL.

An environmentalist beat Walt to the microphone, asking what Hillabrand intended to do about a high fence that was interfering with the winter movements of an established elk herd.

Hillabrand turned around to address the questioner and, in doing so, spotted Walt. There was a pronounced hitch to his movement, like a film having been cut and spliced back together.

A minute later, Walt stood at the aisle microphone and introduced himself to the committee, all of whom he'd met on other occasions. He carried copies of maps, photographs, and a time line of his own investigation to the dais, then offered Hillabrand copies.

The committee chair fingered the documents and then leaned into his microphone. "Sheriff Fleming, Mr. Hillabrand comes here in good faith. He is not on trial."

"I'm aware of that," Walt said into the mic.

"This is a hearing. We're just getting Mr. Hillabrand's semiannual report and his appraisal of the condition of the facility and where it's going over the next six months."

"Yes."

"If you have a public comment, then—"

"I do, Senator." Walt turned slightly to address Hillabrand. "The witness is under oath?"

"He volunteered an oath at the start of his report," the senator answered. "It is by no means binding or legal."

"Be that as it may, I would hope it counts for something." He looked directly at the witness. "Mr. Hillabrand, would you please view the photograph labeled 'B' and answer this question?" Photo B depicted the aerial view of the massive earthmovers, working alongside one of the newer INL buildings. "Are you aware of any current threats to health, *including* any spills, leaks, or mishandling of nuclear waste at the INL, recent or not?"

There were not enough people in attendance to throw a murmur around the room, but clearly the question caught everyone on the committee by surprise.

"I will answer the question," Hillabrand replied confidently. "But, first, I would ask if the committee is aware of your having been detained by INL security just last night, Sheriff, and if this questioning of yours is being done at the hand of politics, in an attempt to salvage the damage last night's incident will have upon your current reelection campaign?"

"Sheriff?" the chairman asked.

"This has nothing to do with politics, Mr. Chairman." Walt never took his eyes off Hillabrand, whose bitten-back smile bordered on arrogance. "I have a follow-up question or two, if Mr. Hillabrand only will answer the first."

The chairman seemed intent to not allow this to be a duel between Walt and Hillabrand. "The committee would like to set the record straight as to your detention. Did this, in fact, take place?"

"It did. Yes, sir. My glider was accidentally blown off course and intercepted by INL security. We were forced to land, questioned by INL security, and later released without charges."

Hillabrand snorted into the microphone. Without permission from the chairman, he waved the photograph high in the air and said, "Carrying him conveniently over our facility, I see. I feel it important to inform this committee that the existence of this photograph is a violation of federal law and that the viewing of this photograph will likely require investigation."

The statement surprised Walt. Hillabrand had just thrown Fiona under the bus. Walt had hoped that Fiona's involvement with Hillabrand might mitigate how seriously he intended to prosecute the photography.

The committee turned in on itself for internal discussion. Indiscernible whispering floated through the room, as the steam radiators popped and clanked. Walt felt desperate to at least get his first question answered, though it now seemed obvious that Hillabrand was willing to lie.

"You said you would answer the question," Walt reminded.

"I'm unaware of any spills or leaks or any health threats posed by our operations at the INL."

"Have you or any of your employees," Walt asked him, "had contact with, or offered payments to, Lon Bernie, James Peavy, or Daniel Cutter in exchange for their silence, their participation in a cover-up concerning contamination of groundwater in the Pahsimeroi Valley?"

This question sent the committee into gasps and further consultation; harsh glances at both Hillabrand and Walt. Someone left the room behind Walt, and, within seconds, a dozen spectators hurried inside, including a few reporters, judging by their busy notepads. The chairman took notice of the arrival of the press, cupped his mouth, and went back to whispering to his panel members.

"Sheriff Fleming," the chairman finally said, "while this committee respects and applauds your service in law enforcement in the great state of Idaho, we do not feel that this is the proper forum for your line of questioning."

"Isn't this a hearing on environmental impact?" Walt asked.

"It is."

"My position, Mr. Chairman, is that the INL, under Mr. Hillabrand's governance, has contaminated an eddy in the Northern Rocky Mountain Intermontane Basins system, the deep groundwater beneath the Pahsimeroi. I have personally witnessed the burning of over fifty head of sheep. What rancher would dispose of his sheep by fire, Mr. Chairman? Buck—Senator Oozer—you run sheep. Have you ever burned any?"

Buck Oozer shook his head no.

"I also have medical records for two employees of Trilogy Springs bottling who were admitted to a hospital in Salt Lake City and, after extensive testing, were determined to be suffering from radiation poisoning. You can see on this map," Walt said, stepping toward the dais, "the relative proximity of—"

"Ask the sheriff," Hillabrand said, raising his voice and interrupting, "if he's an expert in radiation poisoning. If he has ever heard of radon, an underground source of radiation known to riddle the sediments of central Idaho."

"Radon does exist, Mr. Hillabrand, and has existed for thousands of years—millions, I suppose. But it doesn't just turn itself on. These ranchers have had no problems until very recently. Now there's sickness all around that region."

"If there has been depredation of livestock and sickness in employees of bottling companies," Hillabrand said to the chairman, "don't you think we'd have heard about it before now? Is a county sheriff our best source for such accusations? Are you an expert on such matters, Mr. Fleming?" He turned around. "There's James Peavy, right back there. Why doesn't the chairman ask the Honorable Senator Peavy if his livestock is suffering from radiation contamination?"

Peavy stood.

The chairman looked bewildered. He mumbled, "It's not in our purview to treat this like a trial, Mr. Hillabrand, Sheriff Fleming. It's a hearing. Your complaint is noted, Sheriff Fleming, and it will be looked into. Sit down, please, Senator Peavy."

Peavy sat, but his apparent willingness to testify registered with the committee.

The chairman asked, "Are there any other comments from—"

"He's paid off Senator Peavy," Walt said. "Just as he's tried to pay off Daniel Cutter to remain silent about the sickness out at his bottling plant." The gallery stirred. "I'm sorry, Mr. Chairman, but taking note of my complaint is not enough. There are lives at stake here."

"The accusations are baseless!" Hillabrand said. "Totally and utterly baseless!"

"Sheriff Fleming," the chairman said, "please sit down!"

Walt held his ground. "Baseless, Mr. Hillabrand?" Suddenly, it was just the two of them in the room.

"Completely."

Walt held up a finger to buy himself a moment and returned to his seat.

"Finally," the chairman said, loud enough to be heard.

"I'm not done!" Walt said, digging into his briefcase. "Mr. Hillabrand!" He threw something toward Hillabrand, who reached out and caught it one-handed.

"A twenty-ounce bottle of Trilogy water, identified as part of a two-week run, all of which has subsequently been held off the market, quarantined, because of possible contamination. Since you're so sure the aquifer has not been poisoned by a leak at the INL, have a glass of water. Convince me."

Hillabrand looked at the bottle, at Walt, and then at the dais. A reporter in the back stood up and shot a photograph of Hillabrand holding the bottle. When Hillabrand next met eyes with Walt, his own had hardened. He broke the seal on the cap and poured himself a glass.

"Don't drink that," Walt said, running toward the witness table. "It really *is* from the quarantined run. That is contam—"

But Hillabrand put the glass to his mouth and began to drink.

Walt knocked the glass out of his hand. It shattered on the floor in front of the dais.

Hillabrand brushed spilled water off his tailored suit.

"Are you crazy?" Walt asked Hillabrand, loud enough for everyone to hear. "Why'd you drink it? I took readings on Lon Bernie's sheep: they're so hot they should glow in the dark. I have an expert on the aquifer confirming there's an eddy that passes directly under the INL and then turns north into the Pahsimeroi. It . . . is . . . over."

"If you're right about any of this, would I risk this?" Hillabrand upended the plastic water bottle and chugged. Walt fought him and managed to get it out of his hand. Walt recognized Sean Lunn from Fiona's description as Lunn rushed the table. Hillabrand waved the man off.

Walt threw the water bottle to the floor, where it spun, discharging its contents.

"That's good enough for me," the chairman said. "You're done, Sheriff. In fact, this hearing is over. Our next public hearing will be in approximately three months' time. Good day!"

Walt and Hillabrand, both breathing hard from their struggle over the bottle, were locked in a staring contest.

"Why?" an exasperated Walt said to

Hillabrand. "You know what that did to Cutter's employees. I know you know."

Hillabrand steadied his breathing. "Buck's office," he whispered. "Ten minutes."

Hillabrand stood, still brushing water off his suit. "Thank you, Mr. Chairman."

Lunn waited alongside like a well-trained dog.

"You think you can bribe me too?" Walt said, just as softly.

Hillabrand stopped brushing and glared at him.

"Hopefully," Hillabrand said.

# 50

BUCK OOZER'S OFFICE SMELLED PLEASANTLY OF pipe tobacco. A wide partners desk sat between two flags, with a credenza pushed up against the only wall with windows, sunlight spilling over the tall leather chair and flooding the desktop.

Oozer was nowhere to be seen. Only Hillabrand and Lunn occupied the office, as Walt entered.

"I'm going to ask Sean to check you for a wire," Hillabrand said.

"The hell you are."

"Or we cannot do this," Hillabrand said.

"I'm not wearing a wire."

"Then you won't mind. Also, Sean will take your briefcase, cell phone, radio, and portfolio in the hall with him."

Walt studied him, deciding it did him no good to fight. He didn't happen to be wearing or carrying a wire. He took off his belt, which held everything from a gun to a pair of handcuffs and a flashlight, eased it to the floor, and raised his hands.

Lunn ran an airport wand around him, asked him to remove his watch, and then pronounced him clean.

Hillabrand gave a nod, and Lunn carried Walt's briefcase and portfolio out of the room. Lunn pulled the door shut with a convincing *click*.

Hillabrand stood, with his back to the flickering gas fireplace. For several minutes, neither man spoke.

"Where to start?" Hillabrand began.

"I'd settle for something resembling the truth," Walt answered. He carried his heavy belt over to a chair and placed it on the seat. The two men remained standing.

"It's pretty cut and dried for you, isn't it?"

"I suppose it is," Walt said, still seething over Hillabrand's manipulation of the hearing. "You drank that water." He still couldn't believe it. "You knew it was contaminated and yet you drank it."

"It occurred to me you might be bluffing."

"I wasn't."

"I forced myself to vomit just now," Hillabrand confessed. "Hopefully, that helps."

"And if it doesn't? If you're contaminated?"

The man shrugged. It struck Walt as oddly arrogant, as if what made two people sick could have no effect on him.

"You can't hide this forever," Walt said. "I'm not going to be the only one to figure this out."

"Have it all figured out, do you?"

"Pretty close, I suspect."

"Another government contractor raking in the millions in fees and covering up his mistakes as fast as he can backfill."

"Something pretty close to that, yes."

"Let me clarify some things," Hillabrand said. "The death of the vet, Randy Aker, not us. His brother going missing, not us."

"I wish I could believe that."

"You will."

"I don't think so. No."

"You might want to sit down."

"I'm fine."

"Did you really see fifty head of sheep burning?" Hillabrand asked.

"Yes. You were sloppy."

"Me? I don't think so. It's the damn ranchers over there. You want a glimpse of America a hundred years ago? Drive two hours east of Hailey. Jesus, what we have to put up with."

"Must be a real hardship."

"Read that," Hillabrand said, pointing to Oozer's desk, where a fax was positioned to face Walt. The hairs on his arms and neck rose, as he identified the federal government letterhead.

"It's an NDA."

"Yes. A federal nondisclosure agreement," said Hillabrand. "Airtight. They'll take your firstborn if you so much as think about what you're about to hear. That's right: it's worth careful consideration."

Walt read the opening paragraph. "I'm not signing this. I can't use whatever you tell me."

"Who said I'd tell you anything?" Hillabrand countered.

Walt looked between the man and the document on the desk. "It's dated today."

"It was faxed here about five minutes ago."

"You work fast."

"You're kind of forcing my hand, Sheriff. I'd just as soon the hearing had stayed on the train shipments."

Walt thought he understood. "There are no shipments from Russia," he speculated.

Hillabrand didn't answer. He didn't have to.

"You created that—the new shipments—to keep that hearing where you wanted it: well off the recent events up there."

"I signed one of those," Hillabrand said, indicating the document. "I can't go any further unless you join the club."

"I'm not a big one for clubs," Walt said. "The last thing I joined was Costco."

"Just the same."

"Why would I ever agree to sign this?" Walt asked. "I have ninety-nine percent of this in the bag. I don't need this."

"To know the truth. Your precious truth." Hillabrand shifted in front of the fire. "And so I can tell you everything I know about your missing friend."

Walt felt his face flush. "But signing this prevents me from acting upon it."

"No, I don't think that will be the case. I can almost promise you'll be able to use that information. But one thing ties to the next, and . . . there you have it."

"I don't have anything."

"But you will. Some will be prosecutable, some won't."

"Let me guess which part won't," Walt said.

"I understand how it's in your nature to be suspicious. Rightly so. I'm not asking you to be someone you can't be. And I'm not even asking you to trust me because I believe at this stage that's beyond your instincts. Am I right?"

"You think I wouldn't sign this even if it would mean saving Mark Aker?" Walt asked rhetorically. "You think I'm too . . . suspicious . . . proud . . . whatever?"

"*Distrustful* is the word, I think."

"I'm certainly that."

"It's not that I can help you with Aker. Not really. But I believe it might help you to know what wasn't done, who isn't behind it, because sometimes that can lead one in the right direction. As an investigator, you must understand that better than most."

"Yes, we call that *mis*information," Walt said sarcastically.

"But it's not, you see? Once you sign that NDA, I won't have to lie to you any longer."

It was difficult for Walt to see Hillabrand as the victim of the government the way Hillabrand wanted him to. The portrayal seemed unlikely and insincere. He wanted to believe he could find the truth on his own—that he already had most of it—but the truth could take time, and Mark Aker had all but run out of it.

He pulled a pen out of his pocket and signed the document.

"Hand it to me, please," Hillabrand said, taking no chances Walt might try to destroy it, burn it in the fireplace, once he had the truth.

Hillabrand carefully folded the document and slipped it into his suit coat's inside pocket. He then stared at Walt and Walt stared back.

"It wasn't a spill," he said. "And it wasn't my company's money."

"You paid off the ranchers to cover their losses, the same way Danny Cutter was made a similar offer."

"My company made those arrangements, but the money comes from the tax-
payers."

"If not a spill, what, leakage? Seepage?
Or what?"

"You're still so determined to see me in
a particular light you can't quite wrap your
mind around it, can you? What if I'm considered innocent until proven guilty? That
would be a novelty."

He was right: Walt had seen Semper,
and Hillabrand in particular, as the perpe-
trators. He'd had little choice but to do so.
The INL director's rebuffs had been the ic-
ing on the cake. But now the existence of
the NDA made itself felt: perhaps no one
had agreed to meet with him because
they'd been bound by the same contract.

"Sabotage," Walt mumbled, stunned by
the way the events suddenly looked so
different when considered in this light.

"A domestic terrorist attack," Hillabrand
said, his voice low, his words carefully chosen. "Not a bunch of crazy Muslims. A
bunch of crazy rednecks."

Walt felt a sickening dread in his belly.
"The Samakinn." Walt recalled the alert
that had been sent.

"You've heard of them?"

"Only recently."

"They targeted a well-secured facility with the remnants of forty-two reactors spread over an area the size of Manhattan," Hillabrand said. "They attacked an outlying building and caused a rupture. Thankfully, small, but it's still radioactive material. We think it was accomplished by four people, maybe less. This comes at a time when this administration is in back-channel negotiations with Pakistan, North Korea, and Iran on their nuclear policies. We're trying to dictate policy in order to control world safety. The last thing this administration needs is to be seen as a government that can't secure its own fissionable material. When the breach was discovered, the administration informed us this would not go public. Any blowback would be covered by them. Thankfully, it happened in a mostly uninhabited area. The substrata contamination flowed north into the Pahsimeroi. It wasn't until the livestock became ill that we even understood the degree of the sabotage. We've been working around the clock to repair the damage ever since. Thankfully, the few ranchers affected are patriots. They signed the same NDA that you did, took some money for their troubles, and kept their mouths shut. Two things we didn't see coming."

"Mark Aker and Trilogy water," Walt said.

"We should have known about Trilogy. That was a horrible oversight on our part. We didn't even know that bottling facility existed. Very stupid of us."

"The ranchers had contacted the vets before you got to them."

"Aker saw how sick the livestock was. He was in the midst of trying to help when we had to ask the ranchers to turn him away. They made excuses that they'd switched to a local vet. And that might have stuck if the local vet had been made to play along. But Aker must have run into him, or followed up with him, and the lie was exposed. And Aker came looking."

"But then Randy Aker was your doing," Walt said.

"My people say no. Perhaps to protect me, but they say it wasn't us. Our best guess is that it has something to do with the Samakinn. They left a note, long since in the hands of the FBI, a rambling manifesto about the wrongs of the country. They want their message heard. You know the drill."

"And by covering up any news of the leak . . . the sabotage," he corrected, "you've pissed them off."

"A dozen miscreants don't dictate how this country is run. They called some newspapers to make their claim. We fielded some calls as a result. We denied any mishap, as did the administration. No harm, no foul. Another group of wackos making unsubstantiated claims. No damaging articles ever ran. The Samakinn blogged about the spill on the Internet, but without any kind of proof . . ."

"Which is where I come in," Walt said. "Why should I believe any of this? An NDA isn't proof of anything."

"No, it's not." He paused. "I thought you might go there." He walked over to the office door and opened it, murmuring to someone on the other side. A young woman entered, and glanced at Walt as she crossed behind the senator's desk.

She spoke on the phone for several minutes while working the senator's computer. Walt and Hillabrand waited in silence.

When the aide spoke, Walt thought it was to him. But it was, in fact, to the computer.

"Are we ready?" she said.

"We're good on this end," a voice returned.

Hillabrand moved to the door and waited for the aide, who motioned for Walt to take the chair.

She said, "You don't have to do anything. Just sit."

Walt moved around the desk to see the face of a twentysomething man on the screen.

"Sheriff Fleming?"

"Yes," Walt said, sliding into the comfortable chair.

"Stand by for Vice President Shaler."

The man vacated the screen. Walt saw only a set of drapes and some framed photographs. The ski mountain in the nearest photo was all too familiar to him.

Walt glanced over at Hillabrand, who

stood half out the door. "Hopefully, you'll believe her. I'll be waiting just outside." He pulled the door shut.

"Walt?"

She had sneaked onto the screen while Walt had been distracted with Hillabrand.

"How great to see you!" she exclaimed.

"Madame Vice President . . ."

"Enough of that, Walt. It's 'Liz,' and you know better."

"You look well."

"I am, thank you. And you? You look tired."

"I know your time must be limited. I was just speaking to Roger Hillabrand. He said you might clarify some of this."

"Everything I presume Roger has told you is accurate, Walt. We were attacked, and we've had to play hardball to protect current negotiations. Its important for you to know that both houses have been briefed through committee. There is no cover-up taking place. It may take twenty-five years and the Freedom of Information Act for any but a handful of people to know about this incident, but that's how the game has to be played sometimes."

"They tried to frame Danny Cutter on a drug charge," Walt said. "Is that protocol?"

"I can't speak to specifics. I have heard that, in certain instances, pressure points were determined and taken advantage of in order to ensure full cooperation. They have to make absolutely sure that everyone will sign the NDA and cooperate fully. They can't risk anything short of that. If a witness hesitates, there has to be backup. Some of this behavior is despicable, and I apologize for that. I've expressed my displeasure at some of the tactics used."

"My wife? My children?" Walt suddenly saw Gail's intrusion differently.

"What about them?"

"Never mind."

"Tell me. Please."

"It's unrelated."

"It may not be, Walt," she said. "Please, tell me."

He briefly explained Gail's claiming the girls for herself—this after leaving the marriage because she felt overwhelmed by motherhood. It hadn't added up until just this moment.

"I'm wondering if she didn't get an anonymous phone call implying some kind of failure on my part. I'm wondering if there wasn't some behind-the-scenes look at my divorce papers."

"Walt, I would never condone such a thing. I want you to know that. The president and I are briefed regularly about the situation out there but certainly haven't heard all the details. Nothing about what you claim happened to Danny Cutter, and most definitely nothing to do with you. I can, and will, make some calls."

"A thing like this," Walt said, "the sabotage, it can't be contained. Not once it's in the water. You know that, right?"

"Do you mean the news of the event or the contamination itself?"

"Both."

"As to the contamination, it was minimal. There's a tremendous volume of water we're dealing with. Levels are well off of where they were two and three weeks ago. Another two weeks, we're told, and we're in the clear." She pursed her lips as her attention was drawn offscreen. "As to the spread of information, we believe it can be contained,

has to be contained. We need your cooperation, your assistance, in seeing that happens."

"I signed the NDA, Liz. I'm not going to
risk a stay in Leavenworth. I won't say
anything."

"It's more than that. It's Mark Aker. We
need to extract him before he's forced to
publish something that could be damaging."

**"Publish?"**

"Maybe Roger didn't tell you everything.
What the Samakinn seek most is notori-
ety. Credibility. They believe credibility
comes through verification, confirmation
the sabotage was effective."

"Scientific proof," Walt said. "Like a veterinarian's report on the sheep."

"The sabotage is under investigation.
The Samakinn must have had inside help.
Roger's people have been working
twenty-four/seven with the Bureau, attempting to turn up the mole. Our information is that the Bureau has surveillance in
place. They are ready to strike. We both
know what happens to Mark Aker if he's
anywhere near them when that strike oc-
curs."

"I need whatever intel's available," Walt said, sitting forward in the chair.

"I'm not privy to the details. It's too far out of my area of operations."

"But you said yourself, Mark has to be extracted."

"There's a genuine fear of Ruby Ridge here, Walt. It's one of the things holding the Bureau back. If they make this into a standoff, the Samakinn win the press coverage they so desperately seek. It's a no-win for us. And that's got all of us looking at alternatives. But if Mark Aker's out of the equation, there's a lot more leeway. There's still time for you to help us fix this."

"I have nothing," Walt said. "I can't do anything without something to work with."

"Work with Roger. Cooperate with him, Walt. He's not the enemy. That's the purpose of this call: to try to bring you two closer together. His people have their suspicions, suspects. Maybe between the two of you . . ."

Walt had focused on Hillabrand as a suspect for too long to now reverse himself and make him an ally. Just the suggestion of working with him turned Walt's stomach: the man had pursued Fiona, possibly in order to monitor Walt; he'd denied knowledge of Randy Aker's death, which seemed unlikely.

Worming inside him was the realization of how misplaced his suspicions had been, how biased he'd been against Hillabrand's big money, how eagerly he'd labeled Semper the corporate villain, the ranchers as easily compromised accomplices. Senator Peavy had tried to steer him toward Washington, had repeatedly said how he was trying to help Walt, and Walt had reacted negatively, immediately distrusting the man. Perhaps the plan had been for Shaler to seek him out in person and explain the events. It all played out so differently now.

"Listen," Liz Shaler said, "I've got to go. But I want you to think about everything I've said. Follow your instincts on this, Walt. I've always trusted your instincts."

"Thank you." But he was questioning his instincts, and her praise only drove home that point.

"We need to pool our resources, find this group, and extract Mark Aker. Nothing short of that is acceptable."

"Agreed."

Even over a webcam, there was a look to Liz Shaler's eyes that would haunt him. A fierce determination that flirted too close to fear. A take-no-prisoners defiance that mixed with the terror that any mention of radioactivity brought. She seemed to be telling him, without words, that if Mark had to be sacrificed for the "greater good," then that was what was going to happen.

# 51

ROY COATS LIVED WITH THE PAIN. THE DOC HAD stolen all the serious meds; aspirin hardly helped. He felt his best when sitting quietly by the woodstove, the brand name of which was reversed on his cheek in angry blisters. The wound in his leg left him a cripple; it was a caked, spongy mass of scab and infection. His armpit wound was less of a concern. It hurt far less. But if he tried to venture outside into the biting cold, his face lit up in pain. He waited—impatient, hurting badly, and foul of mood—ready to tear the head off the next thing that came through the door.

The required knock on the cabin door won his attention.

He grunted loudly, admitting whoever it was. The burn's infection kept him from speaking much. He could move his lips enough to get a few words out, but that was it.

The doorknob turned, and Newbs poked his head through, then stepped inside cautiously.

"'Bout time," Coats said.

Donny Newbury was twenty-three but looked thirty due to the width of his round face and the thick scrub of a beard that he wore. He ducked his head, coming through the door, and filled the cabin with his wide shoulders and barrel chest.

"I brought Shilo," Newbury said. He eyed Coats warily and stayed close to the door. "A collar and the radio gear. Fresh batteries, like you said. If you'd told me in time, I coulda brought something for . . . your face and all."

Coats grunted. He took everything that had happened to him as a test. "What about Lakely?"

"Not happening," Newbury said, tensing, in case it provoked something unexpected from Coats. "He went to the Mel-O-Dee, like you said. To meet that scientist girl for you. To make the deal and get the drum of waste and all. But it was fucked-up, Roy. I kept watch, like you said. From my pickup. He was in there too long, you know? He was going to drop the stuff and get her keys, or whatever, and make the switch. But it was fucked-up. The thing is, he shoulda checked the makes in the parking lot. Doesn't take a fucking genius to spot the SUVs. At the Mel-O-Dee? Are you kidding me? Pickups and maybe an old Caddie or two. But spanking brand-new SUVs?"

"Get to the point," Coats said painfully.

"Feds. I could see the flashes in the window. Fucking serious firefight. Couldn't have lasted that long unless Lakely had gotten himself hunkered down. He put up a good fight. When it was over, the ambulance arrived. Only one ambulance there in Arco, so two of the body bags went in the back of a pickup. Three in all. Lakely, one of 'em, because he never walked out or nothing. But shit, Roy, he gave 'em hell, I'll tell you that. And there was plenty of wounded on top of the other three."

For Coats, the room wouldn't stop spinning. Blood thumped at his temples and rang in his ears, and he thought his head might explode.

"The drum," he muttered through clenched teeth.

A fifty-five-gallon drum of contaminated waste. Enough for a dirty bomb. *His dirty bomb*. Enough to make the world take notice. He'd have had the front page of every newspaper in the world. The Samakinn would have been heard.

But now he'd lost the drum. He'd lost Lakely.

"The girl?"

Newbury shook his head.

He'd lost the girl.

"But just because I didn't see her come out don't mean nothing."

The feds had the girl. How much did she know about him? How much had he revealed in his lame-ass attempts at conversation? Most important of all, had she seen his truck? Did she know about his truck? If she'd seen his plates, he was done. Gone. They'd be on him like flies on shit.

It was all down to the doc. Again. *They had to find him.*

"You and Gearbox split up. Gearbox'll take Shilo. You take the old road. We need the doc."

They both heard the approach of the snowmobile. A moment later came the knock on the door.

"Huh!" Coats grunted.

Gearbox entered, looking half frozen.

"Newbs'll fill you in," Coats said. "You find the doc and you bring him back here. He's gonna write that letter. We can still pull this off."

He glanced down at his swollen leg. Maybe the doc could help with the leg. He could hardly move the thing without the scab cracking open. He needed some stitches.

If the doc hadn't stabbed him, it would have been him in the body bag instead of Lakely. *Everything happens for a reason.*

"What the fuck are you looking at?" he managed to say. "Find the doc and bring him back here."

Then he caught sight of himself in the

window's reflection and understood why Newbs had been staring so intently: the blisters had torn open, spewing a yellow fluid down his cheek. It looked as if his face was melting off.

# 52

WALT WENT THROUGH THE JAIL'S PERIMETER door shoulder first, following the shiny spot beneath the comb-over belonging to his deputy, Jimmy Magna, who everyone called "Magnum." The forty-five-year-old county jail suffered from poor design. Its security doors were like hatches on a submarine. At twenty-eight inches wide, they were so narrow that the stretcher carrying Taylor Crabtree had to be angled to fit through. The young man was missing a couple of front teeth, and his dislocated right shoulder was in a sling. Otherwise, he'd been lucky. Inmates didn't look kindly on those accused of molesting girls young enough to be their daughters.

"You okay?" Walt asked Crabtree as the stretcher was maneuvered through a second doorway. He'd have done anything to reverse the beating the boy had taken. He'd warned his jailers that Crabtree was at risk and was pissed at the obvious neglect that had occurred.

"I want out of here," Crabtree said through a swollen cheek.

"We'll figure something out. We're going to get you to the hospital first. Maybe a dentist." Walt was eager to question the boy further, to look for a possible link to Sean Lunn and a way to pressure Hillabrand, but the injuries came first. He had to hold himself back from in any way delaying Crabtree's medical care.

"I'm not going back in there," the boy said.

"It's not how it works," Walt said. "We'll get you isolated somehow."

"Please," the boy said. It was more than a word; it was an apology, a confession, something he hadn't spoken to anyone in years.

The plea revealed a contrite Taylor

Crabtree. Walt had hoped remorse existed somewhere inside the boy. He understood the importance of the moment. If Walt delayed the medical care, and Crabtree later filed a grievance, Walt would face review. But he sensed an opportunity.

"When we get him out," Walt instructed his deputies, "unstrap him. Let's get him into the Sit room and put some ice on that lip. Have the ambulance stand by."

"I don't need an ambulance," Crabtree complained.

"Procedures," Walt explained. "You're in the system now. There are ways we have to do this."

"Fuck the system."

"That's how you got in here," Walt said, "but it's not how you get out."

THE SITUATION ROOM smelled of sweat, coffee, and doughnuts. Just as an athlete recognized the particular smell of locker rooms, any cop could identify the combination.

Crabtree sat nursing his mouth with a baggie of ice.

"This is not supposed to happen in my jail," Walt said.

"What if I change my mind and decide to talk to you?"

"I could tell you it would make a difference, depending on what you had to say, but, honestly, Taylor, I don't want to lie to you. I don't know what, if anything, will help your situation right now. You've built a long sheet. A judge is going to review all that. You'll be seen as one of those kids that can't turn the corner and get your act together."

"But I can. Ask Elbie."

"I believe you. And I'll be happy to speak on your behalf, but the system is fairly unforgiving. If we could get you back into the Alternative School and if you *stayed* there. No more stupid stuff. Maybe a judge would be more lenient."

"Can you ask Mr. Levy if I can try again?"

"If he takes you back at the school, what's to say you'll toe the line?"

"Ask Elbie. I'm reliable. I'm never late. I don't cheat on lunchtime or anything."

"I'll speak to Barge."

Crabtree nodded, holding the ice gingerly. "I lied about Kira." He threw it out there.

"Before you dig yourself in any deeper," Walt said, "let me tell you a couple things I know. First, you didn't pick up Kira Tulivich on the side of the road. Second, I know she was in your car and that you dropped her at the hospital, as you've said. Third, that bruising on your face—it's still faintly there—wasn't Kira's doing and it wasn't a snowboarding accident. There are no indications she resisted."

Crabtree's eyes widened with surprise. Or maybe it was concern that he had little to offer Walt now.

"We have no evidence connecting Kira to your trailer. We found no drugs in your trailer. It seems unlikely you're the one who doped her. So what happened to her and where it happened remain a mystery to me, but I now know why it happened, and I think there's a possibility I know at least one of the parties involved. So whatever you do, Taylor, don't lie to me, because I'll likely know you're lying and that's not going to help anything." He paused, giving the boy a few seconds. "And if you don't say anything, that's okay too. Better to not say anything than to try to slip something past me. You get that?"

The boy nodded.

"So should I call the ambulance guys in?"

He shook his head.

"You're afraid." Walt could see it on the boy's face. "Of what, retaliation? By who?"

Only Crabtree's eyes moved. A quick, surgical strike, locking onto Walt.

"Who?"

Crabtree didn't answer.

"It's natural for a young man in your situation to gravitate toward a group. A gang? Are you in with the Mexicans?"

He coughed up a laugh. "Oh, sure."

Walt said the next thing that came into his head. "The Samakinn."

Crabtree's face froze.

"I want you to think very carefully, Crab," Walt said, feeling a rapport developing. "Association with the Samakinn is not, in itself, a crime. Participating in certain activities may be, but if you get in front—"

"You don't fucking get it, do you?"

"I'm afraid not. Help me out, Crab. I want to get it."

"Shit."

"The bruises. The ones you already had

when I saw you at Elbie's. Did Kira give you that face?"

"I did *not* do anything to Kira."

"And you did not get those bruises snow-boarding."

"I rescued her." His eyes, unflinching and bloodshot, glared at him. "You've got it backwards, Sheriff. I'm the one that saved her."

"Okay? From?"

"Them. Coats and the other guy." He broke the eye contact. "He lives up there, you know? Triumph. Coats does. He and his dogs. Fucking dogs *never* stop barking. But is anybody going to complain about it? No way . . ."

"Roy Coats," Walt said. Coats was one of the last true mountain men left in the area. A tracker. Some said *illegal* tracker. He'd been accused more than once of using collared dogs to track down mountain lions for anonymous clients. Walt rolled around the rumors surrounding Randy Aker and poaching. Coats? Fish and Game had tried to bring charges against Coats several years back. He hadn't heard the name since then.

"I saw him take Kira out of a dog crate.

Back of his pickup. This was really late at night. Snowing bad, and he's got her in a dog crate."

Walt looked around. He longed for a tape recorder and yet didn't want to put Crabtree off his statement. Pulling a note-pad from his shirt pocket, he said, "I'm go-ing to write some of this down."

Crabtree nodded. "He dragged her in-side."

"How close is his place to yours?"

Walt's nephew, Kevin, had taught him well about when a teen shifted into avoid-ance mode. Crabtree's eyes went to a cig-arette burn on the edge of the table. His shoulders folded forward. Walt's impa-tience and his lack of sleep almost got the better of him. He nearly marched around the conference table and took Crabtree by the shirt and shook some sense into him. But he'd learned self-control a long time ago, had learned to make these interrogat ions—confrontations—less personal. Crab-tree *wanted* to improve both his current situation and his future. Walt could play the catalyst, if he could get his own frus-tration out of the way.

"Can you see his house from your mobile

home?" Walt asked, his voice calm and collected.

"I'm not saying anything."

"Taylor . . . help yourself out here. You can do this. It's the right thing to do. Forget about you for a minute. Think about Kira. You're helping Kira. You want to help Kira, right?"

The look on his face showed anger and frustration. Walt knew all about both. "What?" Walt said.

"I can't tell you."

"You have to tell me."

"But I can't."

"Okay, how about this? We start the clock right now. Anything you tell me for the next five minutes is off the record. It never happened. I never heard it."

"That's a cop game. You ever seen *Law and Order*? I know all about cop games."

"Four minutes," Walt said, looking at his watch. "No tricks. I give you my word."

Crabtree looked Walt up and down. Something about Walt's promise resonated.

"Coats isn't there much. He hunts with the dogs, I think. Maybe has some other place. Not there much at all. But the dogs . . . a lot of them stick around. And there's this girl . . . watches the place for him. Takes care of the dogs. Smoking-hot, this girl." He dared a glance at Walt, who tried to convey no opinion in his expression. Crabtree was apparently going to leave it there.

"A good-looking girl," Walt said.

"Asked me to take care of the dogs for her one time her mother got real sick and she couldn't stick around. I said sure. And she gave me a key."

Again he paused. Again, it seemed as if he wasn't going to continue.

"A key to Coats's place."

"Correct," Crabtree said.

"And you helped her out by feeding the dogs. Does this connect with Kira, Taylor? I'm a little short on time."

"I put a pair of webcams in there." His head was hung in shame.

Walt's heart raced in his chest. He looked around for a glass of water. There wasn't one.

"*Inside* the house."

"His cabin, yeah."

Walt's jaw dropped. He sucked up his surprise, cleared his throat, and tried to sound as normal as possible. But, inside, he was both churning over the invasion of privacy and jumping at the thought that Taylor Crabtree might have witnessed the assault. Depending on if he ever found Mark Aker, depending on his condition, proving the abduction could be difficult. But a witness to a sexual assault, a rape, tried and convicted in Blaine County, could put Coats away for most of his adult life. It would be a poor trade-off but one that Walt would be happy to have in his back pocket.

"Taylor, I understand that your concern here is prosecution over the existence of the webcams. It's a legitimate concern, given your being expelled from the Alternative School for the same offense. *If* we charged you, a judge wouldn't like that at all. But I can guarantee you—*guarantee*, Taylor—that that will not be the case here. If you witnessed what I think you witnessed, those charges will never be filed. Not only that but others will be lessened or eliminated. But most of all, I need you to be honest. Do you get that? Absolutely honest. The slightest embellishment will hurt everything."

The boy nodded. "I have hours of DVDs," he said.

"Of?"

"The girl. In the shower. Dressing. Undressing. In bed. She had a boyfriend who . . . you know. He came over a lot when she was there. And they . . . you know."

"You recorded it," Walt said, his voice shaking slightly. He couldn't hold himself back. "The assault, Taylor? Crab? Did you record the assault?"

"I didn't burn it, if that's what you mean."

"I'm not exactly what you'd call a techie."

"It's on my hard drive. I've got like fifteen hours on my hard drive."

*Fifteen hours.* "Including the assault." Walt made it a statement.

Crabtree nodded, clearly ashamed. "How do you think I got in there to get her? You think I was going to take on those guys?" Walt noted the plural. "But they took a break. Jesus . . . the things they did to her.

Poor Kira. But I got her out of there and into my car. And I was in such a fucking hurry, I planted my face into the car door as I opened it. I was carrying her. Bashed my face into the door." He reached up and touched it. "It fucked me up bad. Was me who needed the emergency room. Drove like mad. Got her to the hospital. They never figured it out. That it was me helped her. Yesterday, when you came by, I wasn't afraid of your cop car—"

"The pickup trucks." Walt remembered them.

The kid nodded again. "I keep expecting a knock on the door and someone crushing my head in. Coats is fucking out of his mind. He'll kill me, he figures out it was me. All I want is those cameras out of there. They're still in there. Get it? He's gonna find them at some point and then I'm, like, totally fucked."

"I can probably help you there," Walt said, his head spinning from the information. "The night of the assault, Coats had company?"

"Yeah."

"A black Escalade? The guy's in his late thirties. Pretty buffed out. Dresses well."

The boy looked stunned. "How could you know that?"

"It's my job, Taylor," Walt said, and then mumbled to himself: "It's my job."

# 53

"WHY AM I BEING MADE TO WATCH THIS?" FIONA asked, standing alongside Walt in the sheriff's office command center. The door was shut and locked, the television's sound turned down low, so that Kira Tulivich's agony remained contained within those walls.

"I'm sorry," Walt said, "but you're my photography expert."

"They should be hung. No, castrated with a kitchen knife, then pulled, limb from limb, drawn and quartered. And even that would be too good for them."

On the screen, Coats and an unidentified male took turns violating Kira Tulivich. The horror played out in the grainy black-and-white of Taylor Crabtree's webcam, his computer having been confiscated from the RV he used as shelter.

"You may be able to spot a frame we could enlarge or something, to give us a better look at the second man."

"It's not that at all, is it?" she said accusingly. "What is it with you, Walt? Always having hidden agendas. Never admitting them. Why don't you just come out and say you think it's Sean Lunn?"

"Is that what you think?"

"Oh . . . give me a break."

"Is it?"

"That's what I think, yes. Does anything I see here confirm it, make me absolutely certain? No. But you won't even speak his name."

"I can't," Walt said, winning a surprised look from her.

"You need me as a witness?" she speculated.

"I need to identify the second man. Yes. That could prove extremely helpful."

"So you don't mention his name because, if you did, it could be construed
later that you led the witness."

"Something like that."

"I'm sorry." She ran her fingers through
her hair and tilted her head back. She had
an elegant neck, long and regal. "I confuse the professional with the personal,
don't I?"

"It's easy to do."

"So why don't you?" she asked.

Tulivich was held in place by Coats. She
let out a horrible scream. Fiona looked
away. "Well, if anything will put you off sex,
this will."

"I want them both to pay for this, Fiona.
Not just Coats. Coats . . . I'm going to take
care of Coats."

"Do you have him?"

"No."

"Know where he is?"

"No. We do know the Bureau had a confrontation with a man believed to be a
member of the Samakinn—an extremist
group, part Ted Kaczynski, part Aryan Nation. A second suspect, a woman, is in
custody. She's a meth addict and is proving

difficult to deal with. We have a description of a man that's close enough to Coats to do the trick. It's all very fluid."

She dared to look at the screen again. "Jesus . . . I can't take any more of this. That poor girl."

Walt had not taken his eyes off the screen. "Yeah. How 'bout there?" he asked. He used the keyboard's space bar to stop the video. Used the mouse to back up the footage. "Is that a mirror on the wall? Is that his face in the mirror?"

"It's too grainy," she said. "You'll never get anything. This is incredibly low resolution, Walt. Really poor. Even with enhancement, you're going to need a shot that's very strong."

They watched another thirty seconds, Fiona needing to look away repeatedly.

"Wait!" she said.

Walt paused the video.

Fiona leaned forward and pointed not at the man's face, but the pants crumpled at his knees. "Look. The back belt loop. It's ripped. Attached at the top but not the bottom."

Walt craned forward. "How did you ever see that?"

"I was trying not to look at what was going on."

He played a short segment repeatedly. Sure enough, the belt loop flapped loose. It was seen only briefly, but there it was on video.

Walt said, "It's not enough to win a warrant. I can't say because of that it's Sean Lunn. I need to see Sean Lunn in those pants. That would give me probable cause for a wider search. It's not much, even at that."

"But you're going to search the cabin, aren't you?"

"Awaiting a warrant. The judge is golfing down in Twin Falls. It's still warm enough down there to keep the courses open. One of my guys—we're working on a phoner warrant."

"Am I coming along?"

"That's the third reason you're here and why I asked you to bring your gear."

"I'm still mad at you, you know?" She said this proudly.

"I know."

"Roger hasn't called."

"I may have been wrong about him," Walt

said. It came out as a confession, which was not the way he meant it.

"Your timing could be better."

"I'm a work in progress, Fiona. I don't have any of it figured out. But losing Mark like this . . . I know it all has to do more with friendship than we think. More than I understand, at least. It's what's important at the end of the day. Right? I need to find him. Dead or alive, I need to know. I don't understand exactly. I screw up a lot of stuff, but I intend to keep working on my friendships. Starting with you. At some point. I don't want you mad at me."

She glared. A hostile, unforgiving look that showed Walt just how far he had to go.

"Okay," he said. "I get it."

"You know why I really hate you?" she whispered.

"I didn't even know you did."

"It's because I can't stay mad at you." She pushed her chair back. "You'd better turn that off because I'm leaving the room." Standing by the door, she dug around in her purse and came up with a business card. "Sean Lunn," she said, waving it. "The night he was trying to talk me onto the corporate jet. Said to call if I needed anything. So I'll call him. The thing about men? They pretty much wear the same thing all the time. What do you want to bet he shows up in those same pants?"

"You'd do that?" Walt asked.

"I thought you said it's all about friendship?" she questioned.

"I thought you hated me."

"You're not a very good detective, Sheriff. I'm sorry to have to tell you."

# 54

THE WARRANT WAS CALLED IN FROM THE TENTH green by Judge Dan Alban. Within twenty-five minutes, Walt had six of his eight available deputies in strategic positions surrounding Coats's house, including a sharpshooter positioned up a hill among the ruins of the defunct mine. This kind of deployment wreaked havoc on his department, as it left only two on-duty deputies to patrol a county roughly the area of Rhode Island.

The house was situated so that its detached one-car garage blocked it from view of the other houses and abandoned

RVs scattered around the sterile wasteland of pale gray mine tailings. It stood off
on its own, out of sight, surrounded by
an abnormally high post-and-rail fence
topped with a single strand of taut razor
wire. The front gate carried two inauspi-
cious signs: BEWARE OF DOG and NO SOLIC-
ITING.

Walt and his deputy, Bill Noland, led the
way as they pushed through the gate and
approached the house at a run. Noland,
who was in his late twenties, carried a
four-foot stun stick for use on the dogs, if
necessary. Walt carried a "flash and bang,"
a white-phosphorus stun grenade. Both
men also had their Berettas out and at the
ready. Behind them came two more men,
one carrying the ram, a three-foot, seventy-
pound steel maul capable of disintegrating
most doors.

Walt tried the doorknob: locked.

The ram took out the hardware and the
door swung open. Walt tossed the grenade inside and his team turned their
backs. The flash and bang would momen-
tarily blind, deafen, and typically physically stun anyone within the confined
space where it detonated.

His team charged through the door, led by Noland. Walt brought up the rear. The space was small—a living area, a bathroom, and a single bedroom. It all looked familiar to Walt from the webcam video.

"Clear!" his men announced as they inspected the closets and rooms. They moved on to stun-bomb a crawl space, the hatch for which was found cut into the floor in the bedroom closet. It too proved to be empty.

By the time his men reconvened in the central living area, Walt had the two webcams in a pouch on the inside of his windbreaker.

"We'll get that door closed as best as possible. Bring in Fiona and forensics. We'll watch the road—both directions—and keep the house under round-the-clock surveillance. Questions?"

"Sheriff?" It was Noland, calling from the galley kitchen.

Walt faced the refrigerator, where a number of postcards, bill reminders, and hand-scrawled notes had been attached with various pieces of a magnetic poetry set.

| energy | and | persistence | con-
quer | all | things |

"It's Benjamin Franklin," Walt said, consumed by the subtext: Roy Coats was a
determined man.

"Not that," Noland said. He pointed to a
photocopied collage of snapshots. Handwritten at the bottom, it read: "Thanks for
the guiding. Happy hunting!—Ralph." The
center picture showed three men with rifles in their hands, standing in front of a
rustic cabin. The cabin was small, with an
outbuilding on the right in the photo. Walt
picked Coats out immediately, recognizing
him both from the driver's license photo
he'd pulled and by the fact he was the biggest among the three: a burly man with a
full beard who looked as if he hadn't
showered for weeks. The rifle he held
was smaller than those held by the others, a modified .22—a dart rifle, Walt
guessed. The small-gauge rifle Walt had
heard on two separate occasions, losing
a friend both times. The center photograph was surrounded by five other snapshots, three of which featured the cabin

or what appeared to be its outbuildings. In each of the three, the landscape rose in the background; and, in two of these, the background was jagged mountains.

"Plain-sight search," Walt told his deputy. "I want any other photographs of this cabin we can find." He tapped the collage. "I want property tax records for every county in the state, starting with ours and working out through connecting counties, cross-checked for anything owned by Coats. Get on the horn and get that started. It's damn good work, Noland."

"Yes, sir." Noland hurried off, a slight spring to his step.

Walt studied each of the photos carefully. When combined, they presented about three-quarters of a panorama. But it was the two that showed the distant mountains that most captivated him. His index finger traced the line of the peaks against the cobalt blue sky. There were ranges he knew the look of by heart, though admittedly only from one or two angles, typically from a road or similar perspective. Put him on the opposite side of the same range and he wouldn't recognize it. It didn't come as a surprise that he couldn't identify this particular range, though it was certainly a frustration.

Again, Walt traced the silhouetted line in each of the photos where the mountains met the sky.

"Maps!" Walt called out, a little too loudly for the small space. He stood and addressed his small team. "I want any maps, any photos. We're abandoning plain-sight search. I want everyone wearing gloves. We toss the place, but *neatly*, gentlemen. Carefully. And put back everything the way you find it."

He caught himself holding his breath as he watched his men take to the search, a little too eagerly as always.

Coats stood in the center of the middle photograph.

# 55

WALT DIDN'T LIKE TO THINK THAT CHANCE PLAYED a role in his work. He'd spent too much time in continuing education seminars, field exercises, and classrooms to put much credence in the flip of a coin or happenstance. But, more than that, it was the issue of control. He'd been trained to control the investigation, not to allow the investigation to control him. So as he entered the women's side of his decrepit jail—two cells on the northeast corner of the small cellblock—and found Taylor Crabtree engaged in a video game, he fought to accept that a possible solution to this investigation could just materialize out of thin air.

A local film star had donated his son's outdated PlayStation and a dozen games for the entertainment of the inmates. Crabtree was engaged in combat with guns blazing, a pair of headphones over his ears. Walt could hear the dull *zing* and *pop* of explosions through the headphones. He caught a glimpse of the screen, a small computer monitor. It showed a landscape like Afghanistan, rugged high desert; it showed a distant mountain range, angular against a bomb-flashing sky.

The thing was: that landscape looked impossibly familiar. Not all that different than many parts of Idaho.

Walt grabbed the cell bars with either hand.

He knew how to find Coats's cabin.

THE COMMAND CENTER'S scarred oval conference table held four computers, including the one confiscated from Crabtree's RV. Walt studied the intent faces of the four boys at the keyboards: Crabtree; Walt's nephew, Kevin; a boy of sixteen named Wilder; and one other, Jason. Jason and

Wilder had been recruited from the Alternative School by Crabtree; he knew them to be serious gamers.

As he passed Kevin, Walt ruffled his hair and patted him on the back.

The idea had come to Walt as he'd witnessed Crabtree at the PlayStation, the Afghan mountain ridges slipping past. The boys were all currently using the satellite imaging software, Google Earth, in an attempt to reconcile the distinct ridges seen in the refrigerator-collage photographs with the true Idahoan landscape. The boys, experts with either a joystick or mouse, could place themselves into Google's virtual landscape, tipping the horizon, zooming in or out, and even spinning a full three hundred and sixty degrees around a single point, while attempting to match the skyline in the photos to the satellite imagery.

With thousands of mountain peaks to compare, this task might have proved interminable, but Crabtree had further contributed with a simple observation: four of the peaks were snow-topped. Three of the four photos were time- and date-stamped, as was the postcard itself. A phone call to the Forest Service, followed by a second call to the National Interagency Fire Center, in Boise, which tracked snow cover, put the elevation of the snow line at nine thousand feet on the day the snapshots had been taken nearly a year earlier.

Walt's staff had narrowed the candidates by marking all mountain peaks over nine thousand feet on a topographic map; they narrowed it further by color-coding any ranges that contained three such adjacent peaks within a twenty-mile radius.

Now, with twenty-one circles drawn on the map in overlapping rings, the boys were working the computers, using Google Earth, trying to match horizon for horizon— the photographs to the computer screens.

It would have taken Walt's deputies hours to understand and control the Google software; the boys were at it in minutes. He walked around the table, watching over the boys' shoulders. To the untrained eye, the images moved quickly. It felt as if he were flying down to ground level and spinning around, eyes wide open. More than once Walt wanted to tell the kids to slow down, but their eyes worked differently than his, their motor control tied to the mouse or joystick: where he saw a blur, they saw distinct images.

Forty minutes into the experiment, Crabtree used a look to call Walt to his side. The boy raised his finger to the screen, pointing out several peaks. Then he pointed to the same peaks on the enlargements of the photographs from the collage.

"Uh-huh," Walt said, noting the similarities. Excitement rose in his chest, but he said nothing more. There had been five false alarms prior to this.

"These shacks," Crabtree said, indicating objects in two of the photographs, "are here . . . and here." He pointed to the screen, helping Walt to spot the small geometrical shapes created by roofs, mostly hidden beneath the abundance of conifers. Two triangles. A piece of a rectangle. They looked like little more than shadows. Walt would never have seen them.

"And these shots," Crabtree continued, "look to me like they were taken back here. There's a field about a quarter mile behind the cabin. This creek is on one side."

Walt's nephew, Kevin, was out of his chair, also looking over Crabtree's shoulder. He picked up a coordinate and then quickly found the same location on his screen. Walt stood between the boys, watching the two screens fill with images. Kevin's locked onto a view that perfectly matched one of the snapshots, while Crabtree obtained a perspective where the computer-realized mountain peaks on the computer matched point for point with those in the photograph.

"Write down the coordinates," Walt said.

He leaned into Crabtree and whispered, "Don't look now but you just bought yourself a free pass."

# 56

BY TWO P.M., WALT HAD NOTIFIED THE FBI THAT he was leading an exploratory team into a remote area of the Challis National Forest. He did this out of necessity: he needed the Bureau's assistance in arranging air support and he hoped to gain political backing for his decision to hold back the information about the raid from the Challis sheriff, as he feared there was a mole in that office.

The timing of this announcement was critical. He made it far enough in advance of the operation to allow the Bureau to feel included but not enough time for the

Bureau's direct participation. Having recruited a team of eighteen by cherry-picking the various police and sheriff departments in the valley, he had assembled a formidable group. But the final decision of who was to accompany him on the lead attack had yet to be made.

The eighteen did not fit well around the command center's table. Half of the men were standing. Walt directed the group's attention to a PowerPoint presentation put together by Nancy.

"Our challenge," he said, now halfway into his briefing, "is accessibility and, therefore, timing. There are no roads within six miles of the cabin. In the summer, there must be trails, but that doesn't help us. You either know your way in or you don't. Given the probability of a hostage and the physical layout of the terrain—note the surrounding hills—there's no easy way to advance assets on the ground without risking being seen or heard and therefore putting the hostage at risk. For this reason, we will divide into three groups—Alpha, Bravo, Delta—and take a different approach.

"Snowmobiles can be heard nearly two miles off in the backcountry, as many of you know. Helicopters, well beyond that. For this reason, and because we anticipate sentries, teams will abandon the snowmobiles in these three locations," he said, pointing to the screen, "and snowshoe in from there along these routes. The leaders will have GPS coordinates to follow. These routes are through difficult terrain but take the teams away from the most likely routes used to access the compound. We expect those routes may be under guard or even trip-wired.

"I, and one other, will be flying in, in a glider, just ahead of you, in an effort to secure the hostage in advance of a possible firefight."

"So the feds gave it back?"

Walt didn't catch who'd said that. A half-dozen heads hung, to mask snickers.

"My glider happens to have been confiscated, yes," he allowed. "But Luke Walen's stepped up and offered his. Now, if you don't mind, I'll continue the briefing?"

The heads came up and a sense of mirth filled the room. He didn't mind it coming at his expense. He thought they might pay more attention now.

"We will land here, in this open field, and proceed on foot, north-northwest, toward the cabin. If possible, using infrared, I will have identified the number and position of warm bodies down there, providing intel that should aid your advance. Radio traffic will be limited. Just remember: at least two, hopefully three, of us are friendlies. We'll bring a vest for the hostage, but do me a favor and verify your targets."

A nervous chuckle passed around the room.

"The individual team leaders will brief you on your group's route and your role in the operation. Some of you are perimeter control, some a strike force, and some are holding back for extrication. There's a shock and awe component to this that I want you to all be aware of: once our attack has begun, at least one helicopter, possibly two, will secure the airspace above the compound. They're there to help get us out, but my hope here is also to confuse and intimidate the enemy. Our teams need to be braced for that. We don't want anyone made jumpy or trigger-happy by the noise and chaos that follows. Questions?"

Walt fielded a dozen routine questions. It was to be a night raid. Some of the team would be wearing night vision equipment; others would not, and the mixture made clarification important. He appreciated the nervousness and tension that filled the room; better that than overconfidence. He still had to pick his partner for the attack. Together, they would attempt to reach the cabin and rescue Mark Aker, or at least position themselves to do so, ahead of the main assault. It gave Mark the best chance of survival and hopefully would preempt his being used as a bargaining chip.

Walt scanned the group for the right person. Then, through the glass, he saw Tommy Brandon enter the building and approach reception. Brandon, who had likely aided Gail in the abduction of his daughters. He was wearing street clothes, not his uniform. He'd removed the sling.

Walt excused himself from the team, turning it over to his deputy, and met Brandon in the foyer. For a long moment, the two just stared at each other.

"It wasn't my idea," Brandon said.

"I want them back," Walt said.

"I think she knows that." Brandon hesitated. "Look, I want to help on this."

Walt took a deep breath. "What about the arm?"

Brandon showed he had range of motion, though it clearly hurt him to move it. "I'm fine," he said. "Good enough, at least. I want to be part of this."

"She had no right," Walt said. "Did you drive her?"

"I had nothing to do with it."

"And I'm supposed to believe that?"

"We talked about it, if that's what you mean. I told her to talk to a lawyer. She didn't want to hear that. She was all freaked-out about you having a girl in there. You know how she is."

He looked the man over: Tommy Brandon, the deputy he wanted in the glider with him; Tommy Brandon, his wife's lover, a man he wanted nothing to do with.

"How are you in small planes?"

"I hate 'em."

"Good. Get dressed."

# 57

FIONA KENSHAW HAD BEEN GREETED WITH suspicion, AS she arrived at the Tulivich's front door. Someone—from the hospital, perhaps—had leaked to the local press that the sheriff had interviewed their daughter, Kira, in connection with the Mark Aker disappearance, and so the family had put up with several unwanted visitors over the past week.

Fiona's county employee ID, which she carried in order to enter and photograph crime scenes, put off those suspicions and granted her access. A few minutes later, she was on a leather couch, in front of a log fire, awaiting Kira. The girl looked sheepish and shy but not at all bruised or damaged.

The date-rape cocktail had blocked her memory of the assault, she explained, though she still ached all over, leaving her feeling like she was inhabiting some other girl's body. There were some follow-up doctor visits yet to come, and counseling had been recommended, though she couldn't figure out why she would get counseling for something about which she had absolutely no memory.

But for all her claim to remember nothing, Kira had a sullen look, her eyes distant.

"I won't stay long," Fiona said. "And I should be clear that I'm not here in any official capacity. I wanted to see how you're doing and to wish you well. And the sheriff wanted me to pass along that, as it turns out, you've played an important role in a very high-level investigation."

"Seriously?" She feigned interest.

"Small change, I know, but I thought you might want to hear that something good came out of what happened."

"Something good for *other* people, you

mean?" Delivered with an ice-cold asser-
tion.

"I know it's not much."

"What am I supposed to say: happy to
do my part?"

Her mother entered the room, trying to
appear hospitable—a failed effort.

"I've got it, Mom," Kira snapped. "We'd
rather talk alone."

The mother pursed her lips, and re-
treated. The exchange sent shivers through
Fiona.

A victim was like a pebble in a pond,
Fiona realized; the ripples traveled out a
great distance.

Kira whispered to Fiona, "I can't brush
my teeth without one of them hovering
over me. It's like I'm on suicide watch or
something."

*You probably are,* Fiona thought.

"You actually came here to try to make
me feel good about what happened?" Kira
said incredulously.

"Of course not! Nothing like that. I came
to give you these," she said, handing Kira
five photographs from the wedding.

The girl flipped through them. A smile
flickered across her face, quickly wiped

away by a realization. "Ancient history," she mumbled. She blinked repeatedly. "It's weird. I remember this like it was a year ago."

"That's someplace to start."

Biting her lip, Kira studied the photos more slowly. "This one of the bouquet . . ."

"I didn't take that one. I threw it in no charge."

"That's you."

"Yes."

"I don't remember you there."

"I was working. Not exactly dressed for the occasion, as you can see."

"You caught it."

"Technically, no. But that's how the umpire ruled."

Another smile. Small victories.

"Can I keep these?"

"Of course. They're for you."

"Thank you." She made a point of meeting Fiona's eyes.

"There's one other thing. I'm not sure I'm allowed to tell you this, but that's never stopped me before." She winced. "And it's really none of my business. I should say that right off the top. But your family is ob-

viously of some means, and, well, it's one
of those things I feel compelled to do. You
know? Have you ever felt that way? Despite your better judgment?"

Kira nodded.

"Good." Fiona collected her thoughts.
"There's a boy named Taylor Crabtree."

"That loser?"

"You know him."

"I see him around. I don't know him."

"Well, that's the point, I guess. He's the
one who rescued you." She watched this
sink in. "From the cabin. He's who drove
you to the hospital."

"That dork?"

"The same."

"But why? How?"

"He saw you . . . abducted. He was
able to get you out. No one knows this, by
the way. He might be hurt, or even killed,
if word got out, so I'm trusting you on
this."

Kira nodded. "I understand. I promise."
She looked around the room in an effort to
avoid Fiona. "I just don't *get* it. Taylor Crabtree?"

"He's had a rough time of it. Lousy family

scene. Tough conditions. Has found his way into a lot of trouble."

"I know all about it. A friend of mine was at the Alternative School with him."

"He works at Elbie's down in Hailey."

"You're thinking some kind of reward, aren't you?"

"Maybe not quite that obvious. A letter from your father would do a lot. A job that's better than changing tires. Something to give him a leg up. Then again, maybe it's not appropriate. I felt obliged to let you know about his role in it. Maybe I shouldn't have. Let's leave it at that."

"I am *not* writing a thank-you note."

"You do, or don't do, whatever you feel is appropriate."

"He actually got me out of wherever they had me?"

"He did."

"And you're sure it wasn't him that—"

"We are," Fiona answered.

"Alone?"

"Yes."

"Taylor Crabtree?"

"The word *hero* is tossed around a lot. The real heroes are often the most un-likely."

"He saved my life."

"We don't know that."

"Oh my God."

"Anyway . . . I should be going. It's good to see you up and around."

"You did this just because you felt sorry for him?"

"I did it because I had to. Because guys like Taylor Crabtree are often seriously misunderstood, and I know my attitude toward him changed a lot when I heard what he did. I had formed a pretty strong impression of him because of a previous situation—"

"The webcam stuff?"

"No, before that, actually. And this being a small town and all . . . A person like you could help turn opinion around—among his friends, I mean. Not now, of course, but maybe when it's all over."

"When will it be over?"

Fiona said nothing.

"For me," Kira said, "it feels like it'll never be over."

"It's early yet. But, honestly, that's the kind of thing a counselor can help a lot with."

"You'd know all about it, would you?" Kira said sharply.

Fiona waited until the girl dared to meet her eyes. It took a long minute.

Then she said, equally firmly, "I was in a very destructive relationship before I moved here. I went through some of what you went through but without the drugs. I came here today, in part, because no one ever came to me. No one ever knew what was going on. What was happening. I needed someone to talk to, but I was too scared. I thought it would change people's opinion of me, lose me my friends. Ruin everything. And then one day I realized I was ruined beyond anything mere opinion could change. And I took action. I promised myself that if I ever even thought someone was going through what I went through, I would intervene. I would *do* something. I don't know exactly why I came here. You don't need me. But maybe I need you. I needed to tell you it gets better, a little better, day by day." Kira was crying now, her head hanging, her hair falling forward. "You feel it was somehow your fault. A way you acted. Something you wore. That you asked for it. But that's bullshit. And I'm here to tell you that you have to push those voices from your head."

Kira was sobbing now. "I feel so . . . dirty."

"Talk to someone, Kira. It's so much better if you talk to someone."

The head bobbed.

Fiona breathed differently; Kira was the first person with whom she'd shared any of this. It came as a huge relief and terrified her at the same time. Some secrets were more dangerous than others.

"You waited to tell me," Kira said. "Why? Why didn't you just tell me this first?"

"I'm still scared. Of him. Of the truth. Of men. Don't think you can do this by yourself. Memory or no memory, you can get better faster if you let someone in."

Fiona stood.

"Will you come back?"

"If you want me to."

Kira looked up, her eyes wet. "I think I'd like that."

Fiona forced a smile. "Me too. Be seeing you, then."

# 58

BRIEFLY, WALT WAS WITHOUT CONCERN. SITTING in the pilot's seat of the glider had this effect on him, gave him a sense of quiet and peace. But then a flurry of radio traffic brought him back: first Brandon complaining about the updrafts, then the pilot of the towplane double-checking the release point as both pilots attempted to measure winds aloft by checking their heading against their actual track over land. Walt asked to be hauled farther north. He was cautioned against this delay by the tow pilot: daylight was bleeding out of the sky, forming a gray haze below, and making what promised to be a challenging landing all the more difficult.

Walt wanted the straightest approach possible. He consulted a handheld aviation GPS, premarked with the lat-long identified by Crabtree. He had one shot at the snowfield a half mile behind the compound. It would be an ugly landing at best. If he missed the field entirely, there would be no second chances. It was all trees and mountains past that one field—a jewel of flat in a narrow valley situated between the tall spines of two ranges. He hadn't told Brandon any of this, only that they were using the glider to approach silently. Eighteen deputized men were by now waiting on the far side of two different passes, some of whom had begun to advance on foot; the rest would follow by snowmobile on Walt's command.

The logistics of the strike were as complex as they were dangerous. A week of preparation would have been preferable to a matter of hours.

"I think I'm going to barf," Brandon said from the seat behind.

"There's a bag in the seat pocket. Just remember to remove the oxygen mask."

Walt smiled. Some things were worth the wait.

His radio crackled and a male voice called out his tail numbers. Walt confirmed. The man introduced himself as "a friend from the east," reminding Walt that they were on an open radio frequency that could be monitored by pilots and ground stations alike.

*FBI,* Walt thought.

"We have confirmed heat signatures," the voice said.

Walt processed the information: the FBI had tasked a satellite capable of infrared and had obtained a heat signature from the compound. It was active, not shuttered for the winter. People were down there.

"Three bogies," the voice said.

*Good odds,* Walt thought.

"Roger that," Walt said. "Thanks."

"Was that what I think it was?" a distraught Brandon inquired.

"We're going in," Walt said. He eased the joystick forward and the nose of the glider tilted almost imperceptibly. He had one chance at a landing.

In the dark.

In the mountains.

"When I say, 'Brace for impact,'" Walt schooled, "lean forward and clutch your chest to your thighs. Don't attempt to look out or sit up until we've come to a complete stop. It's going to be a hard landing."

"Why does that not sound promising?" Brandon interrupted himself with another spout of vomiting.

"We're going in," Walt said.

# 59

THE ANNOYING AND ALL-TOO-FAMILIAR SOUND OF a snowmobile roused Mark Aker from a deep and unintended sleep. Even as he drew himself from his slumber, he could tell the vehicle was moving toward him, not away. His back was to the hibernating bear. The cave no longer smelled bad to him, which informed him he'd been there a long time and had slept much longer than he'd intended.

The bear had wedged itself into the cave's extreme recess, with little space between the rock, root, and caked mud that it was backed up against. Mark lay in front of the bear, facing the mouth of the cave. His watch face had lost its luminescence. He had no idea what time it was but was guessing evening. He was hungry and thirsty and had to relieve himself, but didn't dare move for fear of disturbing the bear. The experience of cozying up to a hibernating bear might have once been a grad school dream of his. Now it seemed surreal. He wouldn't have believed such a story if he'd heard it himself, and yet here he was . . .

*Dogs.* Barking.

The snowmobile had gone silent. What he heard now sent a chill through him, for he knew Roy Coats owned and trained hunting dogs. Scent dogs. Dogs that could follow a mountain lioness for miles— days—into the wilderness. The handler tracked and followed the dogs by radio collar to the prey, which was typically pinned up a tree. Mark was now convinced that he was the prey; he was the one pinned.

The barking grew louder and more ferocious. The dogs were on a scent—*his scent,* more than likely. And whereas a human being on a snowmobile might not make anything of a dark shadow that turned out to be a cave entrance, the dogs would follow their noses straight to it.

Mark had been around animals all his adult life. As a vet in Idaho, he'd seen cases that would have never made it into medical school textbooks and would not have been believed if they had. He was more exposed to animals in the wild, or the results of confrontations with such animals, than an average vet. And because of this, he could foresee the events of the next few minutes. They played out before his eyes on the darkened walls of the cave, as if a projector were running. And he didn't like what he saw.

As if reading his thoughts, the bear stirred as the barking drew closer.

Mark had a decision to make, and neither choice was viable. If he stayed where he was, the bear would shred him when coming awake; if he fled, the dogs would either tear him to pieces or tree him.

But if he could climb over the bear, getting away from the animal's keen sense of smell, then the noise and the scent of the dogs might hold the waking bear's attention. The hungover animal would be far from alert as it awakened. Bears did not see well. With the bear facing the mouth of the cave, Mark thought it just might work: what the animal first saw and heard as it awakened would become its focus.

The barking, incredibly close now, lifted the hairs on the nape of Mark's neck: the dogs were charging up the hill.

Coming right for him.

# 60

THE GLIDER WAS TOO LOW, BUT THERE WAS nothing to do about it now. With no source of thrust, only the wind and its forward momentum kept it aloft. The lower he flew, the darker it got. He'd circled once above the narrow field, just to the north of the small frozen river, spiraling down toward the treetops, over a sea of gray-green spires accented by the white carpet at their feet. It felt as if a cloak had been thrown over the narrow valley; the sun had left here hours before. And where the sky still glowed a pale blue, the earth beneath it was giving up on twilight.

There was no such thing as a missed approach, no second chances at a landing. He got one chance and this was it.

As he reached the near side of the field, Walt eased the joystick back, lifting the nose while avoiding a complete stall. For a moment, the glider seemed to stand still, its tail actually brushing the very tops of the tall pines.

"What was that?" Brandon panicked as the sound of the contact reverberated through the frail frame.

Walt's focus remained on the field before him, a gray wash of indiscernible length, its surface impossible to read. If he judged this wrong . . .

The beauty of the glider landing in snow was that there's no superstructure supporting the wheels; a glider lands on a very small nosewheel recessed in the frame and an even smaller wheel below the tail, meaning it is well streamlined for a landing in snow.

"Brace yourself," he called out.

Walt held the nose up as long as possible, then eased the glider down into the snow with a lunge that rapped both their heads against the Plexiglas dome. His feet automatically pushed both pedals forward, attempting to brake, but it was his right hand on the joystick controlling the flaps that served that purpose. Snow streamed over the nose, blinding him. The right wing struck something, turning the glider sharply. The glider bounced and groaned and barely slowed, Walt convinced its light frame would come apart.

It submarined and then jumped up, actually lifting fully off the snow before smashing back down and finally grinding to a stop.

"You okay?" Walt said.

"Shit . . . shit . . . shit . . ." Brandon managed from behind him.

Walt shut down the electronics; he had no idea how they'd ever get the glider out of there, but that was the least of his worries. He popped open the dome, checked his GPS, and hand-signaled Brandon toward the far side of the field. Brandon gave him a thumbs-up and climbed out. The two men separated without a word.

Walt dug into his pack for the night vi-

sion headset. Though not fond of the technology, he appreciated the results: he
could see far more clearly and much farther, the electronic landscape black and
an eerie green but vivid. For now, he wore
the contraption, not thrilled with the way it
limited peripheral vision.

It took him a moment to distinguish
what he heard: not coyote, not wolf, but a
dog's barking. Maybe two. Well away to
his left—south—quite possibly across the
river.

Then another sound: snowmobile.

Had his own guys jumped the gun and
raided the cabin ahead of his signal? If
Mark Aker was indeed out there, his life
had just been put in great jeopardy.

Then a second thought flashed through
his mind: had Roy Coats somehow seen
the glider or been warned in advance of
the raid?

Trudging on snowshoes, Walt hurried
in the general direction of the cabin, ig-
noring the barking for now. If Mark was
being held in the cabin, then the existence
of the snowmobile meant one less man to
guard Mark.

He would cut around to the east of the compound, leaving Brandon to approach from the northwest. Careful not to fall, he picked up his pace, believing time was suddenly in his favor.

# 61

BRANDON MOVED CAUTIOUSLY, THE LANDSCAPE ahead of him green and black through the night vision goggles. A slight glow of greenish white in the sky ahead suggested the cabin—the exhaust from a woodstove, more than likely. But judging distance accurately was difficult, and, though he'd trained with the goggles, he had no idea if that glow was a hundred feet away or five hundred yards. Worse, the forest was immature, a victim of a massive forest fire a decade earlier, resulting in a mixture of towering dead tree trunks and a dense undergrowth of twenty-foot pines, bramble,

and piles of decomposing slash from the
earlier fire. Finding a way through it was
challenging, due to the thick undergrowth.
Had it not been for the GPS, Brandon
would have lost his way. Instead, he found
himself forced to take a long way around
to the cabin because of a spine of rocky
hill that separated the cabin from the field
where they'd landed the glider.

His trailing leg felt the tension, though too
late. The snowshoe had caught on something. Looking down, he saw the trip wire
pull free and go slack.

He quickly took five long strides and
dove into the snow, covering his head, expecting an antipersonnel mine to blow. He
waited for a count of five. Then ten.

No explosion.

So the trip wire was a perimeter warning device.

He'd just officially entered the compound. And now, due to his stupidity, they
knew he was here.

He placed his glove to his throat and
squeezed, initiating radio contact with the
sheriff.

"I tripped a wire," he said. The radios

were digital; there was no way any communication between the task force would be intercepted.

"Roger that." The sheriff's voice, calm and collected.

"I've got some highlights at tree level."

"Three hundred yards north-northeast of my position," the sheriff said, confirming he'd seen them too.

"North-northwest for me," he said, checking the GPS, "so we've got good angles."

"Find some high ground. Or some place defensible. Let them come to you. Stay in radio com. If you hear them coming, let me know. I'll create a diversion and bring in backup. Keep 'em guessing."

"Roger that."

"No heroics."

"Out," Brandon said. He felt lousy for tripping that wire. The sheriff might feel obligated now to bring in the others. Their arrival would make Aker's situation all the more tenuous.

The purpose of Brandon and Walt advancing the raid was to capitalize on the element of surprise. They had to squeeze the cabin from two directions to be effective.

There was no way he was letting up his end. He wasn't one to go against orders, but he did so now, knowing full well the sheriff wasn't going to wait. He wasn't going to let him go in there alone.

*THE PREY RETURNS,* the narrator's voice said inside the head of Roy Coats as he saw the LED flash on the wall-mounted box, indicating a perimeter breach. *A hunter's patience is his greatest asset.*

He wanted this to be fun.

He leaned forward and grabbed for the walkie-talkie. His leg stung, and he worried he'd busted open the scab again. The damn thing wouldn't stop bleeding.

"Newbs. Area three's been tripped. Looks like the doc's coming back home for some reprovisioning."

"I'm on it," Newbs reported.

"Let me know when you have him."

**Starved and dehydrated, the prey returns to camp, driven by the uncanny will to survive. Having foraged for nearly two days, he sees the camp as**

his only hope and reluctantly returns to his keeper. But the hunter is aware of the return. His patience has paid off. He will be only too happy to welcome him back.

# 62

FOR ALL HIS STUDY, ALL THE READING HE'D DONE, mark Aker was shocked to witness first-hand how a bear—even a drugged bear—could come out of hibernation so quickly. As the bear sat up, Aker slipped farther down behind it so that, had the creature lay back down, it would have crushed him.

The bear fixed its attention on the mouth of the cave and the barking just beyond: a dog had reached the entrance, jutting its snarling snout in and out of the cave, teeth glaring, while held back by the cave's pungent odors, the dog's persuasive survival instincts.

The blinding darkness prevented Aker from actually seeing the bear glance back toward him, but there was a moment's hesitation, followed by the sound of the animal's sniffing, when Aker knew he'd been found out. The bear had definitely smelled him, but, distracted by the dog's ferocity, had turned in that direction.

Then light caught the top of the cave—a flashlight—silhouetting the massive bear as it charged and swiped. The dog yipped and howled. The beam of the flashlight wavered.

"Shit!" he heard a man shout, also incredibly close.

A single gunshot rang out, followed by the man's sickening wail, as the bear lunged farther from the cave. Another cry, more desperate.

Coats, or Gearbox, had followed the dog too closely, had approached the cave too quickly, had been stunned to discover a bear instead of the escaped veterinarian.

As the bear broke out of the cave, Aker followed closely. The man—Gearbox, judging by his size—had dropped the flashlight. It was blood-covered. The bear was lumbering off in the direction of the road, far faster than his simple movement implied, but too drugged, or wounded, to pursue with much enthusiasm.

The dog was gored at the neck, lying in the snow. The blood surrounding the fallen flashlight was not the dog's. The quantity of spilled blood implied the bear had gotten a fair piece of Gearbox as well.

Weak with fatigue and hunger, and stiff from his lack of movement, Aker picked up the flashlight and trained it on the dog, then in the direction of the noises. The bear was still in pursuit of Gearbox, who was himself surprisingly fast and able on snowshoes. If Aker had any chance to get away, it was now.

The bear might have been wounded by the gunshot, but, if so, it had only made it more angry.

Aker looked down at the wounded dog again and found himself unable to leave it there to bleed out and die.

He bent down, hoisted the dog over his shoulders, and, holding the animal's legs around his neck, made his way through the close-set rocks, knowing the terrain would discourage the bear from following. All the bear wanted was some sleep.

In a moment, the snow would get too deep for just his boots. Twenty yards from the cave, he realized he had no snowshoes, but he was not about to turn back. The bear would return at some point, the drugs contributing to its bad temper. For now, he wanted to put as much distance between himself and the cave as possible.

He heard the sound of a snowmobile's engine turn over. Again, and then it caught and roared like a motorcycle. He switched off his flashlight, not wanting to reveal his location. The headlight from the snowmobile swept through the woods and illuminated the side of the hill. Aker stood stone still.

The snowmobile made a half circle and then accelerated into the darkness, its engine's high-pitched whine receding along with it.

# 63

WALT CAME UPON THE SNOWMOBILE TRACK AT nearly the same instant he heard the single report of a powerful rifle. Adrenaline charged his system the way only gunfire can. His hand went to his pistol as he moved in the direction of the sound.

A pair of lights flared in his goggles. A good distance away. He could not put together what was going on but hoped Brandon was not the target of that report. His fears were settled by Brandon's voice in his ear.

"Your twenty?" Brandon's voice said.

"On a snowmobile track, still north of

the cabin. The gunfire was several hundred yards northeast of me. I've got a possible heat signature from the snowmobile. Hold your position."

"Yeah . . ."

Walt knew that tone.

"Your twenty?"

"I didn't exactly hold position. I should be closing in on the cabin shortly."

"Those were orders."

"I wasn't going to hang you out to dry, Sheriff. Besides, I had to shut down any chance of a getaway. We reviewed all this stuff."

"That was prior to the trip wire."

"It is what it is. Was that shot thrown at you?"

"Doubtful."

"Not at me."

"Hear this, Deputy: HOLD YOUR POSITION! I'll get back to you."

"Out."

Walt saw a second, hotter flare of light through the goggles, and, when coupled immediately with the sound of a snowmobile starting, he understood what had to be done. He jumped off the track, threw his pack on the ground, and unclipped the eighty-foot climbing rope from it. The rope was gray with a red twist, which required him to bury it after tossing a decent length across the track. He moved fluidly and efficiently, living for such moments, for he was briefly free of all else; no thought entered his mind that didn't directly have to do with stopping the snowmobile. It was its own weird kind of ballet, police work; a combination of efficiency and purpose. Walt secured the bulk end of the climbing rope to a tree, punched the slack rope down into the soft snow as he crossed the track, and reached the other side charged with excitement.

The engine sound told him the snowmobile was quickly approaching. He would have one chance. He took a full wrap around the thick tree trunk with the loose end of the climbing rope. Drew in the slack to where the rope barely lifted out of the snow impression, a few feet from the tree trunk.

The snowmobile's headlight glanced the surrounding branches, as if setting them all afire. Walt could barely breathe. His mouth had gone dry, his eyes stung. He carefully lifted the night vision goggles so the headlight wouldn't blind him. It took several seconds for his vision to adjust, and, in those several seconds, the snowmobile raced closer.

There was little time to think this through; he'd acted on instinct alone.

He made one last adjustment to the loop of rope around the tree. He'd rather catch the driver than the vehicle.

The white light filtered down through the branches and onto the dull bark of the tree trunks as the whine of the two-cylinder engine grew progressively louder.

There it was: weaving through the forested obstacle course, a single, blinding headlight.

Walt couldn't make out the driver or the snowmobile, only its penetrating bright light. And then it was upon him. All at once, as if it had jumped a hundred feet ahead.

He waited . . . waited . . . then pulled hard on the trailing end of rope, hand over hand.

The rope popped out and lifted from where he'd buried it in the snow and formed a taut, slanting line leading from the opposite tree, across the track and directly to Walt.

It struck the snowmobile's Plexiglas screen, was lifted higher by the contact, and caught the driver in the throat. The snowmobile shot out into the woods as its driver did a full backflip, landing on his head. He punched through the track's packed snow, buried up to the middle of his chest.

Walt drew his weapon and hurried to the man. He pulled him from the snow, only to find his neck broken, his head at an unnatural angle. More surprising was the quantity of sticky blood. It wasn't until Walt found his flashlight that he saw the lacerations—cougar? bear?—across the man's shoulder and chest. Deep gashes, the flesh of his chest ripped from his ribs. How he'd managed to drive a snowmobile in that condition not only impressed Walt but warned him: Coats and his posse were tough.

Walt caught up to the snowmobile. Inspected it. Righted it. Dug it out of a snowbank and used its engine to help lift it back to the track. He climbed on.

Called out on his radio so Brandon could hear. "I'm on the snowmobile. Please copy: I'm riding the snowmobile into the compound." He waited for the acknowledgment.

Waited some more.

"Brandon? Copy? . . . Brandon?"

No reply.

"Alpha," Walt called out over the airwaves.

"Alpha," came a male voice he identified as Andy Cargill.

"Give me five minutes. If I haven't checked in, contact Beta and Delta and begin your advance on the compound."

The team leader acknowledged.

Now all that stood between Walt and the compound were a few hundred yards of snow.

# 64

BRANDON PICKED UP A WHITE GLOW OF A HEAT signature in his goggles and ducked behind a tree. Human, not elk or deer. Close: fifty yards or less. The shape was coming straight for him, moving with a surprising quickness given the deep snow.

Brandon quietly slipped the M4 assault rifle in front of him. He set the trigger to fire in three-round bursts and touched his chest subconsciously to remind himself the vest was in place. His heart sped out of control, and, while he was hungry for a firefight, he was also terrified.

"Aker!" a male voice cried out from across the field.

Brandon couldn't believe the man had called out.

"I've got the wrong end of a thirty-aught-six aimed at that tree you're hiding behind."

The sheriff's voice interrupted, and Brandon yanked out the earpiece.

"I know you're there, and you know you're there, so why don't you come out and show yourself? I'd really rather not shoot you, but I will if I have to. We've got food and water, and the cabin's warm. I know you're there and I know what you want. So what do you say?"

Mark Aker had escaped. It was the only explanation. The information so surprised Brandon that he gasped, then tried to process what the hell was going on.

"I'm not showing myself until you do, Aker. And if you don't come out from back there right now, then I'm going to have to make you, and I'd rather not do that."

Brandon considered his options: for the moment, he retained the element of surprise; the longer he dragged this out, the worse his position. But was the man wearing night vision goggles? If so, he'd spot Brandon's weapon and start firing. Was he too wearing a vest? How good a shot was he? How powerful was the flashlight he must be carrying?

He tried to lose the snowshoes, but he was strapped into them and they weren't coming off. He'd have to bend over to unstrap them and that would mean exposing himself beyond the protection of the tree, unless . . .

He turned his back to the tree to lessen his profile. He quickly swatted and loosened the straps of both snowshoes and stepped out. He had to make himself shorter by sinking into the snow—he had six inches on Mark Aker. He slipped the M4 around his back so that only its strap would show. With his feet on firm ground, he had a practiced move, a perfected move—a sudden twist—that could throw the rifle around his body and into his grip. But in snow, and with bulky clothing in the way, he wasn't sure he could pull it off. He stuffed the gloves into his pockets, wearing only thin liners.

His hands were shaking, either from the cold or from nerves. He had to regain control; adrenaline had gotten the better of him.

"Aker, don't be stupid," called out the voice.

**Closer.**

The man had moved nearer. *Twenty, thirty yards away*, Brandon guessed.

Then, well beyond the man, the distant whine of a snowmobile. It took a second or two to determine it was drawing closer.

"Water," Brandon croaked at the man. He was ready now. He had only to step out into the clear and yet every aspect of his training forbade him from doing so.

"I told you," the voice answered. "We got water and food. Warmth. A woodstove. Hot coffee. All you got to do is show yourself. Come on."

Knowing he might get popped, Brandon took a deep breath and stepped out from behind the tree.

# 65

WALT STEERED THE SNOWMOBILE TO FOLLOW the existing track, passing a pair of trees where the trip wire had been taken down and pulled to the side. An extension of the same perimeter warning system that Brandon claimed to have tripped.

Passing this point, he crossed into the enemy camp, driving one-handed. His other hand held the M4, hidden behind the snowmobile's front panel.

He slowed. The track curved to the right and rose to meet what was likely a dirt road in the summer. This road showed much more travel than the track he'd just been on, reminding him how outnumbered he likely was. Bracing the weapon at his side, barrel out and ready, he slowed even more as he caught sight of a cabin in his headlight. Behind it, two, possibly more, outbuildings.

Smoke rose from a stovepipe in the roof. Three windows—two in front, one on the side—bled a pale yellow light. He'd so prepared himself for a conflict that he nearly fired on what turned out to be nothing more than a shadow cast by his own headlight.

He stopped and shut off the snowmobile and spun a full circle as he climbed off, fully expecting to see a muzzle flash. He shook off his nerves as he realized that the snowmobile's return must have been expected. It was the only explanation he could come up with to explain the lack of a reception. He darted off into shadow, the only light the pale wash from the cabin. He crept closer, the night vision goggles raised onto his forehead, eyes flickering in every direction.

He single-clicked his radio com.

His earpiece sounded with three distinct clicks, silence, then four clicks. Walt tried again: a single click.

Silence, followed by three and then four clicks. Two clicks was Brandon—still not reporting. Three and four were Alpha and Beta.

Brandon was AWOL, injured, captured, or dead.

He ducked low and crept forward in a long, strong shadow cast by a wall of the cabin. He reached near enough to see a window shade was not just pulled down but sealed—with Velcro?—to the sill and jamb. It was a patch job, and a small amount of light escaped the effort, accounting for the dim yellow glow.

He forced himself to breathe. He didn't want to attempt taking the cabin without Brandon, without some backup. But Brandon's silence necessitated action. With his back to the cabin—possibly only a matter of inches away from Mark Aker—Walt slipped quietly toward the front, wondering what would come next.

# 66

ROY COATS ATTEMPTED TO SORT OUT THE EVENTS of the past few minutes, his mind racing. He had little to go on beyond a single gunshot and, minutes later, the tripping of the perimeter wire.

Had he checked with Gearbox after hearing that gunshot? He couldn't remember. His brain had just about lost its wheels, the pain too great. He squinted and tried to recall what had happened.

He remembered speaking with Newbs about the perimeter wire. And just now the snowmobile—*that would be Gearbox*—had returned to camp.

There was a loud, uninterrupted ticking going on in his head. The top of his mouth itched. He had to relieve himself.

Had he talked to Gearbox or not?

He picked up the walkie-talkie and called out for his man. Waited. No answer came.

Why such a long time between the return of the snowmobile and Gearbox knocking on the door?

"Gearbox?" Coats shouted loudly enough for his voice to carry through the walls. "Get your ass in here and explain—"

His command was cut off by the sputter of semiautomatic weapons fire. *Two hundred yards*.

Coats processed the most important part of that information: *semiautomatic*. Their AKs had been customized by Rupert Folkes in Jerome to be single-shot and full automatic; they weren't rigged as semiautomatics.

At the same moment, the doorknob turned *without knocking*. His guys were trained to show him the respect of announcing themselves.

Coats snatched the .45 off the table and delivered three rounds into the cabin door before the damn pistol jammed. Pissed off at the self-loads, he hurled the gun across the room at the door before instantly regretting his action.

He looked around for another weapon.

The smell of cordite filled his nostrils. Blood trickled from the broken scab, as he stood painfully from the chair.

Another quick burst of semiautomatic fire.

The camp was under attack.

# 67

ONE OF BRANDON'S ALL-TIME FAVORITE MOVIE scenes was in *Indiana Jones,* where Harrison Ford, faced with a sword-wielding Egyptian, simply ignores the flamboyant swordplay, pulls out his sidearm, and shoots him. Stepping out from behind the tree, hands in the air, he waited for the man shouting at him to show himself. Once he did so, Brandon gave it all of about five seconds before lunging to his left with a hip check, the momentum from which carried the M4 around his body and straight into his open hands.

He squeezed off a semiautomatic

burst—three rounds—and watched the guy's kneecaps explode. The guy went down like a folding chair, his weapon flying out of his hands and catching on a branch stump sticking out from the trunk of the tree he'd used as shelter. The gun strap caught under his chin and snapped his head back as he fell, so that he bobbed like a puppet; his obliterated knees folded, so that he looked like both legs had been crudely amputated. The gun then disengaged from the branch stump, and the man fell face-first into the snow, which swallowed him like sea-foam.

Brandon saw all this dimly, in the haze of a partial moon, knowing enough to make for cover as the rifle dropped down into the snow and on top of the man.

Brandon dove.

The fallen man fired at him.

Brandon returned two more quick bursts and got lucky: a piece of the man's head took off like a frightened bird.

The dead guy, his skull open, sat up on the injured knees, waved his hands frantically like a drowning man searching for a rope, then fell forward again before Brandon could get off another shot.

Brandon came to standing in the lee of a wide fir, lowered the night vision goggles, and confirmed the kill.

Ugly.

His hands were trembling; he felt frightfully cold all of a sudden.

Just then he heard three pops from the direction of the compound. Forty-five Magnum. It wasn't the sheriff's gun.

# 68

WALT LAY FLAT ON HIS BACK, HIS CHEST HOT WITH searing pain. Two of the three shots had scored; the third had narrowly missed, so close to his left ear that he'd heard its whistle. Keeping the gun aimed at the cabin door, he wiggled off his left glove and felt for his chest, his fingers worming into a hole in the Kevlar vest where the bullet was still warm. The other was embedded in his radio. The pain when he breathed was unrelenting due to a cracked rib, and it took him a moment to fully understand—to believe—he wasn't on his way out.

Then he rolled and pushed himself up to standing, knowing what it felt like to be hit by a bus. Keeping the thicker logs that formed the cabin wall between himself and the shooter, he ducked and twisted the doorknob and threw the door open.

"Sheriff!" he announced.

**Where the hell was Brandon?**

Now, in the very far distance, came the mosquito buzz of approaching snowmobiles. Both teams were converging on the compound from a mile out.

Walt struggled for breath. Every movement caused blinding pain. He stood, banged off the door, throwing it fully open to make sure no one was hiding behind it, and then pushed himself into the doorway, fell to his knees and rocked forward, his gun gripped in both hands.

**Clear**.

The .45 was on the floor to his right. He grabbed it, ejected the magazine, and tossed both halves out the door into the snow.

He used the furniture as screens, flipping the only table and hiding behind it, then working past the woodstove to the only doorway. Trying to draw a deep breath and then regretting it for the agony it caused.

He turned the doorknob. Tested the door. Swung it open.

A bunk room: two bunk beds, meeting in the near corner. No closets. Clothes on hooks on the wall.

**Clear.**

Open window, the blind undulating in waves, still in motion.

Walt poked his head out the window, then quickly back inside. Right. Left.

**Clear.**

He followed out the window.

A confusion of tracks in the snow.

But one line of tracks called to him above all others, leading directly to a shed fifteen yards behind the cabin. The right leg was wounded and trailing badly, dragging behind, the left leg doing all the work. Walt thought this explained why the shooter— *Coats?*—had not rushed the cabin's front door to finish the kill.

Walt pulled down the night vision goggles and the landscape before him came alive in monochromatic green and black. But it was as if someone had turned on a searchlight: he could see not only the shed and the corral next to it but well beyond to a stack of chopped wood.

His weapon extended, his arm braced and steadied, he punched his way through the thick snow toward the shed, the beat of his heart painful in his bruised chest.

**Where was Mark? Did they have him in the shed? Had Coats moved toward his bargaining chip?**

A sound from behind turned him. He dropped to one knee, swung the gun around, and took aim: the figure stood over six feet tall, with shoulders as wide as a truck. Walt blinked, and he eased his finger off the trigger.

A bear. A *big* bear raised onto its hind legs. Ten, fifteen yards. Even through the goggles, Walt saw the foaming saliva spilling from its mouth. An angry bear. A *mad* bear. And then: the dark spot on its shoulder. A *wounded* bear.

He could try to kill the bear, though it would take most of the contents of his magazine, and the bear would likely maul him before actually succumbing. It took a perfect heart shot to drop a bear. Walt had heard stories of direct hits to the skull that glanced off without effect. He turned and ran for the shed. He didn't need a rearview mirror to know the bear was following at a gallop.

He blew through the shed door and slammed it shut, turning and once again dropping to one knee. The eerie black and green played out through the goggles, depicting a garage and slaughterhouse in one. It was cluttered with tools and sacks, tires and lumber. An enormous dead cow hung from a block and tackle, its long black tongue swollen and drooping toward a dirt floor where a slimy mass of afterbirth and a fetal calf lay cut open and splayed. The smell was suffocating—not even the cold could freeze out death.

The entire wall shook behind him as the bear collided. Past the hanging cow was an old tractor or truck on blocks, reduced to a steel skeleton and surrounded by parts. He heard the wheeze of his own painful breathing and then another crash as the bear bid for entry. The thing hit the door so hard that a shovel fell from the wall and clanged into some fuel canisters.

Then silence.

The front half of the rectangular shed

was clear, meaning if Coats was in here he was hiding back amid the remains of the tractor. Walt stood and moved carefully forward, keeping his back to the wall, staying as close to it as possible, without getting his feet caught in the tangle of clutter. Several seconds had passed without an effort from the bear, but Walt found himself stealing glances in that direction, where the door hardware was now splintered and partially torn from the jamb. He crept a few more paces forward in the churchlike silence.

Glass shattered behind him. Walt turned in the spray and squeezed off two shots, expecting to see Coats, but it was the bear's giant mitt that swiped at him through the broken window, five grotesque claws tearing through Walt's shoulder and into his muscle. Walt fell into the dead cow, starting it swinging, slipped in the slime on the floor and scrambled quickly to his feet. By the time he did, there was no sign of the bear, only two splintered holes in the log wall where his wild shots had landed.

The chain holding the swinging dead cow creaked like a clock slowly winding down.

He briefly lifted the goggles, wishing he could do without them, but the difference was astonishing: the shed held only a faint glow of moonlight. Back in the world of green and black, he moved cautiously toward the tractor, stepping toward the center of the room to avoid a pile of clutter.

He stood there, panting from the rush of the bear attack, his shoulder throbbing, working the goggles left to right, searching out the hidden recesses and hiding places while anticipating a surprise attack.

Behind him, the swinging cow slowly twisted and spun as its metronomic tick-tocking wound down. Unseen by Walt, the crude knife slice running down the center of the gutted animal twitched open and a human hand slipped out. Then another, this one bearing a bloodied meat hook. The gap widened to reveal the feverish face of Roy Coats.

Walt heard the icy crack of the cow carcass opening and spun.

The meat hook sank into his right hand. His gun dropped. His body followed the sinking weight of the hook as he screamed. The goggles bounced off his head. He crashed onto the dirt floor, his bruised chest sending shock waves of pain racing through his body.

Coats struggled to free the hook, but it had penetrated the meat of Walt's hand and did not come loose. The two men were briefly connected by the hook, Coats unwilling to let it go, Walt unable to shake it loose. Walt, on his knees, punched out with his left hand and hit something spongy. The man wailed and released the meat hook.

Walt grabbed hold of the hook, gritted his teeth, and pulled it free. With his left hand, he sank the hook into Coats's chest just as the man raised his head. His left arm was not nearly as strong or coordinated as his right, and, though the hook hit Coats, it did little more than graze him.

Walt punched the man's leg in the same spot again and then kicked up, as Coats craned forward. He caught the man's chin and heard the cracking of teeth.

Coats somehow had the hook now. He swung out at Walt, who scrambled back— one swipe, two—narrowly missing him. Walt collided with a pile of junk, and here came the hook again. He blocked it with a

length of pipe seized from the pile. The
hook came free.

Walt smashed the pipe into the man's
ankle and Coats screamed again.

The shack shook; it sounded like an
earthquake.

Walt saw the gun: five feet to his left.

He dove for it.

Coats threw a knee into Walt's face,
stumbled forward and inadvertently kicked
the gun away. It disappeared in the darkness into a pile of debris along the wall.
Walt scrambled to his knees, swinging the
pipe and connecting again. Then he pulled
himself to his feet.

Coats backed up, away from the pipe,
his right leg dragging awkwardly.

Walt staggered forward, barely conscious, his right arm and hand useless.

Coats snagged a fallen shovel and
swung it madly into Walt's left side. The
blow knocked Walt into the hanging cow
and he spun to fend off the next attack. The
shovel glanced off the frozen cadaver.

The door broke from its hinges and
crashed to the floor—first a rectangle of
moonlight, which was then blotted out by
the massive presence that filled it. The

bear charged the first thing it saw: Roy Coats.

The shovel was lifted high but fell to the floor, handle first, the blow never delivered.

Walt heard the tear of clothing, followed quickly by the bubbling slobber of Coats attempting to cry out. But his cheek was no longer part of his face and his left eye was missing.

Walt knew better than to run for the door: he didn't want the bear substituting him for his present target.

Hands on the cow, he realized where to hide and pulled himself into the frozen womb, the sounds of terror continuing in a relentless stream until Roy Coats was silenced forever and the bear wandered off and out.

# 69

AS FIFTEEN OF THE BACKUP DEPUTIES SEARCHED for mark Aker, he stumbled into camp of his own accord.

Walt's wounds were being tended to in the cabin as word arrived.

"Sheriff!" Brandon said from the doorway in a voice so urgent that Walt jumped up as one of his team attended his hand.

Brandon led Walt around to the side of the cabin and whispered, "He was just . . . standing there."

Mark Aker was, in fact, standing between the shed and the woodpile in two feet of snow, an animal draped over his shoulders and held by its feet around his neck. A dog, Walt saw on closer inspection.

"I approached," Brandon informed him, "but he stepped back, saying your name over and over. He's in shock, or worse."

"Mark," Walt called out. "It's me."

"Sheriff Walt Fleming," Aker called out again, as if he hadn't heard. He took another step back.

"Your flashlight," Walt said to Brandon. "Shine it on me."

As the light struck Walt, revealing a scarred and battered man, Aker started walking toward him. Walt held a hand out, stopping Brandon from meeting him. Mark was clearly in shock or had hypothermia, skittish and unpredictable.

Aker fell to his knees, a few feet from Walt. At least, that was what Walt thought. In fact, Aker had only gone to his knees to unload the dog. With the dog now in his arms he stood, with difficulty, and passed it to Brandon.

He turned and faced Walt. "What took you so long?"

"The cabin's warm. We have a medic." Walt motioned toward the cabin.

"Coats?"

"Dead."

"You found the test tube?" Aker was moving toward the cabin now. Brandon stood there holding the dog, wondering what to do with it.

"I could have used a note along with it," Walt said.

"Needed to buy myself time." His voice was distant. Walt realized they were losing him.

As they led him inside the cabin, Aker began to shiver uncontrollably in waves that bordered on seizures. The medic began an IV, as they undressed him and wrapped him in wool blankets. Forty minutes later, he and Walt were Life Flighted out and flown to Boise for medical attention. Aker slipped into unconsciousness on the way and could not be revived. He remained in a coma for three days when, miraculously—or so the doctors said—he sat up, fully alert.

Walt never left the man's bedside, running his office and writing reports from room 317.

It wasn't until Aker regained consciousness that they were finally able to contact his family, all of whom had been holed up in a Holiday Inn in Ogden, Utah, on Aker's orders.

They might have arrived sooner, had the press gotten hold of the story, but not a sentence had been—or would be—written about the events of the past weeks. A task force of federal agencies had descended upon all concerned to debrief Walt and his team, requiring their signatures on nondisclosure agreements.

*The rights of a few for the good of the many,* Walt thought.

A cover story was invented for Mark Aker that involved his family's desire for privacy and his father's fictional heart condition. The efficiency and thoroughness of the government surprised everyone involved; even Danny Cutter had been silenced by its efforts, not an easy task.

THREE WEEKS LATER, the first rumors began to circulate around the valley. Walt declined comment but knew the stories had helped with his reelection.

On a wintry Halloween night in Hailey, limping and unable to use his right hand, he accompanied Gail escorting the girls as they went house to house in town. While the girls waited in line at a busy house, Gail spoke to him for the first time since "Hello."

"If you want them back . . ."

"Of course I do," Walt said. He knew it would come to this; Gail had never been comfortable as a mother. The excuses would follow next.

"I may have overreacted," she said.

The girls returned, displaying their goodies; Emily got a chocolate bunny she was especially proud of. Walt wondered if it was left over from Easter and wanted a look at it.

They walked as a family down the street to the next house, Walt marveling how uncomfortable he felt in Gail's company. The girls hurried to the next door.

"I don't like who you've become," he said.

"I know."

"I don't want the divorce to screw up the girls."

"I seem to screw them up without even trying. Why I can't do this, I have no idea."

She looked across the street where there was nothing to see, but it kept her face averted.

"Quite a pair," he said.

"We aren't a pair," she corrected. Then she apologized.

"They need us both," he said. "We need to work this out."

"I don't know what you want me to say."

"I'd rather we work it out than the lawyers. I don't want lawyers deciding what's right for the girls."

Gail didn't say anything, saved again by the arrival of the girls. The trick-or-treating continued for another forty-five minutes. Snippets of conversation passed between them but none with any content. The mention of lawyers had broken the spell or they'd simply run out of things to say. Over a decade spent together, and they couldn't find five minutes of things to talk about.

The girls looked anxiously at Walt, then followed their mother to her car. But she stopped them, withdrawing a small overnight bag and handing it to Walt. Emily's eyes brightened. Nikki took her father's hand. Gail stared dully at the three of them, forced a grimace of a smile, and, kissing the girls, climbed behind the wheel.

When Walt got home, he put the girls to bed, taking extra time to read to them, wishing he didn't have to turn off the light.

Returning to his own bedroom, he stopped and looked around. He emptied her closet. Set four black garbage bags of clothes out on the back porch, but that barely scratched the surface. He took off his wedding ring and put it in a drawer with some cuff links he never used. He drank two beers in front of the television and fell asleep in the chair.

# 70

THE DRIVE UP TO HILLABRAND'S MOUNTAINTOP estate reminded Walt again of the man's power and position, of the enormous wealth in Sun Valley and how carefully one had to tread. He was greeted by an aide and shown inside, exceptionally aware that Sean Lunn was nowhere to be seen.

Hillabrand met him in the living room, with its panoramic views of Ketchum and Sun Valley. He'd lost his tan, replaced by a gray pallor.

"You look better than I'd have expected," Walt lied.

"Looks can be deceiving. I've seen the

worst of it. It was only the one glass, after all. I'm told my liver will scar and I'll pay for it later in life. For now, they say I'm recovering, though it doesn't feel like it."

"I was wrong to put you in that position. That's what I came to say."

"Yes, you were."

"So . . . it's done."

"Yes, it is."

"That's all I had." Walt turned to leave.

Hillabrand stopped him. "You ignored James Peavy's warning. Why was that?"

"I don't know. I guess it egged me on more than discouraged me. It led to the discovery of the sheep pit. I'm trained as an investigator. What can I say?"

"People like Coats . . . We can't let five or ten people have that kind of effect on our country. That has nothing to do with democracy. It's vile and wrong."

"Where does warning innocent people about contaminated water come into play?" Walt asked.

"I know you don't believe it, but we had that pretty well under control. If you tested it now, you wouldn't find a trace of that spill in the aquifer. We were buying time. Trilogy Springs . . . that was an oversight. A costly oversight. A mistake that cost us dearly. I don't have any excuses for it."

"I thought I had you," Walt admitted. "It never for a minute occurred to me the INL could possibly be the victim."

"The real victims were the ranchers," Hillabrand said. "They were willing to stay quiet to benefit their country."

"They were willing to stay quiet because you paid them to," Walt said. "And there's the rub."

"How's that?"

"You, and a couple of others in Washington, convinced yourselves that what you were doing was for the good of the country."

"Yes. And your point?"

Walt hesitated and looked around the sumptuous room with its stunning views.

"What makes you any different than them? The Samakinn? Weren't they doing the exact same thing?"

Hillabrand began to speak but bit back his words. Then he said, "But we're the good guys."

Walt slipped the DVD out of his pocket and placed it down. "Are you so sure? I want you to watch this. I want you to look real closely at the guy with Coats, the guy doing the girl. I'll expect Sean Lunn to turn himself in to me within twenty-four hours. If he doesn't, then it's a manhunt. And I will personally see that this entire story gets into the papers, NDA or no NDA. I'll take my chances."

Hillabrand handled the DVD, flipping it over. He looked into Walt's fierce expression. "Okay," he said. "I'll look at it."

Walt thought about that: a man with enough power to make a suspect simply walk through his office door.

"Coats worked for Lunn," Walt said. "Lunn hired him to take down Mark Aker and find out what Mark knew. When that went bad, they targeted Mark's assistant." Walt pointed to the DVD, as if Hillabrand could see poor Kira Tulivich. "At some point, Coats turned against him, seeing Mark as an asset to his own cause. But don't you see what that means?"

Hillabrand's face went red, his neck veins bulging. "No, Sheriff. What does it mean?"

"If Coats worked for Lunn, then he worked for you," Walt said. "It was your money."

Hillabrand rolled his eyes trying to dodge the accusation. "If Sean Lunn did as you say, it was without my knowledge. He went rogue. He probably thought he could earn points with me by handling this himself. It happens. I would never condone such methods. Not *ever*."

"That may or may not be true," Walt said. "The courts will sort it out. But given the events, exactly how does that make you the good guys?"

He turned and left Hillabrand in the living room, in the middle of his private panorama, the indicting DVD pinched between his fingers.

# 71

SHE AGREED TO MEET ON HER TERMS. SHE CHOSE a bench on the snow-covered bike path, overlooking a turn in the Big Wood River. Behind them, the traffic on Highway 75 hummed a little loudly for the picturesque setting. They sat shoulder to shoulder, closer than he'd expected. Some mallards came and went on the river below, their wings etching V's on the darkly moving water.

"Hate me?" he asked.

"This isn't seventh grade, Walt."

"For some of us it still is."

"I . . . There are things . . . I visited Kira, and it brought up some stuff."

"I wasn't using you and your relationship with Hillabrand. I know what you thought, but it wasn't true. When you mentioned it, it made some sense, but that wasn't how it was to begin with."

"I want us to be able to work together."

"Of course." His voice cracked, belying his attempts to keep his feelings out of this. Her words sounded so final.

"Thank you."

"What about a dinner . . . sometime?" He added quickly, "If it was seventh grade, it would have been a movie or an ice-cream cone. At least give me some credit."

"Being your photographer is good. I like the work a lot."

"Are you seeing someone?"

She watched a great blue heron fly the length of the river until it was nothing but a speck.

"There was someone," she said. "Before I moved here. Two, nearly three years ago now. It wasn't good. I ran away by coming here. All it took was talking to Kira to remind me. Which is a long way of saying a cup of coffee, sure. A movie, maybe.

But not dinner. Not for a long time. Not with you, not with anyone."

"A person's got to move on."

"Remind me of that after your divorce is final."

He drew in a breath of sharp, cold air.

"Out of bounds," she said. "That was awful of me. I'm so sorry. That's just it, you see? I don't even know myself."

"When you get to know you," he said, "you'll find you like you a lot." He added, "I do."

"Some wounds heal from the outside in and some from the inside out."

"Who said that?" Walt asked.

"I just did."

A fly fisherman came around the corner of the river in his waders. He worked the far, snow-covered bank, his casts a thing of beauty.

"Freaks," Walt said.

"Aren't we all?" she asked.

"Yeah, I suppose so."

They talked for a while about the confiscation of her photographs and computer, and how she still had the images from the glider on an SD card in her camera. They weighed the rights of the individual versus the rights of a democracy and argued semantics for a while.

It was the arguing that made Walt feel better. There was comfort in disagreement.

"So none of this ever happened," she said, after a long bout of silence.

"That's what I hear." He added, "Only I didn't hear it from you."

She smiled. He warmed up a little.

The fisherman caught something. They heard his cheer well up the ridge where they sat. The fisherman extracted the catch from his net and turned it loose back into the river.

"Catch and release," Walt said. "I guess now I understand it a little bit better than I did before."

"Before what?" she asked. Then she gave him a look.

"Exactly," he said.

Note: The government's INL experimental nuclear facility has existed in central Idaho under a variety of names for the past fifty years. The atomic submarine engine was developed there, as was the world's first nuclear-generated electricity. There is a cold fusion experimental lab active today at the facility. Over two dozen reactors have been opened and closed over the years. No civilians know exactly how many reactors remain operational or how the decommissioned reactors rate in terms of safety requirements.